Suffer a Witch

Claudia Hall Christian

Cook Street Publishing
Denver, CO

By Claudia Hall Christian
(StoriesByClaudia.com)

ALEX THE FEY SERIES
(AlextheFey.com)
The Fey
Learning to Stand
Who I Am
Lean on Me
In the Grey
Finding North

THE DENVER CEREAL
(DenverCereal.com)
The Denver Cereal
Celia's Puppies
Cascade
Cimarron
Black Forest
Fairplay
Gold Hill
Silt
Larkspur
Firestone

JORNADA DEL MUERTO
(JornadaDelMuerto.net)
Prisoner Days

THE QUEEN OF COOL
(theQueenofCool.com)

SETH AND AVA MYSTERIES
(SethandAvaMysteries.com)
The Tax Assassin
The Carving Knife

SUFFER A WITCH
(SufferaWitch.com)

ISBN-13:   978-1-938057-23-6 (print)
              978-1-938057-27-4 (digital book)
              978-1-938057-22-9 (digital chapters)

Library of Congress: 2015913233

PUBLISHER'S NOTE:
This is a work of fiction. Names, characters, places and incidents either are
either the product of the author's imagination or are used fictitiously.

First edition © serial fiction June 10, 2014 – September 22, 2015
Cook Street Publishing
ISNI: 0000 0004 1443 6403
PO Box 18217
Denver, CO 80218
CookStreetPublishing.com

For Rose

Chapter One

"Shit."

Emogene "Em" Peres pulled her 1968 Land Cruiser FJ55 into the Walgreen's parking lot in Danvers, Massachusetts, just as the drugstore's giant outdoor digital clock said "10:15 a.m." She winced at the time. June 10th had rolled around again, and she needed to be on Gallows Hill at 10:18 a.m.

She parked in a space behind the drugstore next to the embankment. Hopping out of the truck, she jogged between the large granite boulders up the six-foot embankment. Once there, she continued to the flat spot on the northwest corner of the hill. From her vantage point, she could see the drugstore's digital clock.

10:17 a.m.

She'd made it with a minute to spare. She pulled a vial of rose water, a sage bundle, and a white candle from the back pocket of her denim jeans. She managed to coax a stream of smoke from the sage bundle and splashed the rose water around. Closing her eyes, she muttered a combination of the Buddhist Metta prayer, a Puritan prayer from her youth, and some new-age nonsense. She had just finished when she heard footsteps coming in her direction. She opened her eyes.

"Bridget!" Emogene said. "You can't be here."

Even at this distance, she could see that Bridget had been crying. As if it were still 1692, Bridget was wearing a floor-length black cotton dress with a red paragon bodice. Her long, dark hair was arranged in the prim Puritan style. She even wore a handkerchief hat.

"Em!" Bridget rushed to Em's side.

Bridget threaded her arm through Em's elbow.

"You can't be here," Em repeated.

The women watched the digital clock flick over to 10:18 a.m. The wind picked up, and a breeze blew through the small hill. Bridget sighed.

"I read online that people have seen the ghost of Bridget Bishop here," Bridget said. Her eyes welled with tears. "Right here. Her specter is supposed to be here at the exact time she was hanged."

"And here you are," Em said with a wry smile.

"That's not what they mean, and you know it," Bridget said and scowled. "I thought . . . I thought . . ."

Bridget began to cry.

"You thought you'd come here and see the evil ghost that had tortured those poor, innocent girls." Em's voice was hard with ancient grief and rage.

"I always felt badly for Mercy Lewis because her boyfriend died in the war." Bridget bit her lip and nodded. "She lost her whole future. I mean, what else was she going to do?"

"She could have chosen not to accuse hundreds of innocent people of witchcraft," Em said. "Including you and me."

Bridget sighed at Em's logic. Em gave Bridget a compassionate smile, which caused Bridget's eyes to seep tears.

"They were just stupid little girls, Em," Bridget said. "They didn't mean ..."

"I know you believe that," Em said. She put her arm around Bridget's shoulders — for her own comfort as much as Bridget's.

"I *have* to," Bridget said. "Look ..."

Bridget dug around in her small tote bag until she found her cell phone. She poked at the phone for a moment until she found a video. She held it up for Em to see and pressed "Play."

The video opened with a couple of teenagers talking about the Salem Witch Trials. They went through their research and their logical conclusion that Gallows Hill Park wasn't where the accused witches of Salem Village were hanged. Instead, they climbed the hill where Em and Bridget were standing.

"Shit, Bridget!" Em said. "Now everyone's going to ..."

"Hush!" Bridget said. "You have to see this."

Em looked around the hill. Seeing no one, she returned to watching the video. The teenagers stood on the hill behind the Walgreen's and spoke of the ghost of Bridget Bishop. They claimed that Bridget Bishop's ghost was breaking lights and scaring cats in the area. The ghost of Bridget Bishop was angry.

"I don't know why they say that," Bridget said. "I'm not angry."

"You *do* hate cats," Em said.

"I'd never scare them," Bridget said. She glanced at Em. "Sweet things. You know they are guards for witches."

"I've heard that once or twice," Em said.

"From me," Bridget said.

"From you," Em said.

"You sure they're not seeing a ghost that looks like me?" Bridget said. "I mean, those girls *said* they were tortured by something that looked like me, and . . ."

"The girls were liars, Bridg," Em said. "The entire thing was bullshit."

"Don't swear, Em," Bridget said. "It makes you seem like a lesbian."

"There are worse things in the world than seeming like a lesbian," Em said.

"Like being a lying, stupid girl?"

"Yes," Em nodded.

Bridget smiled. Em sighed.

"I'm a witch, not a lesbian, Bridget." Em's voice was impatient. "So are you. We were made witches on this very hill by the people who . . ."

Bridget sighed, and Em stopped talking. They had had this conversation at least once a year for more than three hundred years.

"Witches don't have to swear." Em parroted Bridget's usual point to appease her. "Even though we're cursed with immortality and magical powers, we don't have to be coarse."

"Exactly," Bridget said.

She turned on the video, and they watched the young men and women. The ghost hunters were going to have a ceremony around noon to try to soothe Bridget's soul.

"Are you going to that?" Em asked. "I bet you'd make it fun for them. Plus, you're dressed for the part."

"Oh." Bridget looked surprised. She shook her head.

"No."

Em nodded. The women stood together on the tiny piece of grass and granite where their lives had been irrevocably changed. Bridget sighed.

"God, I hate it here," Bridget said.

"It's a pain in the neck," Em said. "That's for sure."

Despite herself, Bridget laughed.

"You going to say a prayer for me?" Bridget asked.

"Already did," Em said. "Do you need more than one?"

"Well . . ." Bridget gave Em a wheedling look. "You're so good at prayers."

Ignoring Bridget's comment, Em said, "Would you like to light your own rest-in-peace candle?"

"Let's do it together," Bridget said.

The women knelt down. Em pushed a small, thin, white candle into the ground on the location where Bridget had been hanged on this day so many years ago. Em snapped her fingers, and flame formed in the palm of her hand. Bridget did the same. The women blew, and the flame jumped from their hands to light the wick of the candle. Bridget sniffed.

"I wish . . ." Bridget started.

"Me, too," Em said.

Em stood up and helped Bridget to her feet. She scowled at Bridget's feet. Bridget was wearing shoes that looked suspiciously like those she'd been hanged in.

"You're wearing your hanging outfit?" Em asked.

"What else would I wear?" Bridget asked. "It is my hanging day."

Em scowled at Bridget, and the woman smiled at her. They started walking toward the parking lot.

"I did not die in this dress, if that's what you're thinking," Bridget said. "It's a copy. I told the seamstress that I'm such a *big* fan of Bridget Bishop."

"That you are," Em laughed.

Bridget laughed. Em pointed to a white stretch limousine pulling around the Walgreen's.

"Sarah sent her driver for us," Em said.

"Goody Good has done well for herself," Bridget said.

"Don't call her that," Em said. "She hates it."

"I know." Bridget gave Em a smug look, and Em laughed.

"Are you going to stay here to wait for your young fans or go to brunch with everyone?"

"Are you going?" Bridget asked.

"Uh . . ." Em had planned to avoid this yearly ritual. She glanced at her Land Cruiser.

"Please?" Bridget asked.

Bridget shot Em another pleading look. Em shook her head at Bridget's innate capacity to manipulate anyone. Bridget gave her another pulse of a pleading smile.

"Sure," Em said finally.

The limousine stopped in front of them, and Sarah Good's driver stepped out to open the door for them. He closed the door with a bow.

"Ms. Good asked me to tell you that she will have you back here in time to get to the shop," the driver said.

"Thank you, Percy," Em said.

"Help yourself to the champagne," Percy the driver said.

Em gestured to the bottle of champagne. Bridget nodded.

"You're working today?" Bridget asked.

Em opened the bottle and poured two glasses.

"It's not my hanging day," Em said. She gave a glass to Bridget. Holding up her glass, she said, "To hanging."

"To becoming a witch," Bridget said.

Their glasses touched with a soft clink, and they each took a drink.

"Happy hanging day, Bridget," Em said. "I wish it hadn't happened, either. But it did. We have to make the best of it."

Nodding, Bridget smiled and emptied her glass.

"More?" Em asked.

Bridget gave Em a pleading smile, and Em laughed.

"You're a *witch*!"

A man's voice laced with vitriol echoed off the storefront. Several people walking on the sidewalk stopped to stare at him. Em glanced to her left to see a homeless man wearing ragged, dirty clothing, long, greasy, grey hair, and a filthy beard leaning against a pillar of the building next door to the Mystic Divine, Em's metaphysical shop.

"Repent!" the man screamed and pointed at her. His finger turned to point toward the heavens. "Repent or *feel* the wrath! The *hangman* is not far away!"

Em scowled at the man. He lifted a shoulder in a shrug.

"Old habits die hard," the man said with a grin. "Plus, the acoustics are great here."

Shaking her head at him, Em shifted her paper coffee cup to her left hand and dug around in her purse for her keys. The man walked toward her.

"Ye be a *witch*!" The man's voice came like a

thunderbolt from a pulpit.

Em yelped with surprise. The plastic lid of her coffee cup dislodged, and her coffee spilled on the ground.

"George!" Em said. "You made me spill my coffee."

"Sorry, Em," Reverend George Burroughs said.

"You should be," Em said. "God, you smell awful!"

George gave her a gap-toothed smile.

"That is *not* a compliment," Em said.

George laughed. He leaned in to hug her, and she waved him away.

"Get inside," Em said.

George slunk into the shop. He stopped near the door and turned to hug her. Em shook her head. She gave him a key and waved her hands toward the stairs in the back of the shop. Whistling an ancient hymn, George went through the shop like a pungent parade. He took the stairs in the back and disappeared upstairs.

Em's eyes lingered on the door to her apartment a moment longer than she'd have liked. Shaking her head at herself, she started opening the small shop. She turned on Tiffany floor lamps and put away the few things left out the night before. The Mystic Divine specialized in all forms of spirituality. The most ardent evangelical Christian and the Wiccan could both find the tools and education they needed to live their spiritual life. The store was laid out in such a way that there were nooks for reading, small private rooms for spiritual readings, and two larger group rooms in the loft upstairs. Em picked up a microfiber cloth and dusted the section on Gurdieff's *The Fourth Way*. The shop made most of its income off of religious counseling and psychic readings. George was a particularly popular tarot reader.

She glanced at the door to her apartment and wondered if he was reading tonight. Longing welled up inside of her. In her mind's eye, she saw him standing under a stream of warm water in his shower. Feeling her presence, he smiled and gestured for her to join him.

"No," Em said out loud.

She forced herself to get out her laptop and read her email. The next time she looked up, George was holding a cup of coffee in front of her nose. His long, grey hair was wet and tied back. He'd shaved. He was wearing clean clothes from his side of the closet. She took the mug from him, and he rewarded her with a soft smile. They drank coffee in hungry silence.

"What are you caught up in?" George asked.

"Some kids are into the whole Salem thing," Em said. "I was watching their videos. They've found Gallows Hill, you know — the real one, not the park."

"Oh, yeah?" George asked

"They say they've caught Bridget's ghost on camera."

"How is that possible?" George asked.

"Who knows?" Em shrugged. "Maybe we lost our souls when we were hanged."

George instinctively rubbed his neck. Em smiled at his gesture.

"How did this morning go?" George asked.

"Bridget was on the hill," Em said.

"What?" George squinted with surprise.

"She was even wearing a reproduction of the dress she was hanged in. Shoes, too."

"She can't be there!" George said.

"I told her, but you know how she is," Em said. "What's the point of..."

"...being immortal if you can't do what you want," George joined Em in quoting Bridget.

"Exactly," Em said. "She told me about these kids. You know, Bridget's convinced that there was an actual specter that tormented our accusers."

"Bridget." George gave a sad shake of his head.

"You know, I never thought of it," Em said.

"Of what?" George asked.

"I never gave even one thought to the idea that there might have actually been an entity that tortured those girls," Em said. "I always thought they were..."

"Full of shit," George said in unison with her.

"But this morning," Em nodded, "I mean, Bridget was so sure that I wondered if she was onto something. Let's say there *was* an entity. It presented to the girls in our likeness. And..."

Em shook her head.

"And?" George raised his eyebrows. "Disappeared for the last three hundred and twenty-two years?"

"And nothing," Em said with a shrug. "That's as far as I got. Do you think it's possible?"

"No," George said.

"Why?" Em asked.

"This *entity* would be responsible for giving us immortality and magical powers," George said. "This entity would be a part of us, and..."

"The Devil," Em said with him.

"Or God," George said. "Remember, it was God who marked Cain."

"Yes, Reverend, but Cain was only protected from being killed by others," Em said. "As you know, we are truly immortal. Plus, I never killed my sibling."

"Are you the child of the Devil, Em? Or marked by God?"

"No." Em instinctively shivered. "No. I am only that from which I was made."

"That's because there are no devils, and we were not marked by God, Em," George said. "The girls were psychopaths. They made everything up. You know that."

"I do," Em said. "Anyway, Bridget was hoping to catch a glimpse of this alternate version of herself."

"And do what with it?" George asked.

"No idea," Em said. "It's Bridget. She didn't really think it through."

"Who are these kids?" George came around the counter to stand behind Em. She clicked to the website, and George read over her shoulder.

"High school, maybe college-aged, kids interested in investigating the whole Salem thing," Em said. "They are *huge* fans of Bridget Bishop. They think she was incredibly brave for being hanged first."

"Like she had a choice," George said.

"I think any one of us would have preferred to be hanged first," Em said. "Better than languishing in that stinking jail."

"I honestly never thought they'd actually do it," George said. "Right up to the end. And some days, I still can't believe it happened."

"That's why you're special, George Burroughs," Em said. "You're an optimist. Even after you were betrayed by your fellow man and hanged for your efforts, you still believe they are good at heart."

"Guilty as charged," George said.

Em leaned back into him. He wasn't a large man by modern standards, but he was sturdy and strong. He put his arms around her waist and held her in his warm, loving arms.

"You think this is serious," George said.

"With technology and the never-ending interest in our trials, it's only a matter of time," Em said with a nod. "Someone's going to figure out that we're still here. I showed you that article in the *Huffington Post*."

"The one wondering where our skeletons are?" George asked. "In use, ma'am — thank you very much."

"They're going to go looking, and . . ."

Em swallowed hard. She shifted away from him, and he let go of her.

"And?"

"It will start all over again," Em said in a low voice.

"Maybe that's a good thing," George said. "People should know what they're capable of creating with their hatred and fear."

"Mmm," Em said.

"Mmm?" George said.

"Even in 2014, Americans believe in evil people like they are a separate species," Em said. "It's not that different from 1692."

"We could appeal to their reason," George said.

"What reason is that?" Em asked.

"I know. I know," George said. "I hear the foolishness in my own words and your voice in my head."

"What do I say?" Em asked.

"'How did that work out last time?'" George asked. "'You tried to reason with people who'd been your parishioners; the very same parishioners who had just a few years earlier professed their *love* for you!'"

George shrugged.

"They thought I owed them money," George said.

"You didn't," Em said. "They took your shirt and breeches off your dead body to repay their imagined debt."

"And left me mostly unburied," George said. "Yes, that much I do remember."

George smiled.

"Where's it get you, Em?" George asked.

"Where's what get me?"

"All this cynicism," George said.

"A visit from you," Em said.

George laughed, and she smiled.

"You staying?" Em asked.

"I don't know," George said. "You want me to stay?"

Em turned around to look at him. Her eyes reviewed George Burroughs' worn face. He'd never been a handsome man. The last hundred years or so, his body and mind had taken on a sense of permanence brought by being immortal. He was incredibly alluring.

"Was everyone at the party today?" George asked.

"Everyone but you," Em said.

"How was it?" George asked.

Em shrugged.

"I'm the only stable one," Em said. "I see everyone all the time. Whenever anyone's in town, they stop by. They were happy to catch up with each other, but me . . . I see them all the time."

"How's Giles?" George asked.

"Good. Happy," Em said. "He bought that big horse farm upstate and has a new wife — young, pretty. He's happy for Viagra."

"He's a witch," George laughed. "What would he need Viagra for?"

"Don't tell the wife," Em said. "They don't have kids, but he's not worried about it. I mean, it's not 1690. He's talking about adopting from overseas."

Em shrugged. George kissed the back of her head and moved out from behind her.

"Do you ever wish you were them?" Em asked.

"Them?" George asked.

"John Proctor, Rebecca Nurse, George Jacobs," Em said.

"Those hanged who were reburied?" George asked.

"The human beings who didn't transform, whose souls are at rest, probably because they were reburied by people who loved them," Em said. "Their families' love saved them from this."

"Not really," George said.

"Why?"

"I'd miss this," George said. "I'd miss you."

"And the other witches?" Em smiled. "It's a barn full of frisky mares, Mr. Burroughs."

"Just you," George said.

"You're swearing off the others?" Em laughed at the idea.

"I'm saying I'd miss you," George said. "This."

"You are a charmer," Em laughed.

"Wanna make some magic?" George asked.

"I need to open the shop," Em said.

George clapped his fingertips together. The "Be back later" sign appeared on the door, and an unseen mist appeared around the shop to discourage people from coming to the door. Em smiled. George held out his hand. With a blink of her eye, they were lying on her bed in a cloud of white sheets and comforters. Her bedroom was expansive, with large, double-hung windows that looked out onto the Boston Common. The floors were made of wide wood planks, and the walls were painted a faint yellow.

"I love this room," George said. His clothing disappeared with his words. He glanced at Em, and she was naked. "And the woman inside it."

Em smiled.

"See, this," George nodded for emphasis. "This is what we are alive for."

"Mid-day screwing?" Em asked.

"Love," George said.

"And magic," Em said.

"Let's make some loving magic," George said.

Chapter Two

"OM."

The Mystic Divine vibrated with the sound of thirty people chanting their ending mantra. Em looked up at the ceiling. The few patrons glanced at Em before mimicking her look at the ceiling. Em smiled.

Sarah Wildes taught this crazy yoga and meditation class on Tuesday and Thursday nights. Most of the Salem Twenty, as they called themselves, taught at the Mystic Divine. But Sarah was special. Her innate nonconformist nature drew people to her in flocks. Em got up from her usual spot behind the glass case to light the pillar candles around the shop. Sarah's class would be getting out soon, and the candles encouraged people to buy. Hearing laughter, she turned to look.

George and his client were just finishing up. George kissed the woman's hand, and she thanked him profusely. He gave the woman a mystical nod before going back into his reading room. The woman floated by Em on a cloud of hope. Em watched the client pay for her reading with one of the college-aged helpers. The woman chatted with the helper about the incredible George. When the woman left, the assistant shot Em a cross-eyed look.

Every woman loved George, and George loved every

woman. Em glanced at his room. He had two more clients before the night was over.

"I don't know how you do it, Em," Shonelle Richland, one of her assistants, said. "He's really . . . yummy. How do you let him . . . do that?"

Em turned to look at Shonelle. Even with eleven generations in between, Em could see her son's eyes shining in Shonelle's face. Em shrugged.

"Age, I guess," Em said. "I've known George for a long, long time."

"Mom says you're destined for each other," Shonelle said.

"Your mom . . ." Em started.

Shonelle's mother had worked for Em when she was in college.

"Can't resist a Harvard man?" Shonelle asked. The young woman leaned into Em. "Don't tell mom, but me, neither."

"Oh?" Em asked with a laugh. "Do tell!"

"You have to light the candles." Shonelle gave Em a taunting grin.

"I'm done," Em said. Behind Shonelle's back and hidden from the front, she lit the other candles with a flick of her fingers. "Who is he?"

"He's smart and funny and friendly and . . ." Shonelle's dark skin flushed red. "He has dark, curly hair, sexy facial hair, and these cool glasses, totally hipster, and . . ."

A burst of applause indicated that Sarah's class had ended.

"And?" Em asked.

"He says he's a descendant of a Salem witch." Shonelle

nodded.

"Oh, yeah?" Em raised an eyebrow to show her intrigue. "It's been three hundred years. Given the way people breed, I'd guess there are *a lot* of descendants of Salem witches."

"No. He says he's a descendant of Alice Parker *after* she became a witch." Shonelle dropped her voice to a whisper. "You know, after she was hanged?"

"What?" Em gave Shonelle a dismissive shake of her head to contain the panic she felt inside.

A sweating, smiling woman and a man walked past Em and Shonelle as they made their way through the shop from Sarah's class. Em glanced at Sarah's class participants and turned back to Shonelle.

"Alice got pregnant in jail." Shonelle said Alice's name as if they were best friends. Em bit her lip to keep from commenting. "When she woke up — you know, after being hanged — she went back to her husband and family. She had a baby about six months later."

"Excuse me," said a woman shining with yoga release and chanting bliss. The woman touched Em's shoulder, and Em turned toward her.

"That's just what he says," Shonelle said to the back of Em's head.

"How can I help?" Em said to the woman.

"I'm interested in the CD — you know, the one Sarabelle used in class," the woman said. "She said you had it down here."

"Sure," Em said. She glanced at Shonelle to find her talking to another person from the class. "It's this way."

Em led the woman across the floor to the display of

chanting CDs.

"Sarabelle is amazing, isn't she?" the woman asked in a conspiratorial tone. "I'm surprised she doesn't have one of these herself."

Em smiled to keep from telling the woman that Sarah, like all witches, would only cause the recording equipment to scream.

"She said her vibration can be heard on a microphone," the woman said.

"Vibration," Em nodded.

"Is that true?" the woman asked. She leaned in and said in a low voice, "Is Sarabelle spiritually gifted?"

"Of course, she is," Em smiled.

The woman gave Em a big smile.

"Do you know if she does readings?" the woman asked. "I would love her to read my energy. I just . . . Well, I don't want to burden you with my troubles."

"Sarabelle does do readings," Em said. "You can sign up at the desk or online at our website. You'll see her under Sarabelle Wilderson."

Nodding, the woman held the CD to her heart. Em smiled at her, and the woman went up to the desk to pay. A man from the class asked Em another question. For the next few minutes, Em helped customers from Sarah's class, and everything started to hum. Sarah laughed and talked to her customers from behind the counter. George's next client came in and was escorted to the back with flourish.

And the cash register dinged every time they sold something.

Em loved it when things hummed. From top to bottom, this store and building belonged to Em, and she to them.

When things hummed, it was easy. When no one came in, Em worried. While she could ride out a storm, the store also supported the Salem Twenty. At one time or another, they had each needed Em's help. When the crowd thinned, Em took out her cell phone and placed a call.

"Did you have a baby after you went back to John?" Em asked.

"Hiya, Mama," Alice Parker said in a surprisingly good southern accent. "It was such a treat to see you this morning."

She heard Alice walking to somewhere they could talk more privately.

"Uh huh," Em said.

She followed Alice's lead and went into her office, near the reading rooms.

"I love it when I get to visit the north," Alice said for whomever was with her. "I'll just be a second, hon."

George's voice came as a deep rumble through the wall while Em waited for Alice to come back on the line.

"You know I had a baby," Alice said, slipping into her usual New England accent in her hushed whisper. "I got pregnant in that filthy jail."

"I was with you the entire time!" Em said.

"Then you remember what happened," Alice said in the same low tone. "It happened to you, too, Em, and you know it."

"Why didn't I know you were pregnant?" Em asked.

"It wasn't like I peed on some little piece of plastic and we celebrated with cake and balloons," Alice said.

"You didn't know," Em said.

"I didn't know," Alice said in a disgusted voice. "Shit,

Em, what I didn't know then could fill the entire Atlantic Ocean."

"That's the truth," Em said.

"You feel that way, too?" Alice asked.

"No, just you," Em said.

Alice laughed, and Em smiled at her joke.

"He didn't live long," Alice said. "I'd had such a hard time in jail, and we were on the run when he was born. John loved him like his own, but the child was sickly."

"So he can't be the ancestor of a love interest of Shonelle's," Em said.

"Is that what this is about?" Alice asked. "Shit, Em, he didn't live but five, maybe six, months. He caught the flu, poor thing. We buried him in Charleston."

"You're sure he stayed buried?" Em asked.

"Certain," Alice said. "You remember John. He'd never have left a baby if he thought there was any chance he'd return. We didn't bury him for a week after he passed. There's not a chance that baby is anyone's ancestor."

"Well, there's a guy saying he's your heir," Em said.

"Liars," Alice said. "You, of all people, know that some people will say anything to claim a connection to the Salem Witches. Idiots. Is this a big deal?"

"There's a group of college kids who are investigating," Em said.

"You said that this morning," Alice said. "Why are you worked up about it?"

There was a knock on the door.

"Everything okay, Alicia?" a man's voice said in the background.

"Shit," Alice said in a low voice to Em. She said in a

louder, southern-accented voice, "I'll be right there, sugar. My mama's having a crisis over her no-good boyfriend."

Alice was quiet for a moment.

"Listen," Alice said in a low tone. "I *have* to go."

"Client?" Em asked.

"Rich client," Alice said. "Hung like a horse. We're at the Boston Harbor for the rest of the week."

"You know you can always work here," Em said. "You can move back into your apartment on the fourth floor. You don't have to do that anymore."

"Don't be such a Puritan," Alice laughed.

"Before you go," Em said. "How did this kid know the story about you transforming *after* you were hanged and about the baby being conceived in prison, if he didn't hear it from you?"

"I don't know, Em," Alice said. "I've never told anyone until just now."

"Never?" Em asked.

"Never," Alice said. "Now, you're going to have to figure out your own mystery. I have something much better to do."

In the background, Em heard Alice flush the toilet and the water turned on and off.

"Love you, Mama!" Alice said. "I'll call again soon!"

Alice hung up. Em looked at the phone. Alice had loved John Parker with her mind, body, and soul. He took her love with him when he died of old age all those years ago. If Alice could die — and certainly she had tried — she would have died simply to be with him, even now, almost three hundred years later.

"Whatcha thinking?" George said from the doorway to

her office.

"About love," Em said. "Client leave so soon?"

"Bathroom," George said. "She got very upset. Had a mascara emergency."

Em nodded.

"What's going on, Em?" George asked.

"Just Alice," Em said.

George gave her a knowing nod. His client came up behind him, and they left for his reading room. Em got up and went to see if there were any remaining customers. Sarah was upstairs cleaning up, so the store was almost empty, and Shonelle was working the register.

"How serious is it with this boy?" Em asked.

"I don't know," Shonelle said. "I met him this morning at the Bishop memorial."

"Bishop memorial?" Em shook her head.

"You know Bridget Bishop?" Shonelle asked.

"Bridget Bishop?" Em asked. She forced herself to make a little shake of her head as if she hadn't known Bridget for the last three hundred years.

"I can't believe you don't know this," Shonelle said. "She was the first Salem Witch to be hanged. Today was the anniversary of her hanging."

"Oh, that's right," Em said. "That Bridget Bishop."

"Yeah." Shonelle gave Em a "You're-old-and-useless" look. Em smiled.

"How was the memorial?" Em asked.

"I cried," Shonelle said. "Poor Bridget. Can you imagine? They didn't break her neck, so she choked and gasped for breath for more than ten minutes."

Shonelle's eyes filled with tears, and she shook her head.

"Pretty awful," Em said.

Em bit her tongue to keep from telling Shonelle the truth — Bridget thrashed on that rope for closer to thirty minutes before she died.

"So you met this guy at the memorial?" Em asked.

"He was running it," Shonelle said. "They're having another on July 19th. But get this . . ."

Shonelle watched a customer walk by them. She leaned into Em.

"He says he caught the spirit of Bridget on film," Shonelle said. "You know what that means, don't you?"

"No," Em said.

"She's still here," Shonelle said. "They're going to try to see if they can communicate with her."

"Why?" Em asked.

"So they can relieve her suffering!" Shonelle said. "Maybe help the poor thing move on."

Em scowled.

"You should come," Shonelle said.

"Come where?" Em asked.

"To the séance," Shonelle said. "I told him all about the store. He said he'd come in for supplies."

"When is the séance?" Em asked.

"You should have it here!" Shonelle's face brightened.

"Here?" Em asked.

"George is in town," Shonelle said. "I bet George or one of the other women can lead it — Lizzie or Marie."

Shonelle nodded.

"It would be a great way to get more people into the store," Shonelle said. "Think of it! The Salem Witch séance — right here in the Mystic Divine!"

"Sounds . . ." Em said.

"You hate the idea." Shonelle looked heartbroken.

"'Hate' is a strong word," Em said.

Shonelle grinned.

"What just happened?" Em asked.

"I know you'll give it a chance," Shonelle said. "Whenever you say that — 'hate is a strong word' — you give things a chance. Plus, George is here."

"What does George have to do with anything?" Em asked.

"Let's just say you're more *relaxed* when George is home," Shonelle giggled.

Em shook her head at the vibrant girl.

"I'll think about it," Em said. "I'll have to talk to the store investors."

"Why?" Shonelle asked. "They should be thrilled. These guys have thousands of YouTube subscribers. Their site is growing every day. Everyone wants to know what happened."

"What happened to what?"

"To the bodies!" Shonelle said.

"What bodies?" Em asked.

"Of the Salem Witches," Shonelle said. "Didn't I say that?"

"What are you talking about?" Em asked.

"They're missing," Shonelle said. Her voice dropped to a conspiratorial tone. "Just vanished."

"What vanished?" Em asked.

"The remains of the Salem Witches," Shonelle said. "That's why John, that's his name — John Parker — that's why he says they are among us. Isn't that creepy?"

"Creepy," Em said with a nod.

"We have to find their remains and put them at rest." Shonelle gave a solemn nod. "That's what John says."

"Sounds like a lot of work," Em said. "How would you know it was their remains?"

"Forensics!" Shonelle said. "U of Mass has already told John they will do DNA testing on anything we find."

Shonelle bounced up and down while clapping at the same time. Em's scowl deepened with every bounce.

"So, you'll do it?" Shonelle asked.

"Do what?" Em shook her head.

"Have the séance here!"

"I can't promise anything," Em said.

"But you'll check into it?" Shonelle asked. "I told John you would."

Em gave Shonelle a vague smile. Shonelle was a bright girl with a lot of interests. It was likely that Shonelle would forget all about this tomorrow.

"Oh look, he's here!" Shonelle said.

A young man waved at Shonelle through the window to the shop.

"Can I go?" Shonelle asked. "He's going to show me ghost-hunting techniques in the Common Burying Ground."

"You know how to ghost hunt!" Em said. "You've been doing it since you were a little kid!"

"I know that, but he doesn't!" Shonelle said. "I mean, he can come in and wait for me, if you want. You don't want to meet him now, and really . . ."

"Go." Em smiled at the girl.

Shonelle waved to the boy through the window,

indicating she'd be right out. She ran to Em's office to clock out and practically skipped out of the store. Em watched Shonelle hug the young man. They walked off arm in arm toward the Boston Common.

"What was that?" Sarah asked.

"Danger," Em said.

"Oh?" Sarah asked. She turned to watch Shonelle and the young man jaywalk across Tremont Street. "Looks like young love to me."

Em turned to watch them for a moment.

"He says that he's a descendant of the child that Salem Witch Alice Parker had after she was hanged," Em said.

"Oh?" Sarah glanced at the couple again. "What's Alice say?"

"Child died when he was five or six months old," Em said. "They waited seven days before burying him, to be sure. Buried him in Charleston."

"And you believe Alice?"

"It's not like her to lie," Em said.

"So something's happening, but we're not sure what," Sarah said.

Em nodded. Without warning, Sarah hugged Em.

"It's going to be all right, Em," Sarah said. She let Em go and started counting her class receipts. "We've survived all this time. What could happen now?"

"We could get found out," Em said.

"Who would believe it?" Sarah gave her a doubtful look.

"It could all happen again," Em said.

In spite of her doubt, Sarah shivered. Em nodded. Sarah regained her composure and shook her head. She hugged Em again.

"You're such a mother hen," Sarah said.

She put a rubber band around her class receipts and held them up to Em. Em nodded.

"I know," Em said.

"Whatever it is, Em, we'll get through it," Sarah said. "We have for more than three hundred years. We will this time, too."

Sarah gave Em a firm kiss on the cheek. She stepped back, nodded at Em, and left the store. Em thought through Sarah's logic. Turning back to the store, Em used her senses to check to see if anyone was there. Feeling no one, she took her seat behind the glass counter. She created a wall of white light around her body for protection. Her body and mind would go through the motions of taking George's client's payment, helping his next client, and even closing the store. She didn't need to be there for that. Using her breath, she calmed her soul.

Em stepped back from the store. She pulled her soul out of her body, out of the store, and into the world. She floated high enough to see what had been Salem Village and the store. If she squinted, she could pick up faint tendrils of historic energy. Her own move from Salem Village to Boston in October of 1692 came as a faint yellow line. George's more mercurial energy flitted back and forth. She watched until she saw the seventeen witches' faint energy lines as they fled what had been Salem Village. Hoping to catch a sense of what was happening now, she watched for tendrils of energy stretching from Salem Village to the store and back again.

There were new energy lines. This energy was new and vibrant. She called the energy to surround her. This new energy was filled with bright curiosity, giddy enthusiasm, and something she couldn't place.

"Em."

The sound reached her high above the world. Em worked to stay with the energy just a little bit longer so that she could understand this unknown component. The more she stretched toward it, the more it evaded her.

"Em. Come back to me, my love."

Em's soul was drawn back into her body. She opened her eyes. She was sitting on her stool behind the glass counter, and George was kissing her lips. He smiled when she'd returned.

"Time for bed," George said.

Before she could protest, he swooped her off her stool and carried her up to bed.

Chapter Three

MALICE.

Black capitalized word floated like a leaf on top of multicolored streams of energy.

MALICE.

Dreaming, Em watched the word until the current of the energy river broke the word into separate letters. The letters floated apart from each other like separate leaves on top and within the rivers of energy. The word became unrecognizable as individual letters.

Suddenly, she was at the party this morning. The letters swirled around each of the drinking, laughing witches on streams of multicolored energy. Seeing Em, the letters lined up to present themselves to her. Sarah Good's mansion was gone. The Salem Twenty were gone. Em was standing alone in front of the word "Malice."

She sat up in bed.

The letters began to spin in a tornado-like formation. They spun and spun until only the dark color of the letters was visible. Her ears filled with the sound of people whispering to each other. Like words being carried on the wind, people's evil gossip whipped the tornado into a frenzy. More and more gossiping voices joined in the chorus. The louder their voices grew, the faster the tornado spun. Em covered her ears with her hands.

"Stop!" Em commanded.

The tornado stopped spinning. The letters fell to the ground, revealing a figure — more shadow than living being — that had been hiding inside the vortex. Em made out his cloven feet and a single horn. She screamed in terror at the form of the devil that had haunted her Puritan life.

"Be gone!" George's voice came into her range of hearing.

At his command, the demon's leathery snout poked out from the shadow. He sniffed in George's direction and stepped into the light. He had the charcoal-grey, leathery skin of a rhinoceros. A horn jutted out from where his hairline should be. He wore a black, fitted tuxedo vest and a top hat over the crown of his head. His muscular shoulders and thick arms ended in human hands. His cloven hooves jutted out of the bottom of tight, black leather chaps. Feeling Em's horrified stare, the creature turned in her direction. His black, beady eyes, shaded by his pronounced browridge, glimmered beside a jutting nose and masculine jawline. He gave Em a ragged-toothed smile before sauntering back to the multicolored river of energy.

"Be gone!" George's voice commanded again.

The demon laughed at the repeated command. He hopped onto the letter "M" and floated down the river of energy. Just before he disappeared over the horizon of her vision, he took off his top hat and bowed to Em.

"Em!"

George's hand came into view. He grabbed the vision,

and it burst into flame with a pop.

"Em!"

George's hands went to her shoulders. He gave her a gentle shake.

"Are you stricken?"

She was shaking so hard that he wrapped his arms around her. She shook her head.

"Can you speak?" George asked.

"Ter . . ." Em tried to say "terrified."

"Yes," George said.

He pulled her out of bed. Pushing and prodding, he got her under the shower spigot. He turned on the water, and a blast of cold water fell onto her head. She gasped at the cold. He threw a handful of salt over her head and reached to change the water temperature. There was a tremendous *Pop!*

The bathroom windows blew outward, showering the street below with glass. The power went out, and she collapsed.

Wrapped in three thick blankets, Em sat with her knees against her chest in a tattered armchair in her living room. She held a large mug of chamomile tea up to her nose while she watched George talk to Ann Pudeator. Ann had been a midwife in Salem Village and now ran the midwife department at Brigham and Women's Hospital. Since the Salem Twenty had unique medical issues, Ann had always been their medical doctor. Plus, she loved delivering babies. It wasn't hard for her to continue in this profession.

She was one of George's lovers. Em peered over the mug of tea to watch them talk to each other.

Em wasn't jealous, mostly because she wasn't a jealous person. She didn't feel possessive of George. If anything, she relished the time he was away serving the homeless and the nights he visited the other women. She knew that George considered her apartment home because she held him so lightly.

Em didn't have real relationships with human beings. Since Salem Village, she'd met only a few unique, human beings she felt she could truly trust. Human beings killed that which they didn't understand. She had always been something that human beings didn't understand. Since they'd killed her once, she figured she'd just leave them alone.

She had George and the others. Most days, that was enough for her. George caught her eye and smiled. He nodded to Em, and Ann looked up. They walked over to her.

"What's the prognosis?" Em asked.

The lights came on in the apartment.

"The power's back," George said.

He left the room to turn off the lights and appliances they'd turned on to test the electricity. Ann sat on the arm of her chair.

"Do you feel any better?" Ann asked.

"Sure," Em said. "Maybe. I don't know what you're asking, really."

"You had a terrible fright this morning," Ann said.

"You think I made it up," Em said.

"No," Ann said. "Of all the things that I believe, I don't

believe that you made up seeing a demon last night. I'm just not sure why *you* saw the demon or *what* you were doing to cause the demon to look at you."

"I was trying to figure out what those kids are up to," Em said. "Mostly it seemed like they were fun, curious kids, but there was this other thing."

"Malice," Ann said.

"Malice." Em nodded.

"Are you sure you didn't go looking for the devil and so you found one?" Ann asked.

Em drank her tea and thought it through. After a few minutes, Em shook her head.

"No, I think it's connected to this," Em said. "I think it's looking for us."

"Looking for us?" Ann shook her head. "Why?"

"No idea," Em said.

"Why now?"

"No idea," Em said.

"Do you think the Devil made us immortal?" Ann asked. "Gave us these powers?"

Em shrugged.

"George always said that it's a mark of God, like Cain," Ann suggested.

"I don't know about Gods and Devils," Em said. "They aren't my thing."

"But you think . . ."

"I think this demon creature did not leave when George commanded it," Em said. "I think . . . Well, honestly, I don't know."

"George said that Shonelle wants to do a séance for the Salem Witches here," Ann said, "at the Mystic Divine."

Em nodded.

"Would you..." Ann started. "No. You wouldn't, would you?"

"If you're asking if I'd have a séance to trap a demon, possibly the entity that did this to us and brought all of that pain to Salem Village..." Em looked up, and Ann nodded, "No. I'd be happy if I never saw it again."

"What about your ever-burning need to know?" Ann said with a smile.

Em shook her head. She loved mysteries, but this was different.

"It must have been horrifying," Ann said.

"How am I, Doc?" Em asked to change the subject.

"You seem fine," Ann said. "Your physical body doesn't show any effects of the episode. Your spirit body shines pure white, as always. You just seem tired."

"Is the demon draining me?" Em asked.

"Oh, I doubt it," Ann said. Ann's eyes flicked to where George had gone. "It's more likely that your partner came back from a month-long trip and you've been catching up."

"Are you offering to take him for a night?" Em grinned at Ann.

"It does sound fun," Ann said. "But, no. As you know, I'm seeing the head of surgery. He's... fun, young, no baggage, doesn't have time for kids. He also gives me nice little presents."

Ann held up a large diamond ring on her left hand.

"Congratulations," Em said.

"Thanks," Ann said. "I thought it was time for another husband."

"Probably," Em said. "I'm sure you'll be very happy."

"I don't have the hang-ups about humans that you have."

Em smiled.

"I don't like this, Em," Ann said. "Neither does George. I'm going to talk to Margaret. I'm seeing her today for lunch. She's good at long-term prediction. Do you mind?"

"No." Em shook her head at the idea that her friend, and fellow witch, Margaret Scott, would look into her long-term future. "I think we should all be on our guard."

"Why?" Ann asked.

"I don't know," Em said. "Just feels like . . ."

George came back into the room with another cup of tea, which he gave to Em. He put his arm over Ann's shoulder.

"Just feels like?" George said.

"We're in danger," Em said. "Something has changed. For us. What do you think?"

While Ann closed her eyes to think, George didn't take his eyes off Em.

"I think you're right," Ann said in a low voice. She glanced at George. "You?"

"I don't know," George lied. "I think Em needs some rest."

"I'll go," Ann said. "I need to be at work by nine, anyway."

George walked Ann out. They kissed at the door, and Ann left. George came back into the living room. He stood about a foot from her, half staring at the wall and half looking at her.

"What is it?" Em asked.

"What is what?" George asked. He scowled but didn't look at her.

"You and I don't do this," Em said. "We don't lie to each other or sugar-coat the truth. What do you think about this 'demon' or whatever?"

"I think that I had to burn the vision to destroy it," George said. He glanced at her and flushed with emotion. "I think I had to cleanse you with water and salt to clear the presence from you. I think the burst of energy blew out the power for a mile radius and destroyed our bathroom windows. I think . . ."

Em's eyes scanned George's face.

"I think that I love you," George said with a sigh and a shrug. "I'm scared for you, for us, for all of us."

"This darkness . . . this thing . . ." Em said.

George tipped his head to the side to listen deeply to her words.

"It belongs to us in some way," Em said. Her voice dropped. "To me."

George scowled at the idea.

"And it's coming," Em said.

"It's going to be powerful — and not very nice," George said. "Was the vision a warning, then?"

"I don't know," Em said. "Maybe a test . . . for me. He bowed to me."

"As if you were his master?" George asked.

"No," Em said. "No, of course not. He bowed as if to say . . ."

Em finished her tea and looked up at George.

"I'll be back," Em said.

"Ta ta for now." George bowed with a flourish. "Yes, I

think you're right."

Em nodded.

"Come," George held his hand out to her. "I've called our employees and told them you were sick. I'm taking you back to bed to rest and recover."

Em opened her mouth to argue.

"We've lived ten human lifetimes and worked hard through every one of them," George said. "We can afford to rest on the bad days."

Em closed her mouth and nodded.

"Good," George said.

He held out his hand and led her back to bed.

Unable to sit still anymore, Em went to spend time in the honeybee colonies she kept on the roof of the building. Two hours later, she was hot, sweaty, and happy. There was nothing like the ordered chaos of honeybees to make everything in the world seem right. She kept her Italian honeybee hives in two Top-Bar hives and three traditional Langstroth hives. She looked up when a shadow came over the Langstroth hive she was working.

Sam Wardwell had dressed in one of the beekeeper's white jumpers and head net that Em kept in the bee shed. He was standing near the hive. She gave him a wooden frame of wax comb covered with bees. He held the frame up to his eyes to look at the rice-grain-sized honeybee eggs.

"They've settled in," Sam said.

"Hopefully they'll thrive," Em said with a shrug.

Like most beekeepers in the United States, Em had lost more than half of her hives over the winter due to a combination of a long, hard spell of cold weather and pesticides. In early May, she had replaced the ones she'd lost with new beehives in the hope they would survive. Sam had picked up beekeeping in the early 1800s, when he lived with Em for a few years while getting back on his feet. He now kept his own hives at his suburban home in Lincoln, Massachusetts.

"I replaced the windows," Sam said.

He had been a carpenter in Salem Village. After getting sober and addressing his inner demons, he'd opened a small carpentry shop. The business had flourished and was now a multimillion-dollar construction company.

"I replaced them with double-paned," Sam said. "They're nice and will keep you warm next winter."

"At least the bathroom won't be drafty," Em smiled. "Next winter, I'll live in there."

"You should let me replace all of them," Sam said.

"I can't afford it," Em said.

"Em . . ." Sam started.

Em shrugged.

"If I don't save as much as I can, what will we have when we need it?" Em asked.

"We could put in more . . ." Sam started.

"Everyone does what they can," Em said. "Immortality isn't for the meek of heart."

"Or Bridget," Sam said.

"I was going to say 'Susannah.'" Em smiled and turned her attention back to the open beehive in front of her.

"You know, I hear myself talk, and . . ." Sam laughed. "I know I'm ridiculous. You've bailed me out of more than my share of expensive disasters. I guess I'd like to give back a little."

"I appreciate the new windows," Em said.

"Nothing, really," Sam said. "If I write you a check, will you put it in the fund?"

Em looked up at him. For a moment, their eyes held. She nodded.

"Thanks," Sam said. "You're our rock."

"I'm kind of your crazy rock," Em said. "Did George tell you what happened last night?"

"George, Alice, Ann, Margaret,..." Sam nodded. "Everyone's downstairs waiting for you; even Giles managed to show up."

"Gee, that sounds fun," Em said. "An inquisition of witches."

"Kind of a role reversal," Sam said. "George is cooking."

Em looked up at him.

"It smells divine," Sam said. "That man of yours ... You don't think he'd swing over to my side?"

"I don't," Em said. "I think you and John will miss out on George."

"And Giles?" Sam asked.

"That man never left the 17th century," Em said.

Sam laughed. They settled into beekeeping. They went frame by frame through the beehives together. They managed to find the queen from one hive. Another hive looked like it had been split in half by swarming. The split hive was healthy enough, but Em marked the cover so she'd remember to keep an eye on it. They moved on to the next hive. The hot, satisfying work took all their attention. When they finished reviewing the hives, they placed special compartments, called "Supers," where the bees could collect honey.

"Thanks, Sam," Em said as they hung their bee suits in the bee shed.

"For what?" Sam asked.

"Beekeeping, new windows, friendship ..." Em smiled. "I owe you."

Sam snorted as if she'd made a joke.

"Ready to face the music?" Sam asked.

"Not really," Em said.

"Hey, you guys!" Margaret Scott appeared on the stairwell. "George has readings to do tonight. You need to ..."

"We're coming down," Sam said.

Margaret smiled at Sam. He passed her on the stairwell and continued down to Em's floor.

"How are you, Em?" Margaret asked.

"I'm okay," Em said.

"Any darkness today?" Margaret asked. She squinted as she scanned Em's physical and spirit bodies.

"Not that I can tell," Em said.

Margaret had been in her late seventies when she was hanged in Salem Village all those years ago. In modern life, Margaret looked like she was a fit woman in her mid-forties. She worked as an economic forecaster for the state of Massachusetts.

"See anything?" Em asked.

"Not a thing," Margaret said. "You're such a radiant light. I'm sure you'd just block out any darkness."

Em smiled. Margaret's words were always in inverse relation to her forecasts. If Margaret saw a negative outcome, she'd always say something incredibly kind and nice. Margaret must have seen something that she didn't like in Em.

"Yes?" Em asked.

Margaret blushed.

"It's okay," Em said. "We can talk about it at dinner."

Em trotted down the two flights of stairs to her apartment, and Margaret followed. Em opened the door to her apartment and felt the wave of warm friendship and noise of talking voices. Margaret slipped in behind her. Rather than going straight into her living room, she slipped into the bathroom for a quick shower and inspection of the new windows. She had just stepped into the shower when the door opened.

"Hello?" Em asked.

"Just brought you some clothes," Sarah Wildes said.

"Thanks, Sarah," Em said. "Are you . . .?"

Sarah Wildes' face appeared around the shower curtain.

"I'm sniffing around," Sarah Wildes said. "I hate the subterfuge, but Margaret asked me to check and . . ."

"And?"

"Finish your shower!" Sarah Wildes smiled at Em and left.

"Witches," Em said under her breath.

She made quick work of her shower and got dressed. She brushed out her long hair before opening the bathroom door. Giles Corey was standing on the other side of it.

"You've brought this on yourself," Giles said.

Em rolled her eyes and tried to move past him. Angry, he grabbed her by the arms.

"You should have listened to me," Giles said.

Em shook her head. He yelped and let go. There was an

odd rumbling in the apartment, and everyone stopped talking. Now furious, Giles took a step toward her.

"How dare you?" Giles asked. "You've brought this upon all of us."

"You have no more idea of what's going on than I do," Em said. "Don't pretend you do."

"I know who's at the root of it," Giles said.

"Who?" Em asked.

Their energies pressed against each other's in the tight hallway. Angry, Em refused to give him any ground.

"Giles?" Sam asked from behind them in the hallway.

"What?" Giles asked.

Giles tried to overpower Em. She kept him off her. She was at least twice his strength, which infuriated him even more. She could have easily overpowered him, but she refused to do to him what he'd always wanted to do to her.

"You remember what happened the last time you went after Em?" Sam asked.

Giles didn't let up his press upon Em.

"Why don't you come out of there, and we'll talk about it?" Sam asked again.

"She's the root of all of this!" Giles said.

"Come out of there so we can talk," Sam encouraged. "She's not your problem alone. We all want to talk to Em. You can have your say then. If you're right, we'll back you. You know that."

Exhausted, Giles let go of his press with a sigh. He shot Em an angry look but was clearly relieved to have a way out. Giles spun around and stormed away from her. Sam touched Em's arm to make sure she was all right. She nodded. Sam followed Giles into the living room. For a moment, Em stood in the hallway to catch her spiritual breath.

When she looked up, George was standing in the hallway. As if to say that she couldn't help it, she shrugged. He smiled. He held his arm out, and she tucked herself into him. He held her close for a moment. Kissing her neck, he stepped back, gave her a nod, and took her hand. They went into the living room to face the music.

Chapter Four

Em stepped out onto Boylston Street. Turning, she pulled closed the door to the back stairs, which went to the living areas. She looked both ways down Boylston Street before setting off across the street. While she would survive being hit by a car, she didn't have time for the hassle today. She stopped walking to let a man running with a baby stroller pass before entering the Boston Common. She'd gone only a few feet into the Common when she picked up a familiar ghost.

"Where you going, Em?" the woman asked.

Em put in the wireless earpiece to her phone so that no one would notice that she was talking to the air. Even though the Common was quiet this early in the morning, Em couldn't be too careful.

"Good morning, Ann," Em said to Ann Hibbins, who'd been hanged for witchcraft on the Common in 1656. The wife of a wealthy merchant, no one, including Ann, was sure why she was hanged for witchcraft. She'd lingered in the Common since 1656. She was one of the first souls Em had met when she moved to Boston in 1692.

"I saw all those *witches* at your house this morning," Ann said.

Em inwardly groaned. Ann was feeling sorry for herself

this morning.

"Why *I* was hanged and died?" Ann gave an angry snort. "But you *witches*! You get to live on and on and on . . ."

Em let her continue in her "on and ons" until Ann got tired of saying the words.

"You could move on," Em said.

"I could move on!" Ann said. "You could have the decency to *die*!"

"Many of us would love to do just that!" Em chastised Ann. "It's not like we planned this!"

"I know," Ann sighed.

Em kept walking while Ann floated along beside her. They weren't exactly friends. They just belonged to the same club of innocent women who'd been hanged for witchcraft. Ann had the dubious honor of having been widowed by one of the magistrates who condemned witches. Em glanced at Ann.

"Why don't you move on?" Em asked.

"I lost the light, Em," Ann said.

"'Lost the light'?"

"I don't know if I can anymore," Ann said.

Em shot Ann a glance. Ann was smart and sly. Em wasn't sure if Ann was trying to manipulate her. Catching Em's look, Ann gave Em a sad shrug.

"I'm stuck here, Em," Ann said.

Em snorted.

"Why did you make that sound?" Ann asked.

"I'm stuck here, too," Em said.

Ann laughed. Em kept walking. Knowing Ann would stay in the park, Em stopped at the *Freedom Trail* near Beacon Street.

"Your hanging day is next week, right?" Em asked.

"June 19th," Ann said.

"Why don't I see if we can't help you?" Em asked. "We'll have a little celebration and see if we can't send you on your way."

"Would everyone come?" Ann asked.

"By everyone, you mean George and John?" Em asked.

"Sam's my favorite," Ann smiled.

"Yes," Em said. "I can promise George, and I'll call John and Sam. I'm sure some of the others will want to come."

"That would be nice," Ann said.

"We'll see if we can't help you transition," Em said. "What if you change your mind?"

"I won't," Ann said. "I've wanted to ask you about it for a long time. I just never got around to it."

Em smiled her goodbye and started walking.

"It's time," Ann said. "I need to do it before . . ."

Em spun in place.

"Before what?" Em asked.

Ann had disappeared. Em cursed herself for trying to help the hanged-for-witchcraft crowd. It only ever caused her grief. Em scowled and continued down Beacon Street to Joy Street. It was a little less than a mile from the Mystic Divine to the Vilna Shul. After last night, Em needed the walk to clear her head.

Everyone thought Em was in trouble. As soon as George said that he thought they were *all* in trouble, everything erupted. Of course, Sarah Wildes, Sam Wardwell, and Elizabeth Howe were loyal to Em. They agreed that if Em was in trouble, they were all in trouble. Giles banged the drum that Em got herself into this trouble and should get herself out of it. No one ever listened to Giles.

Margaret Scott agreed with George. She felt like something was changing. She couldn't define the "something" — she was just sure that it had changed.

"For whom?" Wilmot Redd had asked.

"For all of us," Margaret had said.

Em watched the flicker of hope dance across Alice's face. When Alice realized Em had noticed, she made a sad shrug. Em had no doubt that, if there were ever a chance that they could leave this life, Alice would be the first one to go. John Willard jumped in to say that he'd not heard even a whisper about the Salem Twenty at the FBI, his current employer. He thought people were more concerned with terrorists from other places than homegrown witches. A sigh of relief went through them.

Then Martha Carrier spoke up. She said that Em was right. Increased technology meant increased surveillance. Their days of anonymity were numbered. As general counsel for the CIA, Martha knew of nothing that would stop various government agencies from detaining and extracting the information they needed from the Salem Twenty. A wave of frost went through the group. Never one to hold back, Martha went on to remind everyone to be careful of what they said — anywhere.

Susannah Martin and Mary Eastey piped up to invite everyone to live with them in their Amish community in Pennsylvania. No cell phones. No worries. This led to a huge fight with Susannah, Mary, and Giles arguing a return to Puritan life, against everyone else.

Of course, John thought they should leave for their islands in French Polynesia and wait for a more reasonable generation. This irritated Sarah Good, who thought of the islands as her personal property. Sarah Good said something smug, and they argued again. Ownership of the islands was put to rest by Martha, their resident lawyer, who assured everyone that the islands were owned by the Salem Twenty, LLC, which Em ran.

Fighting her bruised ego, Sarah Good had to have the final say. Never one to mince words, she told Em that, since she had seen the Devil, it was up to her to work it out. They would expect either a resolution to the problem or Em's report on *her* progress by July 19th — Sarah Good's hanging day.

After everyone left, she and George had argued over a best plan of action.

"If it's up to me, then you can be damned sure *I* will take care of it," Em had said.

"You don't have to take care of it yourself!" George had said.

"Who's going to help me?" Em had asked. Angry and exhausted, she couldn't keep herself from saying, "If I count on you to help, you'll just schedule another trip to save some stranger!"

George's hurt face was icing on her already awful night. He'd grabbed his jacket and gone down to do readings. She pretended to be asleep when he returned. He wasn't fooled, but at least she didn't have to talk to him. She got up this morning before he was awake.

If this was her problem, she was going to deal with it. Em groaned at herself.

Why did she have to be so stubborn?

Why couldn't she share her life?

Em had always taken care of her own problems. No matter what happened in life, she soldiered on. Alone.

George hated that. She swallowed hard at what she knew was true. He loved her. He wanted to share her burdens. Certainly, he told her that enough.

But Em could live only one way: her problem, her responsibility. She'd gotten up this morning to get it done.

Turning onto Phillips Street, she saw George standing on the sidewalk up ahead, staring at Vilna Shul. She stopped walking. He turned to look at her. Even from this distance, she could see him grinning in a kind of "I found you" way. She dropped her head and rolled her shoulders forward in defeat. His shoes appeared on the sidewalk before her, and she looked up.

"How?" she asked.

"I'm a witch," George grinned. He held out his arms, and she let him hug her. "I've survived my fair share of Em winters. I don't really want to go through it again, especially now, when you're in real trouble."

"'Em winter'?"

"When you push me away and decide you're going to do it all yourself," George said. "God gave me immortality so I could spend it with you. I'm going to do just that."

"And . . ."

"No 'ands.'" George cut her off. He kissed her hair. "Do you want to tell me your plan?"

"My plan?"

"Why are we standing in front of a Jewish cultural center?" George asked.

"Have I ever told you about leaving Salem Village?" Em asked.

"No," George said. "Not a word. Ever."

"And how I got this name?" Em searched his face.

"I know that you've always hated your given name," George said. "I've always called you 'Em.' I know that you insisted on being called 'Emogene.'"

Em looked away from him. They were a building away from Vilna Shul. She took his hand and led him to the Vilna Shul. Taking a key from her purse, she unlocked the metal gate and gestured for him to go up the short flight of cement steps in front of the historic Jewish Center. He took a seat on an outdoor chair on the porch. She sat down next to him.

"I've never been here," he said.

Em nodded.

"How . . .?" he started and then shook his head. "How is it that I feel like I know you so well, and you have a key to the gate? When did you become Jewish?"

Em smiled.

"How does one go from being a woman of Christ's gospel to . . .?" George gestured around him. "And when? I rack my brain. When was the first time we reconnected after . . ."

He looked around to see if anyone was observing them.

"I'll tell you, if you ever stop talking," Em said.

"I do talk a lot," George smirked. He made a show of closing his mouth. "Are you going to tell me?"

Em smiled. George tipped his head back and laughed. His laughter brought a large, middle-aged man with short, dark hair and a beard with a white Yarmulke on his head to the door of the cultural center. Seeing Em, the man rushed to her, pulled her from the chair, and hugged her.

"Welcome, Grandmother," the man said. "Welcome."

The man let her go to look at her. He glanced at George.

"Is this George?" the man asked. He looked at Em, and she nodded. "Welcome, Reverend Burroughs!"

The man looked back at Em.

"This is a very good day," the man said. The man looked expectantly to George and then to Em. "Are you going to introduce me?"

Em blushed and nodded.

"George, this is my grandson, Rabbi Isaac Peres," Em said.

"Great-great-great — and then some — grandson," Isaac said.

George's face flushed with emotion.

"Yes, I know," Isaac said. "One rabbi a generation with knowledge of our grandmother. That is how it's been in my family since . . ."

Isaac looked at Em.

"1692," Em said.

"1692," Isaac said. "Will you come in?"

"George wants to know our story," Em said to Isaac.

"Please do come in," Isaac said. "We can talk in my office. I have pictures and . . ."

The man opened the Vilna Shul door and ushered them into the cool building. Em took the blue-grey lace scarf from around her neck and covered her head. George gestured to his head.

"Don't worry," Isaac said. "You are welcome here in any form, George Burroughs. Please, come inside our little center."

They walked down a hall but had to stop as a class of

third- or fourth-graders came past them.

"My father will be jealous," Isaac said when the class had passed.

"You know he's teaching Kabbalah at the store," Em said.

"No, I did not know that," Isaac said with a smile. "Stinker. He always has something up his sleeve."

Em smiled. They turned a corner and then another before going through an open door to a warm, friendly office. Isaac took a seat behind his desk. George stopped to look at the photos on the wall. He pointed to one, and Em nodded.

"That's 1905, Reverend," Isaac said.

"Please, call me 'George,'" he said. "As you may know, I wasn't ever ordained, and, anyway, I haven't been a Reverend in a long time."

"George," Isaac said. "I'm Isaac."

"Plus, Em only calls me 'Reverend' when I've annoyed her," George said.

Isaac laughed.

"How can I help?" Isaac asked.

"I wanted to know... everything." George spoke up before Em could say anything.

Isaac looked at Em, and she gave a slight nod. Isaac got up and closed his office door.

"I have never heard the beginning of the story," Isaac said. Used to helping people tell their truths, Isaac encouraged Em with a kind nod. He sat down. "You start. I will fill in what I know."

Em swallowed hard and nodded.

"I remember waking up," Em said.

"In your coffin?" Isaac asked.

"We were thrown into a mass grave," George said. "They stacked us up in a crevice right next to the tree they hanged us on. I was hanged in August, so I was below Em. Em in September. She would have been near the top."

"My group was the last of the hangings," Em said. "I *was* near the top. I'm not sure why because I was hanged right after Sam. And . . ."

Em took a deep breath and sighed.

"I remember waking up," Em said. "It was dark and close. I couldn't feel my body. I tried to scream, but nothing came out. I was terrified that this was the afterlife. There was no heaven, no God — nothing but this awful, dark closeness . . . and silence."

Caught up in her memory, Em stared into space.

"I smelled rotting flesh first," Em smiled. "It was probably George rotting somewhere below."

"Your first physical experience was the stench of me?" George laughed.

"True love," Isaac said. Em and George laughed. "What happened next, Grandmother?"

"First the awful smell," Em said. "And then I could hear things: the wind in the stand of Oak trees, the North River spilling into the bay, crickets, and animals moving in the dark. I'd lost my right eye in the hanging and . . . Well, there was nothing to see. I was under Alice — no, under Ann. I wiggled and moved and shoved and . . . Suddenly, the moon shone, and there I was — sitting in a crevice on the barren hill above town next to the bay.

"I reached for Ann, and she woke with a scream. I mean, we still looked like we'd been hanged. Our heads were like watermelons — bruised — our tongues hanging out. Our garments were soiled with the release brought by death. We couldn't speak. Alice woke next and then Mary Ayer. We were horrified to be awake and terrified of being found out. Always the doctor, Ann got us to wash on the edge of the bay. Sam woke, Margaret . . . I think Wilmot — no, Mary woke last. By that time, we had a kind of assembly. Ann took them to the water. I helped stick their tongues in, straighten their heads, things like that."

"Your necks didn't break?" Isaac asked.

"Short drop and a slip knot," George said. "It took most of us more than ten minutes in excruciating pain to suffocate. Full death took at least twenty minutes. It's why they put the bag over our heads. They didn't want to see our faces turn purple."

"A couple of us had heart attacks," Em said.

"And still came back?" Isaac asked.

Em nodded.

"You touched me," George said. "I remember feeling this bright warmth come to me. I have dreams about it sometimes, and I feel . . . so safe, like I was finally safe after such a long time of wandering."

George nodded.

"You were out of the ground," Em said. "They didn't bury him well. After a month . . . Well, you can imagine."

"Took more than a year to heal," George said.

Isaac nodded.

"How are you handling all of this?" Em asked.

"I've tried to work out every detail since I was told, Grandmother," Isaac said. "My father as well."

"And you're all right with all of this . . . detail?" Em

asked.

"Fascinated at the power of God," Isaac said.

Em smiled at him and sat down in one of the armchairs in front of his desk.

"Where were we?" Em asked.

"Hanging, awakening," George said. "Martha and John were hanged on my day."

"George Jacobs and John Proctor, too, but their families came for them," Em said.

"They didn't become immortal?" Isaac asked.

"Not that we know of," Em said.

"Just those of us in the crevice," George said.

"It's hard to explain," Em said. "I thought . . . I mean, I don't know why I thought this, but I did."

She looked at George and then at Isaac.

"I thought maybe our hanging wasn't done well," Em said. "I mean, by the time I was hanged, people were already talking about ending the witch trials. I guess I figured we woke up because they'd botched the hangings. We hadn't really been dead."

"You weren't revived from death but recovered from passing out," Isaac said. "That's denial. 'They didn't really do this to me. It didn't really happen.'"

"Exactly. That's what I believed until . . ." Em looked at George. "George and Martha . . . They were . . . rotten. Small animals ate more than one meal from George."

"And we woke up," George said. He took the armchair next to Em.

"They woke up," Em said. "The rest were worse — Sarah Good, Susannah, Elizabeth, and Sarah Wildes."

"They were hanged in July," George said. "Bridget in

June."

"If you can imagine, there was no embalming. It was a warm summer," Em said. "It was . . . disgusting. The weird thing, well, the whole thing is weird, but *a* weird thing was that the people who were rotten didn't mind being rotten."

"We were happy to be alive," George said.

Em nodded.

"I don't know how long we were there," Em said. "Gallows Hill was outside of town, but you could see it from every part of town. We were there most of the night, cleaning up and getting our functions back, some."

"It took years for some of it to come back," George said. "Especially for those of us who had been dead a while."

"Giles," Em said. "He had been pressed to death a couple days before I was hanged."

"He was there, too?" Isaac asked.

"He was in with us," Em said.

"The refuse pile," George said.

"You remember that I had sons?" Em asked George.

"Two," George said.

"An hour or so before dawn, I went to my teenaged son," Em said. "He and I were very close. I knew he wouldn't be afraid; I knew he would know me regardless of how crazy I looked. He didn't say a word. Of course, I couldn't talk. He got the horse and wagon he used for his apprenticeship and brought it to Gallows Hill. He and I moved everyone in the wagon. We had to move fast because dawn was coming. He took Alice home to her husband because she was so adamant. Everyone else, he took to a homestead ten miles or more outside of town."

"Whose was that?" George asked.

"Mine," Em said. "Well, my late husband's. He'd bought it for his parents. He hadn't used it because his parents died before they made it to the US."

"They died in England?" George asked.

"Right," Em said. "We'd been married in England. They asked us not to go, but ... Anyway, the house had been torn down, but the barn was still there."

"Barn," George said. "Yes."

"Someone had to go, get out of Salem Village, and figure out how we would survive," Em said. "I was in the best shape, so it had to be me. My son dropped me with Alice. Luckily, John, Alice's husband, let me tag along with them as far as Boston. They went on to the South — North Carolina, I think."

"You just 'woke up'?" Isaac asked.

Chapter Five

"I did," Em said.

"I remember Em touching me," George said. "That's the first thing I felt since the crushing realization that they weren't going to stop, that they were going to hang me."

"And you didn't know any of the ... others," Isaac said. "You weren't friends or familiars."

"I'd been in the Boston jail with the other women since April," Em said. "We'd been through so much together that we were more than acquaintances. Still, I think if we never saw each other again, that would be fine, too. I felt strongly that it was up to me because I was in the best shape physically and mentally."

Em smiled at Isaac.

"Alice and John let me off on Beacon Hill," Em said. "It was just dawn. Like I said, I looked frightful. I needed to find a place to hide. When I did, I found Isaac and the children there."

"My grandfather," Isaac said.

"Rabbi Isaac Peres," Em said. "His wife, Emogene Peres, had been hanged for witchcraft in Spain. He knew what had happened to me by looking at me. He and their three young children — two girls and a boy — moved to America to get away from the religious persecution disguised as witch trials. Emogene was supposed to go with them, but . . . She saw them coming for her, for all of them, so she tricked Isaac into leaving with the children. She saved them. He could only watch as she was tried for being a Jew and hanged under the name of witchcraft. Isaac had all of her papers and everything. He offered me a deal right then and there. If I helped him with the children, he would say that I was Emogene."

"I didn't have much of a choice; it was also a pretty great deal," Em said. "I'd studied religion, so Judaism wasn't a huge stretch for me. Isaac taught me. He found work on the docks. He found us a home. He lived in the outside world, while I took care of our home. I wasn't able to say a word, not one, for almost a year. I had to wear something over my face for six months or more. It wasn't easy, but we made a life. After a year or so, we were happy, and the children thrived."

"Sephardic Jews such as us had been chased through Spain and Portugal, hunted in the name of witchcraft," Isaac said.

"He was furious about what had happened to me and the others," Em said. "And he never got over the sacrifice Emogene made for him and their children. He helped me feed and care for the others."

Em smiled at the great man's descendant sitting before her.

"He was a good, decent man," Em said.

"They built a Jewish community here in Boston," Isaac said.

"Orphanage," Em said. "There were so many children who'd lost their parents, and Jewish orphans had nothing, no one."

"They had you," Isaac said. "Isaac's son, Solomon, became a rabbi like his father. Isaac's daughter, Devorah, had married Isaac Lopez, and they'd opened a mercantile in 1716."

"You loved him," George said. "I remember that."

"She saved him," Isaac said. "It's family lore that my great-great-grandfather would never have survived America without his Emogene."

"I don't think I could have ever replaced Isaac's Emogene," Em said. "The loss of her never ebbed for Isaac, but we were happy. Yes, I loved him, his children, and their children. After so much horror and crazy goings-on, it was good to live such a simple life. I loved the big, anonymous city. Still do."

"They read every book they could get our hands on," Isaac said. "It's our family tradition to read widely and talk about ideas. Even the youngest child is expected to share what they know. While it's fairly common to do that now, it was unusual in the 1700s."

"The Salem Twenty scattered to the winds," Em said.

"After the fire," George said.

"Fire?" Isaac asked.

"Five or six years after moving to the homestead — around the turn of the century, I guess — a fire moved through the area," George said. "We had to move out. I went to England. Sam and John fought the Indians in the Crown colonies. The women went everywhere —to Boston, New York; some joined immigrant populations all along the Eastern seaboard."

George shrugged.

"We had to scatter," Em said. "By that time, we were healthy and getting around well."

"And well known," George said.

"People could have easily recognized us," Em said.

"Did you have ... powers?" Isaac asked. "I don't know what you call them."

"Magic?" Em asked. "I did. You?"

"I didn't know what it was or how to use that," George nodded. "That was Em. In her reading, she found books on how to manage this mastery of the elements — fire, water, time, space, air, that kind of thing."

"I didn't have the skill to control them," Em said. "There was no real guidebook. We picked up one thing here, another thing there. Anything we could find."

"A lot of it was trial and error," George said.

"Em put a spiritual section in Devorah's mercantile," Isaac said. "It's the first religious bookstore in Boston."

"I thought it would be a good way to meet anyone who knew anything," Em said.

"Did you?" George asked.

"Mostly charlatans and some people who knew a tiny bit of how things worked," Em said. "Since I had all the time in the world, I started to put it together into something that made more sense."

Em fell silent. She could feel George's eyes on her face. She smiled at Isaac.

"While I'm deeply glad for it, I'm not sure why we're here today," George said.

"Oh," Em said. "I need a favor."

"Grandmother, I am always at your service," Isaac said.

"I need a human to join a group of ghost hunters," Em

said. "I'm going with Shonelle, but I can't really go with a bevy of witches."

"Ghost hunters?" Isaac asked.

"They are ghost hunting in Danvers, you know, where Salem Village was," Em said. "They say they've filmed Bridget Bishop's ghost."

"Have they?" Isaac asked.

"Something I'd like to find out," Em said.

"They seem to have stirred up a kind of presence," George said. "We think this shade is connected to Em in some way."

"Grandmother?" Isaac looked worried. "What is this?"

"I don't know any more than that," Em said. "If I get more information, I think I can figure out what's going on. But for now, I just have this devil or demon or... dark thing... and an annoying bunch of kids talking about putting the spirit of one of the witches to rest."

"Do you think it's the same kind of apparition that caused all of this?" Isaac asked.

"That's the question, isn't it?" George asked at the same time Em said, "No."

Isaac smiled.

"When do they meet?" Isaac asked.

"They are meeting tonight," Em said. "They are going ghost hunting on Saturday."

"My eldest, Asher, and I will go," Isaac said. "It sounds fun."

"Thank you," Em said.

"It's my pleasure," Isaac said. "Now, if you're not doing anything, I was thinking about getting some breakfast. Interested?"

Em smiled.

"George?" Isaac smiled. "Let's take this woman out to eat."

"As you wish," George said.

Isaac hopped to his feet. They went through the facility and went out the back. Em was standing with George while Isaac went to get the car.

"Are you okay?" Em asked. "That's a lot to . . . process."

"You realize these people . . ." George gestured around him, "they are *human*."

"Not really."

"Oh, yeah?" George asked.

"They're family," Em said.

George chuckled. She let him hold her.

"I will tell you . . ." George started. He gave her a peck on the lips and let go.

"Yes?"

"I've learned something important," George said. He walked away from her as he talked.

"What's that?" Em asked.

"We were in suspension until you touched us," George said.

"What?"

"*You* are the reason we're immortal witches," George nodded.

"Me?" Em pointed to herself.

George turned to look at her. She looked so surprised that he had to smile.

"Why me?" Em asked.

"It's a good question," George said. "Why were you able to awaken us? If Rebecca and John and George had been there, would you have awakened them as well?"

Em shook her head.

"No — why do you think it's me?" Em asked.

"You touched us, and we awakened," George said.

"But I don't think I touched everyone," Em said.

"But someone you awoke touched someone else," George said.

Em made an exaggerated weaving motion to indicate that he was creating a big circle. He smiled.

"I'll tell you," Em said. "If I made us witches, I should be able to undo it. I've tried for Alice."

"We've all tried for Alice," George nodded. "It's not straightforward — that's for sure."

"It's not even crooked," Em said. "It's some kind of inter-dimensional weirdness."

"Inter-dimensional?" George smiled. "Maybe it's destiny."

Em shook her head.

"I don't think I was destined to be hated and hanged by witch-hysterical little girls," Em said. "You, either."

"We'll have to talk about it more," George said. He put his head down and kissed her lips. "I'm glad I came this morning."

"You are?" Em asked.

"Very," George nodded.

Em smiled. Isaac's car pulled up. Em got in the passenger seat of Isaac's SUV, and George stepped into the back.

"Do you have a favorite place?" Isaac asked.

Em shook her head.

"I have just the place," Isaac said. "I hope you don't mind. I called the family and told them you're here.

They're all meeting us for breakfast."

"Sounds nice," Em said.

"They want to meet Grandmother's smoking-hot boyfriend," Isaac laughed.

Em turned around and looked at George. If she didn't know him better, she would have sworn that he was blushing. He caught her look and smiled.

"What's going on?" Em asked.

"Family," George said. "It's been a very long time since I was around the noise and chaos of family."

"Three hundred years?" Em asked.

"A little longer than that," George said.

Isaac looked at him in the rearview mirror and laughed.

At Isaac's suggestion, Em offered to host the Salem ghost-hunting meeting at the Mystic Divine. Shonelle had called this John Parker, the young man running the meeting, to set it up. The young man and his group had the use of one of the upstairs rooms. The meeting was to go from eight to ten that evening. People began arriving more than an hour early to make sure they got in. By seven-thirty, Em realized they were going to have a problem.

There were too many people and not enough space. Em and Shonelle set up folding chairs in the little sitting area upstairs.

"Who knew the Salem Witches were so popular?" Em asked.

"I knew! Look — the store is packed." Shonelle leaned into Em. "*And* people are buying things. You should give me a cut of the profits for my brilliance."

"Sure," Em said. "How much would you like?"

"You could pay for my college," Shonelle said. "Oh, wait — you already do that."

"How . . . ?" Em opened her mouth with surprise, but Shonelle flipped her hair and went down the stairs. Em shook her head.

"And you're the witch," Sarah Wildes said under her breath as she went by on the way to her class.

Em had offered to pay for Shonelle's college, like she had her mother, on the condition that Shonelle didn't know. Clearly, Em needed to talk to Shonelle's mother. She scowled after the girl before going into the meeting room. George was at the front of the room getting John Parker's computers hooked up to the overhead. He caught her eye and nodded. They were all set.

"Okay, it's going to be tight," the young man who went by the name "John Parker" said. "Try to find a seat."

People poured into the room. Em went to the doorway to make sure she was available if anyone needed anything. Every seat in the room filled or was being saved. There were people sitting cross-legged in the front of the room and along all the aisles. A row of adults stood beside Em at the back of the room. Sarah Wildes threaded her way toward Em.

"My class wanted to go to the meeting," Sarah Wildes said. "I know there's not room, but . . ."

"We can set up the overheads to match." Em waved to George to get his attention.

"Like we do for the Wiccan holidays?" Sarah Wildes asked.

Em nodded. George moved through the crowd toward Em. Knowing what needed to be done, he left with Sarah Wildes. John Parker followed them out the door. This Salem ghost-hunting endeavor had taken over the store. As if they knew them personally, people whispered the names of the Salem Twenty.

"That was weird," Bridget said in a low tone to Em.

"What?" Em asked.

"I passed someone talking about me," Bridget said. "Did you know that I'm fantastic?"

"No." Em shook her head, and Bridget laughed.

They watched Alice come in with her gentleman client. She moved the sweater Em had put down to save them a seat. He sat down, and she came back to say hello.

"He wanted to come," Alice said. "Turns out, he's been interested in the Salem Witches since he was a kid. At least, that's what he said. He's become quite fond of me."

"Who hasn't?" Em asked. "Did you hear Bridget is fantastic?"

"Don't worry, Em," Bridget said. "They said you were a bitter old shrew."

"Isn't that the truth?" Alice laughed.

Bridget giggled, and Em shook her head.

"Are you going to be okay with..." Em leaned in to Alice, "John Parker?"

The young man came through the door at the exact moment. John Parker looked from Alice to Em.

"Can I help with something?" John Parker asked.

"My friend, Emogene, here was just telling me you were leading the meeting," Alice said in her southern accent.

Like most of the Salem Twenty, Alice gave off a radiant

sexual energy. The young man flushed and glanced at Bridget, who gave him a sweet-but-sexy smile. To cover his arousal, he moved into the room without saying another word. Bridget giggled.

"Anything?" Em asked Alice.

"That's no relation of mine," Alice said. "He's most definitely not the descendant of one of my children."

"You know all your children's descendants?" Bridget asked.

Alice pointed to her head to indicate that she used her skills as a witch to track them.

"Don't you?" Alice asked. She glanced at Em, who nodded.

"Sure, I just thought ... I wasn't sure that was ..." Bridget held her hands up to make quotation marks and said, "Approved."

"Try to stop me," Em said. Alice laughed.

"I do, too," Bridget said.

"Of course, you do, dear," Alice said. She gave Bridget a light hug. In a low voice, she said, "Don't let the bitter shrew get to you."

They laughed. Em watched John Parker for a few minutes while Alice and Bridget caught up. She touched Alice's arm.

"Could he be a relative of John's?" Em asked. "He kind of looks like him."

"No way." Alice shook her head. "I can smell my John on his relations."

"We think he's someone who's named 'John Parker' but has no relationship to you or John," Em said.

"I do," Alice said. She looked at Bridget, who nodded.

"I wonder why he looks like John," Bridget said.

"Good question," Em said. She glanced at Bridget, "Don't . . ."

The time between Bridget wanting something and her getting it was always short. Before Em could get the words out, Bridget had cast a spell. Em watched tiny particles of yellow light fly across the room to the young man. The tiny particles circled the young man from head to toe before coming back to Bridget. John Parker continued talking to the co-owner of the group and didn't seem to notice the magic surrounding him.

"Plastic surgery," Bridget whispered.

"That's not good," Em said.

"Why?" Alice asked.

"He's manipulating the situation for his gain," Em said.

"Con man?" Alice asked.

She turned to look at the young man. She glanced at Bridget before nodding in agreement to Em. The lights dimmed, and her gentleman waved to her. Alice smiled and trotted forward to her seat. Isaac and his college-aged son, Asher, came in the door. Em pointed to two seats she'd saved for them near Alice. He stopped for a moment, cupped her elbow to say hello, and they went to sit down. Bridget found a stool and pulled it over to where Em was leaning against the wall.

"Okay, let's get started," John Parker said.

Em watched people settle in their seats and open their minds. There was a crackle of excited anticipation in the air.

"Hello," John Parker said. "My name is John Parker. Yes, *that* John Parker."

There was a faint rustling in the crowd. This crowd knew that John Parker was a fisherman who was married to Alice Parker. One of Sarah's middle-aged yoga participants' hand shot up in the air. A waif of a woman, she didn't wait for his acknowledgement to speak.

"Can you tell us about Alice Parker?" the woman asked. "She's always been a mystery to me because there's nothing in the books or websites about her and John. I did find a reference that John packed up his family and left Salem Village the *very night* Alice was hanged."

The crowd mumbled their agreement with the question. This John Parker wasn't about to let the meeting slip away from him. He gave the women a thin smile and turned his attention to the crowd.

"We'll have time for everything," John Parker said. "Let's get started."

"That's smart," George said in her ear. Em startled at his voice. She hadn't seen him come in. She turned her head to look at him. "He needs to let the knowledge of who he says he is linger in people's minds for a while. Makes it more believable."

"He certainly knows what he's doing," Bridget whispered from the other side of her.

George looked at Bridget, and they nodded.

"We'd expect something emotionally charged next," George said. "Either graphic violence or an emotional gut punch. Better to have both."

Scowling, Em nodded.

"Can you get the lights?" John Parker asked. He nodded to Em.

Em flicked off the light switch on the wall behind her.

John Parker hit a button on his computer, and the drawing of Bridget's hanging came on the screen. People gasped. Em looked at Bridget. She was scowling. Bridget gave a quick shake of her head. She leaned into Em.

"I'd never wear that outfit," Bridget said. "Look at the bows."

Em's lips moved to form a smile. Just then, John Parker launched into a vivid description of Bridget's botched hanging. A wave of nausea went through the crowd. Somewhere in the area outside the room, a woman began to cry. Em's face stalled in her almost-smile.

"Told you," George said in her ear.

"He's performing magic," Em whispered to George.

George jerked with surprise. He turned his full attention to John Parker. Bridget stared at the young man in the front of the room. As the crowd slipped under his spell, Alice turned to look at Em. She nodded to Isaac and Asher. They were enraptured with this John Parker. Em gave Alice a slight nod, and Alice turned her hand over to surround herself, Isaac, Asher, and her gentleman with a protective bubble. The humans jerked awake the moment the bubble was completed.

Tiny sparks of magic seemed to emanate from the area around John Parker's head and surround him. The magic flowed over the crowd like a fog before flowing out of the room to capture every human in the store.

The crowd was enraptured.

Sarah Wildes came in the door and stood next to George. The line of witches openly gawked at John Parker. Somehow, he didn't seem to notice. In fact, he couldn't see the protective bubble Alice had placed around Isaac,

Asher, and her gentleman. As if he were a pawn to the magic, John Parker's mind and spirit seemed caught up in the gruesome story he was telling.

"What the hell?" Sarah Wildes said in a low voice. "Any ideas?"

"None," George said.

"Ever see this before?" Bridget asked.

George and Sarah Wildes shook their heads. Em kept her eyes on John Parker. Despite the intensity of her gaze, John Parker never looked in her direction. He kept talking. He gave a brief description of their trials and the eventual end in their hanging.

"Possessed?" Sarah Wildes asked.

George shook his head.

"Under someone else's power," Em said.

The demon appeared the moment the words left her mouth.

Chapter Six

He looked exactly as he had in her vision, down to his black leather chaps and top hat. As if he didn't have a care in the world, the demon sauntered out from behind John Parker. Grinning at Em, he took off his top hat and put it on John Parker's head.

The room became silent. John Parker's mouth was moving, but Em couldn't hear a word he was saying.

"Do you see . . .?" Em asked.

Em turned to look at Bridget. Her face was slack and her eyes vague. She glanced at George. He looked puzzled by something in the front of the room. With her touch, his eyes lost their focus, and he fell into a trance. She looked past George to Sarah Wildes. She was entranced by this demon.

Em's heart raced with panic. She swallowed hard. The demon had taken control of the room. Em's panic grew. George had to burn the vision to get rid of the demon the last time. The creature gave Em a cocky grin. She was alone this time.

"I see him, Em."

The words appeared in her mind. She had no idea who'd said them. Em's eyes scanned the audience.

Alice stood up.

"Be gone!" Alice screamed at the demon.

The creature turned to look at Alice. His eyes went from black to glowing red.

"Don't look at his eyes," Em yelled. "You can get caught in his gaze!"

"Be gone!" Alice said.

The demon hissed. Secure in Alice's protection bubble, Isaac and Asher jumped to their feet.

"Be gone from this room!" Isaac said. His words echoed through the store. "This is a human dwelling, not made for the likes of you. You are not welcome here!"

"Go!" Asher yelled in support of his father.

Alice's gentleman got to his feet. Em could see only the back of his brown suit. He turned to look at the door. Em saw panic on his face. Horrified by the entranced people and the demon, the man was ready to bolt. He reached his hand out to push Alice behind him.

"Be gone!" Alice said.

The demon crouched, making ready to spring onto Alice.

"No!" Em said to Alice. "This is my battle."

Em stepped away from the wall and walked to the middle of the aisle.

"It's my fight," Em said.

"Em!" Alice yelled with fear. "You can't . . ."

"Stay there," Em said. "Protect the humans."

Em glanced at her before turning her full attention to the demon. Alice's gentleman stepped in front of Alice to shield her from the demon.

"Enough!" Em said.

Her hands came together in a sharp clap. Bridget,

George, and Sarah Wildes awoke from their trance. The demon turned its red eyes to Em.

"You are not welcome here," Em said.

"Em!" George yelled. He tried to get to her, but Em tossed an invisible wall around him and the witches. He banged his fists against it. As he had on the gallows, George began reciting the Lord's Prayer in his preacher's voice. From behind the protective wall, the others joined him.

"*Our Father, which art in heaven, hallowed be thy name . . .,*" George, Sarah Wildes, and Bridget said .

The demon hissed at Em.

"You will leave this place," Em said.

" *. . .thy kingdom come, thy will be done, on earth as it is in heaven . . .*" the witches said.

To the demon's dismay, his legs began to fade from under him.

"I built this building from the ground up," Em said.

" *. . .Give us this day our daily bread, and forgive us our trespasses . . .*"

"This is *my* building, *my* store, *my* home. You are *not* welcome here. It is protected from the likes of you. You will leave."

Em reached the palm of her left hand up to the heavens to pull down the power of the angels.

" *. . .as we forgive those who trespass against us . . .*"

She pushed the palm of her right hand out in front of her. She looked up to see a sparkling figure eight shining above her head.

" *. . .Lead us not into temptation . . .*"

"Be gone!" Em said.

" *...but deliver us from evil!*"

The demon sprang into the air to attack her. She pointed the palm of her right hand at him. There was a flash, like a firecracker, and the room fell into pitch-black silence. Sarah Wildes and Bridget screamed in horror. The smell of smoke rose from the front of the room.

"Light returneth," Em said.

The gloom vanished. The room lights flickered and came on. The room was absolutely still. The demon had vanished, leaving only a wisp of smoke in his place.

"We believe we've found the actual site of the Salem Witch burials." John Parker's voice cracked through the still silence.

The young man had been speaking the entire time the demon was there. He stopped talking and looked confused at Em, who was still standing in the aisle.

"Is there a problem?" John Parker asked.

"Spider emergency," Em said.

She took a tissue from the boxes along the aisle and pretended to capture a spider. John Parker glanced at Isaac and Asher, who were sitting down.

"My son is terrible allergic," Isaac said in a thick Yiddish accent that would rival his ancestor. "Very bad, very bad."

Asher nodded. Em held up the tissue indicating that she'd captured the spider. With great flourish, George took the tissue from her and jogged to the bathroom. Em went back to her spot next to the door.

"I had no idea there were horrible spiders here," Alice said in her southern accent. "I'm terrified of those spiders."

She turned to her gentleman. Touching his arm, she

cleared his memory of the demon. His face went from care worn to a bright smile for the lovely Alice.

"Come on, Shug. Let's get out of here," Alice said.

The man looked at John Parker and then at Alice. She held out her hand, and he took it. They walked down the aisle and left the building.

"Now, where was I?" John Parker asked. "That's right . . ."

When George returned, Em pointed out the door. George, Sarah Wildes, and Bridget followed her to her office. Em didn't say a word until her office door was closed. Em took her seat at her desk. Bridget sat down in a chair while George and Sarah Wildes stood.

"What the hell was that?" George asked.

"No idea," Em said.

"But you . . .?" Sarah Wildes asked. "How?"

"No idea," Em said. "Have any of you seen this demon before?"

"No," Bridget said. Sarah Wildes shook her head.

"George?" Em asked. "Have you read about such a thing?"

"Never," George said. "We covered devils and demons in theology school, but that guy never came up. And I assure you, I've never seen him before."

"Have you ever felt his presence?" Em asked. "Any of you?"

"Yes," Sarah Wildes said. "Yes. I have."

"Do you remember when?" Em asked.

"Have you?" Sarah Wildes ignored Em's question to ask Bridget and George. "Have you felt him before?"

Bridget nodded. George was staring off into the

distance. Sarah Wildes touched his arm, and he looked at her.

"Have you felt this demon before?" Sarah Wildes repeated.

"Yes," George said.

"Where?" Em asked.

"Salem Village," George said. He glanced at Sarah Wildes. She and Bridget nodded their heads. "They came for me in Maine. They dragged me from my dinner table and brought me back to Salem Village for trial. I remember being astonished how much Salem Village had changed. There was a cast over the town, a kind of grey fog or shadow. Returning to Salem Village, that's the first time I felt this demon. That's why I was so terrified for Em. The very same creature who'd descended Salem Village into madness has returned."

"What are we going to do?" Bridget asked.

"No idea," Em said. "But one thing's for sure. This is definitely between me and him."

George went to her. He nodded, and she stood from her chair.

"Sarah?" George said. He touched her shoulder. "Bridget?"

"Well?" Em smiled.

"Clear," Sarah Wildes said. Bridget nodded.

"You're 'clear,'" George said. "What does it mean?"

"It means the demon is gone," Em said.

"For now," Sarah Wildes said.

"Gone is gone," Em said.

"And these kids?" Bridget asked.

"We need to keep an eye on this John Parker," George

said. "He may be the entire scope of our problem or the tip of the iceberg. You saw him the day you had the vision, right?"

"He was waiting outside the store for Shonelle," Em said.

"But not inside," Sarah Wildes said.

"He didn't have an invitation to come inside until tonight," Em said.

The witches gave remarkably similar worried nods of their heads. Em smiled.

"We had success tonight," Em said. "We should feel good about that."

"We're going to have to be careful," Sarah Wildes said. "All of us."

"Protection," George said. "We must keep up our psychic protection at all times."

"And stay connected to each other," Em said. "Now is not the time to wander off to the island for fifty years."

Sarah Wildes and Bridget nodded.

"I'll tell the others," Sarah Wildes said. With a nod, she left the office.

"I'm going back up to see what else he says," Bridget said.

"Want to see the photo of your ghost?" Em smiled.

Bridget blushed. She raised a hand in goodbye and darted out of the room.

"Well?" Em asked George.

"I think you're incredibly brave," he said.

"But?" Em asked.

"I don't know what we're up against," George said.

"I don't, either," Em said.

"Why has he come?" George asked. "While I have an idea of *how* he took over Salem Village, I have no idea *why*.

Or why he is here *now*."

Em looked at him, and their eyes held.

"I'm wondering when we *ever* knew what we were up against — *or* why," George said. "When I started my life, I never thought I'd be hanged as a witch. I was a man of God, after all. When I was hanged as a witch, I never thought I'd live three hundred more years. And I never thought I'd have all of this and all of you in my life."

Em blushed.

"I guess I'm trying to say, 'Situation normal.'" George grinned at Em. She nodded. "You want to go up?"

Em shook her head.

"I don't, either," George said.

"What about . . .?" Em pointed up.

"We're going with them on their ghost hunt, right?" George asked.

Em nodded.

"We'll end up having the séance here," George said. "That is what you were thinking, right?"

Em nodded.

"Then there's no reason to listen to the blowhard," George said. "Let's get Isaac and Asher and go to dinner."

Nodding, Em puckered her lips and blew a short burst of air to call them to her. Ten minutes later, Isaac and Asher came into the office.

"We were thinking of getting dinner," Isaac said. "Would you like to join us?"

"Sounds fun," Em said.

"I know just the place," George said with a smile.

"Lead on, my friend," Isaac said.

Em peered out her bedroom windows at the pre-dawn fog. She went to the closet for a thick, wool Aran sweater. She pulled the sweater over her long-sleeved T-shirt and jeans. Turning, she caught a glimpse of herself in the full-length mirror. Even after all of this time, she was still startled by her image in a mirror. She stopped.

Her long, dark hair was tucked up in a thick knot — the way she liked it. The fog had made ringlets out of the wisps of hair around her face. Framed by the curls, her dark eyes looked enormous. Out of habit, she touched the cleft in her chin. Her father used to say that he'd made that cleft with a kiss when she was born. Of course, he never could explain why he had one, too. She smiled at herself and revealed her pretty, straight, white teeth, courtesy of modern dentistry. She never thought of herself as beautiful — tall, skinny — but not beautiful.

History remembered her as an elderly crone with a sharp tongue. For an old bird, she didn't look half bad. Hearing a noise, she looked up to see George coming in from his run. He wrapped his arms around her from behind.

"What . . .?" she asked.

He turned her so she would look in the mirror.

"I wanted you to see us," George said. "You and me."

Em turned toward the mirror but closed her eyes. About her same height, he looked over her shoulder. He gave her a little shake, and she opened her eyes. Her unfamiliarity with the mirror caused her to see them — George and Em — as if they were other people.

"And?" he asked.

"They're a lovely couple," she said.

"We belong together," George said. "We look like we belong together."

"But . . ."

"No 'buts,'" George said. He kissed her neck and shoulder. In a thick voice, he whispered, "Say it."

"We look like we belong together," Em said in the flat voice she used when he made her say things. He grinned, and she laughed. "But . . ."

"No 'buts.'"

"I need to go," Em said.

"Give me five minutes, and I'll be there," George said. He pulled off his sweatshirt on his way to their bathroom. "Who's coming?"

"No idea," Em said. "I told everyone."

"Susannah and Mary are back in Pennsylvania?" George asked. "Giles is upstate."

"As far as I know," Em said and wondered if they had time for coffee.

"The pot's on," he said, answering her thought.

"I'll get it," she said, but he was already in the shower.

Her apartment stretched over the entire third floor. The windowless kitchen took up most of the back west corner of the building. While George always got the credit for being the chef, he mostly turned on appliances and warmed up things. She loved to cook and was fairly good at it. She loved excellent food more than getting credit for making it. This kitchen was exactly as she wanted it. She took down two travel mugs, added a scoop of homemade chocolate and a dash of cinnamon, and filled the cups with coffee. George took cream, but she liked her coffee just like this. She was pressing down the cover of his mug when he appeared. With a nod, they took the stairs to the street.

It had been a week since the demon had appeared at the Mystic Divine. Despite everyone's dire predictions, everything had gone back to normal. They went ghost-hunting with the teenagers and had seen no spirits, ghosts, or anything paranormal. Alice had finished her work with her gentleman and had even humored Em by returning to her apartment on the fourth floor "just for the summer." Sarah Wildes's weekend meditation retreat had gone off without a devilish hitch, and Elizabeth's knitting group had been unscathed after meeting in the room where Em had seen the demon. To be certain, Mary Ayer Parker, their realtor, had gone through the building top to bottom, and found only love and light.

Everything was back to normal. Everyone was back to normal.

Em and George trotted across Boylston Street and into the Boston Common. They hoped to send Ann Hibbins on this morning. While even a weak witch could send on a spirit, Em wanted to give Ann a proper sendoff. Like the Salem Twenty, Ann Hibbins hadn't done anything that warranted being hanged in the Boston Common. She deserved to live in peace. Em had asked the Salem Twenty to come help Ann rest in peace.

Em waved to Sam. He was a talented finder, even when he lived in Salem Village. He was a master at it now. This morning, he was looking for the exact location where Ann had been hanged. Unjust death leaves a stain that can tie the spirit to the ground. Sam easily found the stain.

"It's over here." Sam waved Em and George in his direction.

Em went over a rise and saw that most of the Salem witches were waiting for them. Giles, Susannah, and Mary lived too far away to make it. Sarah Good had flown her helicopter from New York. She waved to Em and George. As they approached, the others looked up. Elizabeth ran to Em.

"Wait 'till you hear what John and Martha found out," Elizabeth said. "From the NSA, no less!"

John and Martha walked over to them.

"What did you find out?" George asked. He looked at John and Martha.

"John Parker?" John said.

"The little shit with a demon inside?" George asked.

"Him," John said.

"Yeah?" Em asked.

"The records show that he's Ann Putnam's great-times-ten-grandson," John said.

"Our Ann Putnam, Junior?" Em asked. "The little shit from Salem Village who got us all hanged?"

"Not me!" Elizabeth said.

Em grinned at Elizabeth and looked back at John.

"Turns out being a little shit runs in the family," John said. "He's on an NSA watch list."

"Any idea why?" George asked.

"Some ideas, no proof," Martha said. "The agency is looking into him for sending money to groups outside of the country."

"Terrorists?" Em asked.

"Maybe," Martha shrugged. "I'll tell you, no one was happy when I asked about him."

"Right," John said. "When I called about him, the field

desk acted like a thousand people had been asking about him."

"Huh," Em said, and shrugged.

"We need to get going!" Wilmot said. "Or we'll lose the power of the dawn."

The Salem witches made a circle around the patch of grass where Ann was hanged on June 19, 1656.

"Ann?" Em asked the wind. "We're ready if you are."

The specter of Ann Hibbins appeared in the middle of the circle.

"Since I'm the strongest witch, I figured I would do it," Wilmot Redd said.

"Go ahead," Em said.

Em glanced around the circle. Over the last three hundred years, this group of strangers had become something of a family. John Willard took her hand, and she took George's hand. George took Sarah Good's hand and kissed the back of it. Sarah Good smiled at him and took Elizabeth's hand. John took Martha's hand, and Martha took Sam's hand. They continued around the circle until Ann Pudeator reached out her hand to Elizabeth. The women smiled at each other and turned to the center of the circle, where Ann Hibbins and Wilmot stood.

Wilmot began:

> "We call to the light of dawn."
> "We call," the Salem witches repeated.

> "We call for the love and peace of the mystic divine."
> "We call," the Salem witches repeated.

"We call for peace."

"We call," the Salem witches repeated.

A stiff wind blew the fog from the area.

"Ann?" Wilmot asked. "Is there anything you'd like to share?"

"Good luck," Ann said.

"Good luck?" Wilmot asked with surprise. "Don't worry, Ann. We've done this many times before."

Ann's eyes locked on Em, and Ann nodded as if Em knew exactly what she'd meant.

"Anything else?" Wilmot asked.

Ann's ghost shook her head. Wilmot held her hands out in front of her with her palms together. A dim light grew between her palms. The light blazed — blinding, white light — and Wilmot struggled to hold onto the light and power as she waited for the dawn.

The sun hit the horizon with a resounding crack, and Wilmot let go of the ball of light. Her ball of light rose above Ann.

"Be at peace, Ann Hibbins," Wilmot said.

"Be at peace," the Salem witches chanted. "Be at peace."

Ann Hibbins looked around the circle until her eyes fell on Em again. She mouthed "Thank you," before rising to follow the ball of light. While they watched, her spirit followed the ball to the great divide. A hand reached through the other side for Ann. She lit up with delight and took the hand. The ball of light sealed the divide. They fell silent. George stepped forward. Em grabbed Sarah Good's hand.

"Please join me in a silent prayer for our sister, Ann Hibbins," George said. They bowed their heads and spent a few moments in silence. When it seemed like everyone was done, George said, "May she spend eternity at peace. May her soul heal from the injustice put upon her."

"May she be at peace," they said in unison.

They clapped and cheered for Ann. Wilmot gave a little bow for her role in the ceremony. With a nod to each other, the witches left the park. George stayed to talk with John. Alice and Em walked back to the store. Alice threaded her hand through Em's elbow. They were almost to Boylston Street when Sarah Good's helicopter buzzed overhead on her way back to New York.

"I saw you," Alice said.

"You saw me what?" Em asked.

"You made that ball of energy, not Wilmot," Alice said.

"I did not," Em scowled at Alice.

"I saw you move your finger," Alice said.

"I had an itch," Em said.

"I don't have any idea why you put up with her 'I'm the strongest witch' crap," Alice said.

"Practice," Em said.

Alice laughed. Em opened the door to the stairwell, and they went up. Alice stopped on the landing to Em's apartment.

"Are you going to ask me in?" Alice asked.

"Are you eating breakfast?" Em asked.

"I will," Alice said. "Mostly I wanted to know . . ."

"What?" Em scowled.

"Are you ever going to tell me what you did to Ann Putnam?" Alice asked.

Chapter Seven

"Who?" Em asked.

"Very funny," Alice said.

Alice brushed past Em as she went into the apartment. Em began pulling food from the refrigerator while Alice poured herself a cup of coffee. Alice drank her coffee in one swallow and poured another.

"Should I make another pot?" Alice asked.

Em looked up from her review of the ingredients on the butcher-block table in front of her.

"Please don't," Em smiled.

Alice laughed. Em turned back to the food in front of her.

"Eggs and toast, Emmy," Alice said. "That's what I like."

"I know," Em said. "I'm just trying to figure out what *George* is making for breakfast."

Alice laughed. Em smiled at Alice and set to work at making some oat-blueberry muffins. She gave Alice a mixing bowl and a carton of eggs for her to crack open. They worked in companionable silence. When Alice finished her task, she picked up her coffee cup and watched Em put together the muffins.

"You're not going to tell me," Alice said.

"About what?" Em asked.

"You and Tituba did something to that poor little Ann Putnam," Alice said.

"Who?" Em scowled.

"Tituba, the slave," Alice said. "I know you bought her because she helped take care of us that first year, as soon as you got her out of the Boston jail."

"Sweet girl."

"You're pretending not to remember the Putnams?" Alice laughed. "Surely you remember the horrible insane girl — who said you made her that way — and her awful mother."

"I remember them," Em said.

"Remember them?" Alice gave an angry snort. "That Ann Putnam, Junior, put that noose around my neck as sure as if that little shit was the hangman herself. And her mother..."

Em touched Alice's arm as she moved past her to the coffee pot.

"Bacon?" Em asked. "I can't remember if we're eating pigs or worrying about our arteries."

"You're really not going to tell me," Alice said.

"Not today," Em said as she dumped out the spent coffee grounds.

She gave the empty pot to Alice, who rinsed it out from the tap and filled it with filtered water. Em checked that they had enough coffee beans, replaced the filter, and took the pot from Alice. A moment later, she pressed the button, and the coffee maker responded with the loud whirl of coffee being ground. Em turned her attention to the muffins.

"Then tell me about you and George," Alice said.

"What about me and George?" Em asked.

As if the question were obvious, Alice laughed. Em nodded with her eyebrows toward the cabinet. Alice took out the silicone cupcake baking cups. Alice put the baking cups in the holes of the cupcake pan, and Em ladled in the dough. Alice gave Em an irritated sigh.

"When did you *know* you were in love with George?" Alice asked.

"1681," George's voice came from the entrance to the kitchen.

Alice put her hand over her mouth and gasped in mock horror. She looked from Em to George.

"What?" Alice said in her fake southern accent.

Laughing, Em shook her head at Alice.

"You knew when you asked the question," George said with a laugh.

"Well, I'll be, Reverend Burroughs, whatever are you talking about?" Alice asked with a flutter of her eyes.

George laughed. He picked up the tray of muffin dough and slipped it into the oven just as Bridget and Elizabeth came into the kitchen.

"What did you make us, George?" Bridget asked.

"Oat-blueberry muffins," Em said. "Eggs, bacon."

"Fabulous!" Elizabeth said.

Elizabeth made a cup of coffee for herself and Bridget before they continued on into the living room. Sam and John came in. When the men started talking about their beloved Red Sox, Em shooed them out of her kitchen. Mary Ayer came in with her cell phone glued to her ear. She waved to Em and Alice before heading into the office for privacy. Em set to work on the eggs and bacon.

"So . . ." Alice said in a low tone. "It's true?"

"What's true?" Em asked.

"You and George?" Alice asked.

Em's eyes drifted toward the doorway George had gone through. She gave a slight nod.

"Henry had been ill for a long time," Em said in a low tone. "George came to see if we needed anything."

"Mm-hm," Alice said.

"He wanted to bring me to Christ," Em said. "We just studied the bible and talked. I was interested in religion, so he brought me everything he could find."

"No woman can resist the Burroughs charm," Alice said.

"It wasn't like that," Em said. "He was married to Hannah."

Alice winked.

"He was," Em said with quiet emphasis. "He never strayed on his wives."

"I know," Alice said. "Slutty behavior after death. I think that's true for all of us."

Em smiled.

"Except you," Alice said.

"Not my thing," Em shrugged.

The egg timer rang to indicate that the muffins were done. Em gave Alice the spatula and went to check the muffins. George came in before she could get there. He opened the oven to check them.

"A few more minutes," he said. Em went to turn on the timer. "Did she tell you?"

Alice shook her head.

"I fell for Em," George said. "Hard."

"But you were so much younger!" Alice said.

"The heart doesn't care," George said. "Henry was ill. My Hannah had just died."

Alice gaped at him.

"What?" Em asked.

"*He's* Benoni's father," Alice said.

"My son?" Em asked at the same time George said, "What?"

Em recovered first.

"What pot are you stirring, Alice?" Em shook her head at Alice.

George looked stunned. He turned to Em, who was focused on putting the scrambled eggs onto the serving plate. She gave him the plate of eggs and gestured for him to bring it out to the dining room. He asked the question with his eyes. She answered with a veiled smile.

"He doesn't know," Alice said in a low voice.

"Know what?" Em asked.

Alice laughed and shook her head.

"Listen," Em said. Her tone was so serious that Alice stopped laughing and turned to look at her. Em's accent slipped into her native 1600s' English. "Henry was very ill. Thomas was a toddler. My family and friends were in *England*. I belonged in *England*. I was loved in *England*. I was *stuck* in awful Salem, in this *horrible* colony. I was so alone, so very alone. George was the first person who'd spoken even two kind words to me in . . . a very long time. His mother had raised him in Roxbury on her own, so he understood what I was going through. We were friends. He saved me and introduced me to Christianity, brought me to the church. I was so overwhelmed, just outdone by this New World and the frontier . . ."

"The Indians," Alice interrupted.

"Those horrible Indian raids," Em said. "I was terrified. Every day. Terrified. Not that I blamed the Indians. But for me, it was . . . awful. I wished every day that I could go home, just to see England again. George came along . . . He'd survived many Indian raids. He'd been to battle and overcome the horrors."

"And was still kind," Alice said.

"Solicitous," Em said.

Em shrugged. She took the muffins out of the oven and gave Alice a plate of bacon.

"Every woman in Salem Village loved George Burroughs," Alice said. "He was so kind and incredibly handsome. He paid attention to us."

"Listened," Em said.

"Except those awful Putnams," Alice said.

"I guess they had the last laugh," Em said.

"I always knew he loved you," Alice said. Em looked up at her. "I think everyone knew. Even Sarah."

Em swallowed hard at the idea that George's second wife knew that he loved Em. Alice nodded her certainty and brought the bacon into the dining room. Mary Ayer came out of the office. Lost in her own thoughts, Mary Ayer poured herself a cup of coffee on her way through the kitchen. George swooped back to the kitchen for a reassuring kiss and the butter. When he was gone, Em spent a worried moment washing her hands and wondering if Giles was right.

By loving George, had she gotten everyone killed?

She swallowed hard and stared at the large painting of the English countryside. Shaking her head at herself, she took down a serving plate and transferred the muffins onto the plate. Alice returned.

"Why didn't you tell him about Benoni?" Alice asked.

"What's to tell?" Em asked.

"You let everyone think you'd had some dalliance with... someone exotic and..." Alice said. "History records you as having a 'questionable' sexual past."

Em set the plate of muffins in Alice's hands to shut her up.

"Then, who was Benoni's father?" Alice asked.

Em gave such a sad shrug that Alice kissed her cheek. Em poured the last of the coffee into a serving thermos and started the coffee maker again. She'd just pressed "Start" when they called for her. Rearranging her face from worried to smiling, she went into the dining room for breakfast with the family.

"Em promised to tell us what she did to the Putnams," Alice said when she entered the room.

Em laughed and took her place at the table.

The hurt and confusion in George's eyes when he'd said, "What?" had torn a hole in Em's conscience. She saw those dark eyes staring at her across a chasm of sorrow.

Even though it had been a long day. Even though she'd laughed with John, Sam, and Mary on their way to work. Even though Bridget and Elizabeth had begged her to come for a spa day. Even though the day had been full of customers and employees and questions and problems and laughter.

Even though she hadn't seen him since this morning,

George's dark eyes burned like an ember in her psyche.

She cursed herself for not dealing with this a hundred years or so before.

She knew he was furious because he'd taken special care to avoid her all day. When the store closed around ten, she made her way upstairs. She was standing in the kitchen, drinking a glass of water, when he came in.

"You were waiting in your office," Em said.

"Of course," George said.

"I . . ." Em started at the same time George said, "I . . ."

Em looked down, and away, from him. He turned his back to her.

"You . . ." George started at the same time Em said, "You're . . ."

He walked out of the kitchen. She could tell by the sound that he'd plopped down on the couch. Not sure if she should follow him, she lingered in the kitchen. Finally, sick of her own nerves, she clicked on the electric kettle and went out into their living space.

"What?" she asked.

"What?" His voice rose. His eyebrows rose with insult.

"Right," she said. "You're clearly angry with me. What's going on?"

"What's going on?" he mumbled, almost to himself. He shook his head and looked up at her. "Are you truly this dense?"

"Dense?" Em asked. "What are you talking about?"

George patted the cushion beside him. Em scowled.

"I promise not to have a fit," George said.

She hesitated. George had a terrible temper. Abusive only to her eardrums, he could storm around screaming for an hour before he was ready for any kind of a conversation.

"Really," George said.

She sat down next to him. They sat in uncomfortable silence for a few minutes.

"Do you love me, Em?" George asked finally.

Em tucked her foot up under her and turned to him. He stared straight ahead.

"Do you love me, Em?" George asked again. "Even a little bit?"

"I do," Em said. She smiled at him. "More than a little bit."

He slowly turned to look at her. She nodded.

"Everyone loves George," he said.

"Everyone does love George," Em said.

"So you . . ."

"No." Em's hands surrounded his face. She looked deep into his dark eyes. For the second time today, her voice slipped into her ancient accent. "I believe we're two halves to a whole."

"But Giles and Isaac and . . ." George shook his head.

"You know this." Em's voice was low. "You said it first in 1681, when we were in Salem Village."

His head went up in a slight nod. She leaned forward and kissed his lips.

"Why didn't you *tell* me?" George said in an accent similar to hers yet completely foreign to the modern man.

"Tell you what?" Em asked. She pulled back to look at him.

"About Benoni," George said.

Em groaned.

"You're angry over something Alice made up?" Em asked.

"I'm angry that you..." George started. "Something Alice *made up*?"

Em nodded.

"Who was Benoni's father?" George asked.

Em looked away from him.

"You know, I've thought about it all day," George said. "Benoni had just started his apprenticeship the spring before we were hanged."

Em nodded.

"He was ten," George said.

"Eleven," Em nodded.

"Henry died in 1684," George said.

"I guess so," Em said.

"Benoni was mulatto," George said in a low voice.

"That's what the neighbors said," Em said. "They also thought I was a witch."

"I never thought he was... dark," George said.

She waved her hand over his head. His long, grey hair and kindly, wrinkled face gave way to long jet-black hair, a bushy black beard which covered the deep facial scars dug by war, and darker, suntanned skin. George looked like the dark Celtic warrior he'd been in Salem Village. George's eyes flicked to the mirror on the wall. For a moment, he looked at himself; then he looked at her.

"Your skin is darker than mine," Em said. "But together, we're not as light as some."

"Why wouldn't you tell me?" he asked finally.

"I don't have anything to say," Em said. "Henry was very ill. Thomas was a baby. I got pregnant. That's what I know."

For a moment, George watched her.

"Was the baby Henry's? Probably not, but maybe. Yours? Possibly, but we were together only twice. Or..." Em looked away from him. "In 1681, I couldn't have conceived of the science we know now. Eggs. Sperm. Moment of conception. Little tests you buy at the store. All of that."

Em shrugged.

"I fell pregnant. And Henry was still ill, and Thomas was still a toddler."

"Something else happened," George said. "After I left?"

"You were in Salem Village." Em made a slight nod.

"Indians?" George asked.

Em nodded. George looked at her for a moment and then nodded.

"Henry was ill," Em repeated. "Thomas was a baby."

"Why didn't I know?" George asked.

"Your Hannah had just died," Em said. "You were confused by Henry and Thomas. You had three babies who desperately needed their father and a bickering congregation and all that ridiculousness about your payment."

"They wouldn't pay me," George nodded. "I had to take out loans and... We were broke. The pressure was..."

"Tremendous," Em said. "I wanted to be a place of peace and joy for you. I wanted to be the place where you felt your burdens lifted, if only for an hour. I needed my own burdens lifted. I looked forward with tremendous joy to your visits, even if we only drank tea and talked about Christ."

"I did as well," George smiled. "My time with you has always been the highlight of my life — then and now."

"Takes three hundred years to finally talk about it," Em said.

George smiled.

"Benoni was a wonderful person," George said. "He came every night to take care of us that first year, after you had left for Boston."

Em smiled.

"I took him home to England with me," George said.

"And came back with his daughter," Em said. "I know."

"She was like a granddaughter to me," George said.

"Why did you marry Sarah?" Em asked.

"You had Henry," George shrugged. "He was ill, but he wasn't dead. Thomas was young. I was a pastor with a large congregation and three children under the age of three. I needed a wife. Sarah had just been widowed."

George shrugged.

"I never would have guessed that her brother-in-law, Hathorne, would . . ."

"Examine us for witchcraft?" Em asked. "Set the bullshit in motion so that we were hanged?"

George gave a curt nod.

"I always felt like he was angry with me for how I treated Sarah, and . . ." George abruptly stopped talking.

"And me," Em said.

He turned to look at her.

"Alice says that everyone in Salem Village knew that you loved me," Em said. "Even Sarah."

He raised an eyebrow in acknowledgment. He looked away in shame.

"Sarah was the mother of four of your children," Em said. "They were great kids."

George turned to look at her.

"You knew them?" George asked.

"Of course," Em said. "I tried to help them when they came to Boston. I worked with orphans, and they were orphans. I don't think they ever guessed who I was."

"There's so much we haven't talked about," George said.

"Why did you marry Giles?" George asked.

"He was almost eighty years old," Em said. "He needed someone to care for him — cook, clean, that kind of thing. He was fairly addled; still is."

"That's the truth," George said.

"I'd spent all that time caring for Henry that it seemed fairly natural," Em said. "Giles was kind to Benoni and helped Thomas join the church."

"His testimony sealed your fate," George said.

"He was pressed to death for his efforts," Em said.

Out of words, they stared straight ahead and listened to their own thoughts.

"Why didn't you tell me?" George asked.

Em chuckled.

"Why is that funny?" he asked.

"You are the most stubborn man I've ever met," Em said. "You're like a dog with a bone. You won't set it down even when you know all the facts."

George grinned.

"You know as much as I do," Em said.

"I do?"

"You do," Em said.

George nodded but didn't respond. In response to his

silence, Em picked up a ball of yarn and needles from a basket next to the couch. George raised his eyebrows to ask what she was making.

"Socks for my man," Em said. "Your socks are destroyed. It will be winter soon enough, and you'll be out with the homeless again."

He smiled at her. "You are good at taking care of your man."

"Thank you, sir," Em said with a nod.

George put his arm around her, and she nestled into him.

"What I want to know is why all this is coming up now," Em said. "I've seen Alice at least once a week for more than two hundred years. She's never asked about the Putnams or Benoni. Suddenly, she wants to know what happened to them and who Ben's father was and . . ."

"I want to know what Ann Hibbins meant by 'Good luck,'" George said.

"That did seem ominous," Em said. "Any ideas?"

"You did just see John Parker's demon inside," George said.

"I wonder if something is happening astrologically," Em said.

"Astrology?" George sneered.

Em laughed.

"We're witches, George," Em said. "Astrology goes with the territory!"

"Feels . . . anti-Christ to me," George said.

"Oh," Em said with a sigh. "I doubt Christ cares about astrology."

"What would he worry about then?" George asked.

"How 'bout the demon inside John Parker?" Em asked.

"Mmm."

The way George made the sound, he could have been agreeing or disagreeing with Em. She looked up from her knitting to find him looking at her.

"What?" Em asked.

"I've wondered what it would have been like to have married you then, in Salem," George said.

"I doubt I would have had so many kids," Em said.

"No birth control."

George wiggled his eyebrows to remind her of how much he liked sex. She laughed. They fell silent. The only sound was the clicking of Em's knitting needles.

"I don't know," George said, finally.

"You don't know?"

"I don't know why all this Salem Village crap has come up now," George said. "While I was running yesterday, I was thinking of suing to finally get my salary."

"Suing the heirs for your salary from 1680?" Em smiled.

"Plus interest," George nodded.

Em laughed.

"What?" George asked.

"Dog. Bone," Em said.

George laughed. When his laughter faded, he turned to Em.

"You're the most powerful witch I've ever met," George said. "Use your skills, Em. Why is this here now?"

"You know what?" Em asked.

"What?"

"I've given enough time today to all this crap," Em said. "Ann's ceremony, questions from Alice, now this. I realized we've had an abnormally long life. I still don't want to waste it. I'd rather enjoy today."

"But . . ."

Em set her knitting down and got up from her seat. She gave him an alluring look before heading toward the bedroom. When he didn't follow her, she pulled off her top and dropped it on the floor. She was unzipping her pants at the door to the bedroom. She turned to look at him.

"Dog," he said. "Bone."

Em made a sharp whistle.

"Come!" she ordered.

Laughing, he followed her into the bedroom.

Chapter Eight

"I don't know why *she* has to be here," Giles's young wife whined.

Not two feet away, Em was perched on a stool in Giles's large, gourmet kitchen, trying to remember the young wife's name. 'Beverly,' who went by 'Bevy'? No, that was the last one. Em squinted at the peas she was shucking. Josey was the one before that. Surely, she knew this wife's name. She glanced at George, who gave her an amused grin and turned back to washing blueberries in the sink.

"She just marches in here every month and ..." the young wife continued.

Giles gave Em a dark look and closed the door to the kitchen. Sarah Wildes sashayed into the kitchen carrying a basket of raspberries. Her flowing, calf-length sundress with the wide, flowered skirt gave her the air of an eternal flower child.

"She acts like *she* is your wife!" The young wife's bellow came through the door.

Sarah Wildes snorted a laugh. She dumped her raspberries into a crate on the kitchen counter and went outside to pick more. Every month, they carpooled to Giles's horse ranch, near the border of Massachusetts and New Hampshire, to spend the weekend working in his five-acre organic garden. This was the Fourth of July weekend, and everyone, except the Amish Susannah and Mary Eastey, had come. Of course, Sarah Good had flown her helicopter in from New York City.

The Puritans were farmers at heart. They relished the sweaty, dirty work as well as the planning that made the garden work. Plus, Giles always said there was no human on Earth who worked harder and enjoyed it more than the Puritans. He was right.

Their hard work was rewarded with more food than they could possibly eat. Giles sold the rest to a high-end, Michelin-starred restaurant down the block. This month, they were harvesting the fruits and vegetables they'd planted in the spring.

"We think we've picked enough B-strawberries for preserves," Wilmot said as she came into the kitchen.

"That was fast," Em said. "And A's?"

"Sam has those in the packing shed," Wilmot said. "We've sold those to the restaurant."

Em nodded. Ever the bookkeeper, Wilmot kept track of this endeavor from the first seed to the last harvest. Her prudent guidance had made their garden efforts profitable year after year.

"*Crash!*" A glass shattered as it hit the door in the next room. Wilmot scowled.

"The new wife?" Wilmot asked.

"Em's acting like Giles's wife," George said.

Wilmot smiled. Em leaned in.

"What's her name?" Em whispered to Wilmot.

"Nancy," Wilmot said.

"No," George said. "That was last century. This is

Treena."

"Trixie," Wilmot said. "That's right."

She waved her hand, and an image of Giles and Trixie's wedding invitation floated in the air.

"Trixie, it is, then," George said before closing the vision with a swipe of his hand.

There was a loud scuffle in the next room. Em nodded to George. He dried his hands on a kitchen towel and took off his apron. When he walked past Em, she patted his rear. He grinned at her.

"Everything okay in here?" George leaned in the room.

Trixie said something in a high-pitched scream, and George went into the room. Not missing a beat, Wilmot asked, "Are we cooking here or at your house?"

Em chuckled.

"What?" Wilmot batted her eyes. "Just a question."

"Here," Em said. "Giles has everything laid out. I thought he'd . . ."

Giles stormed into the kitchen from the other room.

"Are the strawberries picked yet?" he growled.

Not willing to even look at Em, he addressed the room as a whole.

"Yes, Giles," Wilmot said.

She took his arm and led him out toward the back. Near the door to the garden, she turned to Em and winked. Em smiled at Wilmot before turning her full attention to the peas. It would have been easy to use magic to shuck these peas, but Em liked to do them by hand. Magic always left a mark. Magic-shucked peas had tiny bruises on them. While only a witch could see the marks, Em felt certain they affected the taste. She didn't mind the work. After a few hundred years of practice, she was fast and efficient.

A few minutes later, George opened the door and guided Trixie out.

"*Mrs.* Corey had planned to freeze these peas," George said to Em.

"Great," Em said.

"She's a little intimidated by all of us," George said.

"We have a lot of experience with farming," Em nodded. "That's for sure."

"I told her that I would help her with the peas," George said.

Em handed him the bowl of shucked peas. She picked up the bowl full of pea shells.

"I'll head out to help Bridget and Sarah Good," Em said. She dumped pea shells into the trashcan they were using to collect clippings for the compost and wiped her wet hands on her jeans.

"Good idea," George grinned at Em.

She smiled and walked toward the door. She was almost there when the wife said, "I don't know how you stand her," to George. She could almost hear him grinning at her back.

"I don't know how you can stand her," Sarah Good said in a high voice to imitate Trixie. Wearing a pair of designer overalls specifically tailored to her, she looked like a cross between a Midwestern farmer and a rapper. Em smiled at her. Sarah Good hooked her elbow with Em's, and they walked toward the broccoli patch.

"Giles likes them dumb," Sarah Good said.

"Don't I know it," Em said in a tone that clearly referred to herself.

Sarah Good laughed. Bridget looked up from the broccoli to wave them over. When they got near, Bridget stood up.

"Slugs," Bridget said.

"I thought we put out slug bait the last time we were here," Em said.

"The wife took them away," Bridget said. In an irritated imitation of the new wife, she added, "Why waste good beer on some old vegetable that nobody eats?"

Em scowled. The restaurant bought every piece of broccoli they grew. She dropped down to pick the slugs off a foot-tall broccoli plant. She tossed them into a bucket with an inch of vinegar in it. The plants would heal quickly, but someone would have to harvest the broccoli in a week or so. That put them close to the next hanging anniversary, on July 19th. Em scowled.

"She's a menace," Bridget said about Giles's wife.

"She hates Em," Sarah Good said. She dropped to a large broccoli plant and began picking off the slugs.

"If it wasn't Em, it would be another one of us," Bridget said.

"What's that supposed to mean?" Em asked.

"She hates you because she knows you can handle it," Bridget said.

"Why does she have to hate someone?" Em asked.

"I think George is right — she's intimidated," Sarah Good said. "We're all super successful, hardworking, and we like each other. She's an outsider. Wouldn't you be intimidated?"

Em shrugged. Catching her look, Bridget pointed to her and laughed. When Bridget laughed, Sarah Good looked at her and followed her finger to Em. She looked back at Bridget.

"Em's not intimidated by anyone," Bridget said.

"That's not exactly true," Em said. "I'm just not intimidated by her."

Somewhere in the field, John Willard's distinctive baritone voice began to sing Psalm 64, one of their favorite hymns. In Salem Village, every Puritan had taken it as a sacred duty to sing the psalms at least once a week. Now, most of them sang only while they worked. Because George still sang the psalms every day, he usually got them started. Since George was stuck inside, John began. They joined him in song, with Psalm 64 slipping into the rest of the Psalms.

"Em?" Sarah Good asked.

Singing, Em didn't hear her. Sarah Good reached through the plants to touch Em's arm. Em looked up. Sarah Good opened her mouth to say something. Her eyes echoed insecurity. Sarah Good shook her head and looked down at the broccoli plant in front of her.

"Sarah?" Em asked. "What is it?"

Bridget stopped singing to watch them. She looked at Em and then at Sarah Good.

"I . . ." Sarah started.

Sarah Good realized Bridget was looking at her. She shook her head and focused on the broccoli plant. Em and Bridget got up and went to her. Sarah Good stood up.

"What is it?" Em asked. "You're worrying me."

"I . . ." Sarah Good started again.

Bridget put her hand on Sarah Good's shoulder.

"I keep seeing Dorothy," Sarah Good whispered.

"Dorothy?" Em asked.

"Your daughter?" Bridget asked.

Sarah Good nodded.

"Not like she was when she died," Sarah Good said. "She's four years old again."

Hearing a girl's giggle, Em instinctively turned toward the sound. Sure enough, Sarah Good's daughter Dorothy ran from behind Giles's house. Wearing a traditional ankle-length, deep-blue cotton dress and a white hat, the child smiled as she ran toward them. When she was close, she stopped running and looked at them. As if seeing them was a delightful surprise, she burst out laughing and took off running. The child ran with such joy that she seemed to dance across the fertile earth. Dorothy disappeared into the cornfield where John was working.

"Johnny?" Bridget asked in a loud voice.

The singing abruptly ended. They heard John's feet run to the edge of the field.

"Everything okay, Bridg?" John asked.

"Did you see . . .?" Em started.

"What?" John asked.

"Dorothy," Bridget said. "We just saw her."

John's face fell with sorrow. He shook his head. At four and a half years old, Dorothy had been charged with witchcraft in Salem Village all those years ago. The child spent the better part of a year clapped in chains and wearing shackles like everyone charged with witchcraft. If she ever acted like a child, her hands were tied behind her back and she was hung from her wrists in strappado. After Sarah Good was hanged, Em and the others had done their best to care for and protect Dorothy. They'd loved

Dorothy like a daughter. But in such wretched, desperate conditions, their love was nowhere near what the child needed. The poor girl went mad when her mother was hanged.

"She was here?" John asked. The sorrow in his voice was apparent.

Em and Bridget nodded. Still crying, Sarah Good stared at the ground.

"I see her all the time," Sarah Good said. "At work. At home. I came home yesterday, and I'd swear she was sitting on the bed, petting my dog, Rufus."

"The Rottweiler?" Bridget asked.

Sarah Good nodded. John jogged over to them. He gave Sarah Good a tight hug.

"There was nothing you could have done," John said. "Not one thing."

In his strong, tight embrace, Sarah Good began to sob. The sound of her sorrow brought the others. Dorothy was like a gaping wound. Each in their own way, they felt the terrible strain of responsibility tinged with helplessness. When Sam joined them, Em pointed toward the cornfield. He left to see if he could find Dorothy. He returned a few minutes later. When Em looked at him, he shook his head.

Dorothy was not there.

Em nodded to Sam. She wondered if Dorothy had been some kind of shared vision or if she'd actually been there.

"More stuff from ancient history," Alice said in a low tone.

Hearing Alice, Sarah Good said between sobs, "What the hell is going on? All this Salem Village crap keeps coming up."

Mary Ayer put her arm around Sarah Good's shoulders.

"Hand to God," Sarah Good said. "Last night, I woke up from a dead sleep and could have sworn that my husband Will — the lying bastard who testified at my trial — was lying next to me in bed. My children were small and sleeping around our bed, like they did when we stayed in someone's guest bedroom. I could feel Mercy stir inside me. I thought, 'All is well.' I was almost asleep before I realized it wasn't real. I felt so . . ."

"Peaceful," Ann Pudeator said.

"Real," Alice said. "Like all of this is a dream, and that . . ."

"Is reality," Martha Carrier whispered.

"You mean it's happened to you?" Sarah Good asked.

Everyone but Em nodded.

"It hasn't happened to you, Em?" Alice asked.

Em shook her head.

"I don't know whether to feel sorry for you or . . ." John started.

"Jealous," Sarah Wildes said. "I wake up smelling my thick, sweet jasmine patch, the one I had around my house in Salem Village. I feel so . . . safe, hopeful, at peace, in a way that I haven't felt since . . ."

Sarah Wildes' fingertips stroked her throat. Sarah Good held out her arms, and the women hugged.

"I've had this dream every night this week," Giles said. Surprised that he'd spoken in the crowd, they turned to stare at him. "I was on Salem Farm. Martha and I had just been married. I was lying in bed thinking that I was finally safe. The kids had taken over the farm. Martha was there. I mean, I knew about George, but he was gone, in Maine, out of the way. And . . . I knew she'd take care of me to the end."

"I would have," Em said. "I will."

"In that moment, I knew I didn't have to pretend any longer," Giles said. "I could finally live out my years in peace. The feeling was more than safety . . ."

"Everything in its right place," Elizabeth said. "At least for me. It's like whatever happened in Salem Village has haunted me all this time, and, suddenly, it was gone, just gone."

Elizabeth's eyes welled with tears, and she stopped talking.

"Since we were hanged," Margaret said.

"You are all having this experience," Em said.

She looked from face to face. As her eyes turned to them, they nodded.

"You're not?" Giles asked.

Em shook her head.

"But . . ." Em blushed and looked away.

"She doesn't want to say that she wasn't happy in Salem," Giles said with a smile.

"I wasn't happy, either, Em," Sarah Good said. "I have so much more fun, every day, now, than I did in all the years I lived in Salem Village. I know it's crazy, but I still miss it."

Many of the witches nodded.

"Do you think that's why Dorothy is here?" Em asked.

"Dorothy's here?" Alice asked.

Alice's face fell. Elizabeth wiped away a tear. Margaret hugged Sarah Good.

"How did she look?" Sam asked.

"Like a happy four-year-old," Sarah said.

She looked at Em and Bridget. They nodded.

"Em?" Wilmot said.

Em turned to look at her.

"Why don't you hold a séance?" Wilmot asked. "Find out who's here and why. I mean, Alice told me about the demon you saw. Maybe this is just a happy memory for us or . . ."

"The demon is trying to trick us," Ann Pudeator nodded. "Yes, that feels right to me."

A few heads went up and down in a nod.

"We won't know until . . ." Wilmot looked at Em.

"Will you do it, Em?" Sarah Good asked. "For me."

"Not here," Em said.

"When?" Sarah Good asked.

"Monday night," Em said. "We need to finish up here. We'll head back on Sunday night."

"I can fly us to Boston," Sarah Good said. "We can have the séance Sunday night."

"We can finish what's left by dark and drive home," Sam said. "It's only forty minutes or so, without traffic."

"We could do it tonight," Wilmot said.

"I don't mind taking care of the canning next week," Giles said.

"I can help you, Giles," Bridget said. "I'm not doing anything next week."

"I can help, too," Alice said.

Em looked at the sad and desperate faces of her witch family. She gave an acquiescing nod.

"I need to talk to George," Em said.

"I'll do it, Em," Giles said.

He touched her shoulder as he passed. Em widened her

eyes to Sarah Wildes. She smiled.

"Wait up, Giles," Sarah Wildes said.

Giles stopped walking and turned. Sarah Wildes tucked her elbow into his, and they went inside. With nothing left to say, they went back to working the field.

Em and George sat in the far back of the Chevy Suburban John Willard had checked out of the FBI motor pool. Em hadn't said much since the event in the garden. Misjudging Em's silence as her needing time to prepare for the séance, the witches had left her alone, which suited Em. She felt haunted by the familiar curse of being different from everyone else. George had taken one look at her and held her tight. He'd insisted they ride together in the back so that he could simply hold her hand, his gesture of connection to her.

Once at the Mystic Divine, there was no time to talk. The store had already closed, and the employees were finishing up the last details. Shonelle was standing at the door, waiting to be let out when they'd pulled up. She wanted to know what they were doing and if she could be involved. She followed Em around the store trying to convince her to let her stay. Once Shonelle realized they were holding a séance, she was furious that they wouldn't do the same to help John Parker find the Salem Witches. Shonelle ranted and raved, giving credence to the idea that Benoni was, in fact, George's son. In the end, Em promised to think through having a séance for John Parker. Shonelle would call Monday morning for Em's answer.

"And it had better be 'yes,'" the young woman said in the

demanding voice of a child.

Smiling, Em hugged her and let her out the front door.

"Is that it?" Sam asked from the loft area upstairs.

"Yes," Em said.

She locked the store's front door and pulled down the shades to the sidewalk. Turning in place, she saw George standing behind her.

"You don't have to do this," George said.

Em lifted a shoulder in a shrug.

"I can do it," George said. "Any of us can. You don't . . ."

"I do," Em said. "You know it has to be me."

George held out his arms, and she walked into his hug.

"I hate to see you so blue," George said in her ear.

"I'm all right," Em said.

He kissed her neck.

"Are you dreaming of Salem Village?" Em asked in a low tone.

"I only ever dream of you," George said. "You know that."

"But . . ."

"I've dreamt of you in Salem Village and in Boston and on the island and in Europe and . . ."

"Recently," Em said. "Like the others."

He shook his head. She looked deep into his eyes to see if he was telling her the truth; he was. She gave him a soft nod. He kissed her nose and stepped back. They walked through the store together.

Em was powerful enough that she simply had to call in spirits to her. The ritual she was about to perform was for everyone watching. They needed to be present. They needed to be clear. They needed to be ready. Most of all, they needed not to block the action.

Em and George met the witches in the large room upstairs. Giles and Sam were in the process of setting up the large round table. Martha and Mary Ayer were waiting to set up the table. Flower child Sarah Wildes was holding one of her sage bundles.

"Are we ready?" Sarah Wildes asked.

Em gave her a curt nod. Sarah Wildes lit a bundle of sage made from last summer's harvest. Sarah Wildes had used her magic to imbue this sage to enhance its capacity to clear negative energy. This particular bundle was charged with clarity. She waved the sage bundle a foot above Margaret's head. The pungent smoke was to clear any darkness or negative energy.

"Clear and light," Sarah Wildes said.

"Clear and light," Margaret said.

"Clear and light," they said in unison.

Sarah Wildes ran the burning sage bundle around Margaret's body. Margaret nodded and took a seat at the now-prepared large table. Sarah Wildes worked her way through everyone until she got to Em. Sarah Wildes hugged Em before giving her the sage stick. Em repeated the ritual for Sarah Wildes, before giving the sage back to Sarah Wildes, who ran the sage over Em.

"Clear and light," the witches said in unison.

Sarah Wildes went to take a seat across from Em at the table. Em went to her seat in the middle of the table. She looked around the circle at the people who'd become her friends and her family. They were fifteen tonight, since Mary Eastey and Susannah Martin were in Pennsylvania.

"We are . . ." Em said.

"Clear and light," they replied.

Em sat down. She took a white pillar candle from her pocket.

"Remember your psychic protection," Em said. She looked at Giles, the least strong among them, and he nodded. "We don't know what will come in."

Em lit the candle.

"Please," Em said.

The witches took out small white candles and placed them into the candleholder in front of them.

"We are . . ." Em said.

"Clear and light," they repeated as they lit their candles.

"Lights," Em said.

Rather than break the circle, Em clapped her hands, and the overhead lights shut off. Em waited until everyone's eyes had adjusted to the candle-light.

"I call to all spirits and specters from Salem Village who have a direct connection to us and are living within our plane."

She hadn't gotten the first sentence out when a specter began to appear above the white pillar candle.

"Show yourself!" Em commanded.

The apparition solidified. The witches gasped and fell back against their chairs.

Chapter Nine

The apparition of Rebecca Nurse appeared in the center of the table. She was wearing the floor-length, dark cotton dress she was hanged in, complete with a white lace cap.

"Rebecca?" Em's voice expressed her disbelief.

Rebecca Nurse was a kindly grandmother who had been hanged as a witch on July 19, 1692. Her son, Benjamin, had retrieved her body from their mass grave on the evening of her hanging. She was reburied by her family on the large Nurse estate. Em had always believed that she and the other two whose bodies had been retrieved by their families — George Jacobs and John Proctor — were at peace.

"Goodwife Corey!" the ghost scolded Em. "What are you wearing?"

"I . . ." Em looked down at her long-sleeved T-shirt and jeans. "Uh . . ."

George covered Em's hand with his own to encourage her.

"Why, Reverend Burroughs!" Rebecca exclaimed. "What of your wife? Have you no shame?"

"Nice to see you, Rebecca," George said with a smile. "You're as lovely as ever."

Rebecca gave him a stern scowl before looking around

the room.

"I don't think she can hear you," Em said in a low tone to George. He nodded.

"Why . . . you're all here," Rebecca said under her breath. Seeing Sarah Good and Sarah Wildes, she brightened. "My favorite Sarahs!"

"How's our favorite Rebecca?" Sarah Good asked as Sarah Wildes said, "Blessings be to you, Rebecca!"

"And Elizabeth?" Rebecca turned back to Em. "She was hanged just before me."

Elizabeth waved a hand over her bright blond hair and clear blue eyes.

"You missed her," Em said.

She pointed to Elizabeth, and Rebecca spun around to her old friend, now returned to her brown hair and non-descript hazel eyes.

"There you are, dear!" Rebecca said. Rebecca knelt down to Elizabeth. "How are you feeling?"

Elizabeth shot Em a panicked look. Em dropped her head and rolled her shoulders forward in resignation. Elizabeth nodded. An intensely private person, Elizabeth had found the entire process, from accusation to hanging, deeply humiliating. After a particularly brutal "examination," she had fallen into a debilitating depression, which Elizabeth found all the more humiliating.

"I am very well, dear," Elizabeth said. "How are you?"

"Of course, my dear. Lovely to see you, too!" Rebecca said. She looked around the circle. "Where are my sisters? Where are Sarah and Mary?"

"Mary is living in . . . uh . . . in the south," Em said. She added enough magic to her words to penetrate Rebecca's deaf ears.

"Not with that horrible William Penn and those heathen Quakers?" Rebecca looked aghast. "Not *my* Mary."

"No, you're right," Em smiled. "Mary would never live with the Quakers."

"That's right," Rebecca said.

"Mary will be heartbroken to hear that she missed you," Em said.

"Breaks my heart to have missed her." Rebecca put her hand over her heart for a moment, before her countenance became angry. "And Sarah Cloyce? Where is my sister?"

"She was released," Em said. "I haven't seen her since 1693."

"Sarah wasn't hanged?" Rebecca asked.

"No," Em said. "Your family helped to get the trials stopped. They fought hard."

Rebecca beamed with pride.

"They are good children," Rebecca said.

"Rebecca, dear, do you have any idea what year it is?" Sarah Wildes asked in a loud voice.

Rebecca blinked at Em, so Em pointed to Sarah Wildes. Rebecca spun around to look at Sarah Wildes. Em glanced at her, and Sarah Wildes shrugged.

"I wish you wouldn't mumble." Rebecca raised her eyebrows at Sarah Wildes. Turning back to Em, she asked, "What did she say?"

"We're wondering if you realize where you are," Em said.

"Where I am?" Rebecca asked. "It's not like you to beat around the bush, Goody Corey. What is it?"

"What do you remember?" Em asked.

"I was hanged." Tears fell down Rebecca's face. "Such an awful thing. I thought the suffering would never, ever end. Then, suddenly, there was only love and peace. As you know, Martha, 'For as the sufferings of Christ abound in us, so our consolation aboundeth through Christ.'"

"Amen," George gave a robust response.

"You really are a Baptist, aren't you Reverend?" Rebecca sniffed her disapproval.

The witches chuckled. Rebecca scowled down at George Burroughs, and he beamed at her.

"You didn't wake up?" Em asked to keep them from arguing.

"Wake up?" Rebecca scowled. "Yes. A little while ago, George Jacobs came to see me. Mr. Jacobs?"

The apparition of George Jacobs, Sr. appeared next to Rebecca. Seventy-two years old at the time of his hanging, George Jacobs looked every bit the wealthy landowner he had been in Salem Village.

"Martha's wondering why we have awoken." Rebecca said. "I told her you woke me."

She spun in place and floated over to talk at Sarah Wildes and Sarah Good.

"She can't hear," George Jacobs said of Rebecca.

He pointed to his ears to indicate that, even as a specter, Rebecca Nurse was completely deaf. He shook his head at Rebecca. George Jacobs' body had been retrieved from their mass grave by his children and reburied on his farm. His remains were found in 1864 and reinterred near Rebecca's grave in 1992. The specter of George Jacobs looked around the table.

"What year is it?" George Jacobs asked.

"2014," Em said.

George Jacobs shook his head and looked at each of them again.

"You haven't changed at all," George Jacobs said. He nodded and said, "Giles."

"George," Giles returned the acknowledgement.

"We were turned into immortal witches when they hanged us," John Willard said.

"I'll be," George Jacobs said. He nodded to John in hello. "Where was I?"

"Your family retrieved your remains," Em said.

George Jacobs nodded.

"What do you remember?" George Burroughs asked.

"Always the question, isn't it, Reverend?" George Jacobs asked. "What do I remember . . ."

Thinking, George Jacobs gazed off. His hand came to his face, and he rubbed his beard.

"Good that the scar's gone, Reverend." George Jacobs glanced at George Burroughs.

"Yes, sir," George Burroughs said.

"I remember hanging, Em," George Jacobs said. "You still go by 'Em'?"

Em nodded.

"Nice that some things don't change," George Jacobs smiled. "Let's see. I remember that awful choking. I remember looking at the Reverend. He was so confident they wouldn't do it, wouldn't hang us. I remember thinking that he would learn."

George Jacobs snorted.

"I'm such a self-righteous prick," George Jacobs said.

"George Jacobs!" Rebecca said.

"Curse, and her hearing is perfect," George Jacobs smiled. "It's a miracle."

Rebecca scowled at George Jacobs and turned back to continue talking at Sarah Wildes and Sarah Good.

"I was at peace when a man's voice called to me by name," George Jacobs said. "Something like: 'George Jacobs, awaken now.' A command. Then I was walking in this . . . foggy land. I heard the man's voice. He called to me and Rebecca and someone else . . ."

He spun to look at John Willard, who was sitting next to Sarah Good, and then shook his head.

"John . . ." George Jacobs paused to think. "I'm not sure he was clear which 'John.'"

George Jacobs nodded.

"Then I found myself lying down," George Jacobs said. "When I stood up, I was standing next to Rebecca."

George nodded.

"We were in that grey area for . . . a long time," George Jacobs said. "Suspended there, awake, but not able to move or think. I tried to leave the grey, return to my peaceful rest, but I wasn't able to act upon the world around me."

"What happened?" Em asked.

"You called," George Jacobs said. "I recognized your voice, Em. Why did you call us?"

"We saw Dorothy," Em said. "I thought if I opened the space for spirits close to us, caught in the in-between, she would come."

"I haven't seen her, Em," George Jacobs said.

George Jacobs' face reflected the guilt they all felt about Dorothy's situation. He blinked at Em.

"We're dead, aren't we?" George Jacobs said. "And you? I mean, that's Bridget . . ."

"Hi there, George." Bridget gave a little finger wave to George Jacobs.

"She was hanged two months before I was hanged," George Jacobs said. "The Reverend was with me on Gallows Hill."

"We died when we were hanged," Em said. "We came back as immortal witches. Giles was pressed to death."

"Dear Lord." George Jacobs turned to look at Giles.

"Over three days," Giles said with a shrug.

"You always were a stubborn man," George Jacobs said.

"Still am," Giles said.

"I'm sure that's true," George said. He turned to look at Em. "And the rest of you were hanged."

"Yes, sir," George Burroughs said.

"And you came back?" George Jacobs said.

"We did." Em smiled at his repeated question.

Catching her smile, he said, "Just hard to believe."

"It is," Em said.

"Now, I didn't come back because the kids moved my body?" George Jacobs asked. "Reverend?"

"We believe love protected you from this . . . enchantment," George Burroughs said.

He gestured to himself and Em. George Jacobs nodded.

"Is there anything you can tell us?" Sam asked. "Anything at all?"

George Jacobs turned to look at Sam. He nodded at Sam's question and then looked down.

"I have a sense . . . something . . . I . . ." Biting his bottom lip, George Jacobs looked off into the distance.

"What is it?" George Burroughs asked.

"You must find John Proctor," George Jacobs said.

"Where?" Em asked.

"I can't help you," George Jacobs said. "I know only what I've told you."

"George?" Rebecca asked.

Rebecca disappeared as if a giant vacuum had come and sucked her away.

"Listen to me," George Jacobs said. "This man ... I remember him from Salem Village."

"He was there?" Em asked. "As a living person?"

"Bystander in the crowd," George Jacobs said. "A feeling in the air, a smell, lurking around ..."

George Jacobs' legs disappeared.

"Find John Proctor," George Jacobs said. "They can't stop us if we fight together."

He looked at each of them individually.

"Will you fight with me?" George Jacobs asked as he continued to be sucked away.

One at a time, they nodded.

"We are with you, George!" Em said when only his head was visible.

"Em?" George Jacobs asked. "Find John."

And he disappeared.

Stunned, they sat staring at the place where George's apparition had floated.

"We are not alone," Sarah Wildes whispered. "Em?"

Em nodded. They had planned for any possibilities. It was time to put those plans into action.

"Dorothy?" Sarah Good's desperate voice called for her child.

"Show yourself!" Em commanded.

"Mama?" a young child's voice echoed through the room.

"Dorothy!" Sarah Good yelled. She threw herself onto the table. Her arms reached out. "Dorothy?"

"Hold her back!" Em yelled over Sarah's desperate cries.

Sarah Wildes and Ann jumped up to hold on to Sarah Good. Sam grabbed her from behind and held her to his him.

"It's not her!" Em yelled to Sarah Good. "Ann?"

Ann slapped Sarah Good's face.

"It's not her!" Ann said into Sarah Good's face. "It's a trick."

"Dorothy?" Sarah's frantic voice brought tears to their eyes.

"Mama?" a young child's voice said again.

"Show yourself!" Em commanded.

The air began to crackle with electricity. The incandescent light bulb in the floor lamp popped, blowing glass onto the floor. The pressure in the room rose until their Boston-fog-filled sinuses screamed in misery.

"Hold on!" George Burroughs yelled to the other witches.

"Show yourself!" Em ran her hand over the pillar candles in the middle of the table. The flames grew to a foot high. "Now!"

Whap! She clapped her hands together.

The demon appeared, with the specter of Dorothy Good in its clutches. Em's pinky finger pointed to Alice and George Burroughs. The demon opened his mouth to say something.

"Now!" Em yelled.

George and Alice snatched Dorothy away from the demon. The demon screamed with rage and reached for the child.

"Clear and light," the others chanted. "Clear and light!"

"Away!" Em yelled and jumped to her feet.

The space they'd opened for the séance snapped shut, and the demon disappeared. Exhausted by the effort, Em dropped down into her seat and tried to catch her breath.

"Let there be light!" Giles said, and the lights came on.

The witches cheered. Em nodded to them and took a long drink of water. Sam let go of Sarah Good, and she rushed to hold her child. The witches came to see Dorothy.

"It's not her," George said.

"I know," Em said.

Sarah Good was close enough to hear them.

"It's her sanity," Sarah Good said. "The spirit of her mind."

She glanced at Em, who gave her a solemn nod.

"I release you, my daughter, my love," Sarah Good whispered. She leaned forward to kiss the specter's forehead. "Be at peace."

The child kept a tight grip on her mother.

"Be at peace," the witches said to Dorothy. "Be at peace."

The child began to disappear. Sarah Good and her daughter locked eyes.

"Be at peace, my daughter," Sarah Good said. "I love you."

And Dorothy was gone. They silently stared at where Dorothy had been standing.

"Thank you," Sarah Good whispered.

One at a time, they hugged Sarah Good and left the room, until only Em and George were left sitting at the table. Sarah Wildes and Mary Ayer were cleaning up from their ceremony. Sarah Good sat down across the table from Em. She dropped her head into her hands and wept. Mary Ayer sat down next to Sarah and rubbed her back.

"Whatcha thinking?" George asked.

Em turned to look at him. After a moment, she looked away.

"No, really," George said. "What are you thinking?"

"I'm thinking about my father," Em said.

"Was he like that?" George started to ask. Em shook her head. "Then, what?"

"He always told me to watch out for the demons in this world," Em said in a low tone. "Then he would touch the cleft in my chin."

George reached over to stroke the spot. Em gave him a slight smile.

"My father asked to meet me before I left England," Em said. "Henry and I went to my parents' home. As if they'd planned it, my mother invited Henry out into the garden to give him some rhubarb root to bring to America, I think. And my father . . ."

She looked up at George and then shook her head.

"Not here," Em said.

Alice, who'd left to show the others out, was coming into the room when Em said, "Not here."

"There's not a soul in this world who loves you more than we do," said Alice. She gestured to Sarah Wildes, Sarah Good, Mary Ayer, and herself as she closed the door to the loft.

"Show us," Sarah Wildes said.

"We'll not tell a soul," Mary Ayer said.

As if to say he agreed, George put his arm around her. Em turned her right hand over. An eight-inch version of her father appeared on her palm. The women had to lean in closer to see.

Smaller than her father, Em poured tea from her mother's antique pot and set the teacup onto a small table set into a bay window. Her father held out her chair for her.

"This is my mother's home," Em said.

"You're pregnant," Alice said.

"With Thomas," Em said. "We wanted him to be born here, in the colony. There was talk that the colony would eventually become a country. We wanted Thomas to have every chance."

"Shh." Sarah Wildes pointed to her father sitting down in a chair at the table on Em's palm.

Em and her father drank their tea in uncomfortable silence. Her father cleared her throat, and she looked up.

"I don't think I'd ever been alone with him like that," Em said.

"You look uncomfortable," Mary Ayer said.

"I am," Em said.

"Father?" Em asked.

Her father gave her a long look. She smiled.

"You look so young!" George said.

"I was." Em gave a rueful shake of her head. Sarah Wildes pointed at Em and then at George and shushed them.

"I have something to say," Em's father said. He cleared his throat.

"Father?" Em asked again.

"You are my only child," her father said. "My only heir."

"Yes, father," Em said.

"You . . ." Her father's voice started loud but deteriorated into mumbling. He flushed and swallowed hard. "We . . . Uh . . . Our family, we . . ."

"I'm sorry to interrupt, but we should be going," Henry Rich, Em's first husband, came into the room.

"Yes, of course." Her father stood.

"Aw!" Alice said.

"Wait," Em said.

Em's father leaned down. He took hold of Em's elbow and helped her to standing. As he did, his mouth was next to her ear. He said something. He kissed her cheek. His finger touched the cleft in her chin, and he let her go.

"What did he say?" Alice squealed at the same time George said, "What?"

"I don't remember," Em said. The vision disappeared, and she closed her hand.

"But you actually heard him?" George asked.

"Yes," Em said. "I know I heard what he said. I remember thinking about it all the way to New England."

"The trip must have been brutal," Alice said.

"I can't imagine doing it while pregnant," Mary Ayer said.

"It was hard," Em nodded. "Henry started to show signs of his illness. I knew he wasn't himself, but we hadn't been married long, and I was so young. I . . ."

"Did your parents have other children?" George asked.

"I'm not sure," Em said.

"I remember my mother pregnant with my brothers and sisters," Sarah Wildes said. "You?"

"No." Em thought for a while. "I'm sorry. I haven't thought of this in a long, long time."

"Of course," Sarah Wildes said. "Take your time."

Em scowled at Sarah.

"If that scowl is a question, let me be clear," Sarah Wildes said. "I'm dying to know what your father said. So what do we do?"

Em looked at each of her friends. Alice nodded. Em shook her head at them.

"Can we let this drop?" Em asked.

"No," George said and kissed her cheek.

"Do you know how to do it?" Mary Ayer asked. She looked at Sarah Wildes and Alice. "Maybe she doesn't know how."

"Do you know how, Em?" Alice asked.

"Yes," Em said.

"Well, go on then," Sarah Wildes said in a flip tone. They laughed.

Em sighed and snapped her right fingers. Her father appeared in miniature form. She pushed the vision off her hand, and the memory landed in the center of the table. The image grew to near human size. Em had to lean back in her chair to get any perspective. Alice and Sarah Wildes pulled their chairs a foot away from the table and sat down.

"You are my only child," her father said. "My only heir."

"Yes, father," Em said.

"You . . ." her father flushed and swallowed hard. "We were able to have only one child. Uh . . . Our family, we . . ."

"Did he say that before?" George asked. The memory continued to play. "I don't think he did."

"His voice drops after the first word," Alice said.

"Shush!" Sarah Wildes said. "Em, can you go back? Did he say anything else in these other drops?"

"Maybe," Em said. "Let's see."

"You must understand how special you are." Her father flushed and swallowed hard. "We were only able to have only one child. Uh . . . Our family, we . . ."

"You *are* special." George leaned over and kissed her cheek.

"Shush!" Sarah said again.

"I'm sorry to interrupt, but we should be going." Henry Rich, Em's first husband, came into the room.

"Yes, of course." Her father stood.

Em's father leaned down. He took hold of Em's elbow and helped her to standing. As he did, his mouth was next to her ear.

"You are a truth teller," he said in Em's ear. "We are made of God, the true God. We see only truth, live only in the truth. We are God's truth."

He kissed her cheek and let her go.

"Truth teller," Alice said.

"Gospel Woman," George said.

"What?" Em turned to look at him.

"Hathorne recorded that you told them you were a Gospel Woman," George said. "You were telling him that you couldn't be a witch because you were God's truth."

"The man was paranoid and saw witches lurking around every corner." Em shook her head. "Who cares what he wrote down?"

"You didn't remember your father saying this to you?" George asked.

"No," Em said. "He said something ridiculous and . . ."

"Why did you tell Hathorne, the examiner, that you

were a Gospel Woman?" Alice asked.

"I thought it was crazy that he thought *I* was a witch," Em said. "There's no one more unlikely to be a witch than . . ."

Em flushed bright red and shrugged.

"I guess it doesn't matter now," Em smiled.

"No, it matters," Sarah Wildes said. "I feel it in my bones."

"Why?" Em gave Sarah Wildes a disbelieving shake of her head.

"Listen to what you said," George said. "You knew Henry was ill on the boat. It was years . . ."

"Five years before he was truly ill," Em said.

"You always tell us the truth," Alice said.

"You told Hathorne that you were 'a Truth Woman,'" George said. "He wrote down 'a Gospel Woman' because the words are synonyms."

"*You* are God's truth," Mary Ayer said.

"That's why the devil is after you," Sarah Wildes said. "You're the only person who can stop him."

"I . . ." Em said.

"We are here because you, the God's truth, called us back," George said.

"That's crazy," Em said.

She looked at Sarah Wildes, Alice, Sarah Good, and Mary Ayer. They looked like they'd been hit by a train.

"Rebecca and George Jacobs answered your call," George said. "Just today!"

"Anyone could . . ." Em said.

"Tell me, Truth Teller." Alice's voice cracked, and her eyes filled with tears. "Why are we here?"

"I . . ." Em started.

"Tell me," Alice commanded.

The slight tug of Alice's magic begged her to respond. She looked at Alice's face and saw her determination.

"To fight this evil," Em said. "Before it infects the world."

"That's why we died?" Mary Ayer asked.

"Probably," George said.

Mary Ayer's entire being began to smile.

"What happened?" George asked.

"I believe you," Mary Ayer said. "And, I guess I'm okay with it. I died to protect what would become this country."

"Seems like maybe we're needed now," Em said.

"We've been needed before," Mary Ayer smiled. She leaned over to kiss Em's cheek. "I'll fight with you."

"Em?" Sarah Good asked from across the table.

"Sarah?" Em asked.

"I believe you are a Truth Teller. It's like . . ." Sarah Good nodded.

"I've known it all along," Alice said.

"Me, too," Sarah Wildes said.

Mary Ayer nodded.

"What truth do we need to know now, my love?" George asked.

"That we will have to fight this," Em said.

"Bring it on," George said.

"We have to find John Proctor," Em said.

The women nodded.

"When we're done, we will have the choice of peace," Em said.

George leaned forward and kissed her lips. The women hugged her and slowly made their way out of the room. George showed them out.

Long after they'd gone, Em sat in the room, wondering what her father had really meant. She'd seen him, years later, when she was living with Isaac in Boston. Her father, William Panon, came to New England from London to find out for himself what had happened to his daughter. She would have sworn he didn't look a day older than in the vision she'd recreated. She got up from the table and jogged down the stairs. At the computer behind the counter, she typed his name into the search engine. Nothing came up.

"There you are!" George said. "What are you doing?"

He jogged down the steps.

"You can't be working," George said. "You must be exhausted!"

"Looking for my father," Em said.

"My love," George said. "Benoni didn't survive."

"Thomas, either," Em said.

"Then why . . .?"

"Feeling," Em said with a shrug.

"Let's look tomorrow," George said. "One of the benefits of living more than three hundred years has to be that we let tomorrow work out some of our problems."

"And tonight?" Em asked with a smile.

"Tonight, we shower, rest, and recover our balance," George said.

He held out his hand. She took his hand and kissed it. She got up, and they walked hand in hand to their apartment.

Chapter Ten

She'd known it was him, her father, the man who had sired her, the moment she'd seen his photo on his Facebook page. She would have gone to see him right then and there, but George had come to usher her to bed. She could have gone to see him when George had fallen asleep. She could have gotten up the next day and gone, but they'd slept in. She'd lingered over scones and good coffee until it was time to check on the store.

The next day was Monday, of course, and she had a lot of Monday-like things to do. Tuesday went the way of Tuesdays — lunch with Alice, the afternoon with Wilmot going over the store's books, and closing up after Sarah Wildes' class. She wasn't sure what had happened to Wednesday, but Thursday she'd spent her free time trying to track down a new gasket for her honey extractor.

Friday mid-morning, she found herself in Jamaica Plain, walking down Green Street. Staring at her cell phone, she almost ran into a pungent man clutching a six-pack of beer. She knew what it was like to reek of body odor and grease. She knew what it was like to prefer alcohol or drugs or depression over anything else. She'd spent more time than she'd like to remember just like this man. As if to acknowledge their similarities, he gave her a broken-toothed grin. She nodded and kept walking.

She hadn't told George where she was going, but that wasn't unusual for Fridays. She ran errands on Friday mornings. According to the spell she'd cast, this morning's errands just happened to bring her within five miles of where her father lived.

There was a sign on the side of the brick building that said, "Rooms for Rent" in large red letters. Through the glass door, she could see a dingy closet that served as the front desk. She stopped near the door of the building, where she caught a familiar scent. Magic leaves an odor unique to the person who creates it.

George had been here.

Not recently, probably not within the last year, but he had definitely been here. She scowled and pressed the button for the super.

"Yeah?" A man's voice said on a dilapidated metal set into the wall.

"I wanted to ask you a few questions," Em said. She winced at the neediness in her own voice.

"You the police?" the man asked.

"No," Em said. "I'm looking for my father."

"We're all looking for something, lady," the man's voice said.

There was a click, like the sound of a telephone hanging up, and nothing else.

"Hello?" Em asked. She pressed the button again. "Hello?"

"He ain't very nice," a woman's voice came from behind her.

Em turned around. A towering, curvaceous woman,

whose rich chocolate skin was packed into tiny strips of clothing, was standing behind her.

"I'm looking for someone," Em said.

The woman looked at Em's jeans and her white business shirt and raised a penciled-on eyebrow.

"Someone?" the woman asked.

"Why do you care?" Em scowled.

The woman took her time adjusting her ample bosom in her push-up bra before responding.

"Martha is considering if there's something in it for her," the woman said.

"Martha?" Em scowled at the woman's use of her birth name.

The woman pointed to herself.

"What do you want?" Em asked.

The woman's lip bulged out as her tongue made its way across her white upper teeth.

"I can't know what to offer you if you don't know what you want," Em said.

"Whatchu think Martha is?" the woman asked. "Martha ain't no whore with the heart of gold. Martha is a business woman."

To emphasize her point, the woman thrust her enormous rear backward, causing the fabric to rise above her crotch. A man whistled at her from a passing car, and a delivery truck honked.

"You see what Martha means?" the woman asked.

"You want me to show my crotch, too?" Em asked. "Get them to honk?"

A laugh like an exploding volcano burst out of the woman. She nodded to Em's questions. Em shrugged, unbuttoned her jeans, and began shimmying out them. Before she got very far, the woman shook her head so hard that her wig shifted. Em buttoned back up.

"Breakfast?" Em asked.

"It's ten in the morning!" The woman batted her false eyelashes to indicate that the negotiations had just begun. "I've been up for hours."

"Money?" Em asked.

"Money's always good. But for you . . ." The woman looked Em up and down. "I won't take your money."

"Why?" Em asked.

"I don't know," the woman said. "Maybe Martha has become the whore with the heart of gold."

"Yeah, you're a real Dolly Parton," Em said.

"Hey! Don't you be knocking Dolly Parton!" the woman said.

"Best Little Whorehouse in Texas," Em said. "Plus, Dolly Parton is a businesswoman — like you, like me."

"Oh," the woman said.

Martha raised an eyebrow and turned to walk away. Em watched her amble to the end of the block. When it looked like she was going to keep walking, Em whispered a small encouragement for her to return. The woman turned in place and sauntered back to Em.

"I want to know why you're here," the woman said.

"I'm looking for someone," Em said.

"George ain't here!"

"Who?" Em asked.

"Your man," the woman said.

Em's scowl deepened, and the air became thick with electricity.

"Don't panic," the woman said. "He carries your photo. Gave me this name, 'Martha,' because he said it was the best name he knew. Said it was *your* name."

The woman leaned toward Em.

"You 'Martha'?" the woman asked.

"Everyone calls me . . ."

"Em," the woman said. "He said that."

"How do you know George?" Em said.

"He starts every winter in Jamaica Plain," the woman said. "Like Santa. He stops by to find out who's been naughty and who's been nice, or, more like, who's sick, who's getting the shit beaten out of them, stuff like that. Since Martha is sort of a . . . goodwill ambassador for the neighborhood, I see him every December."

"What does Martha give him in return?" Em asked.

"Martha gets to live another year," the woman said.

"He extends your life?" Em asked.

Em's voice betrayed her doubt. She knew of no spell that could indefinitely extend life, and she'd looked. If there was a spell to extend life, there had to be a spell to help Alice end her immortal life.

"I have liver cancer," the woman said. "Picked it up in Kuwait when Martha was Michael."

Em nodded. There was a spell to strengthen the liver. It lasted about a year.

"So you see, I'm the trannie with the heart of gold," Martha said.

Em smiled in acknowledgement that Martha was transgendered.

"He loves you very much," Martha said.

"Who?"

"George," Martha said. "I met him in Kuwait."

Em nodded. Every few years, George got bit by the war bug. The next thing she knew, he'd joined up and was off to basic training. The Gulf War was one of the few hundred wars George had fought in over the last three hundred years.

"Gulf War sickness?" Em asked.

"Sure," Martha squinted at Em. "Why are you here?"

"I'm looking for someone," Em said. "A man. Goes by the name 'Bill Panon.'"

Martha scowled at Em. She made a hip-swaying journey over to the button on the building and pressed it.

"Yeah?" a man's voice asked.

"Somebody looking for you," Martha said.

"Who?"

"George's woman," Martha said.

The buzzer rang to open the door. Martha grabbed the door and opened it. Em took two twenty-dollar bills out of her pocket and held them out to Martha.

"What's dis?" Martha asked.

"For your time," Em said.

"You're a good egg," Martha said. She took the money and stuck it in her bra. "You want me to go with you so he don't give you no hassles?"

"I can manage," Em said.

"I bet that's right," Martha said. "You going to see the Reverend tonight?"

"Probably," Em said.

"Yeah, that's right," Martha said. "Only George knows what George is goin' to do."

Martha grinned, and Em started into the building.

"You tell George I said hello," Martha said.

Em stopped and turned.

"I'll do it," Em smiled.

Martha raised her hand in a wave. Em plunged into the building. The front lobby was empty, as was the dingy front desk. Em looked around for a moment, before taking a few steps into a dark hallway. Em stopped under a hanging single-fluorescent-tube light in a four-light fixture. The hallway reeked of urine and despair. Em put her finger under her nose to block the smell. A door near the end of the dark hallway opened with a bang. Yellow light and music filtered into the hallway.

"Down here," a man's voice yelled.

On guard, Em shuffled slowly down the hallway. The building had once been a livery stable. The hallway carried some of the old charm. It was light enough for Em to make out the basic features but dark enough to make Em walk down in the middle of the hallway. She reached the door and turned to peer in. The apartment was so bright that Em could see very little from the dark hallway. An enormous man looked like a shadow as he filled the entire apartment doorway.

"Whatchu want?" the man asked.

"I'm looking for William Panon," Em said.

"Who wants to know?" the man asked.

"A friend," Em said.

The man snorted.

"He don't have no friends," the man said.

"Father?" Em leaned forward to peer at the man.

The hallway began to spin. With nothing to grab onto, Em dropped to her knees and covered her head. As she had the time George had talked her into "riding a tornado," Em spun around and around and around. Time lost all meaning. She spun and spun until what felt like days later she passed out.

≈≈≈≈≈≈≈≈≈≈≈≈≈≈≈≈≈≈≈≈≈≈≈≈≈≈≈

"Have you seen Em?" George asked as he approached the front desk of the Mystic Divine.

"No," Shonelle said. "But she's avoiding me."

George glanced at the waning light outside and looked back at Shonelle.

"Why would she avoid you?" George asked.

"You know," Shonelle said.

"I don't," George said. "Hence the question."

"Huh," Shonelle snorted at him.

For the briefest moment, George saw his own irritated face and "you're an idiot" mannerisms on the girl's beautiful face. He scowled.

"So, you haven't seen Em?" George asked.

"Em left to run errands," Sarah Wildes said from the loft upstairs.

George looked up to see Sarah Wildes leaning over the railing.

"Is Em avoiding Shonelle?" George asked Sarah Wildes while raising his eyebrows at Shonelle.

"I don't think so," Sarah Wildes said. "She was going to talk to her about going ghost hunting with her friend."

"*Really*?" Shonelle's voice rose with hope, and she gave a little clap. "And the séance?"

"I told you," Sarah Wildes said. "Hell would have to . . ."

"Freeze over." Shonelle went from elated to pouting.

George grinned at Shonelle. She gave George his own best sneer and pushed past him to go to the back. George chuckled. He turned to see Sarah Wildes coming down the stairs.

"Em's not back?" Sarah Wildes asked.

George shook his head. Sarah Wildes grimaced with worry.

"You set a tracer?" Sarah Wildes asked in a low tone.

"I did," George said.

Sarah looked at her watch and then looked outside.

"Did you make anything for dinner?" Sarah Wildes grinned.

"No, Em hasn't started anything for dinner," George said.

"She hasn't been back?" Sarah Wildes asked. "That's just weird."

"When did she leave?" George asked.

"After lunch," Sarah Wildes said. "What did the tracer say?"

"It didn't," George said.

"What do you mean?" Sarah Wildes asked.

"I mean . . ."

Two of Sarah's students came in the door of the Mystic Divine.

"Sarah!" the students said.

"Hi, ladies," Sarah said. "Why don't you head on up?"

The women looked at George and giggled. They had just started toward the stairs when another set of women came in.

"Try again," Sarah said under her breath.

"I did," George said. "She's been gone for seven hours,

and the tracer..."

"Did you call this newfound *Jewish* grandson?" Sarah said in the same low tone.

"Isaac?" George nodded.

Sarah shook her head.

"Oh, Sarah!" a woman said. "I was hoping to..."

George nodded to Sarah Wildes and walked toward the apartment. He had a half-hour before his next client appointment. Maybe the tracer would work this time.

"George?" Sarah Wildes yelled from across the store. He turned to look at her. "Sometimes it's 'when' and not 'where.'"

He gave her a puzzled look. When she pointed to her watch, George realized she meant "when" in time. George nodded and jogged the rest of the way out of the store.

This time he would run a tracer for what time period Em had disappeared into as well as where she was located. His stomach ached with worry as he set up the spell. To be sure he was tracking Em, he took her pillow from their bed and marched it into their dining room. He held the pillow to his nose and took a breath.

"Em," he said as an exhale.

He set the pillow on the table. As he always did, he heard Em's instruction in his mind.

"You are a strong enough witch to have everything you want," Em said. "That's a gift and a curse. If you're not careful, you can end up with a bus load of marshmallows..."

"Or hookers," George said.

"Exactly," Em said. "You have to train yourself to use magic only when you do something specific."

"Make love to you?" George asked.

He put his arms around her waist and kissed her hair. For a moment, she let him hold her close.

"What's your action?" Em asked.

"Put my hands together and then pull them apart from each other."

Over her pillow, George put his hands together and pulled them apart. A green ball of smoke appeared between his palms. The ball of smoke rose to his eye level.

"Find Em," George said to the green smoke. "Look for 'where.' Look for 'when.' Look for 'who,' if you have to. But find Em!"

As it had every time he'd done this spell today, the smoke hovered in front of him. He'd made this spell four times already today. Each time, the green ball of smoke had lingered in front of his eyes until the smoke dissipated. He was about to give up when the ball of smoke flew through the apartment. The ball of smoke was moving so fast that George had to run to keep up.

The ball of smoke went through their sitting area and into the kitchen, where it threw itself against the large painting of the English countryside hanging over the sink.

"What the hell?" George asked.

The painting was of a field of ripe wheat. In the top right corner, a man, wearing a dark wool coat and a dark cap, worked with two large brown horses to harvest the wheat. The green ball of smoke had left a green mark on the man.

"Shit," George said.

He leaned over and tried to wipe the green off the man. Em was going to kill him. Feeling someone, he turned to see that Alice was watching him.

"Angry?" Alice asked.

"I'm fine." George blew out an angry breath. "What do you want?"

"Your client is here," Alice said.

"She's early," George grumbled. "She can wait."

"Em's going to kill you for marking her painting." Alice pointed to the man in the field. "I assume that's your green dot. It's your color."

George nodded. He was almost out of the kitchen when he turned and looked at Alice.

"What?" Alice asked.

"How is this where Em grew up?" George asked. His voice rose with frustration. "She's from London."

"There was a big fire in London, Reverend," Alice said.

"What?" George's voice reflected his irritation.

"1666," Alice said. "The Great Fire of London? Em and her family moved to some family land in the country — a farm, I think. Probably that one. Em always says the painting is of where she grew up."

Alice gestured toward the painting.

"What are you talking about?" George's voice rose with anger.

"If you don't calm down, I won't talk to you," Alice said. "I'm not Em. I won't put up with your crap."

"All right, all right," George said. "Fine."

Desperate for any information, he took calming breaths and paced back and forth. He stopped in front of Alice when he was calmer.

"Tell me again," George said.

"Em's father was fairly wealthy," Alice said. "They lived in London, where he was a watchmaker. His shop was on the edge of where the aristocrats lived — close enough for them to use him and far enough away to make them think they were getting a good deal. According to Em, the wind whipped the fire into a fire storm. Their entire neighborhood burned to the ground, including her father's shop and their home. The fire was so hot that people's bodies were cremated. No one knows how many people died."

"And?" George gave her an irritated look.

"While her father's shop was being repaired and their home rebuilt, her father moved the family to the countryside. They lived on family land, probably that wheat farm."

"A wheat farm," George said.

Alice gestured to the painting.

"That wheat farm," Alice said.

"The painting?"

"Em's father painted that painting," Alice said.

"He did?"

"Yes," Alice said, her voice rising with her own irritation. "It amused him to document his inept attempt at farming."

"He wasn't any good at farming?" George asked and shook his head. He had no idea what Alice was saying or why she was saying it now.

"They didn't live on the farm. Mostly, the farm ran itself," Alice said. "He didn't need to be there. They spent holidays there, but that's all. When they moved there . . ."

"After the great fire," George said.

"That's right," Alice said. "Em said that they were mostly in the way on the farm. Her father was used to being active, so he tried to participate in farm life. Finally, the farm manager convinced Em's father that his time would be better spent doing anything other than farming. He took up painting."

Like a spokesmodel on a game show, Alice waved her hand toward the painting.

"And the man?" George asked.

"The one with a big 'George was here' *green* mark on him?" Alice asked.

"It's a tracer," George said. "I'm looking for Em. I don't know where Em is."

"You don't?" Alice asked. "I just came to ask where she was."

"I don't know," George's voice cracked. "For the first time in more than three hundred years, I don't have any idea where Em is."

George's phone rang. He answered it without looking.

"George?" Shonelle asked.

"Yes."

"There's someone here to see you," Shonelle said.

"Can you tell my client I'll be right there?" George asked.

"Oh, she knows," Shonelle said. "She's early."

"Great. Thanks!" George hung up the cell phone.

It rang again before he could get it into his pocket.

"It's not your client," Shonelle said. "It's someone named 'Martha.' She says she met you in Kuwait?"

"Tell her . . ."

"She has Em's purse," Shonelle said.

George ran out of the apartment.

Chapter Eleven

George ran down the stairs. He opened the door to the Mystic Divine with a bang. The patrons turned to stare at him as he jogged through the store. He gestured to Martha, and she followed him out of the store. They weaved their way through the traffic on Boylston Street until they were in the Central Burial Grounds on the Boston Common. Moving fast, George jingled his keys for the little red-haired Irish girl who haunted this area of the Common. Obsessed with keys, the child-ghost would harass him until she eventually stole his keys. The girl grabbed his keys and disappeared. He kept moving until he reached a large gravestone which read: "Here were reinterred the remains of persons found under the Boylston Street Mall during the digging of the subway. 1895."

"Friends?" Martha gestured to the gravestone for the eleven hundred British-soldier remains found when the city was digging the nearby subway station.

"Some," George said. "What do you know?"

"Did you fight in this one?" Martha asked.

"I've fought in them all," George said.

"See, I would think . . ." Martha started.

"Where did you get Em's purse?" George asked. He

mingled just enough magic to encourage Martha to tell him the truth without making her suspicious.

"She came to *my* street, George," Martha said, with a bat of her artificially long eyelashes. "What was Martha to do?"

"What did you do?" George asked.

"I ..." Martha said. "You know — I don't like your tone."

George scowled at Martha, and she laughed. Martha's laughter woke the spirit of a British soldier. The soldier used his remaining arm to raise his musket at them. Recognizing George, he stood at attention.

"At ease," George said under his breath.

"George?" the soldier asked. He lowered his weapon. "What are ya doin'?"

"Talking to my friend, Martha," George said. "Sorry we woke you, Buford."

"No problem at all," the soldier said. He looked Martha up and down. "Where's Em?"

Irritated, George flicked his hand in a salute, and the soldier disappeared.

"What did you do to him?" Martha asked.

"I put him back to sleep," George said. "Where *is* Em?"

"Now that's a good question," Martha said.

George spied Buford peering at them over a gravestone a few rows away. He nodded his head, and Buford raised his musket to guard them.

"And the answer is?" George asked.

"I connected her with what she was looking for," Martha said. "That's Martha. Always helpful."

"What was she looking for?" George asked.

"If she didn't tell you, I'm certainly not going to," Martha said with a sniff. "After all, we girls have to stick together."

George glared at Martha.

"All right, all right," Martha said. "I'll tell you on because you help Martha with her liver, and we went to Kuwait together, and we're standing over the remains of your friends."

Martha nodded as if she expected a "Thank you" from George. When it didn't come, she put a hand on her hip and gave him a sour look.

"You have to tell me what she was looking for first," George said.

"Have it your way," Martha said. "She was looking for Bill Panon."

"Her father," George said.

"That's what she said, but that man is so disgusting that I . . ." Martha started.

"How did she find him?" Fumbling, George asked the only question that came to mind.

"Everybody knows Bill Panon," Martha said. "You do, too."

"I do?"

"He manages the building you stay at when you're in Jamaica Plain." Martha shook her head at him like he was an idiot.

"I'm sorry," George said. "You're right. I'd forgotten that was his name. I have a lot on my mind when I'm there."

"It's all right, George Burroughs," Martha said. "You know Martha loves you enough to put up with your BS."

George rolled his eyes, and Martha laughed.

"How did she find him?" George asked.

"Who?" Martha asked.

"William Panon." George's voice rose with frustration, and Martha grinned.

"She probably found him on Facebook," Martha said. "Isn't that where everybody finds everybody now?"

"I don't," George said.

"That's because you're *the* legendary George Burroughs," Martha said. "You put up a profile, and you'll have ladies lined up for blocks to get some lovin' from you. Men, too, probably."

George gave her a hard look, and Martha laughed again.

"What happened?" George asked.

"Martha doesn't know," Martha said. "Last I saw of her, she was walking into that building."

"When was that?" George asked.

"Eleven or so," Martha said. "I forgot all about her until this afternoon. Something made me go in there and look for her. I felt a strong compulsion. I figured you made that happen."

"I might have," George said. One of the side effects of tracers is that people who loved him could hear his plea.

"That's what Martha thought," she said. "I went in the building. Everything seemed on the up and up, so I talked to Panon."

"What did he say?" George asked.

"Nothing," Martha said. "He wasn't home most of the day. Seems like someone stole the bulbs out of that fluorescent light fixture in the hallway."

"Again?" George asked.

"Right — you know how dark that hallway can be if

those bulbs aren't in," Martha said.

George nodded.

"Bill had to go out and get more bulbs," Martha said. "He didn't get back until a half hour or so before I got there. I helped him put the bulbs in. Saw Em's purse when the light came on again."

"Where was it?" George asked.

"Tucked into the end of the hall," Martha said. "You know, in that corner where the window ledge hits the wall. He looked inside and saw it was hers."

Martha nodded toward the purse in her arms. Trying to think it through, George looked away from Martha.

"But here's the thing," Martha said in a low tone. She glanced at the ghost of the British militiaman to see if he was listening. "I talked to old Bill when Em came."

"You did?"

"Talked to him over the intercom," Martha said.

"You're sure it was him?" George asked.

"No," Martha said. "I just . . . well . . ."

Martha fell silent.

"Well, what?" George asked.

"He looked scared, you know, when he found Em's purse," Martha said.

"Scared?"

"Yeah," Martha said. "Like 'Oh, shit!' He played it off, but I think he was rattled."

"Because she was gone?" George asked.

"Because she's your woman," Martha said. "He knows a whole ton of George is going to come down on him."

"He's got that right," George nodded.

Martha nodded. As if she'd run out of things to say,

Martha stopped talking and went strangely blank.

"Do you think someone mugged Em?" George asked. "Stole her purse?"

Martha shook her head.

"Then...?" George started.

"There's this story, you know," she said. "Martha don't know if it's true or if it's a lie, but I think it has something to do with this."

"Story?" George asked.

"There's a story that old Bill is the original owner of the building," Martha said. "Maybe owned the land before it was a livery."

"The same Bill?" George asked.

"Very same," Martha said. "Converted the building from a livery to apartments. There's a couple people who grew up in that building..."

"And still live there." George nodded.

"Still live there," Martha said with a nod.

"I've met them," George said.

"Martha knows you have," Martha said. "They say old Bill hasn't aged even one day since they moved in. Not one day."

"You think the manager is Em's father," George said.

"Martha doesn't know what he is," Martha said. "She just knows that he knows more than he's saying."

George's cell phone rang. Pulling it from his pocket, he realized it was time for his appointment.

"I have to..." George pointed back to the Mystic Divine.

"You go on," Martha said. "Martha will wait right here until you're done. We'll go over there together."

"You don't have to," George said.

"We cleared out them houses in Kuwait together," she said. "Martha would have died without her George — ten times over. Now, George needs Martha's help. She's going to be there no matter what. Martha would do anything for her George."

Martha nodded. George gave her a one-armed hug. When his head was close to hers, she said in her deep Michael voice, "We're dancing with the devil, George Burroughs."

He was so surprised that he backed up to look at Martha. She gave him a coy smile.

"Go on," Martha said. "I'll be right here."

George jogged away.

"Take the purse!" Martha yelled after him.

George ran back to her for the purse. She gave him a saucy look and a wink. Laughing, he jogged toward the Mystic Divine. He picked up the little red-haired girl as he neared the street.

"If you're going to play with ghosts, why don't you play with me?" the girl asked in Irish Gaelic.

"What ghost?" George asked.

"You don't know?" the girl giggled.

He looked back at Martha. She was looking at the gravestone, so he could just see the back left side of her head. For the briefest moment, a car's headlight lit up a small round bullet hole just over her ear on the edge of her wig. The back of her wig was thick with dried blood. As he watched, the person he knew as Martha fell to her knees and then to the ground.

Martha was dead.

George's breath caught with sorrow. Whatever Martha had done or been in this life, she had been one of the very few whom he could call "friend." He'd been so worried about Em that he hadn't even noticed she'd been shot.

"There was nothing you could do," the little red-haired girl said. She dangled his keys in front of his face. "She was already dead."

He whispered a fast prayer for Martha's immortal soul and sniffed back a tear. He looked down at Em's purse. Martha must have been holding the purse when she was shot. There would have been enough residual magic in Em's purse to get Martha here.

Martha wanted him to know that she was dead. Martha wanted him to know what she knew. George nodded. Martha wanted him to find his Em. He wiped away a tear that ran down his face.

George glanced at the British soldier. No wonder he'd awoken when Martha laughed. The laugh of a new spirit always called to old spirits. The soldier moved out from behind the gravestones to stand guard over Martha's body. George looked down at the glimmer of the little girl.

"We'll take care of her, George," the little girl said. "But you should call the police."

George grabbed his keys and ran across the street into the Mystic Divine.

Em opened her eyes.

It was dark. She had no idea where she was.

She remembered this deep, blank dark. She remembered not knowing where she was.

She remembered the granite crevice and soil that surrounded her body and the bodies of her hanged friends.

She closed her eyes again to rest.

The dark enveloped her. Like the touch of a soft blanket, she let the darkness wrap itself around her. In its embrace, she was safe.

No more of life's incessant press. No more bright sunrises. No more witches.

Only darkness. Only peace.

She sighed.

Sitting in that horrible Boston prison in 1692, she'd imagined death to be like this — dark peace and an end of the press of living. No more prison. No more accusations. No more torture or groping hands looking for witches' tits or rape or heavy chains or strappado or gawking onlookers yelling cruelties. No more laundry to do or fields to harvest or children to raise or neighbors to get along with. Just dark peace and an end to the press of living.

She scowled.

She'd imagined death to be exactly like this — same smell, same feelings, and even the same sounds. She shook her head at herself and opened her eyes.

"Nothing in life is exactly what you expect it to be, Martha," she said out loud.

Her voice echoed back to her.

She was lying on her side, with her nose pressed into the dirt. She let out a breath, gathered her strength, and she rolled over. Her body ached from the effort. She stretched her neck and then her arms. Like she did in yoga class, she extended her legs. She felt bruised. If she'd broken something, it had already healed.

"Let there be light," she said.

Light emanated from her hands. She flicked her fingers to the ceiling, and a line of white light appeared on the ceiling. She was in some kind of cellar or tunnel with granite walls. She must be under a large tree because the tendrils of roots filled the spaces between the rocks. She took a deep breath. The soil was clean, moist, and fertile.

She was not in New England.

She jerked up to sitting. When she was young, the bubonic plague had taken London to its knees. She had helped her mother and father stuff bodies into graves like this one. She looked around her.

She was lying in a long, narrow chamber with granite stones for walls. There seemed to be rooms on either side at the end of the passage. There was enough room for a child to stand, but not for an adult. She crawled toward the end of the passageway to peer into the room on her right. It was a standard burial chamber from the Neolithic era.

She grinned. She knew where she was.

She was on Rousay. She had come home.

She laughed out loud.

After the plague and fire, her family had retreated to her father's ancestral family land on Rousay, an island in the Orkney Islands just north of the Highlands of Scotland. After the farm manager had begged her father to stop interfering with the farm, she and her parents spent any free day exploring the ancient ruins that covered almost every square inch of Rousay.

Of course, she'd thought that death would be dark peace, blissful quiet, and an end to the press of living. In a

Neolithic passage tomb, death was dark peace.

She crawled back to where she had awakened. It had been more than three hundred years since she'd been in tombs like this. She didn't remember how to get out of them. She lay back down.

The moment her spine hit the dirt, she missed George.

She'd never told him about Rousay or the glorious days of exploration in these tombs. In fact, outside of telling him she was from London — which was technically true — they had never talked about the details of her life before she'd come to live in New England.

When she'd met him, George absolutely hated the Scots. The Scottish Privy Council had just authorized field executions of Scottish Presbyterians, or "Covenanters," not loyal to the king or caught in arms. In order to stay alive, Covenanters were abandoning their faith in droves. The Reverend George Burroughs found their betrayal to be cowardly and despicable. He had no space for deserters, especially people who abandoned their Puritan beliefs. He had railed against the cowardly Scots.

Her life on Rousay was her secret.

Since she was born in London, no one ever needed to know that her heart and soul belonged in the Orkney Islands. Shaking her head at her stubborn man, she rolled onto her hands and knees again to see if she could find a way out.

She went to the end of the passageway and then back to the rooms. As far as she could tell, there was no way out. This tomb had not been excavated by modern archeologists, so there wasn't a new entrance. Em was effectively stuck here.

Leaning against the wall, she wondered if she could use magic to get out. She wondered whether George had noticed that she was missing. She was just starting to feel sorry for herself when she heard footsteps on top of the tomb.

She doused the light and lay in the dark.

Someone was standing on top of the tomb. Their boots whacked the side of the tree above. The tree's roots showered her with dirt.

She lay still.

For all she knew, John Parker or his demon had brought her here. The boots trotted down from the top of the hill. She listened until she heard only silence and the Atlantic Ocean crashing against the shore.

Her mind went over her day. She'd been running errands when she went to Jamaica Plain. Once there, she'd run into Michael, now Martha, who happened to have fought with George in Kuwait. Em had tried to raise the super at the apartment building, but he didn't want anything to do with her. Martha rang the intercom, and the super changed his mind. She'd gone down the long hallway and then . . .

Nothing.

She had a vague impression of spinning. Her stomach turned over. She had no idea how long she'd been in this passage tomb. Probably hours, but surely not days. She rested in the dark.

She'd lain for a little less than twelve hours in the mass grave on Gallows Hill before waking up with a gasp. The dark crevice and rising moon had transformed death's stillness into a desperate press for air. She'd lain there for another half hour, attempting to take a full breath. After some time, she'd become aware of the pressure of the witches on top of her. She'd heard the water lapping in the river nearby. She'd become overwhelmed by the stench of rotting flesh and thrown up.

Em's stomach heaved. She clamped her mouth closed against the acid brought by horrifying memories and too much dark. She felt this terror every time she lay down. When George was home, she'd reach out for his hand, and, even in the deepest depths of sleep, George's hand would grasp tight onto hers. When George was traveling, he would send her the image of the last thing he'd seen before he closed his eyes for sleep. She would catch the image and hold it to her heart as a reminder that she was not alone in the dark.

She was alone in the dark now.

There was a scraping sound at the end of the tunnel, away from the remains rooms. The person had returned.

Em's heart beat a desperate rhythm. She was completely vulnerable. No one would know if the devil infected her. She would return home and transform the others. As the devil invaded the powerful, immortal Salem Twenty, they would wreak havoc on the world.

She had to get home. She cursed herself for never learning transportation spells. She had no magical idea how to transport her body from this tomb. She scrambled into one of the rooms and found something big to hide behind.

Again, the scraping sound came at the end of the tunnel. She felt a *whoosh!* as the air pressed out of this quiet place. A blast of cold, moist air sent a shiver down Em's back. She rolled herself into a tight ball and covered her head.

"Emmy?" a man's voice yelled. "I know you're there, love. Just hang on for your old man."

"Father?" Em whispered.

"It's me, love," her father said. "Hang on. I'll be right there."

Em scrambled to the passageway and peeked down the hall. An opening, just large enough for her to slip through, had been made in the granite. She said a soft prayer of thanks. A man's hand appeared in the opening. She crawled to the other end of the tomb and grabbed onto the hand. The strong hand of her father pulled her head first from the passage tomb.

"Welcome home," her father said.

He grabbed her in a hug.

Chapter Twelve

Em stood in her father's tight grasp for what felt like a second or maybe a year. Emotion overcame her, and she sobbed for all that had happened since she'd seen him last. He held on. When she was steady on her feet, he stepped back to look at her. Ashamed of her emotions, she looked down and away from him. He tipped her face up to look at her.

"My Em," he said. He wiped her tears. "Always so strong."

"I've had to be," Em said.

"Yes, you have." He gave a quick nod and turned away. "We need to get off the hill before anyone sees us."

"Anyone?" Em asked.

"The island's a hub of activity now, Em." Her father smiled. "Archeologists, mostly. Who'd have ever guessed that anyone with even an ounce of sense would want to live on Rousay?"

Em smiled.

"Come now," her father said. He tucked her arm into the crook of his. "It will be dark soon."

Em noticed the sun was low in the sky. On Rousay in the summer, it got dark around ten at night. She must have been in the passage tomb for at least ten hours. As if he could hear her thoughts, her father gave her a slight nod.

"I'll take you home," he said. "We'll say you're a wandering American lost on the hill. Can you pull off the accent?"

"Sure," Em said.

"I've a wife," her father said. "She's lovely, funny, smart about books, and not so smart about things — loads of university degrees."

"She doesn't know you're five hundred years old?" Em asked.

"Oh, I'm much older than that."

Scowling, Em turned to look at her father.

"We have a lot to talk about."

They took a few steps before Em's "running errands" clogs slipped.

"Change your shoes," her father commanded. "While you're at it, put on something sensible. Good Lord, child, you're on Rousay."

"But . . ." Em started to protest.

He laughed and waved away her protest. Smiling, she used magic to change her shoes into her favorite hiking boots. She added a thick, hand-knit, grey sweater over her clothes.

"So severe," he said. With a snap of his fingers, the sweater became orange, red, and yellow. "To match your hair."

He grinned as her long brown hair transformed into a sunny red.

"You're no daughter of mine," he said.

"I'm not?" she asked.

He grabbed her arms and looked into her face.

"You are my only child," he said with a nod. "But as far as anyone knows, I am barren."

Startled by his severity, she could only nod. He squinted at her.

"Most of your childhood, I thought your mother . . ." He gave a slight nod. "That's why I let you go off to the colony with that ridiculous Henry Rich."

"You didn't like Henry?" Em grinned.

"Long-winded speeches about the purity of the church." Her father shook his head. "Purity of a sixteen-hundred-year-old church. Bah. The man was a loon."

"It was a different time," Em said.

"Your mother . . . she was so free, so strong," her father said. "She knew what I was — told me on her death bed."

Her father shook his head.

"I've never loved another like I loved her," her father said. He raised his eyebrows. "Anyway, I am 'Will,' at your service. I'm married to Justine. We live on Rousay at our old place. I hadn't been here in two hundred years before I met her in Glasgow. She's an archeologist."

Em nodded.

"You still with George?" her father asked.

"Yes," Em said.

"That's a long union," her father said.

"Three hundred and thirty-three years," Em said. "And counting."

"Why not sow your oats?" her father asked.

"It's not my style," Em said. "I'm like my mother that way."

Her father laughed and set off toward their farm. She followed him at a quick clip down the paths carved by ancients. A half-hour into their hike, they were joined by a large red Scottish deerhound and her mate, a grey Scottish deerhound. The dogs surrounded them in greeting and then rushed toward the back door of the house on the bluff. The dogs' bark brought a woman to the door. She opened the screen to let the dogs inside. She gave a worried look out into the field and then turned back into the house.

"She can't see us," Em said.

"We blend in," her father said.

Em looked down at her bright sweater and her father's brown leather jacket. She threw him a doubt-filled look. He laughed. He put his fingers to his lips and whistled. The woman returned to the door and looked out. He whistled again, and she turned toward the sound.

"I'm here!" her father yelled.

She gave a whole-arm wave and went back inside.

"She's mostly blind," he said under his breath. "Lost her sight as a child."

"How does an archeologist work if she can't see?" Em asked in the same low tone.

"She has a husband who knows these ruins like the back of his hand," her father said.

Em smiled.

"You'll like her," her father said. "But first . . ."

Her father stopped walking. They had been walking so fast that Em tripped over him. He caught her before she went down.

"We'll talk when she's asleep," her father said. "We need to talk."

"How did you know I was your daughter?" The words

popped out of Em's mouth before she realized she even had the question.

"I came to America when I heard of the hangings," her father said. "I went to the crevice. I looked in the pit, and you weren't there."

"You went to Gallows Hill," Em said. Her father looked away from her to cover his emotion. "I saw you get off the ship."

He turned to look at her.

"Or I thought I did." She shrugged. "It was just something that happened, you know? A few days ago . . . Well, I've been thinking about a lot of things."

"And?"

"I don't know anything," she said.

"We'll talk," he said.

He grabbed her arm, and they started walking toward the back door.

"Come along, stupid American — let's get you inside," her father said. He went up the three stone steps and into the stone house. "I'm home!"

Em stood at the bottom of the steps for a moment. Through the doorway, she heard her father greet his wife and the excited barks of his dogs. Nodding to encourage herself, she went up the steps and into the house.

"Right this way, sir," the uniformed police officer said to George.

George had called the police at the Mystic Divine. He'd had just enough time to reschedule his clients before a policeman arrived. The uniformed policeman had followed him to the Central Burying Ground to Martha's body. When they arrived, Buford, the ghost of the British militiaman, saluted George and retreated from Martha's body. While the policeman bent down to Martha's corpse, the little red-haired girl pulled at George's pockets for his keys. George managed to slip her his keys without the policeman noticing.

A whirlwind of activity ensued. George was led to a bench and instructed to wait until someone could take his statement. He looked up at the uniformed policewoman and nodded. She waited for him to get up before taking off toward the street. He followed the young policewoman to the sidewalk on Boylston Street, where a salty, older detective waited for him.

"Mr. Burroughs." The detective held out his hand for George to shake. "Detective Shane Donnell."

"Sir," George said.

"You wouldn't happen to be Reverend George Burroughs, would you?" The detective laughed. "You know, from Salem?"

George smiled. He'd learned a long time ago that denying who he was only led to long-winded conversations about Salem Village. By saying nothing, the person usually moved on. The detective was no different. Seeing George's smile, the detective checked himself and gave a curt nod.

"I'll bet you're sick of that," Detective Donnell said.

"George Burroughs had nine children," George said with a shrug.

"That he did," Detective Donnell said. He looked into George's face. "I've heard about you."

"Oh?" George asked.

"You work with the homeless in the winter," Detective Donnell said.

"I do," George said.

"Why is that?" the detective asked.

"They are the insane, the lost, the unwell, the lonely, and the abused," George said. "They are the refuse of our prosperous society. They need help, especially in the winter. They accept my help."

"What do you do?" the detective asked.

George knew that the detective was trying to get a sense of him as a person. He was tempted to use magic to clear any of the detective's doubt. He'd found that any good detective could feel the deception even if they didn't sense the magic. In general, his usual charm, honesty, and a smile worked the best.

"I talk to them," George said. "Reach out to the isolated pockets of humanity that are missed by the usual social safety nets. I have contacts with social services and non-profits. Once the need is found, it's pretty straightforward to get actual help. The trick is making the connection. I happen to be good at connecting with people. I'm able to do it financially. So I spend my winters out in the wilds of Boston."

"You own the . . ." The detective gestured to the Mystic Divine.

"My partner, Em, and I do," George said.

"Partner, not wife?" the detective asked.

"Wife," George said. "'Em' is short for 'Martha,' a nickname her father gave her."

"You're clearly not the Reverend George Burroughs," Detective Donnell said with a smile.

George could have told him that, no matter how many times he'd begged Em, she would not marry him. He could have said that Em was still married to Giles, a fact Giles remembered every time he needed something or outlived another wife. He could have said that, while his wife Mary had been dead for more than three hundred years, in the eyes of God, he was still married to her. Instead, he just smiled.

The detective started flipping through the pages of a pad of paper fit for the television detective Columbo. He took a cheap ballpoint pen out of his pocket. He was just about to write something down when a younger man walked up, holding a smartphone. The young man held out the smartphone to the older detective. Detective Donnell looked at the phone and then gave the young man an irritated look before he shifted his focus back to his pad of paper.

"My partner," Detective Donnell said without looking up.

"Detective Alvarez." The young man held out his hand for George to shake. George shook his hand. "Say, you wouldn't happen to be *the* Reverend George Burroughs."

Detective Donnell looked up at George and then at his partner.

"I see what you mean," Detective Donnell said. He turned to his partner. "George Burroughs had nine children."

"I know, but . . ." Detective Alvarez said. "He could be the real thing. They were *witches*, you know."

George wished that Em were there to hear this. She would have laughed. He flushed with worry for her.

Keeping his panic for her at bay, he grinned at the young man and looked away. Detective Donnell hit the younger detective's shoulder with the back of his hand.

"Focus," Detective Donnell said to the young man. To George, he said, "These young kids have no attention span."

"How can I help?" George asked.

"Tell us what you know," Detective Alvarez said.

Detective Donnell gave him a sideways look, and the younger detective shrugged.

"I don't know what I know," George said.

"Start from the beginning," Detective Donnell said.

"Of today?" George asked.

"'Martha came into the store'?" Detective Donnell read off his pad.

"Sure." George nodded. "I had a break in between clients."

"Clients?" Detective Donnell asked.

"I give spiritual counseling," George said.

"Psychic readings?" Detective Alvarez asked.

"If you like," George said. "I talk to people about their lives and try to help them make good decisions. I use the tarot, angel cards, and other tools to help understand a particular situation. I'm also intuitive. I have a sense of what's going on with people."

"Like what?" Detective Alvarez asked.

"Like that Paleo diet is causing your kidneys to shut down," George said to the young man. "Feeling tired?"

The young man scowled at George. Detective Donnell looked at the younger detective out of the corner of his eye.

"You can go get it checked," Detective Donnell said.

The young man ran to the paramedics.

"Sorry about that," Detective Donnell said. "You had a break between clients."

"I went upstairs for a nap and something to eat," George said. "Em runs errands on Fridays. I tried to call her and couldn't find her. I was talking to Alic...ia, Alicia. She lives in the apartments above us."

"This 'Alicia,'" Detective Donnell said. "Alicia Parker. Pretty, about yay big?"

The detective raised his hand up to about his shoulder height.

"That's her," George said. "She usually eats with us. She came down to see what was for dinner."

"Your Em's a good cook?" Detective Donnell asked.

"She is," George said. "I usually get the credit for it."

"Good work for you," Detective Donnell said.

George shrugged. When the detective didn't say anything, George continued.

"I was looking for Em when Alicia came down," George said. "She hadn't seen Em, either. That's when I got the call that Martha was downstairs and she had Em's purse."

"Let's see." Detective Donnell flipped through pages in his book. "I talked to a 'Shonelle' who said she'd phoned you."

"She's a sale associate at the store," George said.

"I see," Detective Donnell said. Reading off his sheet, he said, "You ran downstairs?"

"Em always has her purse," George said. He closed his mouth and nodded as if he'd said what he had to say.

"You know this *Martha* from..." Detective Donnell

said.

"Before Martha transitioned, she was on my squad in Kuwait," George said.

"Gulf War?" Detective Donnell asked.

"Yes, sir," George said. "We cleared houses together in Kuwait City together."

"I understand *Martha* was a prostitute," Detective Donnell said.

"She broke her back in Kuwait." George gestured to his mid-back. "Fell through a roof. She had veteran's benefits, but . . ."

George shrugged.

"But?" Detective Donnell asked.

"Politicians had a war to pay for, so they gutted those benefits," George said. "Martha did what she could."

"So you and Martha come across here, to Central Burying Ground," Detective Donnell asked. "Why?"

"We're old friends," George said. "I wanted to know how she got Em's purse."

"Did you kill her?"

"No."

"Did you want to kill her?"

"Are you asking about the times I wanted to kill her when she was Martha?" George asked with a smile. "Or the times when she was Michael? If you mean both, I wanted to kill her close to a billion times. But I didn't. I actually liked Martha, thought of her as a friend."

"Friend you wanted to kill," Detective Donnell smiled.

"You had to know her," George said.

"So anybody could have killed her," Detective Donnell said.

George shrugged and shook his head.

"You came over here, and . . ." Detective Donnell said.

"Talked," George said. "I wanted to know how Martha got the purse."

"And how did she?" Detective Donnell asked.

"She found it in the hallway of an apartment building," George said. "She helped Em get inside to talk to the super there, a 'Bill Panon.'"

"Do you know Bill Panon?" Detective Donnell asked.

"I've met him a few times," George said. "I usually stay in that apartment building for a week or so when I'm starting out in the winter."

"When you talked to Martha, did you . . ." Detective Donnell looked at George for a moment and then back down to his pad. "The ME says that Martha's been dead most of the day."

Detective Donnell gestured to where Martha's body had fallen.

"He says blood pooled in her back and head," Detective Donnell said. "It's like she rose from the dead and came over here to give you the purse."

George chose not to respond.

"What do you make of that?" Detective Donnell asked.

"I'm not a medical person," George said. "I . . ."

George shrugged. Detective Donnell nodded.

"You didn't notice anything?" Detective Donnell asked.

"I know what you're asking," George cleared his throat. "How could I have not noticed that there was something wrong with Martha? I . . ."

George shrugged.

"Martha had drug problems all the way back," George

said. "Michael had a tough time getting in the military. Couldn't pass the UAs. He got clean and got deployed. I..."

George shook his head and looked away. Martha's spirit was standing next to the detective, reading his notebook.

"He thinks you killed me," Martha's ghost said.

"You didn't notice anything?" Detective Donnell asked.

"Did I notice that Martha was slurring words?" George asked. "Sure, but she usually does. Did I notice she was tangential and argumentative? Sure, but she usually was."

George shrugged. Out of the corner of his eye, he saw John Willard, FBI Agent and one of the Salem Twenty, moving toward the grave where Martha's body had collapsed.

"Listen, Martha and I came over here," George said. "She was all over the place. I had to bully her into telling me about the purse. I don't feel good about it, but I was anxious about Em. That's what I did. I left her here with a plan to meet up after my clients. She told me to get the purse, which I did. I was at the street when she fell, dropped to the ground, and..."

George swallowed hard.

"Why didn't you check her body?" Detective Donnell asked.

"Check her body?" George asked. "Oh, you mean I should have come over here and taken her pulse or whatever."

"It's usual," Detective Donnell said.

"I've seen a lot of death," George said.

"In Kuwait," Detective Donnell said in an even tone.

"In Kuwait," George said. "In Boston. Every winter,

homeless men, women, and children die out in the cold. Here in Boston, in Salem, in New York City, everywhere here in the US."

"Okay, okay," Detective Donnell said.

"If you're asking how I knew Martha was dead," George said. "I knew by the way she fell that she was dead. So I went to the store and called you."

"Did you shoot her?" Detective Donnell asked.

"No," George said. John Willard moved over toward them.

"Where's your handgun?"

"I don't own a weapon," George said.

"Nothing under the couch, something brought back from Kuwait, some little thing you bought on the black market . . ."

"No," George said.

The detective opened his mouth to ask another question but saw the look on George's face and changed course.

"What was in the purse?" Detective Donnell asked.

"I don't actually know," George said. "Your people took it as soon as they arrived. Do you know what was in it?"

"Nothing exciting," Detective Donnell said. "Wallet, keys, sunglasses, hairbrush, things of that nature. Very practical."

"Em's a practical person," George said.

John stood just close enough to listen in on their conversation but far enough away to not appear to be too interested.

"What errand was she running in Jamaica Plain?" Detective Donnell asked.

"I won't know until I find her," George said.

"Would it surprise you if I told you that a woman's body was found by a 'Bill Panon'?" the detective asked.

Surprised, George looked at the detective and then looked at John Willard. John nodded.

"I need to . . ." George swallowed hard. John Willard started across the grass toward him. "My friend John . . ."

Detective Donnell looked up.

"SSA John Willard, Federal agent," John said. He held up his credentials.

"John Willard," Detective Donnell said. "George Burroughs."

John raised his eyebrows to indicate that he thought the detective was a moron.

"What can I do for the FBI?" Detective Donnell asked.

"I need George to identify a body," John said.

"I was just getting to . . ."

"The body is a part of a federal investigation," John said.

"I thought . . ." Detective Donnell started.

"You thought wrong," John said.

"Don't go anywhere," Detective Donnell said to George.

"If you're done?" John asked Detective Donnell.

When Detective Donnell nodded, John took George's arm. They moved at a brisk pace across the sidewalk. John opened his sedan and put George in the passenger seat. Martha's ghost got in the back.

"How many hours?" John asked George.

"Martha said she saw Em at eleven," George said.

John looked at the clock. It was seven-thirty.

"We have a few more hours," John said. He put the car in gear and sped onto Boylston Street. "Any ideas?"

"I lost my keys to the red-haired girl," George said.

"Irish?" John asked. "Ghost?"

"Yes," George said.

"She gave them to me," John said. "They're in my pocket. I'll get them when I get out."

George gave a slight nod. They drove in silence for a few minutes.

"She likes keys?" John asked.

"She does," George said.

"Got a name?" John asked.

"She don't know her name," Martha said from the back seat.

John glanced at the spirit and shook his head.

"When Em gets back, she's going to . . ." John started.

"I sure hope so," Martha said. "I have no plans to spend eternity with you all."

"And dancing with the devil?" George asked.

"He's gonna be there, Reverend," Martha said.

"For what it's worth, I think the ghost is right," John said.

"I prefer 'specter,'" Martha said.

George groaned. They drove for a few more minutes in silence.

"Ann picked up Em," John said. "The girls are already there."

"They're sure it's Em?" George asked.

"It's Em," John said.

George nodded. They drove in anxious silence to Sam Wardwell's home.

Chapter Thirteen

Em picked up her empty teacup and went into the kitchen. When she had lived here, this area had been her mother's domain. They were wealthy enough to afford a cook, but her mother liked to cook for the three of them. Em remembered this room as a very large space, filled with food, laughter, and her wonderful mother. But standing in her mother's domain tonight, she saw what a small, almost tiny space it was. She clicked on the electric kettle and went back to her spot for the night — the wide, comfortable couch in front of the fire.

Dinner had been an interesting affair. Her father had made Shepherd's Pie. Justine, her father's wife, had told story after charming story about her adventures as a nearly blind archeologist. Justine was the opposite of Em's mother, with blond curly hair, clear blue eyes, and rosy cheeks. While Em's mother insisted on speaking her mind and owning her power, with Justine, it was transparent that Em's father ran the roost. More than once, Em had wondered what her mother would say about this wife.

And yet, Justine and Em's mother had a lot in common. They were both deeply kind, almost over-sensitive to another's point of view and feelings. Tonight, Justine had insisted on making Em comfortable before retiring to the bedroom. Em didn't have the heart to tell her that she'd spent a good portion of her childhood lying on the stone floor in front of this fire. Instead, she thanked Justine and settled in for the night.

Em got up when the kettle clicked off. She took down two mugs from the cabinet and made tea for herself and her father. She was just pouring tea when he arrived in the kitchen. Picking up a mug, he led her out onto the patio. They sat down in two metal patio chairs. The stars blazed above, and the Atlantic Ocean pounded the shore fifty feet in front of them. She held her cup under her nose to drink in the smell of Rousay — one part strong tea, one part ocean spray, one part love. She glanced at her father to find him looking at her. He smiled.

"What year is it?" Em asked.

"1978," her father said.

"How . . .?" Em asked.

"It's a time lock and loop," her father said. "The next time you died, your essence would come to Rousay and I would be notified. I would meet you here as soon as possible. We would talk."

Em nodded.

"I have to say that I expected to see you a lot sooner," her father said.

"I'm not big on risks," Em said.

"Yes," her father said. "And George?"

"He fights in every war," Em said with a shrug.

"Immortality is not wasted on George Burroughs," her father said.

"No," Em laughed. Her father laughed at her laugh. "If I had died again in the 1800s?"

"1778," her father said.

"1878 if I'd died in the 19th century?" Em asked.

"It's not original, but it seems to have worked," her father said. "What year is it for you?"

"2014," Em said. "You're telling me that we cannot occupy the same space at the same time."

"That's correct," her father said. "It's a kind of 'There can be only one.'"

"How so?" Em asked.

"If we're in the same space and the same time, we will want to kill each other," her father said.

"And now?"

"A physical manifestation of your essence is here with me," her father said, with a shrug. "Try it when you get home. Of course, you can always speak to me via astral projection."

"Just not in physical body, mind, and soul," Em said.

"That's correct," her father said.

"Astral projection always leaves me feeling awful," Em sneered and shook her head, "for days."

"It's a family trait," her father said. "You probably get sick like I do when you make a prediction."

Em smiled in agreement. They drank their tea in silence. Her father turned to look at her.

"We are immortal, you and I," her father said.

"Is that what being 'made of God' means?" Em asked.

"'Made of God'?" He looked genuinely confused.

"Just before Henry and I left for America, you told me that you and I were 'truth tellers,'" Em said. "Something like we see only the truth, live the truth."

"We are God's truth," he said. "Yes, I remember saying

that."

"Is that about being immortal?" Em asked.

"It's about being 'made of God,'" he said.

"What does that mean?" she asked.

"It means that there is a creator." He flattened his right hand parallel to the ground and held it about chest high.

"Then us." He placed his left hand, in the same flattened position, below his right hand.

"Humans are below that," Em said.

"We are made only of the creator and this place," he said. "Humans are made of us and the earth."

"Humans are not directly of God," she said.

"The creator," he said with a nod.

"And the truth thing?" she asked.

"Don't you know the truth when you hear it?" He shrugged. "Don't you always tell the truth?"

Em nodded.

"What about the others?" Em asked.

"'The others'?"

"The other witches from Salem," Em said. "Are they like us?"

Her father shook his head.

"Are they immortal?" she asked.

"I've never seen them last more than nine hundred years," her father said. "But I never lived with them, loved them, or spent my time with them. It was always something that . . . Well, when I was a child, we considered them abominations. They usually ended up in the fire."

Em nodded.

"I feel like we've gotten ahead of ourselves," he said. "I'm sure you have a lot of questions, and I have some answers.

Where would you like to start?"

"At the beginning," Em said.

"I don't know everything," her father said. "One of the reasons I spend all my time now among the monuments of our ancestors. I want to know and understand everything. I do, however, know one thing — we were made of the elements on this island — earth, sea, wind, rain, sun, air."

"Rousay?" Em asked.

"Yes," her father said. "We were here long before the human pre-ancestors. There are markings — both here and in Norway — of the ancient ones who lived on an island, this island. For more than tens of thousands of years, people came to Rousay to connect with us. Until the Romans entered Britain, people came here to worship us. They brought gifts, and we gave wisdom and granted fertility. There were large festivals, big celebrations, and smaller, more desperate ceremonies for desperate pleas."

"How old are you?" Em asked.

"I was born a thousand years or so before your Christ," her father said.

"Did you know him?" Em asked.

"Christ?" her father asked. "No. His father."

"God?" Em asked.

"I had a conversation like this with Henry Rich," her father said with a broad smile.

"You knew Joseph," Em said.

"Yes," he said. "He and I were friends."

"I remember you saying something like that," Em nodded. "All of this . . . I guess it was there all the time."

"No," her father said. "Henry Rich brought out my rage and impatience."

"He had a gift for that." Em smiled, and her father laughed. "Why was I able to grow up with you and mother?"

Em's voice caught on the word "mother." There was nothing she would like more than to see her mother again.

"I miss her, too," her father said. He looked away while she gained control of her emotions. "We are not immortal until we've died once. You weren't immortal then."

"And your parents?" Em asked.

"I was badly injured on a hunt when I was a young child of six or seven," her father said. "My parents were forced to leave me here, on Rousay, with the elders."

"You could be with the elders?" Em asked.

"Yes," her father said. "We can live in community with each other as long as we don't spend too much time together. I lived in community with the elders, but I spent most of my time alone in my own dwelling, right here on this spot. Of course, at that time, it wasn't unusual for a male child to be on his own when he was younger than seven. Most children went on the hunt, into the mines, or even worked the fields, but that was considered girls' work. I didn't know to miss my parents. I was doing what every boy *should* do."

"Are you an elder, then?"

"I suppose," her father said.

"If you grew up with the elders, why do you have to look at archeology to learn about them?" Em asked.

"I learned our stories from the elders," he said. "I want to learn our truth."

"Truth again," she said.

"It's a family thing," he said.

"It's not an immortal thing?"

"No," he said. "It's our thing."

"But I thought you didn't think I was your child," Em said.

"I didn't," he said.

"Then why . . .?" She stopped talking when he smiled.

"You were like this as a child," he said. "You needed truth. I thought we had raised you with the truth, so you longed for it. Truth is like bedrock. When you have it, it's all you want."

He shrugged.

"I wasn't thinking well that day," he said.

"Why?"

"The only child I had ever been father to was leaving with an imbecile for a new colony fraught with savages, wars, violence, and pedants like Henry Rich," he said.

She smiled. A wind blew off the sea. For the briefest moment, she felt as if she were standing on the deck of the ship that took her to America. In a blink, she was sitting with her father on Rousay again.

"It will be hard for me to let you return to your beloved Boston," he said.

"I guess I was hoping I'd meet my people," Em said in a low voice.

"There aren't as many of us now."

"Why?" Em asked.

Her father sighed and shook his head. He turned his body away from her to look at the ocean.

"Why aren't there more of us?" Em repeated.

"My opinion is that we don't live on Rousay anymore," he said. "But that's my opinion only."

"Why would that matter?" Em asked.

"We're not fertile," he said. "At least I haven't been. You?"

"I had two boys, but that was before . . . all of this," Em said.

"And the others?"

"To the women's delight and the men's disappointment — nothing," Em said.

Her father grinned, and Em smiled. They drank their tea. Her father took a deep breath and turned to look at her.

"Maybe after you're here," he said.

"My body is in Boston," Em said.

He nodded, and they fell silent. Disappointment welled inside her. She'd wanted to know everything, to connect, but her father was controlled and silent. She felt he would answer her questions if she asked them. She just wasn't sure what question to ask that would get him talking.

"Buddha?" Em asked.

"South Asian princeling," her father shrugged. "Beautiful being with great ideas, but still a prince."

Em scowled. She opened her mouth to ask another question, when her father started talking.

"I know what you want from me," her father said. "You want to know what your place is in this world. You want to know where you fit."

"But?" Em asked.

"I can't give that to you," her father said. "We fit in this world because we were placed here by the creator, your God. We must find our own lives and give them meaning."

"Like humans," Em said.

He nodded.

"A few of the witches want to end this," Em said.

"Sure," her father said. "Did they choose it?"

"I don't really know what happened," Em said.

"Tell me," he said, evenly, but she felt the power of his command.

"I remember being hanged," Em said. "They . . . they hated me. It was so shocking to me."

"What was?"

"How much they hated me," Em said. "I think I said something about my innocence, but . . . George was dead. Giles, my husband, was dead. My children had been tortured nearly to death to get them to testify against me. I was exhausted. I wanted relief."

"Sure," he said.

"I woke up in the crevice," Em said. "I was under a couple of the women and on top of everyone else."

"You touched them after you woke up," he said.

Em nodded.

"That's how they became quasi-immortal," he said. "Witches."

"What do you mean?" she asked.

"After the first death, our kind has the capacity to make people witches," he said.

"Abominations," she said.

"That's how we thought of them when I was a child," he said with a nod. "But I'll tell you — I'd give anything to have made an abomination out of your mother."

"Me, too," Em said.

Her father nodded, and they sat in silence for a few minutes. Her father's eyes went vague, and his face reflected his longing for her mother.

"How did they become witches?" Em asked.

"That's right," her father said with a smile. "That's what we were talking about. The thought of your mother pushed everything else out of my head."

"Yes."

"They became witches because you were first reborn into your power. That's what we call it — 'reborn.' At the moment of rebirth, you had the capacity to make anything you touched quasi-immortal — a witch."

"And now?" Em asked.

"Surely you've tried it," he said.

"Giles," Em said. "He likes young, inexperienced women. He's tried to make them stay that way."

"That is not the way it works," her father said. "We grow and change; we just don't age and die."

"Ever?"

"Well, clearly, we can die," he said.

"How is that possible?" Em asked.

"I don't know," her father said. "Science will probably consume my next cycle. For now, my focus is learning from our ancestors through archeology. Who knows? If you find me in 2014, I might be a geneticist at the University of London."

"You will always be a watchmaker to me," Em said.

"That was fun," her father said. "I still do it."

"What?"

"Fix old watches," her father said. "Now it's my 'hobby.'"

Her father laughed.

"Who would have thought that I would ever have the time and energy to have 'hobbies'?" Her father shook his head and grinned.

"You don't take breaks from the world?" Em asked.

"No," her father said. "When one life ends, I move to another place in the world. This is my first time back on Rousay since we lived here after the London fire. I take it you take breaks?"

"We take breaks," Em said. "We used to take them only every fifty years. But we took more than that in the 20th century."

"Oh?"

"Giles set Salem on fire in 1914," Em said. She glanced at her father when he laughed. She smiled. "You laugh, but he was seen. The whole 'Salem Witch Trial' thing was big then, and . . ."

"He was recognized?" her father's voice rose with disbelief.

"He was," Em said with a smile. "He had to get out of town. A few of the others went with him. Then Sarah Good was working in a molasses factory. Her supervisor tried to assault her. She got upset, and her powers caused it to . . ."

Em gestured with her hands that the tank had exploded and made a sound that imitated the blowing molasses tank.

"She was supposed to have died," Em said. "The rest of us got out of town fast."

"When was that?" her father asked.

"1919 — the Great Molasses Flood," Em said. "

"Where do you go?" her father asked.

"We used to go to a more wild part of the US," Em said. "Now, we own an island in the Bahamas. John Willard got it when he was the captain of a pirate ship. I bought it from him for a dollar."

"But you return to Boston?" her father asked.

Em nodded.

"Always to Boston?"

Em nodded.

"Why Boston?" her father asked.

"I thought I had to be close or lose..." She stopped talking when her father laughed. "Why is that funny?"

"I thought the same thing," her father said.

"It's not true?"

Her father shook his head.

"We are what we are, Em," he said. "Even your friends, the other witches. They are what they are. We can live anywhere."

Em nodded.

"Still, it must be nice to have people around who grew up when you did," her father said. "People who speak your same language, know your history."

She looked at him.

"I'm a little jealous," he said with a smile.

"Is there a way to reverse it?" Em asked.

"For those who want to move on?" her father asked.

Em nodded.

"You have to wish it, Em," her father said.

"I've tried," Em said.

He scowled. Leaning over, he held her hands between his.

"You can have whatever it is that you wish," he said. "Anything. Let's try it."

"Gold," Em said.

He nodded. She opened her hands, and there was a single gold Kroner.

"Try it yourself," he said.

She picked up her teacup. Closing her eyes, she wished for another cup of tea. When she opened her eyes, nothing had happened. He smiled.

"See! It doesn't work," she said.

"You truly are my daughter," he said.

"Why?" she asked.

"You are trying to bend the laws of the world," he said. "When you call for gold, it appears because it exists in the world. You can call for a guppy or a sea turtle, and one would appear."

He opened his hand to show her a juvenile sea turtle. Picking it up by the shell, he set it in her hand.

"Tea exists in the world," she said.

He smiled. Picking up the turtle, he closed his eyes to wish it gone. He opened his hands to show that they were now empty.

"You mean I can't ask for things that need to be made," she said. "I can call a tea bag."

She closed her eyes and focused on her hands. In a moment, she felt the rough edges of her favorite Earl Grey black tea bag. She opened her hands to show him.

"You can call hot water to you, but I wouldn't recommend it," he said.

She smiled.

"You can call something like tea to you, but you'd have to know where it existed," he said. "For example, let's see what your George is drinking."

He held his cup. In a moment, it filled with Guinness

beer. He took a sip.

"It's confusing," Em said.

"And you just want some tea," he said.

Em nodded.

"Your friends," he said. "They can leave only on the anniversary of their making."

"Oh?"

"Yes, there are some rules," her father said with a smile. "You can only undo things on the exact anniversary of your making them."

"So my hanging anniversary," she said.

"The anniversary of their transformation," he said.

"September 22," she said.

He nodded. They sat in silence for a moment before she went inside to make more tea. When she returned with two full mugs, he was watching the stars again.

"Why are you here?" he asked.

Chapter Fourteen

"I'm here because you made it so," she said.

"No," he said. "You had to have come looking for me. That was the criterion. Why did you come looking for me? You said earlier that you've been thinking about a few things."

She nodded.

"What is happening in your world that would bring you here?" he asked.

"A man has entered my life," Em said. She turned her body to face him.

"A lover?"

"Not mine," she said. "He claims to be the child of one of the witches, Alice Parker. She fell pregnant in prison."

"She came back pregnant," her father nodded. "Surely the child didn't survive."

"That's what Alice says," Em said. "My son Benoni's ancestral granddaughter works at the store. She convinced us to have this John Parker — that's what he goes by — into the store for a lecture."

Em swallowed hard.

"And?" her father said.

"A demon came out of him," Em said. She looked up at her father, and he nodded. "We held a séance for those who were killed and not buried with us. They told us that this demon has disrupted their slumber."

"He brought them back," her father said.

"He hasn't brought them to life," Em said. "But . . ."

"Yes?"

"They — the spirits — told us that we should find the last one, John Proctor," Em said. "But I have this feeling that if we find John Proctor's remains, the others will be returned."

"Would that be bad?" her father asked.

"Yes," Em said. "After all of this time, I don't think they could handle it, and . . ."

Em fell silent. She held her Earl Grey up to her nose to smell the Bergamot.

"And?"

"They hanged a lot of women for witchcraft in Boston," Em said.

"I've heard," her father said.

"One of them has haunted the park across the street from my house for more than three hundred years," Em said. "She asked to be sent on last week, which we did. When she was leaving, she wished me 'Good luck.' And before that, she said she wanted to move on before . . ."

"Before?"

"She didn't say," Em said.

Her father gave her a knowing nod.

"What?" Em asked.

"You've met your demon," her father said.

"What does that mean?" she asked.

"We are made of the creator," her father said. "They are made of the opposite — chaos, entropy, devil, demon —

pick a word. Each of us has an opposite."

"And the others?"

"They have only you," her father said. "That doesn't mean that this creature doesn't want some of his own witches. He's likely recruiting ghosts and other malcontents. They are easier to gain access to because they have so much time and so little to do. They also don't have bodies to feed."

"The others," Em started and then stopped.

"Yes?"

"They are having dreams of Salem Village," Em said. "They feel like they're right there. I watched their faces when they told me."

"And?"

"I think they'd go back in a heartbeat," Em said.

"There's nothing to go back to," her father said.

"They would rather die than extend this prolonged life," Em said. "I've heard them say that a prolonged life is like a kind of death."

"And you?"

"Life is life," Em said. "Death is death."

"You are suited for immortality," her father said.

"Suited or not, it's what I have," Em said.

Her father laughed. Not sure how to respond, Em fell silent. She watched the stars and listened to the surf in companionable silence with her father. She was so focused on the dancing stars that she started when he spoke.

"Surely, this is of your devil's making," her father said.

"What is?" Em asked.

"Your witches' longing for the days gone by and their old homes," her father said.

"Why would he doing this?" Em asked.

"To remove your witches from your side," her father said. "Increase his odds of winning."

"Winning?" Em asked.

"The war," her father said.

"War? What war?"

"With you," her father said. "He's trying to reduce your ranks. He must think that the reason you transformed these people is so that you would have soldiers of your own. I would."

"That's not true," Em said.

"Doesn't matter," her father said. "He deals in deceit and lies."

"We are truth tellers," Em said. "George said the demon reminded him of a feeling or fog hanging over Salem Village when he returned. He was surprised at the darkness that seemed to encompass the entire region."

"Truly?" her father looked surprised.

Em nodded.

"That means he's planned this war," he said.

"George?"

"Your demon," he said.

"Where's he been for more than three hundred years?" Em asked.

"Planning a war, no doubt," her father said.

"What?" Em sat up in her chair.

"He's planning a war against you."

"Can he do that?" Em asked.

"He can and will," her father said. "Every new immortal must face their demon, and it always ends in war."

"Why?" Em asked.

"It's part of the deal," her father said with a smile.

"Have you met your demon?" Em asked.

"I have," her father said.

"And?"

Her father shrugged and looked away.

"Did you win?" Em asked.

"I suppose so," her father said. "I . . . You remember the plague? The fire?"

"Of course," Em said.

Her father nodded.

"That was your war?" Em asked.

"Battles in my war," her father said. "We came here for me to recover."

"Recover?"

"From the battle," her father said. "But the demon never stops until . . ."

Em watched rage and sorrow move across her father's face until all that was left was resignation. He glanced at her and noticed her attention for the first time. He cleared his throat.

"It was a long time ago," he said.

"It was."

"I think the final battle was Henry," her father said. "My only child left on a boat with Henry Rich. Did he get sick on the trip?"

"Yes," Em said. "I never knew what happened. He'd been such a vibrant man, and suddenly he was ill."

Her father glanced at her and then looked away.

"Your demon did that?" Em asked.

Her father's head moved just slightly in a nod. He turned his body to stare at the open ocean.

"But . . ." Em said.

"Yes," her father said. "Henry's illness and death set you up for witch accusations all those years later."

"Your demon is the reason I was hanged?" Em asked.

Her father didn't turn to look at her.

"Your demon is the reason I was hanged?" Em repeated.

He didn't respond.

"Answer me!" Em said in frustration.

"I've nothing to say," her father said. "My only child was hanged as a witch. I . . ."

He looked at her and smiled.

"I hate hanging," her father said. "Burned in a pyre is worse, if you can imagine anything worse than hanging."

"Drowning sounds particularly bad," Em said.

"Not really," her father said in a matter-of-fact way. "Fire is awful because it takes so long. You get to watch the wood catch on fire, then your clothing, your feet — inch by inch, it consumes you, while the good people — people you loved and thought of as friends — stand by and cheer."

"Sounds horrible," Em said.

Her father raised his eyebrows in an "of course" gesture.

"Our hangings took up to thirty minutes," Em said.

"Awful," her father said.

They fell silent for a while. Em drank her tea and listened to the waves.

"Do we share the same demon?" Em asked.

"I doubt that very much," her father said.

"But?"

"From what you've said, they've combined their efforts," her father said. "One got you hanged."

"Thus making me immortal," Em said.

"The other is waiting for me, for us," her father said.

"Will you fight with me?" Em asked.

"I cannot," her father said. "We can't . . ."

"Be at the same location in the same time," Em said with him.

"Why would your demon wait so long?" Em asked.

"He couldn't defeat me in my time," her father said. "He needed help."

"My demon is stronger?" Em asked.

"Different in some way that's compatible to my demon," her father said.

"It's just . . ." Em shivered, " . . .horrifying."

"It is," her father said.

Em was looking at the bottom of her teacup and wondering if she could get another cup when her father sighed.

"Your God says he never gives you something you can't handle," her father said.

"And?"

"We should be able to handle this," her father said.

"How?" Em asked.

"I have no idea," her father said.

Em nodded. Her father stood from his seat.

"Let's sleep on it," her father said. "Tomorrow night, we'll go visit the area I remember as the center of knowledge. If this is happening now, it's happened before. There should be something in the library."

"You sure?"

"No," her father said with a laugh. "But we'll try anyway."

Em smiled.

"Come, daughter," her father said.

Em followed him into the house. They hugged in the living room before he left for the bedroom and his wife. Wide awake, she sat on the couch, waiting for sleep. The next thing she knew, her father's wife was moving about, and the sun had risen on the next day.

"Did you drink my beer?" George gestured to his Guinness.

Shaking his head and laughing, John Willard patted George's arm.

"It was just . . ." George started.

"Disappeared like magic," John said with a laugh. "You're pestered with a demon who drinks your beer."

George laughed. Their laughter caused Wilmot and Margaret to give them dark looks. George touched their shoulders as he passed them on his way to refill his beer. They were in the basement of Sam Wardwell's home. Em's body lay on a massage table near the middle of the room. The rest of the witches sat in their usual groupings — Bridget, Elizabeth, and Mary Ayer Parker chatted near the fireplace; Wilmot and Margaret were reading novels on a leather loveseat against the wall; Sarah Wildes, Ann, and Alice were standing near Em; Martha Carrier, Sam, and Sarah Good were working on a puzzle; Giles was sitting by himself; and George and John played pool.

"She should be back by now!" Giles jumped to his feet. "It's been twelve hours!"

"Giles, we don't know exactly . . ." Ann started to say.

"We *do* know!" Giles said. "That *ghost* that came with *George* said . . ."

"She's a ghost," Sarah Wildes said as she walked to Giles. "You know how they are disoriented when they first die."

"I resent that," Martha said from the corner of the room Sam had forced her to stay in.

"She should be . . ."

Em's body gasped for air. George ran to her side.

"Em!" Alice bent over her face. "Em!"

Em's chest moved up and down with her breath.

"She's not here!" Giles wailed.

"Back up!" Ann ordered. "Now!"

The witches took a step back. George put his arm over Giles's shoulder and tried to lead him away. Giles pushed George away from him. Ann started working on Em's body.

"This is *your* fault!" Giles said. "You and your whoring ways! You killed her!"

"Now, Giles," Martha Carrier said. "George didn't . . ."

"You know how he is." Giles pointed at George. "How it *breaks* her heart! Why do you think she married an old so-and-so like myself? You broke her, and now you've killed her!"

Horrified, George took a step away from Giles. John Willard came to his side. Sam put his arm around Giles to comfort him. Bridget, Elizabeth, and Mary Ayer watched in fascinated revolution, while Martha Carrier and Sarah Good grinned at the drama.

"Just breathe, Giles," Sam said. He rolled his eyes to George and shook his head. Turning back to Giles, he said, "We're all scared. You're making it worse."

"She loved you," Giles pointed at George again. "And you . . ."

Giles weaved. His knees went out from under him. Sam caught him before he hit the ground. George and John helped Sam get Giles to the couch. Giles bent over and wept into his hands.

"Did you kill him?" Ann asked from her position leaning over Em.

"Not yet," Sam said with a grin.

"I've got this," Sarah Wildes said.

She sat down next to Giles. She took his hand and interlaced their fingers before leaning over to talk with him. George moved to Em. Ann was hooking Em up to a heart-rate monitor and starting IVs. Alice hovered nearby.

"How is she?" George asked.

"Alive," Ann said. "Of course."

"But?" George asked.

"She's not here," Ann said and looked up at him.

"What does that mean?" Alice asked.

As if she wished she hadn't spoken, she immediately covered her mouth. George put his arm over Alice's shoulder.

"I don't know what it means," Ann said.

"What do you mean you don't know?" Bridget asked.

"I mean, it's never happened before," Ann said. "Not to any of us. Our essences came back when our bodies returned. Em's body is strong. Her vitals are good. Her lungs are clear. Her pressure is good, even in her limbs. She's fit as can be."

"But?" George asked.

"She's not here," Ann said. "Can you . . ."

Ann pointed to a few empty vacuum tubes sitting on a table nearby. Alice grabbed the tubes and brought them to her.

"Where's *my* Em?" Bridget asked.

"Your Em?" Wilmot asked. "Stupid girl. She's . . ."

Bridget started screaming at Wilmot. Elizabeth replied to Wilmot, and Margaret joined in. One at a time, the witches began fighting with each other. Sam Wardwell put his fingers to his lips and blew a loud whistle. Everyone stopped talking and looked at him. He pointed to where Martha was standing.

The ghost of Martha had crouched down and was hissing at something they could not see.

"What is it, Martha?" George asked.

"The devil is here," the deep voice of Michael came from Martha's visage.

Sarah Wildes jumped up from the couch and clapped her hands.

"Surround Em!" Sarah yelled.

The witches ran to Em's side and joined hands, leaving Ann in the middle to work on Em.

"Whatever our differences," Sarah said, looking from face to face. "We all love Em. She is our friend, our rock. And right now, she's in need. George?"

"Why George?" Giles started. "He's . . ."

Sam Wardwell put his arm around the elderly man. Giles looked at Sam and scowled.

"A moment of silence to collect our thoughts," George said.

The witches bowed their heads in silent prayer.

"Let us sing," George said. He took a breath and began

singing Psalms 1 from the Geneva Bible, "Blessed is the man that doth not walk in the counsel of the wicked, nor . . ."

" . . .stand in the way of sinners, nor . . ." Ann Pudeator was the first to join in. She sang as she continued to set up Em's IVs.

Gradually, the witches joined in. Sam shook Giles's shoulder when he wasn't singing. Giles glanced at Sam and returned to glaring at George. But, the sheer joy of singing with the others got the better of him, and Giles joined in at Psalm 3.

"Lord, how are mine adversaries increased? How many rise against me?"

Em looked up at the clock from the couch in her father's home. After a full day of tending the sheep and farm, she waited for him to take her to their ancestors' ruins. For the first time in a very long time, she was excited. Tonight, she might learn the answer to the riddles that had haunted her since childhood — Who created the world? What was the nature of God? How can she celebrate the wonder of life, when she should be dead? What was she going to do about this demon? And . . . And . . . She scowled.

If George were here, he'd know exactly what to ask. On her own, her mind focused more on the demon than the more important meaning-of-life questions. She had a chance to discover the great mysteries of life, and what she really wanted to know was how to get out of the situation she found herself in. She cursed her own practical nature.

And still, she was excited.

Her father came out of the bedroom and nodded to her.

"Ready?" he asked.

"I'm ready," she said.

And then it hit her. What if this wasn't her father? What if this entire adventure was a trick of the demon? She stopped dead in her tracks and gawked at her father.

"What is it?" her father asked.

"I just . . ." Em licked her lips.

"Realized this entire thing could be a setup?" her father asked with a smile.

"You, too?" Em asked.

"After last night," her father said. "It's all seems a little too . . ."

"Perfect," Em said.

Her father nodded.

"How will we know?" Em asked.

"We won't," her father said.

"How did I get here?" Em asked.

"You died in Boston," he said.

"How did I die?" Em asked.

"I don't know," her father said.

"I went to see you," Em said.

"What?" her father asked.

"I went to Jamaica Plain to meet Bill Panon," Em said. "He owns a building that was converted to apartments from a livery stable. The property hasn't changed hands since the 1700s."

Her father nodded.

"Is that you?" Em asked.

"No," her father said.

"The man who runs it is said to . . ." Em stopped talking.

"It's not you?"

"No," her father said. "The only thing I own is this farm, and, even then, it's held in an ancient wildlife trust. That's how I avoid having to take breaks."

"You're not in the system," Em said.

"I'm not in any system," her father said. "Never have been. Your birth wasn't recorded."

"How did you get married?" Em asked.

"We got married," her father said.

"Marriage license?" Em asked.

He shook his head.

"How . . .?" Em asked.

She stopped talking when he shook himself like he was a dog.

"It doesn't matter. She doesn't care," he said. "You went to see someone you thought was me."

Em nodded.

"Why did you come to find me?" he asked.

"I wanted to talk to you," Em said. "I wanted to . . . connect to . . . ask you about the demon and who I am and . . ."

Em swallowed down the sorrow and longing that had welled in her throat. Her father gave her a soft smile and a nod to acknowledge his similar feelings.

"You came to find me, and you found your demon instead," he said.

"But . . ." Em said.

"If I hadn't called you here . . ." Her father looked away from her. When he glanced back, his eyes were filled with tears. "And your body? Is it safe?"

"We have an arrangement with all of the Massachusetts'

coroners," Em said. "By religious preference, we need to take the bodies without autopsy."

"So your body is safe?"

"It's with the witches," Em said with a smile.

Her father let out an anxious breath. For a moment, he looked at Em. She shrugged, and he laughed. Smiling, she thought about what he was saying.

"What would have happened to me if you hadn't . . .?" Em's voice held equal parts horror and awe.

"Your spirit would have been captured," he said. "Do you remember how you died?"

"I remember spinning," she said.

He nodded and raised his eyebrows. Rather than answer the question in her face, he picked up a large backpack and started toward the door to the cottage.

"Coming?" he said with a smile.

She followed him out into the farm. They walked side by side for a while, making sure to skirt the lights from the residences.

"Where are we going?" she asked.

"Do you remember the cave?" he asked.

"I don't think Mom would let you take me there." She shook her head.

He laughed, and they continued their trek.

"It's called 'Covenanters Cave' now," he said. "It was used by your kind during the Killing Time."

"'My kind'?" Em grinned. "You mean, 'religious loons.'"

"Yes, in fact, I mean just that," he laughed.

She smiled at him.

"The cave is hidden from view," he said. "You can find it only on old maps."

"There's just sheep here," she said. "What happened to the crofters?"

She gestured to the ruins of a small family farm that had once been the home of a land tenant.

"They were pushed out by greedy landlords," her father said.

"Landlords?"

"They raised the rents until the crofters couldn't stay," he said. "One of them was a Burroughs. You think there's any relation?"

"Who knows?" Em shrugged.

Her father turned, and they began walking toward the black cliffs of the Kiln of Brin-Novan. Vigorous ocean waves had created caves and natural arches out of the layers of black Devonian.

"Are you all right to climb?" her father asked.

"Sure," Em said.

"We can also . . ." her father started.

"I don't know any transportation spells," Em said.

"That's why you stayed in the passageway cairn," he grinned.

She nodded.

"You have to want it," he said.

He waved and disappeared. She looked over the cliff to find him standing under a natural arch looking up at her. He cupped his mouth and yelled something to her that she couldn't hear over the ocean. She closed her eyes and wanted to be with her father. Much to her surprise, she found herself by his side.

He opened his backpack and retrieved two headlamps. He gave her one and put on the other one. He held out a bottle of water to her. She took a long drink and gave it back. He finished the bottle.

"Be very careful," he said. "This entire area is enchanted. If you use magic, you can bring it down onto you. It won't kill you, of course. It will take you a hundred years of hard work to get out."

"Now you tell me this?" She gave a nervous laugh.

"We're not inside yet," he said with a grin. He turned on his headlamp. "Do be careful, Em. I don't know what charms are placed around these caves. I only know they've kept people out of them for more than two thousand years."

"I will be careful," she said.

He kissed her cheek and set off into the cave. She took a breath, turned on her headlamp, and followed him into the dark.

Chapter Fifteen

They walked along a thin shelf that was covered by the cave ceiling and open on one side to the ocean. After a hundred feet, they came to a six-foot-wide ocean channel that blocked their way into the cave. The channel churned with all of the ocean's wild power. When the waves came in, sea water shot up six feet in the air. Everything within ten feet was slick with water blown by the ferocious wind. The air was thick with cold ocean mist.

"The first defense," Em's father yelled over the roar of water and wind. He held his hands out over the water, closed his eyes, and, in a low powerful voice, said, "Be still."

In response to his command, water from the channel shot up into the air, creating a wall of water. As if drawn by a magnet, the water dropped onto them. They were soaked to the bone in frigid ocean water. Loosened by the wind, Em's hair came out of its tight knot. She grabbed her long hair and leaned forward, hoping that the wave had freed a safe crossing for them. The ocean churned as if nothing had happened.

"Any ideas?" her father asked.

"Only one," Em said. She raised her hand to the sky to pull down the power of the angels and held her right hand in front of her. She said, "Show me the way."

For a moment, while Em held her breath, nothing happened.

"There!" her father yelled and pointed to a small ledge to their right.

A woman appeared. She was standing on a small shelf halfway up the black rock wall. When their headlamps turned on her, she seemed to disappear.

"Turn it off!" Em yelled, and they turned off their headlamps.

Once their eyes adjusted, they made out a woman standing on a black rock ledge halfway up the cave's wall.

"Who are you?" Em's father asked.

"State your business." They could hear the woman's voice clearly — as if she were standing right next to them. Her voice had a power to it that made them feel both safe and in terrible danger at the same time.

"I am William, the truth teller," he said. "I am here with my daughter, Martha of Truth. We are here for information."

"William of Truth," the woman said. "Martha of Truth. This cave is shut."

"But not destroyed," Em's father said. "It's you — Ellen, the Watcher — isn't it?"

"Yes, William," Ellen said. "You should not be here."

The ocean in the channel rose up again and smashed down upon them.

"We seek information," her father yelled. "Wisdom."

"State your claim," Ellen the Watcher said.

"I am William of Truth," her father said. "Born to power on Shetland. Raised in Rousay."

"You are not elder born," Ellen the Watcher said.

"I am what's left," Em's father said. "Me and my daughter — we are all that's left of our kind."

"Surely, you jest," Ellen the Watcher snorted a laugh tinged with derision.

"I am unable to lie," William said. "You know that, Ellen."

"But..."

"We scattered to the winds when the Romans came," William said. "Without each other, our demons caught up with us, and..."

Em watched sorrow and rage move across William's face.

"And you survived?" Ellen asked. "The sickly boy has turned into..."

"A survivor," William said. "As is my daughter. There are billions of humans on the earth now, and only the two of us left."

"And the witches," Em said.

"What is this about witches?" Ellen the Watcher asked.

"Em has a few abominations," William said. "They keep her company. Where are you in time in relation to Christ?"

"The carpenter?" Ellen asked. "Why?"

"Time is measured in relation to his birth now," William said.

"Really? That *is* odd." Ellen thought for a moment before adding, "About a thousand years post Christ."

"They caught you some four hundred years later, in the Spanish Inquisition," William said. "You were burned and quartered."

The woman put her hand on her heart. Em swallowed hard at the idea of being quartered alive.

"Who did that?" Ellen asked.

"Rome and the Christian God," William said.

As if to gather her thoughts, the woman jumped down from the ledge and walked into the cave. Em looked at her father. She was about to ask him what had happened when he gave her a severe look.

"Wait," he said.

Em held her tongue. She braided her hair down her back while she waited. Her icy feet ached. She shifted her weight from one foot to the other to try to get the blood flowing. She glanced at her father, who stood like a statue, staring into the cave, and wondered if she'd ever gain his resolve. She was watching her father when a man flew out. He wore light-colored trousers with a white shirt. His skin was suntanned dark. He looked as if he'd stepped off a Bahamian golf course.

"Argos!" Her father dropped to his knees, and Em followed his lead.

"No time for that!" the man yelled. "You must hurry."

"But how. . .?" William asked.

"If you are William of Truth and Martha, his daughter, you'll know!" the man yelled.

He turned and went further into the cave. Em could make out the outline of his light-colored clothing near the back of the cave.

"Truth tell," William said under his breath. "Any ideas, Em?"

Em's stomach turned over. This "Argos" had indicated that maybe this man wasn't her father.

"Em?" William asked. He put his hand on her. "Ideas?"

"Yes, yes — I see it now," Em said.

"See what?" William asked.

"There is no channel," Em said. "Come, father!"

Em jumped to her feet and helped her father to his. She stretched out her foot over the channel. Instantly, a creature with razor-sharp teeth, a long, serpent-like snout, and a body a thousand times more awful than any map monster flew out of the water. The creature's mouth was closing around Em's foot when her father knocked her off her feet. They fell hard on the wet, rocky ground. The creature extended its neck over them and howled with rage in such a high-pitched tone that Em's ears rang.

"We are not in your space!" William yelled. "Be gone!"

The creature looked William in the face and let out another scream. Their hands went to their ears to try to block out the sound. The creature nodded his head and dove back into the ocean channel. Em's entire body shook in fear. She clutched onto her father until she was able to catch her breath. He held her tight until their ears cleared.

"It's not that simple," he said. "It's never that simple."

"Oh, father," Em said. She threw herself into his arms. "I was afraid that you weren't you, and. . ."

"I know," he said.

They held each other in a tight hug, for warmth as much as for comfort. After a moment, she looked up.

"Father?" Em asked.

He pulled back to look at her.

"We're in the cave," she said.

They had been transported into the cave with their hug. Her father touched the cleft in her chin and smiled.

"Love," he said. "It's the only truth."

"Yes," Em said. She wiped her tear-stained face and

looked around.

"Ready?" he asked.

She nodded.

~~~~~~~~~~~~~~~~~~~~~~~~~~~~~~~

Mary Eastey set Em's hand next to her body and stood up. She straightened her simple Amish dress and gave George a smile. She'd been a deeply compassionate human and was now their strongest empath. She had been sitting with Em since she and Susannah Martin had arrived from Pennsylvania. George held out an arm, and they hugged. Mary Eastey put her hand over George's heart and stepped back.

"What does Ann say about Em's body?" Mary Eastey asked in a low whisper, owing to the late hour and the situation. The witches were resting, reading, or sleeping on the couches and cushions around the room.

"Ann says that Em is well, healthy," George said. "Of course."

"Yes, I was the same when I died last," Mary Eastey said with a nod. "My body was fine, but my soul took a while to recover from the shock."

George gave her an agreeing nod. He put his arm over her shoulder and led her to the small basement kitchen where Sarah Good had made a thick stew. Susannah was leaning against the counter, having a quiet conversation with Sam. She moved aside so that George could ladle some stew for Mary Eastey. He gave her the bowl, and Susannah gave her a hunk of warm sourdough bread.

"Elizabeth's?" Mary Eastey held up the bread.

"She still has the starter," Susannah said.

"From the 1600s?" Mary Eastey chuckled at Elizabeth's capacity to hold onto things.

"Don't laugh," Susannah said. "I want to get some before we leave. Don't want to offend the baker."

"As if you could," Elizabeth said from a barstool a few feet away.

"It's always so wonderful to see everyone," Mary Eastey said.

"Wonderful enough to rejoin the world?" Sam asked.

"Maybe," Mary Eastey said.

"How is Em?" Alice asked from the entrance to the kitchen.

She'd followed Mary Eastey and George into the kitchen to learn the news. Her worry and sorrow over Em made her too impatient to wait. Mary Eastey gave Alice the kind of soft smile she'd have given a child — and Alice bristled. She turned in place to leave.

"I'm sorry, Alice," Mary Eastey said. "I didn't mean to offend you."

Mary Eastey set down her bowl of stew and went to hug Alice. They hugged for a moment. When they released, Alice was crying.

"We're all on edge," George said.

"Understandably," Mary Eastey said. "And I'm afraid I don't have much news."

"What do you know?" Wilmot asked.

Stepping back from Alice, Mary Eastey saw that everyone was awake and looking at her. She blushed at the attention and looked down. The witches became very silent. After a moment of collecting herself, Mary Eastey looked up at them.

"She's definitely not here," Mary Eastey said.

Wilmot made an annoyed sound, and Mary Eastey gave her a kind smile.

"Yes, I'd guess that you know that," Mary Eastey said. "When I got very silent, I could hear Em's voice."

"Calling for help?" Giles asked.

Mary Eastey smiled at Giles, and he blushed.

"No," Mary Eastey said. "She seemed to be talking to someone. Nothing exciting. Just a conversation. Before I got up, she seemed to be moving — running, possibly. I'm not sure."

"What do you think it means?" George asked.

"I believe it means that Em is all right," Mary Eastey said. "We have to trust Em to return to us."

"You believe she will?" Margaret asked.

"Of course, she will," Mary Eastey said with a laugh. "Em loves us very much. Don't you doubt it."

As if to say, "Em loves you," Mary Eastey pointed to each of the witches in turn. With a soft smile, Mary Eastey picked up her stew and moved it to a spot next to Elizabeth at the kitchen bar. She took a seat. The witches returned to their resting spots.

"The one thing I don't understand . . ." Mary Eastey said, and everyone stopped moving.

"Yes?" George asked.

"What did my sister say?" Margaret asked.

"It wasn't your sister as much as George Jacobs," Sarah Good said. "Rebecca still can't hear and wasn't able to understand that she'd been dead or that it wasn't 1692."

"Sure," Mary Eastey said while she shook salt onto her stew. "As we've learned, we are the same in life as in death.

What did George say?"

"'Find John Proctor's body,'" Alice sad.

"Any ideas as to why?" Mary Eastey asked.

"Nothing that made a lot of sense," said Sarah Good.

"To us," George said. "It seemed to make great sense to George Jacobs."

"And Em?" Mary Eastey asked.

George nodded.

"Then we should turn our attention to that," Mary Eastey said.

"Why?" Giles asked. "That won't bring Em back."

"Em will return when she's ready," Mary Eastey said. "In the meantime, we should find John Proctor's body. Anyone know what Em thought would happen when we did?"

"George Jacobs, John Proctor, and your sister would come to life," George said.

Surprised, Mary Eastey's head jerked up from her stew. She looked at George and then Elizabeth for confirmation. They agreed with a nod.

"Maybe we shouldn't, then," Mary Eastey said with a snort.

"What?" Sam asked.

"I've enjoyed more than three hundred years without her... uh... guidance." Mary Eastey chuckled. "Can you imagine my sister trying to work out email or Skype?"

"It's going to happen!" Alice said. Still stinging from Mary Eastey's earlier dismissal, Alice's voice was hard.

"I have no doubt," Mary Eastey said with a nod and took a bite of stew. She nodded and made an "mmm" noise. When she'd swallowed, she said, "What's the rush?"

Mary Eastey laughed. On edge and worried, the witches joined her laugh with relief. The witches moved to their resting spots, and Mary Eastey ate her stew. George went into the kitchen area for another beer. He was pouring his Guinness when he felt Mary Eastey watching him.

"Is there a place... um..." Mary Eastey paused for a moment to come up with the right words.

"A place?" George asked.

"An old place," Mary Eastey said. "With burial chambers and stone circles and..."

"Isle of Man?" George asked.

"Orkney," Sam said.

"I'm not going to Scotland," George said in a scathing voice.

"Get a grip, George," Susannah laughed. "It's been more than three hundred years since the Scots betrayed a king you didn't even like."

George cleared his throat and looked down.

"You have to excuse him, Mary," Sam said and jostled George's shoulder. "It was one of George's first wars. The resentment runs deep."

The witches laughed, and George grinned. Mary Eastey stared at the ceiling for a moment before she nodded.

"I'm not talking about Scotland," Mary Eastey said in a tone meant to get them back onto her question. "I mean, yes, there are sites on the Isle of Man and Orkney. I was with you when we went on the cruise to the ancient places of Britain. We went to the Isle of Man and those amazing ancient places in Ireland. Some of us even went to Scotland."

Mary Eastey winked at George, and he scowled. She

looked at the men.

"Human history is amazing," Mary Eastey said. "But what I meant was is there someplace here, in the Americas?"

"There's a bunch in Mexico," John Willard said. "In the Amazon and Teotihuacan, near Mexico City. I keep asking you to visit with me."

"Let's go in January." Mary Eastey gave John a soft, loving smile. He beamed. One of the reasons Mary Eastey was with the Amish was that she and John were on a break. It was clear to everyone that they were back on again. Mary Eastey turned back to George and said, "I mean, here — in New England. Some place old. Created before Christ."

George shrugged and looked at Sam. He shook his head.

"There's Gungywamp." Bridget's voice came from across the room.

"Bridget?" Mary Eastey asked. "You get over here and give me a proper hello!"

Bridget got up from the couch with a few thick blankets draped over her shoulders.

"Sorry, I'm freezing," Bridget said. She hugged Mary Eastey.

"Same old Bridget," Mary Eastey said with a smile. "How are you, dear?"

"Good," Bridget said with an impatient nod. "You said you were looking for someplace old in New England, created before Christ, right?"

Mary Eastey gave Bridget an indulgent smile. Sam put his arm on Bridget's shoulder.

"No, don't do that," Bridget said. "I know you think that

I'm an idiot."

"You just play that role to avoid responsibility," George said.

"True," Bridget pointed to George. "But I'm not fooling now. There's a place called 'Gungywamp' in Connecticut. No one's really sure who made it. They say it was made by Native Americans. My last husband thought it was made by aliens because there's a chamber there that lines up with the stars on the equinoxes. A stone chamber, no less. We used to go there for the spring equinox — or we used to, before he died."

"How old is it?" Mary Eastey asked.

"At least 2000 years before Christ," Bridget smiled and nodded.

"Are there standing stones?" Mary Eastey asked.

"Not like Stonehenge," Bridget said. "Or that ridiculous 'American Stonehenge.'"

They shot hard looks in the direction of where Giles was lying.

"Hey, you agreed to it at the time," Giles said.

They laughed.

"Gungywamp is amazing," Bridget said. "Not so much that it has a bunch of stuff — I mean, any square foot on the Isle of Man has more of the same thing — but this is. . ."

"Here," Mary Eastey said. "In the states."

"Right," Bridget said. "In the north area, there's short standing stones, a bunch of cairns. . ."

"Is there a circle — no, two — concentric circles?" Mary Eastey asked.

"That's Gungywamp," Bridget nodded.

"We need to get there," Mary Eastey said.

"Why?" George asked.

"Em will be there at first light," Mary Eastey said.

"Our Em?" Bridget's voice rose with delight.

"At this point," Mary Eastey said.

"We'd better get going, then," George said.

The witches launched into action, packing their belongings and getting ready for a road trip.

"Where's Em?" Ann asked.

Everyone stopped moving and looked at her.

"Em's body's gone," Ann said. "Who took it? Giles?"

"Why do you always suspect me?" Giles asked.

"Because you're a moron," Martha Carrier said.

"How dare you. . .?" Giles started.

"There's no time for this!" George commanded.

"But Em's body!" Ann said. "She needs. . ."

"Let's hope it's waiting for us at this 'Gungywamp,'" George said.

"Shotgun!" Alice called as they filed out into Sam's garage and into two perfectly reconditioned 1979 Chevy Suburbans.

"You're sure about this?" Susannah asked Mary Eastey under her breath.

"As sure as I can be," Mary Eastey said.

"Let's just hope she's there," Susannah said.

Mary Eastey nodded and climbed into the back of the SUV John Willard was driving.

"Let's just hope she's there," George mouthed and took the driver's seat of the second SUV.

Her father looked around the cave for a moment before walking at a stiff pace toward what seemed to be a platform or a stage. They were in a wide, open area swept clear of debris by the ocean and the wind. The stone floor was scarred by long-forgotten fire pits. William walked so fast that Em had to jog to keep up.

"We used to meet here," William said. "On the equinoxes and solstices, we'd be here, every one of us. There is something about this room, or maybe this place, which allowed us to be with each other in the same time and same place. We were a small community — only a few hundred — but when we got together . . ."

William gave her a salty grin.

"I've seen artists' renditions of these kinds of things — the community waits for announcements from the elders." William talked as fast as he walked. "They show a severe and anxious crowd. We never worried. The party started early in the morning and continued long after the council was over. I had my first drink of alcohol over there."

He pointed to an area of the cave.

"My first woman over there."

He pointed to another area.

"We were safe here and among each other," he said. "My days here were some of the best days of my life."

When they reached the wide platform, William pointed to the edge.

"I spent my twenties as a scribe for the elders," he said. "I used to attend the meetings and take notes."

"That's why you know about the library," Em said.

"Correct," William said. "Most of our kind never got past this stage. I was not an elder, but I was entrusted with

a. . ."

William reached under his shirt and pulled out a square brass medallion. Em remembered playing with the medallion when she was a child. She'd never asked him what it was or why he was wearing it. Her eyes held the question tonight.

"It's a key, Em," William said. "A key to the chambers here."

He pointed to a short set of stairs up onto the platform. Standing on the stage, he looked out into the larger cave.

"The elders would meet for a day while we prepared meat and set up for the feast," William said. "The crowd was festive, so the work was easy. After meeting, they would stand right here to tell us what they'd decided. It wasn't like politics now, where people feel so hopeless and misrepresented. We believed that our elders knew what was best for us. And you know what? They took their responsibilities very seriously. There was no corruption. They voted their conscience and what they felt was best for us. Mostly, they were right. When they weren't, they were quick to admit it and change direction."

He gave Em a soft smile and turned to an ornate door. The rock door was covered with intricate, swirling designs that, if Em hadn't known better, she would have thought were Celtic in origin. In the center, there was a complicated knot. William pulled the medallion from around his neck and held it to the knot.

"William of Truth," he said.

He nudged Em. She looked at him, and he gestured for her to say her name.

"Em. . . uh. . . Martha of Truth," she said.

The great door opened with a decisive crack. William pushed her back and stepped back himself. The door swung open.

"Ready?" her father asked again.

"I am," Em said.

They stepped into the elders' private sanctum.

Chapter Sixteen

The moment they stepped inside, the enormous stone door swung closed with a bang. Em spun in place just in time to hear the large bolt click closed.

"Don't worry, Em," her father said.

When she turned to look at him, he was noticeably younger. He looked like he was nineteen or twenty. She stepped back with surprise.

"You look about ten," he said, after clearly reading her mind. "It's this place. It shows our soul's age, not our physical age. We are children compared to those who belonged here."

Em gave him a quick uncertain nod and started looking around. They were standing in a small antechamber. The plush, silken fabrics and rich, handspun rugs made her feel like they had just missed someone. Yet this area had been abandoned for centuries.

"Have we moved in time?" Em asked.

"Possibly," William said. "I never knew how these chambers worked. They always seemed magical."

"I can see that," Em said with a smile.

"Come on," William said.

He gestured to the doorway covered in heavy drapes in front of them. He held the drapes aside and stepped through after her. The meeting chamber was carved out of pale granite. Twenty-three unadorned high-backed stone chairs had been carved into a circle with a large opening in the center. The stone was smooth from centuries of wear. Behind and above the chairs, there was a thin passageway. Em glanced at her father. He seemed lost in memory. She touched his sleeve, and he glanced at her.

"They used to sit here." He gestured to the stone seats. "The seats look awful, but they are quite comfortable."

"Magic?"

"Most certainly," William said. "When an elder had something to say, they would stand in the center to speak. The others listened with rapt attention. No one dared interrupt. When they were discussing important issues, everyone took turns to speak. But more often, two or three people did most of the talking."

Her father walked across the circle to a slightly larger chair.

"This is where Argos sat," William said. "He was the eldest, the father of us all. He was incredibly kind and unfailingly fair. He was like a father to me. I adored him."

William glanced at Em.

"Your mother was his granddaughter," William said.

"Immortal?" Em couldn't help but ask the question she knew the answer to.

"Sadly, no," William said. "Her mother was a half-human, and her father was human. Another thing I didn't know until she was dying."

"Is that why you were able to have me?" Em asked.

"Maybe," William said. "I think it was a gift from Argos. He was known as Argos the Kind."

William's face held the pinched look of love mixed with grief. Em put her hand on his back. He looked at her and smiled.

"I used to stand up there, behind Argos," William said. "If you can imagine it, there were about a hundred of us. We stood behind them, ready to do their bidding. They only had to ask, and all of our talents were theirs for the taking. We were absolutely silent until called upon. It's amazing to think of now, but there was no speaker system. Silence was required in order for these great leaders to hear each other."

"Do you think you would have become an elder?" Em asked.

"Maybe," William said. "I thought so at the time. We had lived this way for many thousands of years. I don't think anyone imagined that it would ever end. After the last century and a half of so much change, it's hard to believe anything ever endured like that."

"I could see the world was changing," Ellen the Watcher said. She appeared before a stone seat, which she sat down in. "I saw that our world was shifting. I just never imagined that we would be destroyed. I assumed we would linger here and there throughout the world and return here for the holidays."

Em felt someone looking at her, and she turned to see Argos sitting in his stone seat. He was staring at Em so intensely that William stepped in front of her.

"Argos?" William asked.

"She is both savior and destroyer," Argos said.

"She's only a girl," William said. "Not four hundred years yet."

"She is more than that," Argos said. "She is our future and our past."

William turned to look at Em. She shrugged.

"What do you need, child?" Argos asked.

Em's throat was instantly dry. She shot William a panicked look.

"She would like some assistance with her demon," William said. "It has joined forces with mine and. . ."

"With all of ours," Argos said. "You are dealing with an army."

"But. . ." Em started. "Why?"

"Why?" Argos asked. "You are a truth teller. You know that things are what they are."

"I guess I'm asking: 'Why me?'" Em asked. "You are the eldest — or Ellen the Watcher or any of the esteemed people who have sat in these chairs. Why am I dealing with an army of our opposite?"

"You live at a time when the final battles of the ruling class are being held," Argos said. "Will humankind come together, or will the ruling class be able to assert itself again? Humankind has been at this juncture over and over again. The ruling class has always won. But, in your time, there is a real chance for people to rule their own lives, without masters, and, after a time, peace will reign. This reality is but a breath away. The demons cannot allow that.

"So I ask again: What do you need, child?" Argos asked.

With his words, the rest of the seats filled in. William gasped in wonder. Em looked from one intelligent face to another.

"You have all of our wisdom at your disposal — for now and for the rest of this battle," Argos said. "How can we assist you?"

"First, I would need to be able to contact you at will," Em said. "I don't know exactly what I'm up against, so I'll need to be able to reach you."

"Done," Argos said. "You will only have to think my name, and a part of you will be standing right here. What else?"

"I need to learn about demons, and my demon in particular," Em said. "My father says that his demon and my demon have combined forces. I need to learn about his demon as well."

"I will grant you access to our library," Argos said. "William, you know the way?"

"Yes, sir," William said.

"Anything else, Martha of Truth?" Argos asked.

"I need to know how I can be the past and the future at the same time," Em said.

"You stand at a crossroads," said a woman who stood from her seat and walked toward Em.

"Miriam of Geography," William said in her ear.

"The past stretches behind you," she said. "The future is ahead. You are both past and future. You will bring about past and future."

Em silently wished that George were there. He would make sense of this nonsense and even have questions to ask. As it was, she managed a weak smile.

"Do you want me to bring you back? Bring us back?" Em internally groaned at her simple and practical question. She was surrounded by the wisest of the wise, and all she could do was ask stupid questions.

"It will happen automatically when you defeat the

demons," an elderly, dark-skinned man said. "Benjamin the Warrior, Martha of Truth. And your question was not stupid. Practical, yes, but not stupid."

The man made a slight bow and sat down.

"And you're sure I'm going to defeat these demons?" Em asked.

"Why do you doubt?" William asked.

"Because *humans* tried me as a witch," Em said. "It was humans who jailed me, beat me, raped me, and belittled me, and it was humans who hanged me. Humans — not demons."

When she finished, the elders spoke in hushed tones to each other.

"How do I defeat the demons when human beings are more than willing to do their bidding?" Em asked.

"You *will* find a way," Argos said.

"I'll find a way," Em said under her breath. She shrugged and raised an eyebrow to indicate that Argos' statement wasn't helpful.

"Do you have any other questions?" Argos asked.

"That's all I can think of right now," Em said. She bit her lip to keep from asking again how exactly she was going to beat the demons.

"Very well," Argos said. "The library is yours. William?"

For a moment, William and Argos shared a look. William ended the look with a slight bow.

"This way," William said.

He gestured to a door off the passageway above the stone seats. Em climbed the steep stone steps to the passageway. When she looked back, the stone chairs were empty again. The elders were gone. She felt a sudden chill and shivered.

"What happened?" William asked.

"I have this feeling of . . . foreboding, I guess," Em said.

"You mean, you feel the loss of them," William said. "As if they are truly gone forever."

Em nodded.

"I feel it, too," William said.

He held back the curtains, and Em walked through. She gasped. She was standing in a football-field-sized room. Books lined wall shelves from the floor to somewhere beyond her sight above. Feeling movement, she turned to look.

A small, thin man was standing next to her. His skin was brown and his hair deep black. His dress was something Em had seen in the Ancient Egypt exhibits at Boston's Museum of Fine Arts. He held his hand out to her.

"Weni the Librarian," he said in a reedy voice. He leaned close to look into her face. "I have waited many millennia for you."

He gave a quick sniff, spun in place, and walked away. Em was so surprised that she could only watch him. He was ten feet away before he turned his head back to her.

"Come along, Em," Weni said. "We have much to do, much to do! And your witches are waiting for you."

"My witches?" Em asked.

"We will start here." Weni gestured to a three-foot-high stack of books.

"But, how. . .?" Em started to ask, and Weni laughed.

"I like her, William," Weni said. "But does she not know she is a witch?"

"How is being a witch. . .?" Em started.

Her father put his hand on the stack of books. Words

flew out of the books and into his brain. He winked at her and lifted his hand. More than a little intimidated, Em took a small step toward the books. Weni whipped around her. On his route around her, his shoulder hit hers, and she flew to the books. Her father took her hand and placed it on the books.

"It's controlled by your breath," Weni said. "Breathe in!"

"Uh. . ." Em shook her head.

"*Now!*" Weni screamed.

Startled, Em gasped and the words flew into her brain. She felt like she was watching a movie or listening to an intricate song. Suddenly, knowledge was there. She was so surprised that she stopped breathing.

"*Breathe!*" Weni commanded.

"Focus on your breathing, Em," William said in a low tone. "Like yoga or meditation. You'll see."

Em turned her attention to her breath. She breathed in the knowledge and let out unknowing. After a time, Weni held out a chair for her. Em sat down. For the next few hours, or maybe a few years, Em sat in the chair while Weni brought her the books, charts, and maps she requested. Her father and Weni added to the pile when they thought she needed information. She focused on breathing and absorbing what he brought her. When she looked up next, the table was clear, and Weni was watching her.

"You have a great capacity for knowledge, Em," Weni smiled. "I knew that you would."

"You knew?" Em asked.

"I have watched you for a long time," Weni said.

"Do the elders have to die?" Em said.

"Nothing *has* to happen," Weni said. "But happen, it does. The elders are dead in your time, true. They are not dead in all of time. Through you, they aren't dead at all."

Pretending what he'd said made sense to her, Em gave him a curt nod. Her father helped her to her feet. Her legs were unsteady — as if she'd been sitting a long, long time. William kept her on her feet until she was steady. Weni watched the entire process with rapt attention.

"I have the feeling that you wish to say something to me," Em said.

Weni closed his eyes for a moment. Then he opened his eyes and held out his right hand. In his hand a gorgeous maple tree grew. It started as a seedling and then became a young tree, before it transformed into a ten-inch-high tree with wide limbs and gorgeous, light-green leaves.

"Kill it," Weni ordered.

Em scowled.

"Kill it," Weni ordered again.

Em placed her hand above the tree and slowly pressed down until her hand reached his. Weni shook his head.

"William?" Weni asked.

"No idea, sir," William said. "None."

"Cut off a limb, and the tree survives," Weni said. "Hang one or even nineteen humans on it, and the tree of knowledge will survive. Cut down a tree, and the tree will regrow from the stump."

"Remove the stump," William said.

"Even then. . ." Weni said.

The tree in his hand was cut down and the stump removed. Tendrils began appearing where the stump had been. The tiny tree grew into multiple maple trees.

"Then, how. . .?" Em asked.

"Kill the roots," Weni said. "Plant a poison inside the tree, and it will rot from the inside."

"But. . .?" Em started.

"Yes, what does it mean?" Weni asked. Em blushed. "Never doubt your practical nature, Em. It is your beauty, and it is the reason I know you will win this war."

He held out his arms, and she let him hug her.

"Kill just one," Weni said in her ear. "Poison him. He will bring the rot to the others. Don't let them draw you into a battle with all of them. Focus on poisoning the one."

Em nodded, and Weni stepped back.

"I belong to you," Weni said. "I was given by Argos to William for his great service. William has given me to you."

"I don't know what that means," Em said.

"You will see me in your world," Weni said. "I will bring you the knowledge from this room anytime you request it, and even if you don't."

Em gave him a curt nod.

"Time to go," William said.

"Take her by that path." Weni pointed to a bookshelf, and a door appeared.

"Weni," William said as he bowed.

Weni returned his bow, and the men hugged. Weni glanced at Em. Before she could thank him, he disappeared. Em glanced at her father to see him wiping away a tear.

"He was my teacher," William said. "My friend."

Em nodded.

"I will take you up the stairwell and then take my leave,"

William said. "Dawn is coming. My wife will be looking for me."

Em threw herself into her father's arms, and he held her in a tight hug,

"I could not love you more," William said. "Nor be more proud of you."

"I love you, father," Em said.

In a blink of an eye, Em was standing alone, and light was just peeking over the edge of the horizon. She had no idea where she was. She knew only that she was completely alone. She felt an overwhelming, desperate loss of her father and the world where she belonged. For a moment, she could only watch the dawn.

Then, she heard a man's voice calling her name and smiled.

"I'm here," Em yelled.

George appeared at the edge of the hill. He ran toward her. The rest of the witches crested the hill. Seeing Em, they took off running in her direction, and she laughed. George reached her first. He lifted her up and spun her around. He let her go to allow the others to greet her. As they gathered around her, she went from one to the next, hugging them in greeting. She ended with Ann, who allowed her a quick hug before taking her vitals.

"You're finally here!" Alice said and gave Em another hug.

"And where exactly is 'here'?" Em asked.

The witches laughed.

Chapter Seventeen

Excited to be together, Em and the witches spent the morning touring Gungywamp. Bridget took on the role of their tour guide. She blossomed under their attention. Midway through their first cairn, Em transformed Bridget's usual stilettos into rugged hiking boots. For the first time in a hundred years, Bridget didn't scream about the practical shoes. She just smiled at Em and continued a story of her many adventures around these ancient structures. They ended their expedition with breakfast at a local diner in Groton, CT.

After breakfast, Em finally admitted to her own exhaustion, and George insisted on heading home. Leaving the passenger seat for Sam and his long legs, she took her place next to Alice in the far back of the Suburban that George was driving. Susannah scooted in next to her. Giles, Elizabeth, and Margaret sat in the middle seat. The rest of the witches went in the other SUV.

"So, John and Mary Eastey?" Em asked.

"I know!" Alice said.

"Did they resolve anything?" Em looked at Susannah, who had shared a house with Mary Eastey in an Amish settlement in Pennsylvania.

"Of course not," Susannah said. "She just realized that

John Willard is a kind, decent man."

"How did that come about?" Alice asked.

"Comparison to other men," Susannah grinned.

Em and Alice laughed. Susannah smiled.

"Are you ready to return?" Em asked.

Susannah turned to look at Em. She opened and closed her mouth before nodding.

"I'm ready to rid myself of this old body," Susannah said.

Em grinned. Em took Susannah's left hand, and Alice reached over to her right.

"How young?" Alice asked.

"Oh . . ." Susannah looked out the window. "Thirty? Thirty-five? Is that too . . ."

"Done," Em said.

Alice leaned back to get a better view. Susannah looked as if she were on the young side of thirty-five. Her teeth were gleaming white, her eyes clear, and her nose small and pert. She had always been thin, so they softened her boney features with youthful curves. Em smiled and nodded. Alice leaned forward and touched Susannah's head.

"Blond is in," Alice said with a smile.

"Blond?" Susannah's voice went up with delight.

"Elizabeth? Margaret?" Alice leaned forward so that her head was between their shoulders. "What do you think of Susannah?"

Elizabeth gasped, and Margaret clapped her hands together.

"Beautiful," Giles added.

Susannah put her hand on his shoulder in thanks. Giles smiled. Sam turned around in the passenger seat and whistled "wheet whoo." Susannah blushed. She was so embarrassed that the witches turned away from her to allow her to collect herself.

"What's with Giles?" Susannah asked under her breath.

"Yeah," Alice said. "He's been so . . ."

"Nice," Susannah said.

"I saw you talking to him," Alice said.

Em nodded and looked at the back of Giles's head.

"Tell us," Alice said out of the side of her mouth.

Em grinned.

"Come on," Susannah said.

"He told me that he's been angry with me for everything," Em said.

"Everything?" Alice asked.

"Continuing to live," Susannah nodded. "He has been mad about that."

"When I was gone, he had to face the idea that I might not return," Em said. "He realized that all of this was a gift."

Susannah mock-clapped her hands. Em shrugged.

"About time," Alice said.

"You should talk," Em said and bumped Alice with her shoulder. Alice laughed.

"Did I tell you my client is coming back into town?" Alice asked. "The one who was with us when we met the demon?"

Em shook her head, and Susannah rolled her eyes at Alice.

"I can't believe you still do that," Susannah said.

Em nodded.

"This one's a keeper," Alice said. "He likes me. Anyway, how else . . ."

" . . . is a three-hundred-year-old gal going to meet a nice man?" Em and Susannah joined Alice in asking.

They laughed.

"Hey!" George yelled from the driver's seat. "Don't have too much fun back there!"

Em, Alice, and Susannah fell silent. They batted their eyelashes at him, and he laughed.

"Okay, okay," George said. "Carry on."

They laughed.

"Want to see . . ." Em said.

She held her hand over her head. Her hair turned fire red. It unwound from the bun and fell in gentle waves down her back. Her sweater turned from the neutral grey to bright orange to match her hair. Alice squealed with delight. Susannah touched Em's newly ginger hair.

"It looks so natural!" Susannah said. "How . . . Where . . . ?"

"I saw my father," Em said with a shrug.

Everyone in the SUV fell silent. Margaret turned around in her seat, and Elizabeth turned her head. Sam rotated his body to look at her from the passenger seat. George's eyes watched her in the rearview mirror. Noticing their attention, Em blushed.

"Where did you go, Em?" Giles asked.

"I . . ." Em smiled at Giles and turned to look into the faces of each of them. "My father cast a spell to bring me to him when I died next. Of course, he cast the spell in the 1600s, but you know me. I'm not much of a risk taker."

The witches laughed.

"I promise to tell you everything," Em said with certainty. "I just need to process it all."

"Who loves the hair?" Alice asked in an attempt to brighten the mood.

"Love it," Sam said.

"Me, too," Margaret said. "Will you . . . ?"

Em put her hand over Margaret's head, and her hair turned bright red. Margaret was so delighted that she giggled.

"Elizabeth?" Alice asked.

"No," Elizabeth laughed. "Don't you dare!"

She put her hands over the top of her blond head and ducked down. They laughed.

"You will tell us." George's voice broke through their levity. "Won't you?"

"I will," Em said. "I also have some ideas about finding John Proctor and fighting the demon."

Em nodded.

"When we get home?" Margaret asked.

"When she's rested," George said.

Em winked at Margaret, and she smiled.

"You won't leave us out, will you?" Margaret asked.

"Bring your own shovel!" Em said.

Margaret laughed and turned around. Elizabeth said something to Margaret, and she whispered back. Em glanced at Giles, who was still looking at her.

"Giles," Em said.

"You seem different," Giles said. "More sure of yourself."

Em nodded.

"It looks good on you," Giles smiled and turned forward.

Sam asked Giles a question about their season tickets to their beloved football team, the Patriots. The Suburban slowed to a stop as they reached morning traffic into

Boston. Off the hook, Em leaned back against the seat.

"Could I live with you?" Susannah asked.

Em turned to look at her.

"I mean, in the apartments," Susannah said. "Not with you and George. I know all of that's over."

"What's over?" Em asked.

Alice bent over to see Susannah around Em.

"George and everybody," Susannah said.

"What do you mean?" Em asked.

"You don't know?" Susannah asked.

"Know what?" Em asked.

"George doesn't share himself anymore," Susannah said.

"I . . ." Em shrugged.

"He just stopped," Susannah said.

"That can't possibly be true," Em said. "He visited you on his way home just a couple months ago."

"He stayed with us," Susannah said. "Helped with the upkeep of our house. Stayed up late talking, praying, giving counsel, but nothing else. No romance."

Em's eyes scanned Susannah's face. Susannah had been seventy-one years old when she was hanged. At that time, George was her pastor and her counselor. Immortality created a push-pull relationship between Susannah and George. Susannah had left for the Amish after a blowout argument with George.

"It's why I left," Susannah said. "Alice didn't tell you that he's not 'available' anymore? That's what he calls it: 'available.' He's not available to anyone. Period. Why didn't you tell her, Alice?"

"George and I never had that kind of relationship," Alice said. "I'm too hung up on my husband."

Alice shrugged. Susannah gave a little nod and looked down at her hands. Deeply embarrassed, she pulled her shoulders up and dropped her head. Em reached over to hold Susannah's hand. Em gave her hand a squeeze, and Susannah looked up at Em.

"I never loved him, Em," Susannah said. "Not like you do, not like what you have. I know that now. If I were a better Christian, I would have seen the God in your love. I just didn't want to lose, again."

Em put her arm around Susannah and hugged her. Susannah tucked herself into Em's shoulder and cried. Em held on until Susannah's tears ebbed. Alice reached around Em to touch Susannah's arm.

"You didn't lose," Alice said.

"You can't lose," Em said.

Susannah gave them a watery smile.

"And yes," Em said. "You're always welcome to stay. We've rented everything except the small apartment in the back. It's not much, and the window looks out onto the parking lot. Alice is in the big one for the summer. You could move in there when she moves out in the fall."

"You can share with me," Alice said.

"What about your . . . clients?" Susannah asked.

"This one's loaded," Alice said. "We won't stay there."

"What do you say?" Em asked.

"Sounds really great," Susannah said. "Thanks."

Smiling, she looked forward for a moment before threading her arm through Em's.

"What's the plan for Saturday?" Susannah asked.

"The boys' and Martha's hanging day?" Em asked. "No idea. You?"

"I'm sure they're making a plan in the other car," Alice said.

Em scowled.

"What is it?" Alice asked.

"We have to find John Proctor before his hanging day," Em said. "George Jacobs and Rebecca. We should do that on their day."

"Do what?" Susannah asked.

"Em thinks that, if we find John Proctor, George Jacobs and Rebecca will return to physical form," Alice said. "Like we did."

"Really?" Susannah asked.

Em nodded.

"Do we want that?" Susannah asked. "Mary Eastey has been more than a little relieved that her sister didn't make this . . . trip."

"I don't think we have a choice," Em said.

On that note, the women fell silent. In the seat in front of them, Margaret and Elizabeth were asleep. Giles and Sam were talking in low tones about the Patriots' quarterback, Tom Brady. When Em looked at blonde, young, Susannah, she had also fallen asleep. Em turned to look at Alice. She gave Em a little wave and a smile.

"Glad you're back," Alice said.

"Me, too," Em said. She leaned in and said in Alice's ear, "I found a way to send you on."

Alice didn't respond.

"What?" Em asked.

"And leave you to deal with the demon yourself?" Alice asked. "Not a chance. When this is over, we'll talk."

"But I thought . . ." Em started.

Alice shook her head and looked out the side window. Em stared forward at the road. George caught her eye in the rearview mirror and winked. She smiled at him, and he turned his attention back to the stop-and-go traffic. Em watched the scenery for a while before succumbing to exhaustion. The next thing she knew, George was pulling up in front of the Mystic Divine. Through the glass, she saw a slight, dark-skinned man standing behind the counter inside the Mystic Divine.

"Who's that?" Em asked when she got out of the SUV.

"He's new," Margaret said. "George, who's the new guy?"

"Weni," George said. "You'll like him. He's smart and very knowledgeable."

Feeling her eyes, Weni turned around to look at her. She inclined her head to him, and Weni smiled. Alice got out behind Em.

"Come on," Alice said to Susannah. "Let's get you settled."

Alice threaded her arm in Susannah's, and they went upstairs.

"Ready to get back?" George asked.

"Not really," Em said.

George grinned. They took the outside stairwell to their apartment.

luum un luum luum i lm un mm mt mod my bm

"I wondered..." George said as he came into their kitchen. Em was leaning against the counter, drinking a cup of black tea.

"Tea?" Em held up the pot she'd made.

"Sure," George said.

She waited for him to fill his cup with a half-inch of milk before pouring him a cup of strong tea from the pot. He glanced in the cup and gave her a wry look.

"I need a . . ." he started.

"Fork," they said together.

"Yes, sorry," Em said. "I made tea for William, my father, and fell back into old habits."

"Reminds me of visiting you in Salem Village," George said with a grin.

"You can always add milk," Em said.

"Milk in after?" George scowled. "Heresy."

"You weren't even born in England," she laughed.

George laughed and took a drink of his tea.

"It *is* very good," he said.

She grinned at him and started toward their living room.

"Wait," George said.

She turned around at the door and looked at him.

"I ruined your painting." George gestured to the painting of the wheat field and William.

"What do you mean?" Em asked.

"How . . .?" George took it down from the wall. "There was a green dot."

He pointed to the painted image of William's back as he fought with the wooden plow.

"It's gone," he said and looked up at her.

She gave him a soft smile and started for the living room again. Still holding the painting, he followed her.

"I should check my email, because . . ." Em started.

She turned to see that he was still holding the painting. She looked at the painting and then at him.

"I need to ask you something," George said. "I'm just not sure what."

Em nodded her head to the couch and went to sit down. She set her cup of tea on the end table. Seeing her tea, George realized he'd left his in the kitchen. He leaned the painting against the couch and jogged back to the kitchen. She pulled the painting onto her lap. Looking at the image, she realized the painting would be a great way to contact her father. She touched the image of his back. He turned around and waved. When George returned, the painting was sitting on her lap, and she was smiling.

"What?" George asked.

She turned the painting for him to see.

"He's waving." George's voice was tinged with a touch of awe. "How did you . . .?"

"The painting must be a kind of portal so that I can get his help and wisdom," Em said. "They said they had set something up. I just wasn't sure . . ."

"They?" George asked. "Who's 'they'? What 'they'?"

Em patted the couch. George gave her an irritated look.

"You can't just tell me?" George asked.

"I can," she said and patted the couch again.

He made a show of sitting down on the couch.

"Where is that?" George asked. "And how is it that I don't know anything about it?"

"Well . . ." Em started.

"You're acting so oddly since you got back," George said. "I was worried sick about you, and you . . ."

"I'm sorry you were worried," Em said with a slight smile. "I know what it's like to wait for someone when they've died. It's horrible and heartbreaking. You do get used to it after the hundredth or so time, or at least, I . . ."

"Very funny." George cut her off. "I'm the unstable one. You're the rock."

Em laughed.

"Where is that?" George asked. "Alice said you lived there."

"After the London fire," Em said. "The fire was unbelievable. It burned so fast that people couldn't get out of its way. Entire families were burned alive. And it burned crematorium hot. Living beings — humans, dogs, cats, everything — went from living flesh to dust. They didn't bother to fight the fire because it burned mostly the middle- and lower-class slums, hotbeds for the plague, which had ravaged the city just the year before."

"Alice said your father's watch shop was right there," George said.

"It was," Em said. "We barely managed to escape with our lives."

George threaded his hand through hers and pulled her closer to him.

"We went to Rousay," Em said. "My father has a tract of land that's been in the family for many thousands of years. The whole island used to belong to us, but it's been lost due to greed and the usual."

"Rousay?" George asked. He gave a quick shake of his head. "Where's that?"

Em winced. She scanned his face before taking a guarded breath.

"Rousay is an island in the Orkney Islands," Em said.

"Okay," George said.

"Scotland," Em said.

"What?" George reared away from her. She wrinkled her nose and nodded. "You're a Scot?"

"My father was raised on Rousay. He was born on Shetland," Em said. "Shetland, Orkney, and Rousay were inhabited long before there was a Scotland, long before the Covenanters betrayed their king and were cruel to one Reverend Burroughs, long before there were human beings, for that matter."

George sneered and leaned back on the couch. He stared off into space for a few minutes.

"I suppose you didn't tell me because..." George started.

"You're very prejudiced against Scots and Scotland," Em said. "You think Scots are lesser beings, even after your beloved *science* and *genetics* proved that the Picts were a sect of the Celts."

George crossed his arms and grunted. Em knocked her shoulder against his.

"Celts," Em said. "Like you. Celts."

He gave her a dark scowl, and she grinned.

"You're a Scot?" he asked.

His face was such a mix of disgust and sorrow that Em had to suppress a laugh.

"Why didn't you tell me?" he asked.

"I'm not sure," Em said. "Why didn't you ask?"

"You *said* you were from London," George said.

"I was born in London," Em said. "We moved to Rousay only after the fire. We returned to London when I was sixteen or seventeen. I met Henry in London."

George scowled.

"Are you ready to let go of your prejudice?" Em asked.

"No," George said.

"Even for me?" Em laughed.

He looked at her and shook his head.

"You ask too much of me, Em," George said.

She burst out laughing, and he grinned.

"Can I love you and still hate Scots?" George asked.

"If it makes you happy, sure," Em said.

"It does," George nodded. "Very happy."

Em had to look away to keep from laughing.

"Where did you go?" George asked.

"I went to Jamaica Plain to find my father," Em answered the question she knew he wanted answered. "I found a person using his name. My father thinks it's my demon, but I don't know. It was terrifying, really. I spun around . . ."

Em nodded.

"I met your friend Martha," Em said.

"Martha is dead," George said.

"Oh, I'm sorry," Em said. "I liked her. How did that happen?"

"I'll tell you later," George said. "Now I want to hear about . . . well, everything and . . ."

She turned to look at him.

"Are you really a Scot?" George asked.

Em laughed. When he grinned, she told him about her trip to Rousay.

Chapter Eighteen

Em shook her head at the chaos on her computer. She'd been gone a total of three days. Three days away had created three days of cleanup. If she didn't get out to find John Proctor tonight, she'd run right into Rebecca Nurse, Sarah Wildes, Elizabeth Howe, Susannah Martin, and Sarah Good's hanging day. There was always a big hoopla around the guys' hanging in July. This year, she thought it would be fun to make a big deal for these brave women. She checked the clock and calculated that she had just enough time to get the shovels together before they were leaving. She got up from her desk.

"I have an errand to run," Em said to the woman working the front desk.

"You're leaving?" The young woman looked scandalized. "You just got back!"

Em smiled at the young woman.

"You can get me on my cell," Em said. "It's brand new and charged up. I solemnly promise not to break it."

"It's just that we were so worried about you," the young woman said.

Em put her hand on the woman's shoulder, and the young woman gave her an anxious nod.

"I'm not leaving right away," Em said with a smile. "I

need to get some things from the roof."

"The roof?" The young woman looked even more worried. She leaned forward to Em. "You're not going to..." The young woman looked around to see if anyone was close. Seeing no one, she mouthed, "...jump."

Em had to stifle a laugh. She shook her head.

"I'm here," Em said. "Don't worry."

"I just know that poor George was beside himself," the woman said. She gave a little sigh. "He's really..."

"Yes, he is," Em said and smiled. She raised her eyebrows and shrugged her shoulders. "Off to the roof I go! Call me if you need me."

The young woman raised a hand in a kind of uncertain goodbye. Em went up the store steps to the apartment. She quickly changed into old jeans and a T-shirt before heading up to the roof. She opened the shed and started looking through her shovels. She was there merely a second before a shadow crossed the door. The late afternoon summer sun made the rooftop spotlight bright compared to the dark shed. She could see only the dark outline of someone.

"Em?" the woman asked.

"Yeah," Em said. Assuming it was someone from the store, she didn't look up.

"It's me," the woman said. She stepped into the shed. "Martha."

"Martha!" Em said. She set her shovels down and hugged Martha Carrier. "I couldn't tell that it was you."

Martha nodded. In Salem Village, Martha had grown up in a wealthy family. When she got pregnant at fifteen, her father paid an indentured servant to marry her. She'd been known for being harsh and disagreeable after that. Em found Martha to be sharp as a whip. Martha had the rare gift of being able to think fast and communicate clearly. Martha never suffered fools, which endeared her to Em. This skill made her good at her current job as a general counsel for the CIA.

"I'm getting ready to dig up Proctor," Em said using the name they'd called John Proctor in Salem Village. "You coming?"

"Wouldn't miss it," Martha said.

Em smiled and gave Martha a shovel.

"We can't count on the others to bring shovels," Em said.

"Is everyone coming?" Martha asked.

"Those who can get away," Em said. "Sam's coming. George, of course. They'll probably do most of the digging. You know how they hate to have us 'girls' do 'men's work.'"

"John's working on a case," Martha said.

"Sarah Good is working," Em said with a shrug. "We'll see who shows up."

"Mary Eastey is upset," Martha said.

"I know, I know." Em raised her hands. "I can't blame her. I don't really want her sister to return either. You?"

Martha chuckled. Em went deeper into the shed.

"I wanted to talk to you about something," Martha said. "You know, before everyone was around."

"Yeah," Em said.

"Um," Martha said. Martha followed Em down a pathway between stacks of empty beehives. "Em?"

Em looked up.

"Alice told Susannah, who told Mary Ayer, who told John Willard. . ." Martha swallowed hard.

"What did they say?" Em asked.

"She said you know how to send us. . . um. . . on," Martha said.

Em looked at Martha for a moment. She set the shovels against the wall of the shed and reached out to hold Martha. The woman began to cry. As her tears fell, she spoke of her sorrow.

"I'm so lonely, Em," Martha said. "I don't have friends, except the witches, and you know, I'm not sweet, like Elizabeth. I haven't had a boyfriend for more than a hundred years. Who would want to be with me? I'm so bossy and controlling and. . . I don't have George or John Willard, and Sam, well. . . I miss my kids. I miss my beloved George and our life. Hell, sometimes I even miss my stupid husband, Thomas."

Martha gave a snot-filled snort and stepped back.

"All these years of liberation, and I miss Thomas — that stupid, abusive jerk," Martha said. "I have as much money as I could want. I love my work, but I feel. . ."

"Out of place," Em said.

"Like I don't belong." Martha nodded against her shoulder.

"I know how that feels," Em said.

"You do?" Martha asked.

"I think we all do," Em said. "I think it's particularly hard for you because your work is so intense and takes up so much of your life. You're really in the thick of this paranoid time."

"Always pretending I wasn't born in 1643," Martha said.

"And sometimes I slip. Not a lot, but every once in a while. I'm afraid they're going to rendition me."

"I'll burn them where they stand if they touch even one hair on your head," Em said.

Martha clutched Em again.

"I'm so sorry," Martha said.

"You've been strong a long time," Em said.

"That's what my counselor says," Martha said.

"Therapy?" Em asked.

"I went because I thought it might help," Martha said. "I've never had another love relationship — not after my George."

"You were married for forty years," Em said.

"It was almost a hundred years after Salem Village," Martha nodded. She moved away from Em again. "I went from being called the 'Queen of Hell' to being married to a General, the head of a new country, no less. It was. . ."

"Exhilarating, Mrs. Washington," Em said with a smile.

Martha nodded.

"I just never got over everything that happened, in Andover and Salem Village, you know?" Martha asked. "Add to that how my George died. He was there one moment and gone the next. Even Ann couldn't heal him."

"Awful," Em said.

"It's helped," Martha said. "Therapy, that is. I don't feel like it was my fault that I got pregnant when I was fifteen. My dad was humiliated, so he threw my life away. I've been able to see the good in Thomas, especially how he treated the kids after I was hanged. I even went to the crypt where George is buried and said goodbye."

"He was a good man, Martha," Em said.

"I never loved Thomas or Daniel, for that matter," Martha said. "Only George. In all of this time, I've loved one man. That's all. And he died in 1799."

"I know," Em said.

"And the slaves?" Martha shook her head. "I feel horrible about the slaves. Every day. I read about all the troubles African-Americans have, and I know it's because of us, me, slave owners."

"It was a different time," Em said.

"You never had them," Martha said.

Em shrugged.

"Every historian says that *I* wanted to keep them," Martha sniffed at her sorrow. "They were Daniel's slaves. I wanted to set them free. You know that, Em. But my George never wanted to let go of anything he'd obtained."

"People want George to be pure of what they see now as evil, regardless of the truth," Em said.

"Evil," Martha said. "It's amazing to me how certain we were."

"In 1692?" Em asked.

"We knew what was godly and what was of the devil," Martha said. "We just knew, and slavery was godly."

"Arrogance," Em said.

"It was easier to be certain then," Martha said. "Fewer people. I didn't think about what was happening in Asia or the Middle East. Even when I was married to my George! All that mattered was what directly affected me — Indian wars, slaves, church, family, the children."

"Maybe you just need a break," Em said.

"Maybe," Martha said. "But if I wanted to. . ."

"If you want to end this, I will help you," Em said.

"I knew you would," Martha said.

"You can't do it until my hanging date," Em said.

Martha nodded and hugged Em.

"Alice will kill me," Martha said. "She keeps talking about the war between you and the demons. Is that real?"

"Unfortunately," Em said.

"Will you forgive me if I. . .?" Martha said.

"Of course," Em said. "Nothing to forgive."

"You're a good friend, Em," Martha said.

"So are you, Martha," Em said. "You deserved to be loved, not hanged. George loved you and tried to make up for it all. And now that he's gone, you still deserve to be loved."

"I'm not Bridget," Martha said. "She's had a rich husband a decade."

"Bridget is Bridget," Em said. "You are you."

"Her husbands treat her like a goddess." Martha shook her head. "And I can't find. . ."

"There is a man who works with you," Em said with a smile. "He's wondering when you'll notice him. You never know, but he seems like a nice guy."

"Em," Martha said. "Don't tease me!"

"Never," Em said. "You know who I mean?"

Martha thought for a moment and then nodded her head.

"Maybe you feel this way because your life is about to expand," Em said. "One last chance to quit before everything changes."

"Maybe," Martha said.

"You know, it's okay to love your George Washington and love someone else," Em said with a smile. "He would be the first person to encourage you to find someone to love."

"I guess," Martha shrugged.

"Well, you have until the end of September," Em said. "Why not try it with this guy until then? You can always get out of here if it doesn't work."

"You mean die?"

"Or leave for the island," Em shrugged. "What do you have to lose?"

Martha bit her lip for a moment and then looked at Em. Martha nodded.

"Good," Em said.

"Jeez, it's hot in here," Martha said.

Em gave her two round-head digging shovels and picked up a spade.

"Should I grab the potato fork?" Martha asked.

"I'll get it," Em said.

"How do you have all of these?" Martha asked as she stepped out of the shed.

"Giles," Em said. "They're part of my divorce settlement."

"Really?" Martha asked. She looked at the shovels. "But they're almost brand new!"

Martha caught sight of Em's grin and laughed.

"Do you want to go with me?" Em asked.

"Sure."

"We won't be alone," Em said. "The others are coming."

"That's okay," Martha said. "Can I have some lemonade?"

"Of course," Em said. "Let's leave these by the door and get some lemonade. You know we'll end up waiting on

George anyway. *And*, I just remembered that I made lemon sorbet last night."

"Heaven," Martha said.

Martha smiled. She put her hand on the door and stopped.

"You're sure about the guy at my work?" Martha said. "It's Bruce, right?"

Em nodded, and Martha smiled. Em followed Martha to her apartment. Em was just taking the sorbet out of the freezer when Alice and Susannah came down. Martha poured the lemonade. Em had just scooped out the sorbet when Elizabeth and Margaret arrived. Sam followed Mary Ayer into the kitchen.

"I should have made more sorbet," Em said.

She was acknowledged by a kind of "mm-hm" from the witches. The sorbet was almost done when George arrived. He took the bowl from her hands and finished her sorbet while she groaned at him.

"Are we ready?" George asked. Sarah Wildes came in behind him. She waved off any sorbet.

"Isn't it dangerous to go when it's light out?" Margaret asked.

"We need to try to use the GPS and our other equipment," Em said. "There's no guarantee that they'll work. We have to try."

"Better to try in the daylight," George said.

"Even so, it seems dangerous to me," Mary Ayer said.

"I have permission from the owners of the land to stage a recreation," Em said.

"A recreation?" Alice asked.

Em pulled on her shirt, and their clothing transformed

into what they'd worn in Salem Village.

"This way, if anyone asks, you can honestly tell them who you are and what you're doing," Em smiled.

The witches gave her doubtful scowls.

"We can head out there and find him," George said. "We have to get George Jacobs and Rebecca anyway. After we find Proctor, we'll head to Rebecca's old place. When we have George Jacobs and Rebecca, we can return to get Proctor when it's dark."

"That's a much better plan," Margaret said. She stood up to leave.

"Really, Em," Susannah said with a shake of her head as she walked by.

Em scowled. Sarah Wildes pointed at Em at the same time Alice mouthed, "Your plan?" Em nodded. Sarah and Alice grinned.

"You're brilliant, George," Mary Ayer said.

Sarah, Alice, and Em laughed.

"What?" Mary Ayer said.

Mary Ayer took George's arm, and they left the apartment. Alice and Sarah chortled their way to the Suburban. To spite George, Em got in the passenger seat in Sam's work pickup after putting all her tools in the bed. George followed Sam out of Boston toward modern-day Danvers.

"I hate coming here," Sam said as he took the ramp to MA-128.

Em turned to look at him.

"I know it's childish," Sam said. "I should be over it. I'm just. . . not."

He glanced at Em, and she smiled.

"Are you?" Sam asked.

"Yes," Em nodded her head and then shook her head. "No."

Sam nodded in agreement.

"I'm over the whole thing," Em said. "And I'm still so hurt and confused by it."

"How did this happen to *me*?" Sam asked.

"Exactly," Em said. "I was married, a member of the church..."

"Safe," Sam said.

"I was safe," Em said. "Sometimes I wake up at night and wonder why they hated me so much. What did I ever do to them?"

"Was Mary Eastey as saint-like as they say?" Sam asked.

"She was beautiful," Em said. "She gave this little speech and blessed everyone. She asked them to stop this evil business because it was bad for them. She was wonderful, saintly. Of course, *I* wanted to burn down the town."

"Yeah," Sam said. "I guess Giles got around to it eventually."

"More than two hundred years later," Em smiled.

"Good thing he stopped drinking," Sam said.

"'Good' is an understatement," Em said.

Watching the road, they fell silent. Their tension rose with each passing mile.

"Do you think we'll get over it?" Sam asked. "Forgive?"

"The Gospel of Mary says..."

"Mary Magdalene's gospel?" Sam asked with a raised eyebrow. "Be thee not a Puritan?"

"Very funny," Em said.

Sam laughed.

"The Gospel of Mary says that Mary Magdalene was betrayed by Peter," Em said. She raised an eyebrow, and Sam nodded in agreement. "Peter was her friend and someone she thought of as a brother. Yet, she was forced to leave her home with her children to escape his wrath."

Sam nodded.

"We were betrayed by people we've long outlived," Em said. "They believed that *we* were the evil and *they* were benevolent."

"Like Mary Magdalene's betrayal," Sam said. "To Peter, the 'rock' from which the church was founded, she was just a whore who seduced his savior. To the good people of Danvers, we were witches — *we* rotten to the core — even though *they* were the ones who accused and hanged innocent people for their property and power."

"Exactly," Em said.

"It's more than a little ironic that we are actually witches now." Sam pulled into the Walgreen's parking lot. "What did you do to Ann Putnam, Senior?"

"Who?" Em scowled.

"Her husband?" Sam asked.

"I'm not sure who you mean," Em said.

"Fine," Sam said as he parked in the far back of the pharmacy parking lot. "What did you do to Tituba?"

"I paid off her jail fees," Em said. "My husband, Isaac, bought her from that loathsome Parrish."

"And then what?" Sam asked.

"Then nothing," Em said. "We thought she'd go back to her husband, Indian John, but she didn't want to have anything to do with him."

"Why?" Sam asked.

"She was disgusted at the way he lied," Em said. "He was in cahoots with the evil men who hurt her. Indian John testified against almost everyone, including her. He didn't help her get out. She felt betrayed by him."

"The word of the day is 'betrayal,'" Sam said.

Em nodded.

"Where did she go?" Sam asked.

"We put her on a boat back to Barbados," Em said. "We gave her what money we could spare. John Willard saw her when he was a pirate. By then, she'd lived a full, happy life. She had married again and was a grandmother. After everything that had happened, she deserved it."

Sam nodded.

"Feel any better?" Em asked.

"I'm glad I'm not alone in my... pain," Sam said.

"You're definitely not alone," Em said. "In our own ways, we each feel the pain of betrayal. I don't think any of us has really gotten over it."

"Bridget?" Sam asked with a smile.

"Bridget?" Em asked. "Not a chance. You should have seen her on her hanging day. She was so sure that those 'poor girls' were tortured by something real."

"Better to believe that than feel the full force of being betrayed," Sam said.

"Exactly," Em nodded.

"What do you think it will be like for Rebecca, George Jacobs, and John Proctor?" Sam asked.

"No idea," Em said. "I'm hoping we'll be able to put John to rest. There's a record that his family took his remains and reburied them. But you remember his family."

Sam nodded.

"His wife, Elizabeth, was convicted, like Proctor was," Em said. "She was pregnant, so they didn't hang her with us. While she was still in jail, Proctor's children from his other wives grabbed everything he owned — land, house, even the bed they slept in — with that forged will. They fought tooth and nail over the estate for years. I can't imagine that they would have had the time or inclination to move John's remains. If Elizabeth was out, maybe she would have rallied her family to help. But, given the chaotic state his family was in when he was hanged, I don't believe they retrieved and reburied him."

"You think they just *said* that they reburied him," Sam said.

"When they heard about Rebecca and George. Sure." Em nodded. "You remember what John's older children were like."

"Bitter that the new wife got the goods," Sam nodded.

"I think John's been there the whole time," Em said. Her face filled with sorrow.

"Why didn't he come back when we did?" Sam asked.

"I don't know." Em shook her head. "I fear that he did, and he's stuck there, or. . ."

She shook her head.

"It's not your fault, Em," Sam said.

She gave him an unconvinced nod. George drove up in the Suburban and parked next to Sam. She turned her head to look at him, and he rolled his eyes. He gestured to the back. Weni was sitting right behind him. Em grinned.

"We have help," Em said.

Sam leaned over to look up.

"Who *is* that guy?" Sam asked. "I had a long talk with

him about what it meant to be a man. Incredible conversation. He had insights dating all the way back to the early Egyptians."

"He's the elders' librarian," Em said.

"I thought you couldn't be in the same time as any other elder," Sam said. "How can he be here and you be here?"

"I don't know," Em said. "Let's ask him."

She grinned at Sam, and they got out of his truck.

Chapter Nineteen

"This area," George said, "right here, used to be a part of Gallows Hill."

George gestured to the small road he was standing on. Dressed in their Puritan finery, the witches gathered around him. Weni walked over to stand next to Em.

"According to the old maps, we were buried near this location," George said.

"It is kind of you to let him share your discoveries and your plan," Weni said in a low voice.

"He's better at this," Em smiled.

When she was in the elders' library, she had reviewed every map ever created for this small spot on the planet. Her father thought she'd lost her mind. He thought she should be researching the edges of human knowledge, not where she had been buried. She'd just smiled and continued her research. She hoped it would pay off here at Gallows Hill. Glancing around, she saw that they were drawing curious eyes. She whispered a spell so that if anyone outside their group heard them talk, it would sound like a language they almost understood, but they would have no idea what it meant.

"You remember what it looked like," George said.

"It was a hill," Margaret said as she walked around

George. "There was water and giant oak trees."

"Exactly," George said.

"It wasn't over there?" Martha Carrier asked as she pointed to the spot they'd used to mark the hanging anniversaries.

"Close," Sam said. "It was always close but not exact."

"The closest we could come," Em said.

"That's exactly right," George said. "But in order to find Proctor, we must be exact."

"You know, I haven't been here in. . ." Susannah started.

"Three hundred and twenty-two years?" Em asked.

Susannah blushed and nodded. Alice put her arm around Susannah's waist.

"I'm sure you're wondering what happened," George said. "The railroad built a line right where I stand. Like they do, they blew a path through Gallows Hill."

"I was on that crew," Sam said.

"I was with you," George said. "I never even noticed. Em, with the help of Weni, found a railroad map that shows the destruction of Gallows Hill. And I can tell you: If there were human remains here. . .?"

George shrugged.

"We would have built right over them," Sam said.

"The US railways are a graveyard of the men and women who worked the railroad," George said.

"You're saying that John was blown up?" Bridget asked.

Surprised to hear her voice, they turned in the direction of her voice.

"Sorry, I'm late," Bridget said.

"How did you get here?" Em asked.

"I parked at the houses and walked in." Bridget gestured

to the hiking boots on her feet. These were the same hiking boots Em had given her at Gungywamp. Mary Ayer hugged Bridget to welcome her. "I wanted to see the whole area. And I'd say that George is right. This is the outer edge of where we were buried."

Bridget smiled and nodded.

"Why are you dressed like that?" Bridget asked. "Should I..."

Em used her left hand to point under her right armpit. There was a small, but growing, crowd of people standing close enough to see what was happening but far enough away not to get hurt if they were crazy.

"I brought yours," Em said with a "do it now" raise of her eyebrows. "It's in Sam's truck."

Sam held up the keys. Bridget took the keys and went to change behind the darkened windows of his vehicle.

"Where was I?" George asked.

"The railroad," Margaret said.

"As I said, the railroad blasted through here to create a line," George said. "This road was built over the rail line. In fact, it's highly likely that the rail is still here."

"And John?" Elizabeth asked. Her voice was laced with horror.

"The railroad piled everything over there," George pointed to the hill behind him.

"Oh, I get it," Alice said. "That hill wasn't here."

"They moved it to put the rail line here," George said as he gestured to the road. "That means that John must be there."

Em felt a shiver run down her back. She turned to see Bridget get out of Sam's truck in a drab Puritan dress with her characteristic red bodice. She grinned when she showed Em her boots under the dress. Em smiled at Bridget. Feeling a draw, she looked past Bridget. The man claiming to be John Parker, and the demon who lived inside him, was standing among the crowd. With her look, the transparent image of the demon's face appeared over the young man's face. Em shivered and turned back toward the hill. George was pairing up the witches to search for John's remains on the hill behind them.

"Your look brings him out," Weni said in a low voice. "He is called by you as you are called by him."

"I didn't call him here," Em said.

"Then why are you wearing this costume?" Weni asked. Without turning around, he said, "The child of your line is with him."

"Shonelle?" Em asked.

Em whipped around to see John Parker put his arm around Shonelle. The girl kissed his lips, and Em winced. Seeing Em, the young girl ran to her.

"Why didn't you tell me you were dressing up?" Shonelle asked. She picked up a piece of Em's skirt. "This is horrible."

"Historically accurate," Em said.

"What?" Shonelle asked.

Em whispered a spell so the girl could understand her.

"This is what the Puritans wore," Em said.

"How awful for them," Shonelle said. "Do you have an extra one for me?"

"Sure," Em said. "Sam?"

Sam was standing with Margaret. They were getting instructions and a map from George. He looked up when she called.

"Shonelle wants to wear one of these horrible dresses," Em said.

"Hey, Shonelle," Sam said.

"What did he say?" Shonelle asked. "My ears must be full of wax today."

"He just said 'Hello,'" Em said.

Shonelle waved. Martha Carrier and Alice headed in the direction of the embankment where they usually commemorated the hanging.

"There's an extra dress in your truck," Em said. "Shonelle can wear it. Do you mind?"

Sam threw the keys to Em. She gave them to Shonelle. After a look at their map, Susannah and Elizabeth started down the road, away from the Walgreen's parking lot.

"We're just about to head out," Em said. "You'll have to hurry if you want to go with us."

Shonelle jogged toward Sam's truck.

"We'll wait for you," Bridget said to Shonelle.

Shonelle turned to look at her. She shook her head that she didn't understand what Bridget had said.

"Hurry!" Em said again. Shonelle waved at Em's order.

"You made the dress. . ." Mary Ayer started.

"It's too big," Em said with a smile. "Funny how that happens."

Mary Ayer smiled. George called Mary Ayer and Bridget over to him. Dressed in her drab Puritan finery, Shonelle brought Em Sam's keys. She twirled around to show the shirt while Em and Weni applauded. Sarah Wildes glanced at Em, who nodded in agreement and freed Sarah Wildes' words, before asking Shonelle if she'd like to join her in the quest. Shonelle looked relieved that she was with someone she could understand. Shonelle glanced at John Parker, who waved her on. He smiled at Em and turned to go.

"What was that?" Em asked.

"The man has needs the devil cannot understand," Weni said.

"And that means?" Em asked.

"He has to urinate," Weni said.

Em smiled.

"You're with me," George said. "Is that okay?"

"Can we bring Weni?" Em asked.

"Of course," George said. "We're going straight up here. Is that too much?"

"Lead on, young Reverend!" Weni said.

They scrambled up the embankment. Em paid special attention to any tingle or sensation that might indicate John Proctor was buried nearby. She heard a whistle from just south of where they were. Using magic to hear, she and George cupped their ears.

"We've found a bit of the oak tree that hanged us," Susannah said. "It looks like the original tree was burned, maybe by lightning strike. There are three or four trees that came off the stump maybe a hundred years ago. Each bears the distinctive stench of our hanging."

"That's very good," Weni said.

"But nothing of John?" Em asked in a magic-enhanced normal voice. She cupped her ear again.

"Not a shred," Susannah said.

"You remember the trees were a ways away from where they dumped us," Elizabeth said.

"True," Em said.

"We'll mark it and keep looking," Susannah said.

"Thanks," Em said.

Em looked at her map for a moment. A dot appeared with the marking "hanging tree". She showed the mark to George and Weni, who nodded. They continued hiking up the hill. Weni was light on his feet and soon took the lead. On more than one occasion, George turned to pull Em up behind him.

"Stupid dress," Em muttered.

"You can always take it off," George said with a wiggle of his eyebrows. She kissed him as she passed, and he patted her rear.

"Remind me again why we are doing this," Weni said.

He turned in place to face Em and George.

"Why do we look for the remains of this John Proctor?" Weni asked. "You call him. . .?"

"Proctor," George said. "He ran a popular pub. Everyone called him by his last name."

Weni nodded and glanced at Em.

"Why do we. . ." Weni started to ask again.

"When we talked to the spirit of George Jacobs, he said the demon had awakened them from their slumber," Em said. "He said that they can't stop us if we all fight together."

"They were awakened by the demon," Weni nodded. "Why must they remain awake?"

"They're unable to slumber," Em said. She felt her frustration rise.

"You need this Proctor to help fight the demons?" Weni asked. "This is what this spirit said?"

Em nodded.

"You were there, Reverend?" Weni asked.

"I was," George said.

"And you also knew this George Jacobs as well as this 'Proctor'?" Weni asked.

"And Rebecca Nurse," George said with a nod. "She came back with them."

Weni gave a curious nod. A tree stump appeared next to him, and he sat down. He took out a long-stemmed churchwarden's pipe made of rich cherry wood. With a wave of his hand and a puff of his cheeks, smoke began to rise from the pipe. The sweet, pungent pipe tobacco seemed to heighten Em's senses and speed up her thinking.

"What if they won't come back?" Weni asked.

"I don't think that matters," Em said.

"Of course, it matters," Weni said. "It is the *only* thing that matters."

"I just touched them before, and they came back," Em said.

"But not against their will," Weni said.

"No," Em said. "Most of them didn't want to be here. They've resented me ever since."

"No!" Weni jumped to his feet. He waved the pipe in front of her face. "I am instructing you, Martha of Truth. You must hear this truth. These witches, your friends — they could not have come back unless every fiber of their being wanted to return."

Em blinked. She glanced at George.

"That's true for me," George said. "I wanted to be with you with every fiber of my being."

"You reached out to them with the power of love, which is the power of all life," Weni said. "If they didn't want love, if they didn't want life, they would not have return. They made the choice to return. And so it was."

"But..." Em started. Weni stopped her protest with a wave of his pipe.

"The only person who had no choice was you, Martha of Truth," Weni said. "Only you were *required* to return, due to your blood lineage."

Em shook her head as if she couldn't believe it.

"You didn't want to come back?" George asked.

"Uh..." Em said. She glanced at Weni, and he nodded to encourage her. "I was exhausted. I felt as if the core had been ripped out of me when you died. I had looked forward to a long sleep and a conversation with Jesus. I didn't know you or any of them would come back, George."

George gave her a soft smile.

"This is your father's fault," Weni shook his head. "In that way, it is my fault."

He patted her hand.

"I apologize for my harsh words and attitude," Weni said and sat back down on the stump. "I did not realize how much you do not know. Tell me again. This spirit stated that they had been awakened. He believed that, if you found the third, they would all come back — or you made that up."

"How did you know?" Em asked.

Weni waved his pipe as if her question was irrelevant. He gave a deep, chest-rattling cough before he started puffing again.

"Yes," George said. "He believed that, if we found John Proctor's remains, he and Rebecca would rise."

"Your fear is?" Weni asked.

George shook his head and shrugged. Em blushed and looked away.

"Martha of Truth?" Weni asked.

She looked at him, and he nodded to encourage her again.

"That's a spell, isn't it?" Em asked.

"It is," Weni said. "Does it work?"

"Yes," Em said. "I am afraid that John has been alive all this time but is trapped under the dirt for more than three hundred years of horror."

"Ah," Weni said. "Wouldn't that be awful?"

"Yes, it would," Em said.

"He is not alive now and has not been alive," Weni said. "Does this George Jacobs want to return to life?"

"I don't know," Em said.

Weni gave an exaggerated sigh and puffed on his pipe. George and Em gawked at the man. Finally, he rolled his eyes up as if to implore the heavens.

"You can ask him," Weni said.

"How?" Em asked. "The witches are scattered."

"Yes, I wondered about that," Weni said.

"What do you mean?" Em asked.

"I wondered if your demon was going to attack your witches while they were wandering this hill," Weni said.

"He cannot," Em said.

"You have protected them?" Weni smiled.

Em nodded.

"I did, as well," Weni said with a little chuckle. "Well, let's ask this George Jacobs."

"How?" George Burroughs asked.

"Turn your palm over, Reverend," Weni said.

George held his hand palm side up.

"Demand his presence," Weni said.

"How?" George Burroughs asked.

"State his name," Weni said. "You are his minister and his friend. You have his allegiance. You only have to demand his attention."

"Oh," George said. He cleared his throat. "George Jacobs."

A seven-inch high apparition of George Jacobs appeared on George Burroughs' hand.

"Reverend?" George Jacobs asked.

"I'm wondering if you'd like to return to Earth in human form," George Burroughs asked.

"Or wander in this grey?" George Jacobs asked.

"Good question," George Burroughs said. He looked at Weni. "Can he be put to rest?"

"Of course," Weni said, with a flourish of his pipe.

"Did you hear that?" George Burroughs asked.

"I can be put to rest or come back," George Jacobs asked. "I don't mean to be difficult, but I wonder if I am put to rest — will I be brought back?"

"No," Weni said.

"He says 'No,'" George Burroughs said.

"Who said, 'No'?" George Jacobs asked.

"Em's teacher," George Burroughs said.

"Em's teacher?" George Jacobs asked.

George nodded.

"All right, Em's teacher: Why do you say we cannot be revived after being set to rest?" George Jacobs asked.

"You were placed after death — is that correct?" Weni

asked.

"Yes," Em said.

"I don't know," seven-inch-high George Jacobs said.

"Then your remains were taken by your family and buried," Weni said.

"That's correct," Em said.

"And moved again," Weni said. "Isn't that correct?"

"Yes," Em said.

"He was never put to rest," Weni said.

"What does that mean?" George Burroughs asked.

"He was placed by his tormentors in a mass grave," Weni said. "He was pulled away by family who buried him in secret, without ritual. Then, his physical remains were discovered and reburied. Where is the rest?"

"I think he's saying that we can put you to rest, if you'd like," Em said.

"Rebecca as well?" George Jacobs asked.

"Of course," Em said. She glanced at Weni and he nodded.

"If it's all the same to you," George Jacobs nodded, "I'd rather rest. I was a grandfather when I was hanged. If I were a young man, I'd relish the adventure. But for now, I'd rather just rest."

"Done," Weni said and hopped to his feet.

"Thank you," George Jacobs said. He gave a little bow and disappeared.

"We have work to do," Weni said.

George and Em didn't move. They looked at him. Weni gave them a toothy smile.

"What work, Weni?" Weni asked in an exact imitation of Em's voice. "Martha of Truth, you only have to ask.

First, we need to find this John Proctor and ask him the same question. If we find him, we will put his soul to rest, and then call the universities. They will spend a few decades arguing with each other. That will keep the demons away."

Weni smiled.

"What do we do next, Weni?" Weni asked in an exact imitation of George's voice. "We will find this George Jacobs and give him what he has asked for. And this Rebecca? We will give her peace as well. Good thing you're wearing your finery."

Weni tapped out the ashes from his pipe. He looked at George and then looked at Em. Hopping to his feet, he took off into the forest.

"Come along," Weni yelled after them.

Em sprinted after him. She ran about ten yards when she found him standing in the cover of the trees. She checked herself and stopped fast. George stopped next to her. They were standing on the edge of a clearing. Before them stood the young man, John Parker. He was waving his hands in the air and calling out to the sky. Demons of every shape and size circled him like a murder of crows over carrion.

Across the clearing, the trees shook as if struck by a violent wind. Bridget and Mary Ayer came to an abrupt stop. Martha Carrier and Alice stopped next to them. Margaret and Sam stopped short of entering the clearing on their right. Sarah Wildes was looking at the map when Shonelle came within a foot of the clearing. Sarah Wildes grabbed Shonelle before she stepped into the clearing. Shonelle saw John Parker and tried to get free.

"Give her sight," Weni said.

Shonelle saw the demons for the first time. She squelched a scream and threw herself into Sarah Wildes' arms.

"Forget," Sarah Wildes whispered.

Shonelle stopped shaking in Sarah Wildes' arms. Sarah gave Weni a dark look. He shrugged at her concern.

"This *is* an Indian burial ground. No wonder you were frightened!" Sarah Wildes said. Shonelle stepped back. Sarah Wildes led her away. "You have a real knack for this. You must be intuitive."

"Em's said that before," Shonelle's voice came back to the clearing. "I've heard it runs in my family."

The witches stared at each other in silence until Sarah Wildes and Shonelle were away from the clearing.

"What's he doing?" George asked Weni.

"He is trying to capture your John Proctor's soul," Weni said. "Is there anything special about this soul?"

"Not that I know of," Em said.

George shook his head.

"What did he do in life?" Weni asked.

"He owned a pub," George said.

"He farmed large tracts of land," Em said.

"Nothing else?" Weni asked.

"Anyone?" Em whispered. "Is there anything special about John Proctor?"

From across the clearing, the witches shook their heads. Weni stared at the man in front of them.

"Huh," Weni said. "This John Parker is very . . ."

Em turned to look at the man.

"Inept," Weni said. "It surprises me. He is the last of his kind, the leader of an army of demons, and he cannot wield a simple spell."

Weni took a breath and pushed Em out into the clearing. Em tried to scoot back to protection, but Weni blocked her way.

"We meet again," John Parker said.

Em turned around to look at him.

"I am in your ear," Weni said.

Em nodded that she'd heard him.

"Were you looking for this?" John Parker asked.

He raised his arm. He was holding the spirit of John Proctor by the throat.

"I found him," John Parker said. "He is now ours!"

He lifted John Proctor's spirit over his head. The demons screeched with glee at the sight of the spirit of John Proctor. Dark clouds began to gather overhead.

"What are you going to do about it?" John Parker asked. Em didn't move or say anything. "I see that you're intimidated. I'd be intimidated, too."

"Don't make me come and get him," Em said in a soft voice.

John Parker gave her a taunting laugh. The demons screeched an even more evil laugh. Em started to smile.

"You can't do anything about it," John Parker laughed.

Em grinned and took a step toward him.

Chapter Twenty

Feeling movement behind her, Em turned to see Alice step to her side.

"Give no place to this devil!" Alice shouted a verse from Ephesians in the Geneva Bible. She took another step toward John Parker.

Much to Em's surprise, the rest of the witches moved in a circle toward John Parker, as well. Em took another step, and the witches followed. The demons howled. Dark storm clouds blotted out the clear summer sky. The wind whipped through the clearing, leaving a heavy mist in its wake.

"Put on the whole armor of God, that ye may be able to stand against the assaults of the devil." To encourage them, George quoted Ephesians 6:11 at the top of his lungs.

Lightning cracked. Freezing rain began to fall from the sky. Alice hooted.

"I've spent my entire life preparing for this fight!" Alice yelled with glee. She pointed at John Parker. "Get behind..."

"...me, Satan!" the rest of the witches joined in Alice's quote of Matthew 16.

John Parker screamed with rage. George laughed. Mary Ayer clapped her hands with glee. Em looked from face to face. Her witches were enthralled. As Alice had said, their Puritan background had prepared them for a battle with Satan. Em felt an overwhelming sense of gratitude for her friends. John Parker and his demons did not know what they were in for.

"Thou art offensive to me!" the witches said in unison. Em joined in, "Because thou understandest not the things that are of God."

"Go on, Em," George yelled.

"We've got your back!" Elizabeth yelled.

Em set out across the clearing. The wind buffeted, and the freezing rain pummeled Em. The fog deepened until she could see only the grey contrast of the young man's outline. She filled her left hand with light and raised it over her head.

"You do not frighten me!" John Parker yelled over the wind. "You cannot destroy me!"

The light in her hand reflected off the fog, transforming everything into shimmering white. John Parker was invisible. She doused the light.

"Take up your shield of Faith," George yelled another line from Ephesians 6 to encourage her. The others joined him in quoting, "wherewith ye may quench all the fiery darts of the wicked."

Martha Carrier began singing the Puritan hymn "My Refuge Is the God of Love" by Isaac Watts. Her lone voice was joined by Susannah's before she finished the first line. The other witches joined in. While they sang, Em continued to move through the fog. She'd reached the area where John Parker had been holding John Proctor's spirit when they finished the song.

"Be strong, Em." George's voice came to her through the fog.

The witches cheered. A sharp crack of lightning cast a flash of gleaming light in the clearing. When the dark returned, Em saw that John Parker was standing less than a foot from her. She stepped back.

"I have captured his soul," John Parker screamed over the wind. Holding John Proctor's spirit by the neck, John Parker raised the ghost above his head. "And he will live in hell forever!"

"John?" Em asked.

"What?" John Parker and John Proctor asked at the same time.

"Sorry, young man," Em said. "I was speaking to my friend, Proctor."

John Parker sneered and lunged at her. Em stepped aside with ease. She opened her right hand and put John Parker into a restful sleep. She waited until his eyes closed before turning to her friend.

"Em?" John Proctor asked.

"It's me, Proctor," Em said. "We were transformed into immortal witches the night we were hanged."

"I recall," John Proctor said.

"You do?" Em asked.

"You asked me if I wanted an immortal life," John Proctor said.

"I did?"

"You don't remember?" John Proctor asked.

"No," Em shook her head.

John Proctor's mouth bent into a smile. With John Parker's hand tight around his throat, Proctor's face and bald head looked like a hand-drawn face on a flesh-colored balloon. She scowled.

"I was dozing when I saw the light," Proctor said. "Your light. It was bright behind my eyelids. When I opened my eyes, I heard your voice ask me if I'd like to return."

Shrugging, Em shook her head. When the young man holding John Proctor's spirit growled, Em looked up at him. John Parker's eyes had rolled back into his head, and he was foaming at the mouth. Em glanced at the others. Their faces held their horror and concern for the young man.

"I said 'No,' of course," Proctor said.

"Why 'of course'?" Em asked.

"Three wives? Seventeen children?" Proctor asked. "The never-ending bickering between my older children and my beloved Elizabeth? Not to mention the Godforsaken pub and that worthless Thomas Putnam trying to steal my land! I fought with him for years over that land. A few lies from his evil daughter and wife, and the land was his. All of my hard work lost to that lying... Let's just say that I was ready for a long rest and a much-deserved visit with my Lord."

"I hear you," Em said.

"Are you here to remember?" Proctor asked.

"No, Proctor," Em said. "I have an issue with a demon or two."

"Is that what's happening?" John Proctor's eyes looked up. "That's a lot of demons."

Em nodded.

"Did you take care of Putnam for me?" Proctor asked.

Em gave him a curt nod.

"Are you coming back?" Em asked.

"Not if I can help it," Proctor said. "Can you. . .?"

"Done," Em said. She smiled. "We're settling George Jacobs and Rebecca Nurse tonight. We'll take care of you, too. After tonight, you should rest in peace. I'm sorry it has taken us so long. We didn't know you were here."

"Better now than never," John Proctor said. "You're a good friend, Martha Corey. Thanks."

"It will be my pleasure," Em said. "My only hope is that you rest in well-deserved peace."

"Can you release me from this idiot?"

Em snapped her fingers. As if his hand had been burned, John Parker's fingers popped open. John Proctor was released from his grasp. The demons dove toward Proctor's spirit. Em clapped her hands, and Proctor disappeared.

"This is between you and me!" Em turned to face her demon. "Not them."

She pointed at the demon, and the demon gave an evil laugh. John Parker started screaming at the top of his lungs. He clutched his head and fell to the ground.

"What is it?" Margaret yelled.

"Looks like some kind of stroke!" George said.

The young man writhed on the ground. Em tried to kneel down to help him but met her demon instead. The demon rose up and pushed Em off her feet. She fell back on her rear. The demon towered over her. The demon's presence threatened to overwhelm her.

"Put on the whole armor of God," George's voice came from some faraway place.

Em gawked at the horrifying demon.

"You are a witch," the demon said. "Your powers can change stone into bread and even revive the dead. You are not of your God. You are of me. And I say to you, my child, come with me, and we shall be as one."

Em felt tears well in her eyes. She felt the gaping overwhelm of being betrayed by her friends and townspeople. She felt her own impotence. Mostly, she felt completely and totally alone.

"Why did you take my family, my kin?" Em asked the first thing that came into her mind. Her voice rose, and she asked again, "Why did you kill every single one of them?"

Shaking with rage, she got to her feet.

"Why did you take all of them?" Em asked

"Who?" Her demon looked confused. "Who?"

"Why did you take my entire family?" Em asked. "Everyone like me?"

Her demon shook his head at her. Em's rage pulsed through her veins.

"You will never take me," Em said. "You will never take my witches. You and your kind will leave this Earth and never come back."

The demon was so surprised that it moved back.

"If this is your response, you have already lost, child," the demon said. "You are the last of your kind."

"My kind grows every day," Em screamed at the top of her lungs. With her words, the fog began to clear. The demon began to fade. "Kindness, love, and peace reign throughout the world. You control only the tiny, dark corners of this world. I will see your reign ended. I will see you removed. I will. . ."

The demon was gone. The sun peeked through the clouds. The clearing was calm, quiet, and beautiful. The witches ran to help John Parker. Em's hands dropped to her knees. She bent over and fought for breath. She felt a small hand on her back. She looked to see who it was just as Sam started CPR on John Parker. Martha Carrier was on the phone with Emergency Services.

"You did well, Martha of Truth," Weni said. "Better than I'd have thought."

Em gave him a slight nod and looked down at the dirt.

"I have one question," Weni said. "Who are your people?"

"I belong to the world," Em said. "All people are my people."

"Good," Weni said. "That is very good."

"I have a question," Em said. She stood straight and stretched her neck.

"Yes?" Weni asked.

"Where did the demon go?" Em asked.

Weni shook his head in a gesture of "I don't know."

"My question is a little different," Weni said.

"What's that?" Em asked.

"In all of my years, I've never seen a demon capture a weak human such as this boy," Weni said. "Never. Why did he take this young man? And who will he take next?"

Em nodded.

"I fear this which feels like a victory is actually a devastating loss," Weni said.

"How so?" Em asked.

Weni opened his mouth to respond. His mouth hung open for a moment before he closed it. He touched Em's arm to move her out of the way of the emergency medical technicians rushing into the clearing. When she stepped near him, he spoke in her ear.

"We'll talk later," Weni said. "For now, I need to do some research."

Much to her surprise, the slight man disappeared. Em looked around to see if anyone had noticed. Seeing no one, she watched the paramedics carry John Parker out of the clearing. George helped Sam up. The witches looked at each other and then at Em.

"What's next?" George said.

"We bury our friends," Em said.

"What about calling the university?" George asked. "This morning you said that if we found Proctor, we'd call the university to keep the demons away."

"I said. . .?" Em shook her head. "No, Weni. . .?"

"Who?" George asked. He put his hand on her shoulder and looked into her face. "Are you feeling all right? That was quite a battle with the demon."

"But Weni. . ." Em said.

George hugged her tight.

"It will be dark in an hour or so," George said to the group. "Let's get some coffee and wait. We can get John and bury him at Rebecca's home. Put them at peace."

"Great idea," Sam said.

"They have pie at the shop downtown," Alice said.

"I've marked the location on my GPS," Margaret said.

"Then it's settled," George said. "We'll have coffee and pie before returning to this exact location tonight."

"I'm famished," Bridget said.

The witches began to move toward the parking lot. Em

stood in the clearing for another moment.

Why hadn't George known who Weni was? Was Weni a figment of her imagination?

She looked down at the ground and spotted something unusual. She knelt down. Pipe tobacco. She picked it up and held it to her nose. It smelled like the type Weni smoked. She tucked the tobacco into her pocket. Alice put her arm over Em's shoulders.

"I thought you were brilliant," Alice said.

Em smiled. She stopped to look back when they'd reached the edge of the clearing. The ghost of Martha, George's transgender friend, stood over John Proctor's grave.

"Never forget," Martha said to Em. "You're Martha of Truth. You know what is true — not the demon, not the librarian, not even George — only you."

Em nodded to Martha. She glanced at Alice. Exhilarated by "vanquishing the demon," Alice had been talking this whole time. A quick glance told her that the others were equally excited.

"I'm sorry, Alice," Em said.

"Don't be sorry!" Alice said. "You know how excited I get about pie!"

Smiling at Alice, Em continued on out of the clearing. She was about to start down the hill when Em looked back. Martha was gone.

On July 19, 1692, Rebecca Nurse, Sarah Good, Susannah Martin, Elizabeth Howe, and Sarah Wildes were hanged as witches on Gallows Hill. Because Rebecca wasn't with them now, and Susannah had been living in Pennsylvania, they rarely got together to acknowledge this hanging. Caught between her guilt over her daughter Dorothy and her rage at what happened, Sarah Good usually sulked alone in DC. Elizabeth and Sarah Wildes often spent the day working with underprivileged children.

Em was determined that this year would be different. She asked everyone to meet her at the graveyard at the Rebecca Nurse Homestead before dawn. Twenty-five acres of Rebecca's historic homestead and her colonial home were now open to the public. Em had asked Sam to pick up Sarah Good and Alice to bring Susannah. She and George brought Elizabeth and Sarah Wildes with them. They arrived within minutes of each other.

A barn owl hooted at them from a tall oak.

"Spooky," Ann Pudeator said.

"Just an owl." John Willard pointed at the bird in the tree.

Margaret and Mary Ayer giggled nervously. The rest peered up into the tree to see if they could spot the owl.

"You'd think it was haunted!" Alice said.

Everyone laughed. Bridget pulled in, with Giles in her passenger seat.

"We brought..." Bridget started. She was equally as excited as she was deeply embarrassed. She scooted around her SUV rather than complete the sentence. She opened the back to show five large bouquets of flowers.

"We made them last night from flowers from our garden," Giles said.

He gave them a wide smile and picked up a bouquet. He

gave it to Elizabeth.

"My dear, you are simply the finest human being I know," Giles said to Elizabeth.

Tears fell down Elizabeth's face. She nodded her thank-you. He took another bouquet from the car. He hugged Sarah Wildes.

"You are simply the finest human being I know," Giles said to Sarah Wildes.

He kissed her cheek. She put her nose into her flowers to keep from crying. He selected another bouquet and walked to Sarah Good.

"Sarah, I've known you a long time," Giles said. "I can only say that you are simply the finest human being I know."

"What about... Elizabeth and Sarah and...?" Sarah Good argued.

"I'm a doddering old man who celebrates only the finest things in life — such as you," Giles said. Giles gave Sarah Good a soft smile. "I've seen you suffer for Dorothy. She's at peace now. You deserve to love this life because..."

"I am the finest person you know?" Sarah Good asked.

"Exactly," Giles said.

Sarah Good hugged Giles tight. When they separated, Sarah Good's face was wet with tears. Not one to stand on formality, Susannah grabbed Giles and hugged him tight. They spoke quietly to each other. When they separated, they both looked like they'd been crying. Giles took a bouquet from Bridget and gave it to Susannah.

"We have one last one for Rebecca," Bridget said.

"We're here to put Rebecca, George Jacobs, and John Proctor to rest," Em said.

"I thought we did that already," Mary Eastey said.

They had spent the last couple of days working with their friends' remains. Half of the witches had worked to energetically cleanse Rebecca, George Jacobs, and John Proctor's physical remains to remove all vestiges of cruelty and injustice related to their hanging. The other half of the witches cleansed their friends' souls. It was hot, sweaty work. When they finished, they'd used magic to set their friends remains at peace in the graveyard on the Nurse Homestead.

"We did the work of it," Em said. "Now we need to give them to God."

The witches smiled and nodded.

"We should do it in our old clothes!" Alice said.

Everyone transformed into their Puritan dress. Laughing and talking, they made their way to the graveyard. They formed a circle around their friends' graves. Em nudged George to hurry up.

"It will be dawn soon!" Em said in a low tone.

This morning's dawn would provide the light to finally set their friends to rest. Smiling at Em's impatience, George went to the center of the circle.

"Let's begin," George said.

Chapter Twenty-one

"For a moment," George looked from person to person, "bring to mind all that you know about Rebecca, George Jacobs, and John Proctor. Remember the good times and the bad. Remember when we knew that we couldn't save them?"

His spell caused them to slip back in time. Em found herself standing in the Boston jail. She simply couldn't believe that they would hang these women. Sure, they had hanged Bridget a little more than a month ago. But would they really hang these pious women? Em couldn't wrap her mind around it.

They had been strangers when they were thrown in jail together. Now they were closer than family. Em had watched helplessly while the lecherous guards abused Elizabeth and Sarah Good one last time. When guards had finished, they had pushed Elizabeth and Sarah onto the open wagon. A crowd of vicious spectators had begun to form around the cart. Susannah went to the cart next. Even with Sarah Wildes' help, Rebecca had moved too slowly. One particularly awful guard had dragged the addled woman onto the cart by her hair.

The cart had jerked and tipped. The women in the back had knocked into each other, and the more than three hundred people in the jail became hysterical. Em had screamed with rage. A few people had confessed to witchcraft on the spot. Wilmot had fainted. Giles had ranted like a madman. Martha Carrier had screeched with rage. George had tried to lead everyone in a prayer, but George had been out shouted by the guards. The crowd of bystanders had pelted the women with rotten fruit and awful words. As if to encourage the crowd's abuse, the cart had crept through the muddy streets. Weeping, Em had watched until the women were long out of sight.

She blinked, and she was back at Rebecca Nurse's homestead. Looking around the circle, she saw that everyone had been lost in their memory of that awful day. Susannah was silently weeping. Elizabeth, who looked caught in her own private hell, leaned against Sarah Good.

"Come back," George said. "Come back to the present."

He waited until everyone was back from the past.

"We can only remember the past," George said. "We cannot change it. In the present, we know peace. We know love. We know our Lord. Peace be with you."

"Peace be with you," the witches said.

"It is time to set our friends Rebecca Nurse, George Jacobs, and John Proctor to their final rest," George said. "Peace be with them."

"Peace be with them," the witches repeated.

"Rebecca Nurse." George said her name, and the spirit of the woman appeared. "You are loved. You are remembered."

The spirit of Rebecca Nurse rose from her grave and hung in the air. The elderly woman looked from face to face.

"Mary?" George nodded to Mary Eastey, Rebecca Nurse's younger sister.

"Sister," Mary Eastey said. "I love you and wish for you the silence of the sweetest rest in the bosom of our Lord."

"My dear Mary," Rebecca smiled. "I love you, too."

"Go," Mary Eastey said. "Be at peace."

"You are at peace," the witches said in unison.

The spirit of Rebecca Nurse closed her eyes. Her translucent spirit began to fade until it was mist.

"George Jacobs." George said his name, and his spirit appeared as a translucent image of the man.

"Bless you for this," George Jacobs said. "I long to see my Lord and my beloveds. I yearn to be at peace."

"You are loved, George Jacobs," George said. "You are remembered."

"You are at peace," the witches said in unison.

"Love to you and yours!" George Jacobs raised his hand in a wave before fading away.

"John Proctor," George said, and John Proctor's spirit appeared.

Smiling from ear to ear, John Proctor looked from face to face. He nodded to encourage George to get on with it.

"You are loved," George said. "You are remembered."

"You are at. . ." the witches started.

The charcoal-grey hand of Em's demon reached up and grabbed John Proctor's shoulder. The witches gasped, but John Proctor laughed. He lifted the demon's hand from his shoulder and stood face to face with the horrifying creature.

"I don't choose you," John Proctor said. He nodded to Em. "My friend Em taught me to have power over you! I *choose* light. I *choose* love. I am no longer confused."

"Everyone!" Em yelled.

"We have to complete the spell," George said. "John Proctor, you are at peace!"

"You are at peace," the witches repeated in unison.

"Bless you, friends," John Proctor said.

Like George Jacobs and Rebecca Nurse, his specter faded. He gave one final wave before he was gone. In the grey light of the breaking dawn, they saw that the demon had remained.

"You have no hold here," Em said. "Be gone."

"Be gone!" Alice said.

"Be gone!" the witches said.

The demon snarled at the witches before turning his malice to Em.

"You *will* deal with me," the demon said.

"But not today," Em said. She held her right hand in front of her. "Be gone!"

The demon vanished, and the witches cheered. As if to punctuate their cheer, the first of the sun's rays rose over the horizon. The witches turned toward the sun only to see a Fox News van pull into the homestead parking lot. Em groaned.

"We should keep. . ." Margaret said.

She pulled on her clothing. Em nodded. The reporter scrambled toward them.

"We're not doing anything wrong," Giles said.

He walked to Rebecca's grave and laid the flowers there. Bridget knelt down at the grave to say a prayer.

"What are you doing here?" the reporter asked.

"What are you doing here?" George asked. "This is

hardly the day or the place for mocking the dead!"

Elizabeth, Susannah, and Sam moved toward their cars.

"If you'll excuse me," George said.

He put his arm around Em, and they walked toward her car.

"Hey! You own the Mystic Divine!" the reporter persisted. "Don't you?"

Rather than answer, they kept walking toward Em's car. Em whispered a forget spell. For a moment, the reporter watched them go. The cameraman yelled at the reporter, and he trotted back to the graveyard. The others managed to make it to their vehicles unscathed.

Standing at the passenger seat of her Land Cruiser, Em looked back at the graveyard. Using her senses, she used her intuition to energetically scan the graves. Rebecca Nurse was at peace. Em sighed with relief. George Jacobs was also at peace. Em nodded. Holding her breath, she scanned John Proctor's grave. He was at peace. Nodding to herself, she got into the SUV.

She was just putting on her safety belt when she saw the demon. He was standing under an oak tree with a barn owl on his shoulder. He was watching the reporter talk about the day. When he noticed that she was looking at him, the demon shook his head at her.

"You will not win," Em heard the demon say, as clearly as if he were standing next to her. "You will join me in the end."

Em closed her eyes to avoid looking at the demon. George started the car, and they drove away from Rebecca Nurse's homestead. Turning onto the road, George clicked on the radio.

"Ever wonder what's behind your local pharmacy? Boston University has announced that it has found at least some of the remains of the Salem Witches on a small strip of land owned by the railroad behind the Danvers Walgreen's. BU plans to excavate the site in conjunction with UMass and Harvard. As you may know, today is the three hundred and twenty-second anniversary of. . ."

Clicking off the radio, George grinned at Em.

She smiled.

"Where to?" George asked.

"Sarah Wildes insisted on having the party at her house," Em said. "She wants to use today as a celebration of life, not the celebration of her hanging."

"A day in the country," George said. Sarah Wildes lived on a five-acre horse property outside of Walpole. "Nice."

He glanced at her. His eyebrows rose with anxiety.

"Is she cooking?" George asked.

"Sarah Good's chef," Em said.

"Perfect," George said with a smile.

She grinned at him, and he drove to Sarah Wildes'.

Truth be told, Em loved summertime. George was home. The store was busy. The sun came up early and stayed up well after any reasonable bedtime. The temperature was warm. It was muggy enough to curl even Em's magic-straightened hair. And everything was just right.

After Em's recent death in Jamaica Plains, George decided to show Em a few of the many places he'd died. They camped on the Boston Harbor islands, visited unmarked revolutionary war sites, and went to the Indian frontier in Maine. Sometimes they were joined by other witches; more often than not, they were alone. At each location, George reenacted his death scene, which never failed to leave Em laughing so hard that she gasped for breath.

July slid unnoticed into August. The long, warm days pushed them out of the building and onto the roof at night. They built bonfires and ate s'mores with Alice and Susannah. They spent whole sun-drenched days laughing and spent entire nights watching the Perseid meteor shower batter the world.

But when Friday the 15th rolled over into Saturday the 16th, George began to shut down. As she did every year, she tried to engage George with the things he loved — great food, good friends, and fun times. By the end of the week, he was too withdrawn to speak. There was nothing she could do. He pulled the blinds to the apartment and closed the shutters of his mind. He didn't leave their bed.

On August 19, 1692, the bastards in Salem Village had hanged Reverend George Burroughs. More than three hundred years later, he still couldn't believe it. There wasn't anything Em could do to make it better. This year, he had shut down in a way she'd never seen.

Monday night, August 18, he took himself to bed at six. She'd wrapped herself around him and held on tight. Sometime around three in the morning, she woke to his body shaking with silent sobs. She held on while he wept.

He hadn't cried the night before he was hanged. He'd not cried even one tear any other year. He wept uncontrollably tonight.

She'd never felt more helpless. She tried to surround him with her love and hold on. Sometime around the edge of dawn, he finally fell asleep.

An hour later, John Willard and Martha Carrier arrived. Their faces were tear stained and their voices husky. George dragged himself from the bed to be with them. They took one look at him and began to weep. Em guided them to their living-room couches, and they settled in.

She brought them tea, which stayed in the pot until it was cold. She made their favorite scones, which they didn't eat. She turned on music, which went unnoticed. As if they were in a trance, they held each other's hands and grieved for their catastrophic betrayal all those years ago.

The other witches checked in with Em over the course of the day. She turned away Alice and Susannah. Wilmot dropped by with her wonderful cookies, which went uneaten. She let Mary Eastey in the apartment. John Willard looked up at her for a moment before returning to his gloom. After a while, Mary Eastey joined Em in the kitchen.

"What do you think. . .?" Mary Eastey whispered.

"I think it just caught up to them," Em said. "Maybe. Honestly, I have no idea."

"Do you think it's the demon?" Mary Eastey asked.

Em shook her head and then shrugged.

"I don't know," Em said. "You?"

Mary Eastey shook her head.

"They seem to be sad," Em said. She turned to look at Mary Eastey. "Have you ever let yourself be sad about what happened?"

Mary Eastey gave Em a long look before she shook her

head. Em gave her a compassionate nod.

"What can we do?" Mary Eastey echoed what each of the witches had said.

"Pray for their peace," Em said. "They are strong. They will get through this. But for now, we have to pray for their peace."

"Easy," Mary Eastey said.

She gave Em a partial smile. Em put her arm over Mary Eastey's shoulder. When they returned to the living room, John Willard moved over. Mary Eastey went to sit next to him. She took John Willard's hand to support him.

When the afternoon slipped into the evening, George got up from the living room. He went to the bathroom and took a shower. Martha Carrier came into the kitchen, where Em was hiding. After nodding to Em, Martha Carrier got a glass of cold water from the filter in the refrigerator door. She leaned against the kitchen counter and took a long drink of water before looking at Em.

"I would love some coffee," Martha said. "Will you make me something yummy? It will be my first 2015 post-hanging meal. John?"

Martha went to the doorway of the living area to ask John Willard. He looked up when she said his name.

"I would love some coffee," John Willard said. He took the glass of water from Martha Carrier's hand and drank it down. "And something ridiculously wonderful."

"Full of calories and carcinogens and fat," George said.

He came into the kitchen wearing his robe. Martha left to use the bathroom. George hugged Em hard.

"I love you," George whispered in her ear. Em kissed his cheek. "And I'm starving."

"Me, too," John Willard said.

Martha Carrier came from the bathroom, and John went to use it. Mary Eastey joined Em in the kitchen. Martha went into the bedroom to call her boyfriend, Bruce.

"I didn't know you were the cook," Mary Eastey said, as Em started pulling food out of the refrigerator.

Em gave her a sly look, and Mary Eastey laughed.

"Okay, I should have figured," Mary Eastey said. "I just always thought it was George."

Em shrugged. When the pot of coffee was made, Mary Eastey brought a cup to John Willard and Martha Carrier before getting one herself. They stood in the living room drinking coffee until the call to the open air was too much for them. They went up onto the roof. George joined her in the kitchen.

"Any idea what's happening?" Em asked.

"With what?" George asked.

"*With you!*" Em retorted. "You spent most of the day in a funk. John Willard and Martha Carrier, too."

Scowling, George nodded but didn't respond.

"I've known you a long, long time, and I've never seen you like that," Em said. She raised her eyebrows as a way of asking the question again.

"I can just tell you how it felt," George said. "It felt like the clouds moved in and wouldn't leave. It felt like Salem Village."

George poured himself a cup of coffee and set the mug on the counter.

"No," George said. "It felt like all of the dread and hope and pain and fear and loss and rage was compressed into that final moment — the moment I hanged from that oak tree."

He poured milk into his coffee.

"Sounds horrible," Em said. "Do you think it was a spell?"

George was drinking coffee when she asked the question. He thought about it for a moment and finished his cup. He didn't respond until he'd filled his cup again. Em started making another pot of coffee.

"It feels like a lack of a spell," George said. "You know, like we've been under a spell this whole time, and now we're not. I was overwhelmed with the monstrosity of what they did — to me, to you, even to themselves. Their ancestors bore the shame of what they did to us."

"Some still do," Em said.

"We suffered, sure, but their actions marked the rest of their entire lives," George said. "They could not out live the horror of what they did. Their children and grandchildren lived with that shame."

Em nodded.

"I mean, I knew that Nathaniel Hawthorne added the 'w' to his name out of shame over what happened," George said.

"His great-great-grandfather judged us as witches," Em nodded. "Sent us to the gallows."

"Exactly," George said. "Ann Putnam, Jr., never married. As you know, her parents were tortured and killed right after the trials. The other girls were married off just to get rid of them."

Em nodded.

"We were hanged under the evil cloud of greed and

depravity," George said. "But everyone involved — the entire community! — had to live with the shame, whether they were involved or not."

"They changed the name of Salem Village to Danvers to avoid association with the trials," Em said.

"That's what I mean," George said. "I knew that, but it never really sunk in. I guess I was too caught up in my own suffering."

"And this morning?" Em asked. "How did you feel?"

"I felt so sad for all of us," George said. "It's like this entire thing happened to each of us — accuser, judge, and accused, not to mention the community as a whole. The evil of the deed continues to linger."

"And now?"

"Now, I'm just happy to be here, right here, with you," George kissed her forehead. "Thank you."

"For what?" Em asked.

"For being there for me and asking for nothing in return," George said. "It was the kindest, most generous thing anyone has done for me."

George hugged her and kissed her. Standing nose to nose, she felt his arousal. He kissed her lips.

"They went upstairs," Em said.

"Do you mind if I stay here with you?" George asked.

"Not at all," Em said. "But I should probably cook."

"Gives me something to look forward to," George kissed her again. "I'll get dressed so you won't be tempted."

He gave her a lecherous look, and she grinned.

"Why don't you call the others, and we'll celebrate life-after-hanging tonight?" Em asked.

With a nod, he went back into the bedroom. When he

returned, he sat down at the kitchen bar and began calling the witches. By the time he'd finished, the meat was marinating, the vegetables were ready for the grill, and the party was well underway. George followed her upstairs.

Chapter Twenty-two

Em scowled at the paycheck in her hand. This employee had worked almost sixty hours at the Mystic Divine. Her thumb traced the employee's name: Weni Uni. The paycheck was one of the few artifacts Weni had left behind.

No one remembered him.

The assistant manager who hired him had no memory of the slight man with an Egyptian accent. George thought she had imagined him. Even Shonelle, who'd spent three days training him on how to work the cash register, couldn't remember what he looked like. Everyone said the exact same thing: "I never remember the short-timers. They come and go in the summer." Then they gave an exaggerated shrug.

Em was sure it was a spell. She just wasn't sure who had cast it. Shaking her head, she was just putting the check in her desk drawer when there was a tap on the doorframe of her open door. Em closed the drawer before looking up.

"Yes?" she asked.

A middle-aged man with white hair and a round head was standing in her doorway. He had a blue ballpoint pen tucked over his right ear, and there was a blue ink stain on his right hand. He sported a worn, but clean and pressed suit under a beige overcoat. He was holding a pad of paper in his hand.

"Detective Shane Donnell," the man said. "You Emogene Peres?"

"And if I am?" Em asked.

"Well, first, I'd want to know why your partner George thinks your name is Martha," Detective Donnell said.

"He's an idiot?" Em gave him a broad smile, which made the detective blush.

She got to her feet and waved the detective into her office. She was just closing the door when a younger man pushed his way into the office.

"Alvarez," the young man said. "Had to park the car."

He stuck his hand out for Em to shake, which she did. She waved him into the other chair in front of her desk.

"You didn't ask why we're here," Detective Donnell said.

"I assume you're here to discuss the woman who died in the Common Burial Ground," Em said. "Is that so?"

"Sort of," Detective Alvarez said. Detective Donnell gave him the evil eye, and Detective Alvarez said, "Sorry."

Em raised her eyebrows and shrugged. The young detective chuckled.

"Sir?" Em asked.

"So I did some digging. . ." Detective Donnell said.

He gave her a stern look designed to frighten her. Em smiled at him.

"Vegetable garden?" Em asked. "I envy you. I don't have any real land here. I have to keep mine on the roof. No digging involved."

"I did some digging into you," Detective Donnell said.

"Me?" Em was genuinely surprised. "Whatever would

possess you to do that?"

"For starters, your body was at the morgue," Detective Donnell said.

"My what?" Em asked. She looked down at her chest. Looking up, she shook her head and shrugged. "What was it doing there?"

"It was dead," Detective Alvarez said with a nod.

Detective Donnell gave him a dark look.

"Security cameras cover every corner of the morgue," Detective Donnell said. "We have a video of the attendant wheeling your body into the morgue."

"I take it that my body is no longer there," Em said.

"No, it's not," Detective Donnell said. "We don't know what happened after that. When the body went missing, we took a photo off the security camera and ran it through facial recognition. You'll never guess what we came up with."

"What?" Em asked.

She knew she should shut this conversation down, but she couldn't help but be amused by the sincere detective.

"The body was yours," Detective Donnell said.

"It was?" Em looked down at her body and back at his. "Where was I when my body had this little adventure in your morgue?"

"We talked to Rabbi Isaac Peres," Detective Donnell said, rather than answer her question.

"My grandson?" Em asked.

"Yeah, like you have a grandchild," Detective Alvarez said. "You're like forty years old. You think we're stupid?"

"Um..." Em looked from Detective Donnell to Detective Alvarez. "I realize that I have no idea what we're talking about."

She leaned forward across her desk.

"Do I need a lawyer?" Em asked.

"At the same time Martha or Michael — or whatever you want to call him — was dying, your body was in the morgue," Detective Donnell said.

"Or a body that looked like mine on your cameras," Em said. She gave them a partial smile. "Did you get a clear picture of my dearly departed doppelganger?"

Em knew that even her dead body would short out the video cameras. Whatever picture they had of her would be grainy at best. Detective Donnell gave her a sour look.

"So, you have a body that disappeared, and you decided it was mine because. . ." Em said

"We ran it through facial recognition," Detective Donnell said. "Your driver's license came up."

"God, that poor family," Em said.

"What family?" Detective Donnell asked.

"The family of the person who was killed," Em said. "You know, the body you lost."

"I didn't lose a thing," Detective Alvarez said.

Detective Donnell looked at his partner.

"I never lose nothing," Detective Alvarez said.

Detective Donnell rolled his eyes.

"Well, I don't," Detective Alvarez said.

"I believe you," Em said.

Detective Donnell and Detective Alvarez shared a look. Em gave them their privacy by focusing on tidying her desk. Detective Donnell cleared his throat, and Em looked up.

"So I did some digging," Detective Donnell said.

"To bury the body?" Em asked with a smile.

Detective Donnell gave her an appreciative grin before turning back to his page.

"When did you purchase this building?" Detective Donnell asked.

"We rent it from a corporation," Em said. "Uh... Salem 20. Why?"

"This building was built by an 'Emogene Peres,'" Detective Donnell said.

"Okay," Em said with a shrug. "I share a name with the woman who built this building. Is that against the law?"

"I spoke with Rabbi Peres," Detective Donnell said again.

"And?" Em asked.

"He's not a very good liar," Detective Donnell said.

"He's a Rabbi," Em said. "From a long line of rabbis. Is he supposed to be a good liar?"

Detective Donnell looked down at the page open in his notepad and sighed.

"You're not an easy woman," Detective Donnell said.

"Am I supposed to be?" Em asked. "You came into my business and are asking me silly questions about... well, I don't know what. Why don't you get to the point so I can get back to work and you can get on with your day?"

The detectives stared at her.

"I won't lie to you," Em said. "I'm incapable of it. Ask me what you will."

"What are you? A gospel woman?" Detective Alvarez snorted. "You know, like..."

He looked at Detective Donnell, and the older detective gave a rueful shake of his head. Em blushed. She stood up from her desk.

"Thank you for your time, gentlemen," Em said. "Now, if you'll excuse me, I'm going to get on with my day."

"We're not done," Detective Alvarez said.

"Yes," Em said with a smile. "But I am. If you need anything else from me, my lawyer will be more than happy to help. You can call him to make an appointment. For now. . ."

Em's door opened, and George stepped inside.

"I heard you were looking for me," he said. He looked from Detective Donnell to Detective Alvarez. "What can I do for you gentlemen?"

George's physical presence added to the intensity of the moment.

"Gentlemen?" George repeated.

He stepped back to indicate that they should leave Em's office. Detective Alvarez glanced at Detective Donnell, who nodded. The younger detective left the office. When George looked at Em, she shrugged. Detective Donnell stayed rooted into his seat.

"Detective?" George asked.

Detective Donnell looked at George.

"I believe I am the one you came to speak to," George said. "Would you like to come with me?"

"In a moment," Detective Donnell said. "I need to speak with Ms. Peres."

"Em?" George asked.

Em nodded. George gave Detective Donnell another strong look, which the detective missed by focusing on his pad of paper. George left the door wide open before leading Detective Alvarez away from Em's office. Em listened to George and Detective Alvarez chat in the hallway.

"You're going to want to close the door," Detective Donnell said.

"Why would I want to do that?" Em asked.

"Because I know who you are," Detective Donnell said.

"Who am I?" Em asked.

"Martha Rich Corey," Detective Donnell said.

"From Salem Farms?" Em asked with a grin. "Tried as a witch and hanged on Gallows Hill on September 22. We're having a sale for the anniversary of her hanging. We have sales once a month in the summer to celebrate each of the hangings. And Giles Corey's death by pressing, of course."

Em grinned. The detective gave her an even look.

"You can't be serious," Em said.

"You don't deny it," Detective Donnell said. "Your man is Reverend George Burroughs, isn't he?"

"His name is George Burroughs," Em said with practiced ease. "You do know that the good Reverend had a lot of children, all of whom lived here in the Boston area."

"But you don't deny it," Detective Donnell said.

"I'm beginning to believe you've lost your mental faculties," Em said. "What do you want?"

The detective looked Em full in the face. His eyes seemed to draw in her features.

"You don't look like your pictures," he said.

"My driver's license?" Em asked.

"No, the drawings of you," he said.

"I'm sorry," Em said. "I truly have no idea what you're talking about."

Detective Donnell nodded.

"Maybe if you walk me through it?" Em asked.

"When I spoke with George, he said that he knew what death looked like from his experience at war and in the winters here," Detective Donnell said. "I got curious and wondered what war George Burroughs had been involved in."

"Okay," Em shrugged.

"He's fought in almost every war as far back as the Indian wars," Detective Donnell said.

"You mean that someone named George Burroughs fought in every war," Em said. "If I had to hazard a guess, there are probably more than one George Burroughs who has fought in wars throughout history. It's a very common name."

"This George Burroughs," Detective Donnell said. "The man who was standing in your office just a moment ago."

"And you know this. . ." Em scowled. "How?"

The detective gave a vague nod.

"Are you feeling all right?" Em asked. "Is there someone I should call?"

Shaking her head, Em looked at the man. Every fifty years or so, someone put the pieces together and confronted her about being Martha Corey. Half of the time, they had to pack up and head to the island. The other half of the time, Em was able to convince the person that they were imagining things. She had a sense that the detective was leading up to something. She let him talk.

"I'm pretty sure you didn't come here to talk to me about George and wars or Martha Corey or anything else," Em said. "Please, speak plainly to me — what is it that I can do for you, Detective Donnell?"

He looked at her and squinted.

"Detective?" Em asked.

"I can prove that you are the person who built this building," Detective Donnell said.

"Okay," Em said.

"I can prove that you and George and the rest of your friends are immortal!" Detective Donnell said with growing fervor.

"And?" Em asked. "Is there a law against any of this?"

"No, but..."

"There is a law against slander, Detective," Em said.

The detective's face flushed with frustration. He shook his head.

"Out with it!" Em ordered.

"Do you know who Lydia Dustin is?" the detective asked. "*Remember* — for you, I'd guess it would be *remember*. Do you *remember* Lydia Dustin?"

The image of the Boston Jail flashed before her eyes. Lydia Dustin had arrived at the Boston Jail on the same day as George. Prison life was hard on Lydia. The constant torture and abuse broke her will to live. She was deeply humiliated by the spectators. She'd barely survived to Em's hanging day. The next year, Lydia was released, but she was unable to pay her board for the time she was in prison. Em had been on her way to pay Lydia and her granddaughter Sarah's fees when she learned that Lydia had died. She covered her sorrow at the memory with a confused look.

"Who?" Em asked.

"Lydia Dustin," Detective Donnell asked.

"Uh..." Em shook her head and shrugged her shoulders.

"Fine," Detective Donnell said. "I am a descendant of Sarah Dustin. You probably *remember* her from the Boston Prison. . ."

"Okay," Em said in an even tone.

". . . she was my ancestor," Detective Donnell said. "You probably know that Lydia and Sarah were found not guilty in January 1693, after a new trial."

Detective Donnell raised his eyebrows.

"I'm not all that familiar with the specifics." Em repeated the script she'd spent decades practicing. "As I said, we use the Salem Witch Trial hanging dates as an excuse for a sale. We are a mystic store, after all."

The detective shook his head and started digging around in his pockets. He checked his pants pockets and the one in his shirt. Then he checked his suit pockets. Finally, he leaned to his left to get to the bottom of his right overcoat pocket.

He pulled a silver pictish cross from his pocket. The cross was thin and showed obvious hammer marks. A classic pict serpent was carved into the cross itself. It was hung on a thin, sixteen-inch silver chain with two paired circles of silver interlinked with each other. Grasping it by the chain, he held the cross out to Em.

Em's fingers itched to snatch the cross away from him. She forced them to stay still.

"According to family legend, Martha Corey gave this cross to Lydia Dustin the day she was hanged," Detective Donnell said. "After her grandmother died, Sarah used the cross to pay off her and her mother's debts. Sarah used it to get out of prison."

"How do you have it?" Em asked.

"Sarah married one of the prison guards," Detective Donnell said. "He got it back for her as a wedding gift."

Em tucked her hands into her pockets to keep from reaching for the cross. Her father had found the cross in one of the ancient burial sites on Rousay. He'd given it to her on her tenth birthday. She'd secretly worn it under her garments the entire time she had been a Puritan. Because this kind of ornamentation was forbidden, no one, not even her husband Henry or George, knew that she wore this cross every day.

Detective Donnell let the cross swing in front of her. She bit back her rising desperation that this man had her cross. But there was no way she was going to let him see her desire. She had learned her lesson from the Salem Witch Trial examiners. Silence and restraint were the best policy with the police. She braced her very being against showing any interest in the cross and chain.

"The family rule is that if any of us ever finds Martha Corey, we are obligated to give this cross back to her," Detective Donnell said. He leaned over Em's desk and let the cross fall onto the center of her desk blotter. "You see, Sarah saw you long after the witch trials were over. You and Alice were walking together down a street in Charleston. Sarah knew you were immortal."

"Okay," Em said. She didn't dare move.

"There's a whole bunch of thank-you's and stuff we're supposed to say to Martha of Truth. I won't bore you with it," Detective Donnell said. "We're supposed to also say, 'Only you know what's true.'"

"What did you say?" Em asked. Em was stunned to hear Detective Donnell say the same words Martha the ghost had said on Gallows Hill.

"It doesn't make sense to me," Detective Donnell said. He mistook her shock for indignation. "I had to get this from my great-aunt Florence. She made me repeat it after her and write it down. It's something Lydia learned and wanted Martha Corey to know."

He held up the notebook. Em was too stunned to do anything but nod. He got up from his seat and walked to the door. At the door, he turned around to look at her.

"I don't care if you're immortal," Detective Donnell said. "As you said, it's not illegal. I don't care if you and George and John Willard and whoever else are witches. I don't even care if you fly around on brooms. The broom thing might be illegal, but I'm not in traffic. What do I care?"

Detective Donnell nodded and turned to leave. Em reached for the cross. He turned at the door. Her hand hung in the air.

"You don't have to run off," Detective Donnell said. "You can trust me."

Em nodded.

"I want to be able to ask if I need some help," Detective Donnell said.

"Why would you need my help?" Em asked.

"Something's coming," Detective Donnell said. He gave a curt nod of his head. "I don't know what, and I don't know why, but I know in my gut that something's coming. I may need a group of witches on my side."

"If I can be of service, detective, I'm happy to help," Em said.

He nodded.

"I can't promise witches or immortality," Em said. She

smiled as if she'd made a joke.

He waved away her words and continued down the hallway to George's office. She didn't dare touch the cross until she heard him call to Detective Alvarez. She listened with witch's ears until they left the building.

With a sigh, her fingers stretched out to touch the cross. She felt a pulse of love run through her. She was standing at her desk with her hand over the cross when Bridget came into her office.

"Em?" Bridget's voice edged with concern. "Are you okay?"

"Sure." Em looked up. She tucked the cross into the watch pocket of her jeans. "Why?"

"You were just standing there, like you're in a trance," Bridget said. "I said your name from the door."

Em nodded.

"What is it?" Bridget asked.

Em pulled the cross from her pocket. She held it out for Bridget to see.

"It's something my father gave me when I was little," Em said. "I wore it all the time. I gave it to Lydia the night before I was hanged."

"You dirty girl!" Bridget brightened with delight. "And here I thought I was the only one who liked to wear pretty things. Where'd you get it?"

"That Boston Police detective."

"Wow," Bridget said.

Em smiled and tucked the cross back into her pocket. She looked up when Bridget closed Em's office door.

"I wanted to talk to you about something," Bridget said.

"Okay," Em said.

"You know about Giles and me?" Bridget asked.

"Giles's young bride came into the store a while ago," Em said. "She told me that Giles was all mine. She was leaving town with some young stud. He seemed like a moron to me, which I told her. She got angry and left."

Em raised an accusing eyebrow at Bridget.

"She reeked of magic," Em said. "Someone cast a spell on the poor girl."

"I. . ." Bridget started.

"Then, of course, you two made those lovely bouquets for Susannah, Elizabeth, and Rebecca's hanging. You had one for Martha on her hanging as well." Em smiled, and Bridget blushed. "Will you make one for me next week?"

"Em!" Bridget gave a little stamp of her feet.

"Why don't you tell me about you and Giles?" Em asked.

"When you were dead, we were all at Sam's house," Bridget said.

"Uh-huh," Em said with a grin.

"Then, I got to show everyone around and. . ." Bridget nodded. "You have no idea what a profound effect that had on me. I realized that I wasn't just some fluffly little girl who men need to take care of, and. . ."

Bridget swallowed hard.

"Giles, he. . ." Bridget said.

"I'm just giving you a hard time," Em said. "Giles told me all about it at our weekly breakfast."

"Oh," Bridget said. "What did he say?"

"He said that he realized how much he enjoyed your company," Em said. "Over the last few months, he's found you to be smart and fun. The sex is really good. He's sorry he waited so long to spend time with you."

Em nodded.

"He's smitten," Em said.

"I am, too!" Bridget said with a smile. "I mean, he was always your curmudgeon husband who everyone had to put up with. Now, I see that he can be very kind and steadfast. I guess I value his steadiness more now that I'm almost four hundred years old. I have my own fortune, so we're on equal footing, which he says he likes."

"I'm happy for you both," Em said.

"I am, too," Bridget said. "I need to ask you something."

"Okay," Em said.

"We want to get married," Bridget said. "Really married, by George, with everyone around us."

"Giles told me," Em said.

"I'm wondering if you would divorce him," Bridget said.

"I'm sorry, Bridget. That's simply something I cannot do," Em said.

Chapter Twenty-three

Bridget was so surprised by Em's words that she took a step back.

"What?" Bridget asked.

"I cannot divorce Giles," Em said. "I'm sorry."

"But you don't love him!" Bridget said. "You have George, and. . ."

Bridget crossed her arms, and her head moved forward.

"You don't even love him," Bridget said.

"Not romantically," Em said.

"I love him," Bridget said. "I want to spend the rest of my eternity with him. We are so happy together."

"I know," Em said. "I am thrilled to see that you two have found your way to each other. I couldn't be happier."

"But you won't divorce him?" Bridget asked.

"I can't," Em said. "Does Giles know you're here?"

"No," Bridget said.

"What did he say when you asked him to divorce me?" Em asked.

"I. . . uh. . ." Bridget's cheeks flushed red. Her eyes welled with unshed tears. "I thought he'd want to divorce you to be with me!"

Em gave Bridget a soft smile.

"Why?" Bridget asked. "Why won't you divorce him?"

Em bit her lip and looked away from Bridget.

"It's not a sin!" Bridget said. "It's not like what we said it was when we lived in Salem. It's just a fond parting of the ways! You've already done that. This would make it official."

Em winced and looked down at her desk.

"Please," Bridget reached across Em's desk and took her wrist. "Tell me why."

Em looked into Bridget's desperate face. She closed her eyes against the sight and then nodded. Opening her eyes, she gestured for Bridget to take one of the chairs in front of her desk. She went around her desk and sat in the other.

"We hadn't met until we were in the Boston Jail," Em said.

Bridget nodded.

"What did you know of me?" Em asked.

"I knew about you and the Reverend," Bridget said. "Very salacious stuff, but then everyone wanted to be his lover. We were all just jealous that he was so very in love with you."

Em nodded. She took a breath to speak, but Bridget interrupted her.

"You had that son," Bridget said. "Everyone said you had 'questionable' morals. But my friend Clara said that you had been attacked by Indians. She said your husband was sick so you had to do everything for your family, and that meant you were vulnerable."

Bridget nodded. Em opened her mouth again to speak. Bridget leaned forward.

"Which was it?" Bridget asked.

"None of your business," Em said with a shake of her

head. "Plus, we're not talking about me. We're talking about Giles."

"You can tell me, Em," Bridget said with an ardent nod.

Em scowled.

"Fine," Bridget said.

"After Henry died, I was left with two young sons — Thomas and Benoni," Em said. "Thomas was almost of age, but Benoni was a young child."

"Benoni," Bridget said with a nod. "That was his name. He was wonderful after we were hanged. He used to bring food to the barn. He was our rock that first year."

"Ever wonder why he did that?" Em asked.

"No," Bridget said. "I never did."

Em grinned because, of course, Bridget never thought to question the good fortune that had come her way.

"He and George really hit it off," Bridget said. "Is he George's?"

"Bridget!" Em said. "Stay on track here."

"Oh, sorry." Bridget did her best to pretend to be contrite. "What does this have to do with you not divorcing Giles?"

"Giles came to me after Henry died," Em said. "He was nearly eighty years old. His daughters and their husbands had taken responsibility for the farm. He needed someone to care for him, someone who wouldn't tattle to the world that he was ill."

"Giles was ill?" Bridget asked.

"He was old and a little loopy," Em said. "He'd spent his life breaking the land and fighting the Indians. His body was sore, broken, and his mind going. He kept getting confused and a couple of times stole items he was sure were his own. He didn't want his family to know that he was losing his faculties. He saw merchants and business-people moving into our sleepy town. He feared that his weakness would destroy his children's chances at life in the new world."

Caught in the memory, Em looked away.

"He asked if I would care for him as I had Henry," Em said. "In return, he would allow Benoni to live with us and find him an apprenticeship when he was of age. He also would pay for Thomas to go to Harvard."

"Your sons," Bridget said in a tone of dawning understanding.

"He kept his word," Em said. "Benoni helped you and all the witches because Giles had been such a great father to him. And the pressing. . ."

"He allowed himself to be pressed to death for you," Bridget said.

"He wouldn't have lasted the year," Em said. "Especially without me to take care of him. Most people believe he refused to participate in the trials to save his land from being seized, but his children had already taken ownership of the land. It was never in question, but. . ."

"Thomas and Benoni," Bridget said.

"My sons would have lost everything," Em said. "Giles and his daughters treated my sons like they were their own kin, even to the very end. Because of Giles, Benoni grew up to be a fine young man. He and George went to England, where he went to school. Benoni returned with wealth and status. When he married, Giles's daughters put on the celebration. Their children called him 'Uncle.' And, Thomas graduated from Harvard. He went on to be a successful member of Giles's family. Giles's daughters didn't leave Thomas to live out a half-life because his father was dead and his mother deemed a witch. They made him a part of their family because Giles insisted that he was a part of his family. They were one, seamless family."

Bridget nodded.

"I made a solemn oath that I would take care of Giles Corey as long as we both shall live," Em said. "I'm sorry, Bridget. I won't go back on that oath."

Bridget caught Em's eyes. Bridget gave a little nod.

"Plus, do you really want to keep track of his farm?" Em asked with a smile. "You want to be responsible for the garden sales? His taxes? Making sure he gets in to see Ann every year?"

"I..." Bridget said.

"Wouldn't you rather leave all that stuff to me?" Em asked. "You get to enjoy being his fun life partner in everything, except his care."

"What does George think of this?" Bridget asked.

"He understands," Em said. "He says that I wouldn't be who I am if I thought anything differently."

"But..."

"Bridget, the man was *pressed* to death to save *my* sons," Em said. "He needs me to look after him, and, for the rest of our lives, I will do just that. That doesn't mean you can't spend from now to eternity as his loving partner — just not his caretaking wife."

Bridget looked down at her clasped hands.

"Do you understand?" Em asked.

Bridget nodded.

"And?" Em asked.

"You're right," Bridget said. "I don't want to keep track of the garden or make sure he gets to the doctor or any of that crap. I want to have fun. I want to travel and laugh and... enjoy. That's the thing, Em. Neither of us has really enjoyed the gift of this life. We want to drink deep of all this life has to offer — together."

"You know that he's an alcoholic, right?" Em asked.

"Of course," Bridget said. "But you know what I mean."

"I do," Em said. She gave Bridget a warm smile. "You said you wanted to have a real wedding."

"We were thinking of having it on September 22," Bridget said.

"My hanging day?" Em winced.

"It's your hanging day," Bridget said. "But it's also our return-to-life day. Alice thought of having the celebration, and it's her hanging day, too!"

Em nodded. For the last week or so, Alice had been trying to catch Em alone to talk, but Em had been too busy.

"Ann and the Marys are in," Bridget said. She leaned forward, and, in a low voice, she said, "I wouldn't be surprised if John and Mary joined us in getting married."

Bridget beamed at Em. When Em didn't respond, Bridget continued on.

"We want to have a formal affair — ties, tuxes, formal dresses, lots of flowers, great food," Bridget said. "Alice says we should celebrate vanquishing that demon. And you know? She's right."

"Mmm," Em said. She felt like she'd taken Giles's place as the group curmudgeon.

"We've hired a jazz band and..." Bridget flushed with joy. Em grinned at her. "I was supposed to pretend that we hadn't planned anything, but it's all set up. We're having it in the ballroom at my house."

"On my hanging day?" Em asked. "A week from Monday?"

"I knew you would fuss for a while but then give in," Bridget said. "You always do."

"Mmm," Em repeated. She added a scowl just to show that she was not a pushover.

"Please?" Bridget asked. When Em didn't respond, she reached out to touch Em's hand. "You'll have the morning. You and the others can spend the morning together. We'll get together in the evening to celebrate our love, our amazing lives, and the destruction of the demon."

Em winced and looked away from Bridget.

"We spent our whole lives getting ready for a battle with the demon," Bridget said. "And when the challenge came, we did not back down. I was so scared that I was shaking. But we vanquished all of those horrible demons. They are gone; and we're still here."

Bridget gave an emphatic nod.

"We should celebrate," Bridget said.

"It sounds like you're going to no matter what I say," Em said.

"If you said not to do it, we wouldn't," Bridget said. "You know that. We'd be sad, but we'd know it was for the best."

Bridget let go of Em's hand and leaned back.

"Are you saying 'No'?" Bridget asked.

Em didn't respond.

"I knew it!" Bridget got up from her seat. She gave Em a little wave. "I'll tell everyone."

Bridget was out of Em's office. A moment later, George appeared in her open doorway.

"What was that?" George asked.

"Bridget and Giles want a ceremony," Em said.

"They asked me to marry them," George said. "John and Mary, too. I was going to talk to you about it tonight."

Em nodded. George squinted at Em.

"You okay?" George asked.

"Just a lot on my mind," Em said with a smile.

George nodded.

"You know..." he started. He stopped and swallowed hard. Knowing what he was going to ask, Em smiled. Understanding her smile, he nodded and said, "Let's talk about it tonight."

"Deal," Em said.

George's name was paged on the overhead speaker. He pointed to the sound and left her office. She got up and closed the door. She went around her desk and sat down. For a moment, she stared off into space.

Had they vanquished the demons? While Em wanted to believe that they had, she couldn't help but wonder. There was no evidence that they had destroyed the demons. There was also no evidence they hadn't.

The young man, John Parker, lingered somewhere between life and death. She had no idea why that mattered; she only knew that it did. And, she hadn't seen hide nor hair of the demon. No tingling feelings that he was around. No sense of demonic presence. Nothing.

Her demon seemed to be gone. Em just wasn't sure if it

was gone for good or just gone for now. Em wanted to be sure.

She took the cross out of her pocket. She said the prayer her father taught her when he'd given her the cross. The prayer converted the cross into a dowsing pendulum. Em stood up and pushed her chair back.

Holding onto the chain, Em hung the cross over the blotter. If the demons were gone, the cross would pull to the north, which was away from her, toward the top of her blotter. If the demons were still around, the cross would pull to the south, which was toward her and her chair.

She swung the cross in a wide circle over her blotter.

"Have we destroyed the demons?" Em asked.

The cross swung easily around the circle. It was starting around the circle again when it seemed to pause. The cross shot to the north. Before getting there, the cross shot to the south.

"Be clear," Em commanded.

The cross moved to the center line. Shaking her head, Em sighed. She stared at the cross for a moment. Even before she was a witch, this pendulum had always worked for her. Of course, this cross wasn't in her possession for some three hundred years. She made a fist with the hand holding the chain and pressed it against her forehead. Shaking her head at herself, she knew she had to try one more time.

"Maybe the question is too vague," Em said under her breath.

She held the cross by the chain again. With her other hand, she started it moving in a wide, open circle.

"Is my father alive?" she whispered.

The cross shot to the southern position. *No*. Em gasped in horror. The demon had been correct. She was the last of her kind. Swallowing hard, she gritted her teeth against the pain that shot through her heart. She started the cross in a circle again.

"Should I marry George?" she asked.

The cross swung evenly around the circle until it pointed to the north. *Yes*. Em grinned at her girlish question. Feeling brave, she formulated the question she needed an answer to. She started the cross swinging in a circle.

"Are all of the people like me gone?" Em's voice cracked when she said the last word.

The cross didn't hesitate. It shot straight to the north position. *Yes*. Em took a quick breath to keep from sobbing. Rather than think too much, she swung the cross and asked the next question.

"Does my demon still exist?" she whispered.

The cross shot to the north position. *Yes*. Em swallowed hard and started the cross swinging.

"Are all of the demons still alive?" Em asked.

The cross moved to the north position. *Yes*. Em felt as if the bottom had fallen out of the world. The demons had already won. There was no reason to bother fighting. The demons had killed all of her kin. They would always win.

She held the cross over the blotter to ask one last question. Swinging it in a circle, she swallowed hard before asking:

"Will I find a way to win against the demons?"

The cross shot to the north position. *Yes*. Em smiled.

Then she realized that she'd received a number of "yes"

answers in a row. She needed to check the pendulum. She thought for a moment before coming up with a question with a "no" answer. She started the cross in a wide circle.

"I'm pregnant," Em said.

The pendulum shot to the *Yes* position. Em shook her head at herself. The cross had sat in someone's drawer for more than three hundred years. She shouldn't have expected it to actually work! She shoved the cross deep into her pocket and went about her day.

Her hanging day began with an early-morning phone call from Shonelle. John Parker had died in the night. He'd never regained consciousness after the demon-induced stroke on Gallows Hill. There was no listed next of kin, so Shonelle begged Em to go with her to collect his body.

Em and Shonelle were standing in the Massachusetts General morgue at eight in the morning. The entire place reeked of death. Shonelle didn't smell it. But Em's witch's senses were overwhelmed with the blood, body matter, and decay of death.

"I'll give you a moment with him," the attendant said.

"Thank you," Em said.

"The funeral home is. . ."

"MacIntosh," Em said. "They should be here this morning. We're not having a service."

"Just a cremation," Shonelle said. With the words, she began to weep. "We'll bury him tomorrow."

"And there's no family?" the attendant asked.

"Not that anyone can find," Em said with a smile.

"We've posted his photo on websites and in papers across the country. No one's come forward."

"He... was... m-m-my... boyfriend," Shonelle said between sobs.

The attendant gave his best approximation of a sympathetic nod. When Shonelle looked down, the attendant rolled his eyes. He gave Em a shrug and led them into a small, airless room where the demon-free body of John Parker lay. Shonelle wept into her handkerchief, while Em silently cast a spell to determine the identity of the corpse.

The number 1625 appeared on John Parker's forehead, and Em scowled. John Parker belonged in 1625. They had already tested his DNA and determined he was not any kind of descendant of Alice Parker. Em wondered if this John Parker was actually Alice's father-in-law. She was so deep in thought that she didn't notice that Shonelle had stopped crying.

"Em?" Shonelle's voice caused Em to jump. "Sorry."

"I was miles away," Em said. She put her arm around Shonelle.

Shonelle nodded. For a moment, they stared at the young man's face.

"I wanted... well..." Shonelle's face flushed with emotion. "Did you see those..."

Shonelle looked around to make sure no one was in the room with them. She leaned into Em.

"Demons," Shonelle whispered.

"Demons?" Em asked.

"When you and George and the others were looking for Gallows Hill," Shonelle said. "I haven't slept a wink since. . . since. . . And. . ."

Shonelle started crying again. Em waited for the flood to end.

"I saw something," Em said with a nod. "Why do you ask?"

"I. . ." Shonelle started. "You know how I'm a descendant of Martha Corey — you know, the Salem witch?"

Em gave Shonelle a vague shrug.

"Today is the anniversary of her hanging day, and. . ." Shonelle said.

Shonelle waved her hand at John Parker.

"With the demons and everything. . .." Shonelle leaned into Em. "I haven't really been here for him."

"I don't think there's been much him to be here for," Em said. "He never woke up from the coma."

Shonelle nodded and blew her nose.

"I was *scared*," Shonelle said in a low voice. "And now. . ."

Shonelle gave an exaggerated sigh.

"Do you think it's a coincidence that he died today — of all days?" Shonelle asked.

"Well." Em looked up and gave a little shrug. "There's been more than three hundred anniversaries of Martha Corey's hanging day."

"So you don't think this is my fault?" Shonelle asked.

"Your fault?" Em asked.

"Because I'm like Martha Corey, and she was a witch," Shonelle said. "And the demons and everything."

"In the first place, Martha Corey was a kind, decent woman of great Christian faith," Em said with a sniff. "She was no witch."

"But. . ."

"And in the second place. . ." Em made a conscious effort to relax. She smiled at Shonelle. "We all only have one life — Martha Corey, you, John Parker, me. You're not responsible for what happens in someone else's life."

She gestured to the corpse.

"This young man was very ill," Em said. "And, by the grace of God, he is finally at peace."

"And the *demons*?" Shonelle asked.

"May they be at peace as well," Em said.

Shonelle seemed so surprised by Em's words that she gave a little gasp. She stared at Em, who nodded.

"No one starts their life with the goal of. . ." Em started one of Shonelle's mother's favorite sayings.

". . . becoming a demon," Shonelle finished the statement with a smile.

"Exactly," Em said. "Why don't you go to the bathroom get cleaned up? We're meeting George for breakfast."

"Your pre-wedding meal!" Shonelle grinned.

"Pancakes," Em said. "I'll talk to the attendant and meet you by the bathrooms."

Shonelle smiled and nodded. When the girl had left the room, Em pressed the call button. She was staring at the wall wondering how this John Parker was related to Alice's John when she heard movement. Looking back at the body, she saw the shadow face of her demon on John Parker's face.

"You know what you need to do," the demon said.

"That's the thing," Em said. "I don't know."

The demon opened John Parker's mouth to say

something, but the attendant came in. The demon was gone. Em thanked the attendant and went to find Shonelle. Together, they went to meet George, Isaac, and Isaac's entire family for breakfast.

Chapter Twenty-four

One nice thing about immortality was that Em was the same size and shape she'd been when she died. Em stepped in front of her full-length mirror. She was wearing a calf-length, silver beaded dress that she'd bought in 1917 to marry George. The word came the morning of the wedding — America had entered World War I, and Captain George Burroughs needed to report for duty. While George prepared for another war, Em had packed away this beautiful dress and her dreams of ever becoming his wife.

She turned sideways. The silver beads made a lovely tinkling sound when she turned. Using magic, she made some minor alterations to modernize the dress. Of course, she'd used magic to clean the tarnish from the silver beads and reduce the weight of the ridiculously heavy dress. She smiled. It was lovely.

She'd put her hair up in such a way as to create three roses at the nape of her neck. She was going to carry three long-stem white roses to match her hair. At Alice's insistence, she'd stuck a silver hair comb with a length of tulle under the roses in her hair. She smiled at herself.

"You look. . ." George's voice came from behind her.

Em looked up to catch his face.

"Wow," George said.

"You look pretty 'wow' yourself!" Em said.

George was wearing a light-grey tux with a white bow tie and tails that matched her silver dress. He smiled at her compliment.

"Are you ready?" Em asked. "Two weddings, plus your own."

"I'm excited," George smiled. "This day marks the start of a new era for us, for all of us. The demons are gone. We have from now until eternity to be together. Did you hear Mary's news?"

"I've been so caught up in getting everything ready, I haven't had time for anyone's news," Em said and shook her head.

"She's pregnant," George said.

Em's mouth dropped open.

"What?" Em asked in a shocked whisper. She turned around to look at him. George raised his eyebrows and nodded.

"John is thrilled," George said. "I think that's why they were so adamant about getting married. They want God to bless their union and the child."

George beamed.

"I knew she wasn't feeling well," Em said. "I thought it was just the overwhelm of being back in Boston. I told her she should go see Ann. Did she?"

"Of course," George said. "Wait. . ."

He went out into their living room and returned with a photo. He gave it to her.

"It's called an ultrasound," George said. "John's so happy that he made a copy for everyone."

Em took the image from George. The image showed a yellowish-grey blob. She shook her head.

"I don't know what I'm looking at," Em said.

"I'd never seen one, either," George said. "I guess they can use this *ultrasound* to look inside the womb. It seems unnatural to me, but John assured me it's common for everyone to have one now."

He pointed to a bump on the image.

"That's the nose," George said.

"Oh, I see," Em said. "That's a face, a head.... How cool."

"And that's. . ."

"She's having a boy," Em said.

Beaming, George nodded. They stood with their heads bent over the photo.

"They want to name him 'Isaac,'" George said.

"After Mary's husband," Em said.

George nodded.

"I think that's why they've been so adamant about getting married," George repeated.

"You don't think Bridget and Giles. . .?" Em asked.

George shrugged.

"She was at least sixty when she was hanged," Em said. "But then, Mary was in her fifties."

"Killing the demons has brought youthful vigor to us all," George said with a grin.

They looked at the picture for a moment. George looked up into Em's face.

"Do you think we. . .?" George asked. "You know that I love children."

"You had nine," Em smiled.

"Ten, with Benoni," George flushed. "I... uh... I... um... I'd love to have eleven or twelve or..."

George grinned. Em gave him a searching look.

"Susannah told me you don't have sex with the others anymore," Em said.

George looked into her face.

"I guess... well..." Em said.

"You're wondering why," George said.

Em bit her lip and looked away. George touched the cleft in her chin, and Em turned to look at him. He raised his eyebrows to encourage her to respond.

"I'm surprised, I guess," Em said.

George nodded.

"And I'm surprised you didn't tell me," Em said.

"My sexual promiscuity didn't *ever* have anything to do with you," George said.

Em nodded. She moved away from him to her dresser, where she picked up the silver cross Detective Donnell had returned to her.

"Your cross," George said with a smile.

"You knew about the cross?" Em asked. "I thought no one knew about the cross."

"I've seen you naked," George said.

"But..." Em said.

"I knew you didn't have it when we awoke," George said.

"I'd given it to Lydia," Em said. "Lydia Dustin. Detective Donnell is related to her granddaughter, Susan. He gave it to me."

"Detective Donnell?" George asked.

"Why didn't you chastise me for the cross?" Em asked. "It was against Puritan law!"

"I know. I should have," George said. "But, those moments, with you, in Salem — they were the highlight of my life. They were the best, more meaningful moments of my life. I had never felt more alive, so overcome with love and passion. I memorized every detail. I would replay them in my mind for. . . years."

Em gave him a soft smile.

"There was a moment, when we were done, that you touched your throat." George reached out to touch the cross. "You touched this cross."

He smiled.

"I remember every moment, even now," George said with a nod. He turned away from her. "I guess it seems weird that I was so promiscuous."

"George," Em started.

"No, Em, let me finish," George said. "I was standing on a hill in Laos, 1965. In the valley, our planes were dropping bombs. The sound of people's terror echoed through the forest canopy. Helicopters flew low, with guns blazing. It was pre-dawn. I was following behind the planes. My team was to clear out any resistance. There was this building. Nothing much. It just looked like. . ."

George shrugged.

"A building," George said. "I stepped inside and. . . There was this gold statue at the front — a seated Buddha, I think, although the villagers said it was their monk. The villagers spoke of him as if he were alive, which is why I went there."

George glanced at Em to see if she was following him. She gave him a soft nod to continue his story.

"The statue spoke to me." George raised an eyebrow

when Em's eyebrows pinched together with concern. "It called me by name. God or demon, I had no idea and no faculty or experience to determine which. The statue said: 'Who do you love, George Burroughs?'"

George looked at Em.

"I said, 'Martha.'" George's voice dropped. "The statue said: 'Through her love, she gave you the gift of life. That is powerful love.' I was terrified because this thing knew I was a witch. I raised my machine gun to destroy it, but before I could do anything, the statue said: 'What do you give her in return?' And I realized that I had no idea. My entire life had been transformed by your love. I was nothing, no one, until we met in Salem, and this. . . Your love has always been my prize possession, and I. . ."

George shrugged.

"So I stopped screwing around," George said. "Just until I could figure it out and. . ."

George gave an impish shrug.

"I never wanted to be with another," George said. "Not ever. I was just. . . foolishly playing with the only thing I valued. "

He shook his head.

"Now, I only want to be worthy of your love," George said. "I work every day to be worthy of the love you give so freely."

"Why didn't you tell me?" Em smiled.

"Embarrassed, mostly," George said. "There I was, a Reverend, an expert in God's love. Then a love so profound and boundless is given to me, and I. . ."

George scowled at himself and looked down. She tipped his head up and kissed his lips. He looked deep into her eyes before smiling.

"Will you marry me?" George asked.

"I am doing just that today," Em said.

"That's very good," George said.

"What happened to the statue?" Em asked.

"No idea," George said. "I was called out of there. I never saw it again."

"We should go Laos," Em said. "Find this statue that changed your life."

"You'd leave Boston?" George asked. He voice spoke his surprise.

"Sure," Em said. "Maybe in November, when it starts to get cold."

"Good plan," George said.

He held his elbow out.

"Shall we go?" George asked.

"It would be my pleasure," Em said.

She took his arm, and they left their apartment. Downstairs, a limousine waited to take them to Bridget's Beacon Hill mansion and the celebration.

It was a celebration to beat all celebrations.

George officiated the marriage of Bridget and Giles first. Em walked Giles down the aisle. She kissed his cheek and hugged him tight before leaving him to wait for Bridget. Sam brought Bridget down the aisle. She had never looked more beautiful. George led them in a very traditional Puritan service, with solemn pledges and lots of scripture. For Em, who had attended to no fewer than seven of Bridget's eleven weddings, this was Bridget's most heartfelt and beautiful wedding. Bridget cried through the entire ceremony.

Mary and John had a more modern ceremony. They walked to the front together. While Bridget had worn white lace, Mary had chosen a lovely, fitted, ivory silk dress that highlighted the miraculous bump in the front of her dress. This was both John and Mary's first immortal wedding. They were the very image of joy. George led them through a modern Presbyterian ceremony that echoed its Puritan roots.

They had planned to wait an hour after Mary and John before George led the community in marrying him and Em. Without warning, Isaac arrived with his entire family in tow. Isaac was no George. He took hold of the audience at once. The quiet reverence of the other weddings slipped away as Isaac led them through a rousing Jewish wedding ceremony, steeped in tradition. Em had never felt as loved or as happy.

The party continued all night. Isaac and his family left around nine. Shonelle and her mother stayed until ten. After eleven, only the witches and their human partners remained. Ann and her fiancé danced. Alice and her once-client-now-boyfriend sat talking in the corner. Martha's Bruce told jokes and kept their table entertained. For the first time, Sam brought his human partner to the ceremony. His partner was handsome, funny, and a descendant of George Jacobs. They had a ball. The witches danced, laughed, ate great food, and celebrated vanquishing the demons.

Around dawn, the witches began to slip away. Sarah Wildes offered to continue the party at her home, and the

witches joined her. Giles and Bridget slipped away to a
suite at the Liberty. Mary and John preferred to go home.
As a surprise, Alice had booked Em and George a room at
the Ritz-Carlton. They left Bridget's Beacon Hill mansion
to cross the Common near dawn. The ghosts of the soldier
and the little girl came by to congratulate them. While
George checked them into the hotel, Em slept with her
face against his shoulder. She vaguely remembered George
undressing her. They were tucked into their bed with the
"Do Not Disturb" tag on their door before the sun had
warmed the Common.

Em fell into a deep sleep. In her sleep, she was
transported back to the day she'd seen George for the first
time. She had been shopping at the outdoor vegetable
vendors. Her son, Thomas, had come with her to help
carry groceries. She knew that a new Reverend was due in
town, but she could have cared less. Her life was too
overwhelming for new Reverends, squabbling churches, or
any other nonsense.

She had been standing in front of an apple vendor when
George had walked by. He and his first wife, Hannah, were
being shown around by Thomas Putnam. Em had been so
caught up in trying to determine how many apples she
could afford that she hadn't bothered to look up. She'd felt
him move past her like the heat of fire from a moving
torch. She'd looked up at the same moment he looked at
her. She had felt a shot of electricity run through her. He
had nodded and continued moving.

He told her later that he'd asked Thomas's wife, Ann
Putnam, Sr., the mistress of the home George and his
family were staying in, about Em. Ann had said that Em

was no one, not a member of the church — only a poor woman with a sick husband. A year later, George had arrived on her doorstep as an outreach from the church. In the dream, she found herself opening the door to him.

"Why, you're not poor at all," had been his first words to her.

"My father takes care of us," she'd said.

"I was told you were poor," George had said.

She'd stepped aside to let him into her home. Thomas was at school, and, as usual, Henry was in their bedroom. George kept his hands tightly clasped behind his back as he surveyed the room.

"They are idiots," she'd said with a smile. "They believe you're poor if you do not own land. I have a sick husband, who cannot work the land. It would be foolish to buy land we cannot maintain. And I am no fool."

George turned to look her full in the face. And she was struck. For a moment, they simply stared at each other. She caught herself first.

"Sir," she had said and looked down.

"I came to. . ." Her heart was pounding so loud and fast that she didn't hear a word he'd said. Even in the dream, she felt the sick, nauseous feeling of that moment.

"I love you," she said, in the dream. George stopped talking. "I always have and always will."

"I know," George said. "Because I love you, too. I simply cannot bear a life without you."

Caught in the dream, Em smiled at this rewrite of history. Of course, in real life, it had taken them almost three years to admit what they both knew at the first moment they'd seen each other. It had taken them more than three hundred years to say it in front of their friends and family.

Em drifted into a deeper sleep. Her life flashed before her. Henry died. Benoni was born. Giles came to make a deal. And then she was sitting in the living room at Giles's home, talking to the examiners. She'd been so sure she was safe; she was so wrong.

She was standing in the middle of the torture and violence of the jail in Boston. She'd intentionally kept herself out of the gossip around the witch trials. Instead, she worked every day to keep herself and the others alive. She had no idea who might arrive at the jail.

She's felt the heat of George first and then heard the jeering from the crowd. She'd turned to see who had arrived when George stepped through the doors. People rushed forward to greet him. Within moments, he was leading the accused in prayer. His eyes sought her over their bowed heads. She'd smiled, and he'd nodded.

The days and nights of the Boston jail flashed by in a dizzying kaleidoscope until the guard was wrenching George from her arms. The guards hurled him onto the cart. He'd been so certain that he could convince them that he was a man of God. He'd been sure they wouldn't hang him. The whispers found her only an hour later. Her beloved had been hanged. The men had fought over his body. Em retreated to a small corner to cry.

The images came fast now. Giles refused to participate in the trial, and the Sheriff took him out to the field.

"Surely they won't press him to death," they'd whispered to each other in the jail. Just as surely, one boulder at a time, they did just that.

Her fight seeped out of her. Her heart had broken. She prayed for the quiet peace of death. In a *whoosh!* she had hanged from the oak tree by a bit of rope. She'd swung and spun. As she slowly suffocated, her eyes had moved over the crowd. Tonight, she saw something she hadn't recognized at the time.

Her demon was standing in the middle of the crowd. He wasn't near the front, as a leader, nor was he in the back with the reluctant. He watched her with great intent. Their eyes locked.

"And now it begins." The demon's words were the last thing she heard.

Deep asleep, Em watched her body as it was tossed into the common grave. She saw herself awaken in the pit. In this version of her life, the demon was standing beside the grave.

"Why are you here?" Em asked.

"Because you are here," the demon said.

"Can't you leave me to live my life?" Em asked.

"You know I cannot," the demon said. "We will not be denied."

"What does that mean?" Em asked.

The demon grinned.

"I am supposed to just know?" Em asked. "How can I know what I do not know?"

"How can you, Martha of Truth?" the demon asked.

Confused, Em shook her head.

"Why do you think Weni the librarian went away?" the demon asked. "Where is your father?"

Em was so surprised that she could only blink.

"Yes, Martha of Truth," the demon said, "I have kept

them from you."

"Why?" Em asked.

"Because you need to do your own work!" the demon screamed.

Startled, Em jumped back.

"Em?" She heard George's voice from outside the dream. She felt him shake her shoulder. "Em?"

"My work?" Em asked.

"Your work," the demon said. "I rooted for you. I believed in you. I chose this lunatic John Parker because I believed you would see the truth, and, instead, you. . ."

The demon snorted. Smoke came from his nostrils. He lowered his head so that the rhinoceros horn was pointed at the center of her forehead.

"You will die!" the demon said. "This war will end with your death!"

The demon turned to walk away from her.

"Is there another way?" Em asked.

The demon stopped walking. His shoulders hunched for a moment. She was slipping back into the common grave when he spun in place and stalked back to her. When he neared, she realized that she'd mistaken his mood. The demon seemed happy, almost jubilant.

"Now that's a very good question," the demon said.

"What is your name?" Em asked.

"My name?" the demon asked with a smile. "I knew you were different, Martha. I knew you would save us all."

"Save us all?" Em asked.

Em felt herself flying through the air.

"Save us all?" Em yelled to the demon. "How?"

The demon gave her a little wave. She watched the demon until he was a mere speck on the horizon.

"There is one thing," the demon's voice came to her. "Any attempt to increase your ranks will be seen as an act of war."

Behind her closed eyes, she saw a flash of white light. She felt a burst of cold water. When she opened her eyes, she was standing in the apartment shower, and George was begging God for her release from the trance.

"I'm here," Em said.

George held her tight. He swooped her off her feet and carried her back to bed.

She sat up in bed. The room was dark. George was asleep by her side.

"What is it?" George's sleep-filled voice asked.

"I had the weirdest dream," Em said. "I guess it was a dream."

"You just got in bed!" George said.

Em picked up the clock. They had been in bed for less than two minutes. The champagne in her glass was still bubbling. The blankets were cool, as if she'd just slipped into them.

George leaned up on one arm to look at her.

"Are you okay?" George asked.

"Yes," Em said with a smile. "I'm very okay."

Grinning, George put his head down to go to sleep. Em lay awake, staring at the ceiling.

She'd let Weni and her father tell her about the demons. She'd let her reading of the Bible and other verses color her ideas about the demons. It was time for Em to do her own research. It was time for Em to find out for herself. Nodding to the ceiling, she turned over and fell into a peaceful sleep.

Chapter Twenty-five

Em pulled closed her hotel room door and set out into the hallway. She was in Charlottesville, Virginia, for a week-long seminar on the Salem Witch Trials. In all these years, Em had never looked into what had happened to her and the others. When asked, she always said she'd lived through it and that was enough. But the truth was that historians spoke of a Martha Corey that she didn't recognize. Their Martha Corey was arrogant, cruel, and high handed. History remembered her in the words of the men who, with purpose and malice, set about murdering her. She'd turned her back on history a long time ago.

Now that she remembered the demon's words on the day of her hanging — "And now it begins" — she realized that she needed to take an in-depth look at the Salem Witch Trials. She had a good understanding of what had happened to each individual. She needed to understand what had happened in a larger context. She needed to understand the entire event. She needed to do her own research.

When George left for the fall, Em braced herself against the lies and started researching the trials. She'd ordered every book and read online the books that were no longer in print. While looking for the original documents, she discovered that the University of Virginia's Scholar's Lab had the largest collection of original documents from the Salem Trials. She was scheduling a visit to Charlottesville when she discovered that the Scholar's Lab University Extension taught a popular seminar on the Salem Witch Trials. She decided on the spot that she would attend. Using a little magic, Em finagled a spot.

Em stopped in the hotel lobby for a thermos of hot water and a few tea bags before walking to class. She had no idea how she would respond to the seminar. Would she cry? Would she get so angry that she'd set the auditorium on fire? Both were real possibilities. She decided she would sit in the back, near the door, and drink her tea. She could easily slip out if she became overwhelmed.

A woman near the middle of the back row was saving five or six seats. Em pointed to the aisle seat. The woman smiled and nodded that it was available. Em was just getting settled when a middle-aged woman came in to sit next to her. The woman waved to her friend in the middle of the row and smiled at Em before sitting down. The woman leaned into Em.

"Connie," the woman said in a low voice and pressed her chest.

"Em," she said.

"First time?" Connie said.

Two women waved to Connie and moved to sit in their row. Em stood so they could get by.

"At the seminar?" Em asked.

She was so surprised by the woman's friendly tone that she scowled a bit more than she would have liked.

Not intimidated, Connie nodded and sat down.

"I haven't been here before," Em said finally.

"I thought so," Connie said. "I can always spot the new ones."

Em raised her eyebrows to see if Connie was going to say anything else. The woman was rummaging through her handbag.

"Do a lot of people come more than once?" Em asked.

"Most of us," Connie said and came up with a ball-point pen. "This is my eighth time."

"Eight times?" Em asked.

Surprised, Em looked at the woman as if she were crazy. Connie nodded in agreement that she was, in fact, crazy. Em smiled.

"Why?" Em asked.

Connie scanned Em's face and gave a little nod.

"I guess we feel..." the woman pressed her hand in to her chest. "... for the women."

Connie nodded.

"And men, too," Connie said. "You know there were men hanged, right? Oh, and they were hanged and not burned. Most people think they were burned."

Em gave Connie a soft smile, and Connie nodded as if she'd set Em straight.

"Plus, the man who teaches this course is..." Connie started.

The woman sitting next to Connie leaned over and said, "Dreamy."

"I was going to say 'handsome,'" Connie said.

"Charming, funny." The woman next to Connie gave a little sigh, and Em squinted at the familiar description.

"Doctor..." Em fumbled for her program. She'd been so

focused on getting into the class that she hadn't paid any attention to who was teaching it.

"Burrows," the woman two down from Connie said. "I'm Cassie."

"Em." Em nodded to the woman.

"Charlie," the woman next to Connie said.

"We're the three 'C's,'" Connie said. "We're from Wisconsin. Madison." Connie pointed to herself. "Milwaukee." Connie pointed to Charlie. "And Eau Claire." She gestured to Cassie.

Em smiled as if she knew that these cities were actually different places.

"Em, from Boston," she said.

The women gave Em a little wave.

"So this Doctor Burrows? Any relation to the Reverend?" Em asked.

"Different spelling," Cassie said with a shake of her head. "He's from Boston, though. Maybe you know him."

Em shrugged and started making a cup of tea in the cap of her thermos.

"He owns one of those woo-woo stores," Charlie said. "What is it called?"

"Mystic Divine?" Em asked.

"That's it," Connie said. "Have you been there?"

Em gave them a vague nod and tried to keep the amused grin off her face.

"How long has he been teaching this course?" Em asked.

"Ten years?" Cassie said. Em swallowed hard to keep from looking surprised.

"Longer than that," Connie said.

The women argued among themselves for a moment

until they agreed that they weren't sure.

"He's cute," Charlie said. "But he's totally taken."

"Which totally makes him more attractive," Cassie said.

"He's taken by that Mary who works with him," Connie said.

"Which Mary?" Em asked, with a little too much emphasis. The women looked up at her with surprise. "I know a lot of Mary's."

"You probably *do* know her," Connie said. "She lives in Boston."

"They both do," Cassie said. "You should hear them. Year to year, they always learn something new. This year, they say they're going to reveal where the bodies are buried."

"You know, no one knows the exact location the witches were buried," Charlie said.

"Not witches," Connie said.

Charlie wagged her head side to side.

"We always argue about this," Connie said. "Charlie believes they were actual witches. What do you think, Em?"

The woman looked at her.

"I. . ." Em said. Her mouth went dry. Her heart pounded in her ears. She had no idea why she was panicked. She only knew that she was. "I. . ."

She shrugged to fill in the blank.

"That's how I am, Em," Cassie said. "I wasn't there, so I don't know. And. . ."

"Even if they were witches, they didn't deserve to be hanged," the women said in unison.

"Look at the time!" A woman came rushing into their

row.

Em and the three "C's" got up to let her through. She dropped into a chair next to Cassie, and the women's attention turned away from Em. Relieved, Em took a sip of her hot tea. She looked at her thermos. She never got used to how these thermoses worked. Talk about witchcraft. Thermoses were amazing. She was lost in her own revelry over the tea when Connie touched her arm.

"There he is," Connie said. "Isn't he. . ."

Em looked across the nearly eight thousand people in the auditorium to see her husband move into the room. He wore jeans, a brown sweater she'd knitted, and a beard. As she had the first time, she felt his presence like a hot coal moving across her heart. He seemed to feel her presence as well. He scanned the audience.

"He's got a wedding ring this year," Cassie said with a pretend pout.

"Mary still doesn't." Charlie pointed to Mary Ayer Parker, who was standing next to George.

"It's *not* Mary," Connie said with finality. Charlie shrugged.

"I see some familiar faces. . ." George said as he peered out into the audience.

He put his hand on his heart and whispered what Em knew to be a finding spell. It took him only a moment more to find her at the back of the room. She felt her face get hot and her lips turn up in a smile. His face broke into a big smile. He instinctively touched the beard that she hated and looked down. When he looked at her again, everyone in the auditorium turned around to see what he was smiling at.

"He's smiling at me!" Connie said.

"It's Em," Charlie said with a push of her elbow into Connie's side.

The women looked at Em, and she shook her head as if they were crazy. George said something to Mary Ayer Parker. She found Em and grinned. Before Em had a chance to respond to the women, George started the course.

"We have five days," George said. "Five days seems like a long, long time to talk about something that happened so long ago. However, what happened in Salem in 1692 affected the very creation of this country and continues to affect Western civilization today. Those of you who have been here before know that we'll spend the mornings talking about the environment in which the witch trials happened, or more simply, the 'why' of the Salem Witch Trials. We'll spend the afternoons focused on two of the individuals who were hanged as witches. This year, we will discuss: Sarah Good, Susannah Martin, Martha Carrier, John Proctor, Mary Eastey, Margaret Scott, and Giles and Martha Corey. That is eight."

"George Jacobs!" a voice yelled from the side of the class.

"Elizabeth Howe," a woman yelled.

George nodded and grinned.

"Okay, okay," George said. "Tomorrow, you'll have a chance to vote on the final two people we discuss. Let's get started. Can we lower the lights?"

George began lecturing. Em leaned back in her seat to listen.

Em was just finishing dinner with the three "C's" when an address appeared on her telephone. She waited until the women had finished their wine before making her excuses and leaving the restaurant. The map on her phone told her that the address was for a small house on campus. To avoid being seen, she cloaked herself in darkness and headed off into the fall night. Em felt her heart race with excitement and her breath catch in her throat as it had when she'd snuck out to see George in Salem. Smiling, she made her way to see her lover.

Mary Ayer answered the door. She didn't say a word until Em was well inside the house.

"I can't believe you guys," Mary Ayer said as she hugged Em. "You really didn't know he taught this class?"

"This is his time to do what he will," Em said with a shrug. "Plus. . ."

"There is no talk of Salem in our house," George said.

"That's not exactly true," Em said.

"Pretty close," George said. He held out his arms and crushed her in a hug. He gave her a bruising kiss. "I do not have words to describe how delighted I was to look up and. . ."

He let go of her to look at her.

"What are you doing here?" George asked.

"I thought you hated history!" Mary Ayer said with a laugh.

"I do!" Em smiled. "I need to figure this whole demon thing. . ."

Mary Ayer gasped, and Em looked at her.

"We didn't vanquish them?" Mary Ayer asked.

"I don't think so." Em shook her head. "Sorry."

Mary Ayer looked at George, and he nodded.

"They've declared a kind of a truce," Em said. "They said as long as we don't add to our ranks, they will leave us alone again."

"But Mary's pregnant," Mary Ayer said. "Bridget, too, but I'm not supposed to say anything."

Em nodded.

"Oh, God," Mary Ayer said. She wandered to a worn stuffed armchair and dropped down. "Alice will be so disappointed."

George chuckled, and Em smiled. Mary Ayer turned to look at Em.

"I thought it was too easy," Mary Ayer said. "Is that why you're here?"

"I had another dream," Em said.

George put his arm over her shoulder and kissed her hair.

"The demon said something that made me realize that I'd only ever taken someone else's word for. . ." Em waved her hands and added, "everything."

"You need to do your own research," George said.

Em nodded and looked at him. He kissed her nose.

"I'm surrounded by all of these smart people," Em said. "They all have smart ideas and opinions, but I have no idea if they are accurate. What if they're completely wrong?"

"You think your father and the mythical Weni might be wrong?" George asked.

Em nodded.

"I've felt that way, Em," Mary said. "You remember that jerk Upham?"

"Charlie?" Em asked. Mary Ayer and George nodded.

"He got as much right as he got wrong," Mary Ayer said. "And I thought, 'If this guy could just make stuff up — like that junk about poor Tituba starting it all — I could tell the truth.' So I started researching."

Mary Ayer nodded.

"I'm good at it," Mary Ayer said.

"Mary is the foremost expert on what happened to us," George said. "We work together for a month every year, and it usually ends up with her teaching me what she's learned. I keep telling her she should teach this seminar, but. . ."

George looked at her.

"No one's as good at talking to a crowd as George," Mary Ayer said with a blush. "You know, Em."

Em smiled at her.

"But I could help you," Mary Ayer said with a nod.

"What about your business?" Em asked.

"It pretty much runs itself now," Mary Ayer said. "I have great realtors who work for me. I only have to go in on the weekends."

"And answer when they call with questions," George said.

Mary Ayer nodded.

"I could totally help," Mary Ayer said.

"I don't know what help I need," Em said.

"I'd love to go to that library," Mary looked from George to Em, "you know — the one on Orkney?"

"Would you go, too?" Em asked George.

"We're going to Laos in a month, and after that. . ."

"You need to be with your people," Em said with a nod.

"I. . ." George opened his mouth and then nodded.

"They need me, count on me."

"But I could go," Mary said.

"Let's see if I can handle this week," Em said. "I find it all very. . . overwhelming. You say the words, and the filth and fires and pain and horror and. . . everything invades my bones. I can barely breathe."

Not sure of what to say next, Em nodded. George pulled her in and kissed her hair.

"Okay," Mary Ayer said. She smiled at Em and then at George. "I'm really glad you're here, Em."

She hugged Em and kissed her cheek. She did the same with George.

"I'll see you in the morning," Mary Ayer said.

She turned on her heels and headed up the stairs, leaving Em and George alone.

"What do you usually do when you teach?" Em asked.

"I find it exhausting," George said. "Mary keeps a Puritan schedule. I try to match hers."

Em gave him a lusty smile, and he laughed.

"I have a hotel room," Em said. "You could sneak in and sneak out."

When George leaned forward to kiss Em, she transported them to her hotel room. He laughed when he realized they had moved. He took her hand and led her to bed.

"You didn't tell him?" Ann Pudeator asked Em.

Em shook her head from her vantage point on an exam table at the Mary Horrigan Connors Center for Women's Health.

"I just don't understand why you didn't tell him," Ann said.

"George's work is really important to him, Ann," Em said. "It means a great deal to him to go and check on people in the fall. He gave up two weeks to go to Laos with us. If he doesn't get everywhere, then he has more people to see in the dead of winter."

"You didn't tell him because of some homeless people?" Ann asked. "Strangers?"

"Close to twenty-five percent of homeless people are vets. Many of them are people George knew in the wars," Em said. "He feels a deep connection to them. If he knew I was pregnant, he never would have gone."

"I would have told him," Ann said with a nod. "Put an end to that nonsense."

Ann looked at her and smiled.

"This is why you're his partner and wife," Ann said.

"I want him to live a meaningful life," Em said.

"And you?" Ann asked. "How are you feeling? It can't be easy to be pregnant at your age."

Em grinned, and Ann smiled.

"Practiced that?" Em asked.

"I thought of it after Mary was here," Ann said.

"Mary Ayer said that Bridget is pregnant, too?" Em said.

"With a girl," Ann said with a nod. "Do you think it's because you're married?"

Em shook her head.

"None of the girls with human boyfriends are pregnant," Ann said.

"Do they want to be?" Em asked.

"Did you?" Ann asked.

Em shrugged.

"I'm helping Elizabeth and Sam," Ann said.

"Elizabeth really wants a baby," Em said. "It's her one disappointment in immortality."

"That and not being able to fly," Ann said with a grin.

Em smiled.

"I talked to my fiancé," Ann said. "Told him the score."

"About being immortal?" Em gasped.

"About being infertile except for certain men born near where I was born," Ann said. "It's an acidity thing."

"And?" Em asked.

"He doesn't want children," Ann asked.

"Are you still going to marry him?" Em asked.

"George is going to marry us on Christmas Eve," Ann said. "You know all about it."

"Just checking," Em said with a smile.

"Why do you think we can get pregnant now?"

"My father said that I might be able to get pregnant after seeing him," Em said. "It's common for my kind after a trip to Rousay. I assume everyone's able to get pregnant because I'm able to get pregnant."

"You think I could, too?" Ann asked.

"Probably," Em said.

"With John or George or Sam," Ann said.

"You're forgetting Giles," Em said with a smile.

With a vigorous shake of her head, Ann burst out laughing. Ann pointed at Em.

"No," Ann said with finality. "Wipe your mind."

Em smiled.

"Come on, let's take a look," Ann said. "Lie back."

Em lay back on the exam table. Ann moved the

ultrasound wand over her belly.

"You're not showing at all," Ann said. "Did you before?"

"Not until the last month or so," Em said.

Ann nodded.

"Ten fingers," Ann said. "Ten toes. No horns."

"Horns?" Em asked in horror.

"I'm joking," Ann said. "Would you like a photo?"

"Like Mary had?" Em asked. "Absolutely."

Ann hummed to herself as she worked.

"He's going to be handsome," Ann said. "I can't wait."

"Why Ann Pudeator!" Em said. "You should have a baby."

"Nah!" Ann said. "I'm having too much fun doing what I want."

"We can afford nannies," Em said. "You'd never have to change even one diaper."

"Oh, stop," Ann said, but her smile suggested that she was interested. She printed out a photo and gave it to Em. "You can get dressed."

Em dressed quickly and went to Ann's office.

"You need to take these vitamins," Ann said. She passed a large bottle of pills across her desk.

"Vitamins?" Em asked.

"Everyone does," Ann said. "No alcohol or smoking, but you don't do that anyway. Only one cup of coffee, and limit your tea to just a couple cups. Is that going to be a hardship for you?"

"I can do it," Em said.

Ann stood from her desk and hugged Em.

"What's that for?" Em asked.

"You've been more of a mother to me than my own,"

Ann said. "I know you're going to enjoy having another child. I'm happy for you."

Em blushed.

"Make an appointment to come in once a month until you're close," Ann said.

"Can you tell when that might be?" Em asked.

"May," Ann said. "Bridget and Mary are due in April. Why are they ahead of you?"

"They must have been busy when I was in Rousay," Em said with a smile.

"Probably," Ann said. "I'll be 'Aunt Ann'?"

"Of course, my sister," Em said.

Em hugged Ann, and Ann walked her out to the front desk. Em made an appointment for a month from now, the middle of December. It was a nice day, so she decided to walk to the Massachusetts Historic Society, where she was currently reading Cotton Mather's papers. As she had learned from George and Mary Ayer, Cotton Mather's opinions set the stage for the witch trials, and his later work justified the killing of twenty innocent people. So far, his papers had proved what Martha Carrier had always said about him — the man was pure evil.

She used the beautiful walk in the crisp fall air past the Back Bay Fens to hearten herself. She and Mary Ayer were leaving for Orkney in a week's time. She needed to finish up. Standing outside the Historic Society, Em took a deep breath of clean air before plunging into the building to continue her dark work.

Chapter Twenty-six

Em followed Mary Ayer out of the restroom at Logan International Airport. The new year had just begun, and they were on their way to Orkney. Rather than use magic to jump there, Em insisted on making a trip out of it. They were spending a couple of days in London before heading up through Scotland and on to Orkney. The other witches were joining their trip as they could. Sarah Good was waiting for them in London, and Martha Carrier and Alice Parker had staked out a lovely castle in Scotland.

Of course, John Willard wouldn't let the former Mary Eastey, now Mary Willard, travel in her "condition." Unconcerned, Giles and Bridget were on a cruise to the Greek Isles, enjoying their last months of child-free life. Elizabeth Howe was teaching school. Sam Wardwell was in the middle of rehabilitating a large historic building. Sarah Wildes was covering at the store. And George was out in the wilderness of Boston, helping his homeless brethren.

At their terminal, Mary Ayer stopped under a television blasting the local news. She stared at the television while Em continued to a set of free seats by a window. Mary Ayer gestured toward the television and walked over to Em, who looked up and shook her head.

"What was it?" Em asked.

"Trial for the bomber," Mary Ayer said. "You know, that kid with a funny name."

"Dzhokar Tsarnaev," Em said.

"They sent out the jury summons," Mary Ayer said.

Em nodded and sat down. Mary sat next to her and leaned in.

"Are you going to sit on the jury?" Mary Ayer asked.

"With Christmas and New Year's, I haven't thought about it," Em said.

"Bull," Mary Ayer said.

Em grinned at her friend's curse word.

"I know you've thought about it," Mary Ayer hissed between her lips. "You were there."

Em winced. The marathon was one of Boston's most fantastic celebrations of life and health. It marked the end of winter in Boston. The finish line was only a few blocks from the Mystic Divine, so Em went every year. On April 15, 2013, two young men had left handmade bombs near the finish line at the marathon, just feet from where Em was sitting. Em's eyes flicked to Mary Ayer's face.

"And?" Em asked.

"I just thought you'd want to be on the jury," Mary Ayer said.

"It's not the Super Bowl," Em said. "I can't just buy a ticket."

"Yeah, how about those Patriots?" Mary Ayer asked with a smile. "They just have to knock down Baltimore and Indianapolis, and, *bam!* They're Super Bowl champs again."

"It's basically a done deal," Em said with a roll of her eyes and a grin.

"You can say that again," said the man who was sitting behind them.

Mary Ayer had to bite her tongue to keep from laughing. They had spent New Year's Eve together as a group. Sam, John, George, and Wilmot talked non-stop about their fantastic football team — the New England Patriots. Em smiled at Mary Ayer, and they fell silent.

"So?" Mary Ayer asked after a few moments.

"I don't know," Em said. She whispered a spell so that no one could listen in. "It may surprise you, but I'm not fond of handing out punishment."

"Capital punishment, no less," Mary Ayer said with a nod.

"Sixteen days," Em whispered.

Mary Ayer nodded. Sixteen days after Em and the others were hanged, Governor Phips had declared spectral evidence — the exact evidence used to convict them — invalid for use in court.

"Eleven days," Mary Ayer whispered.

Em sucked in an angry breath. Eleven days after they were hanged, Increase Mather, the father of the horrible Cotton Mather, denounced spectral evidence and the trials. The women fell silent. After a few minutes, Em turned to look at Mary Ayer.

"Are you?" Em asked.

"Maybe," Mary Ayer said. "I... Boston is my home. I watched her rise out of the mud to become a thriving, vibrant city. I will fight with all I'm made of to keep her from returning to the war and wanton violence that marked the beginning of her life."

Mary Ayer nodded. Em put her arm around her friend. They leaned their heads together. There were no words that could express the depth of the bond Mary Ayer and Em shared by being hanged within moments of each other.

"I knew you'd understand," Mary Ayer said.

"I just wish there was more I could have done, you know, that day," Em said. She gave a slight nod. "If I had known... If I'd just seen them leave those backpacks, I could have shielded everyone. They left the pack right in front of where I was sitting, and I..."

"I know," Mary Ayer said.

"Even a witch is powerless over this kind of random violence," Em said.

"You did what you could," Mary Ayer said.

"It's not enough," Em said.

"It's enough," Mary Ayer said with a firm nod. "More than enough."

Each lost in her own thoughts, they fell silent until their flight was called. They were flying First Class, so they boarded with the early passengers. At the door, Em touched the outside of the plane to guarantee their safe flight to London.

Mary sat near the window, and Em sat next to her. Terrified of flying, Mary reached to hold Em's hand and happened to brush Em's stomach. Surprised, she looked up into Em's face.

"You, too?" Mary Ayer asked.

Em nodded.

"Does he know?" Mary Ayer asked.

Em shook her head.

"He'll be home long before the baby comes," Em said.

Mary Ayer's eyes scanned Em's face. The plane filled quickly, and, before they knew it, the flight attendant was asking for their orders. When she was gone, Mary Ayer grabbed Em's hand.

"And if he's not?" Mary Ayer asked.

"I'll have another son on my own," Em said. Another flight attendant started giving the safety instructions. Em turned to look at Mary Ayer. "This time, I won't be quite as alone."

"You'd better believe it," Mary Ayer said. "Soul sisters for life."

Em grinned. Mary put her head on Em's shoulder.

"You can see this is why we need to get this done," Em said. "Now. Before we go to war with the demons."

"We will," Mary Ayer said. "But first we have to get there."

"I'm glad you're here, Mary," Em said. "Thank you for coming with me."

Mary Ayer smiled. She took a breath, and the plane took off.

"Who would have ever thought people would fly through the air like this?" Mary Ayer whispered.

"Next stop, London," Em said with a smile.

"Next stop, London," Mary Ayer said.

Em winked a sleep spell at Mary Ayer, and she dropped off. Grinning at her spell, Em reached under her seat for her knitting. She was working on a little cardigan.

"Can I bring you anything else?" the flight attendant asked as she set down Em's bottle of water.

"No, thank you," Em said with a smile.

"What are you working on?" the flight attendant asked.

Em held up the start to the tiny sweater. The flight attendant cooed over it.

"You clearly have that Puritan work ethic," the flight attendant said.

Unsure of what the woman was saying, Em gave an amused scowl and a little shake of her head.

"You're just industrious," the flight attendant said. "I'm from Boston. We're kind of steeped in the Salem Witch Trials."

Em gave her a vague smile and a nod.

"Well, I'll leave you to it," the flight attendant said and hurried off to attend to other matters.

Em smiled after her. What would the woman do if she knew who they were? Em smiled at the absurdity and settled in for the flight.

Em knocked on the door to her father's home on Rousay and waited. There was a car in the driveway and smoke coming from the chimney, yet Em was sure her father was not here. She waited another minute before turning toward the car, where Mary Ayer was waiting. Em shook her head, indicating that no one was there.

She was almost to the car when she heard the latch click open the door. She spun in place and started back toward the door. An elderly man glanced at her. He had a cloud of thin white hair and a full beard. He wore heavy pants and a thick sweater. He walked to the garden and tapped out his pipe.

"Sir?" Em asked.

He raised an eyebrow in her direction but finished what

he was doing. While his fingers were actively burrowing through his coat pocket, his eyes scanned her face. He turned toward her.

"William's daughter," he said. He squinted. "You look just like him. That you, Martha?"

"Sir," Em said. Closer now, but still a few feet away, Em looked the man up and down. She was sure she'd never met him before.

"No, Martha, we've never met," the man said. "I take care of this place for your Da."

"Nice to meet you," Em said. "You have me at a disadvantage."

The man snorted a laugh. He packed tobacco into his pipe.

"How can an old man like me have any advantage over a witch such as yourself?" the man asked.

"Sir?" Em gave him a much-practiced look to indicate that the man was insane. The man laughed. "Your name?"

"Ah," the man said. He held a flame up to his pipe. His lips puckered, and Em could almost feel the air sucked through the pipe. The tobacco blazed in pulses of glowing fire. He blew out a lung full of smoke. "Bernard Flett."

"Aboriginal," Em said under her breath. This man's last name indicated that he had descended from the original tribes of Orkney and Shetland.

"What was that?" Bernard Flett asked. "Did you say 'Aboriginal'?"

The man laughed.

"Your father used to say that my family had descended from gods," Bernard Flett said.

"The originals," Em said with a nod.

"He was not wrong, my dear," Bernard Flett said. "You live in America?"

"Boston," Em said.

"I can hear it in your voice," Bernard Flett said. "What can I do for you, Martha of Boston?"

"I am looking for my father," Em said.

The easy smile on the man's face fell. He looked up at Em and then down at his pipe. Before answering, he went through the ritual of lighting and smoking his pipe again.

"Your Da's gone," Bernard Flett said, finally.

"Gone?" Em asked.

"Dead," Bernard Flett said.

"That's not possible," Em said with a quick shake of her head.

"You mean because your father lived many thousands of years, he could not die?" Bernard Flett asked.

Em sucked in a breath.

"Was cut up into sections, he was," Bernard Flett said. "Each piece set on the train track. London Overland, North London branch. He'd been there at least a day when they found his head sitting on the bank. Some passenger saw it and took a picture. Thought it was some kind of fancy art project. The photo was on one of them Internet sites for a few days before anyone went to look."

"When was this?" Em asked.

"Four, maybe five years ago," Bernard Flett said. "Tore the heart out of me. How could anyone do such an evil thing to such a wonderful man?"

Em shifted from one foot to the next. Her mind told her that this news was impossible. Her father had to be alive. But, in her heart of hearts, she knew her father was gone forever. She sniffed a long breath.

"Would be worse if they hadn't caught the guy," Bernard Flett said.

"What?" Em leaned forward with surprise.

Bernard Flett raised an eyebrow.

"Said he was possessed by a demon," Bernard Flett said. "He's in Carstairs. Crazy as a loon."

Em gave a slight nod.

"Your Da left everything to you, in case you're wondering," Bernard Flett said. "He said you'd show up one day."

"Thank you for caring for the property," Em said.

"It's not a problem," Bernard Flett said. "You coming home?"

"I hadn't planned to," Em said. "I'm just here for a visit with my friend, Mary Ayer."

Em gestured to the car, and Bernard Flett squinted to look. Mary Ayer waved and Bernard nodded his head.

"If it's all right with you, I'd like to stay," Bernard Flett said. "It took me almost a decade to get used to living in the silence of Rousay. Now, I can't live anywhere else."

"Of course," Em said.

"Good girl," Bernard Flett said. "Hang on."

Bernard Flett left her standing in the cold. Em looked out onto the open field. Until just a few months ago, Em had been sure her father was dead. She'd just adjusted to the idea that he was alive when he was now gone. She felt the cold fog of the morning invade her very soul. She shivered and instinctively hugged herself.

"Here we are," Bernard Flett's voice came from inside the door. He appeared in the partially open door. "You're shivering."

"I..." Em nodded. "It's the shock."

Bernard Flett's eyes seemed to take in her face. She nodded again, and he gave a partial shrug. He stepped back into the house.

"Would you like to come in?" Bernard Flett asked. "I have a fire going, and..."

"No," Em said. "Thank you, though. I have my friend..."

Em gestured to the car. Bernard Flett gave her a curt nod and stepped into the doorway. He held out a manila envelope thick with paper. Em gave him a questioning look.

"That's it," Bernard Flett said.

"That's what?" Em asked.

"It's your father's last wishes," Bernard Flett said. "There is also a private letter to you and a few personal items. I put them all in that envelope so I wouldn't lose them."

"Thank you," Em said.

He gave her the manila envelope. She looked at the seal and back to him. He shrugged.

"I'd like to stay here until I die," Bernard Flett said. "It won't be too long now."

His grin showed his stained and broken teeth. Em gave him a curt nod.

"You are welcome here," Em said. "How will I know when..."

"I'll make arrangements," Bernard Flett said. "Your father set up a fund to take care of the property."

"Do you need more?" Em asked.

Bernard Flett chuckled.

"Sir?" Em asked.

"You are your father's daughter," Bernard Flett said. "These days, everyone pinches every penny. Not William. He was always, 'What do you need, Bernard?' He was special that way."

Em gave Bernard a sad smile.

"So, no, I have plenty of money," Bernard Flett said. "I'll return what's left when I'm gone."

"Fair enough," Em said. "Is there anything else you need?"

"You've made an old man very happy, Martha," Bernard Flett said. "Thank you."

"Of course," Em said. "I'm going to have my lawyer go over everything. Don't be alarmed if you hear from her."

"Fair enough," Bernard Flett said. "You'll find your father's lawyer's card in the envelope."

Em nodded. She took a breath and turned to leave. She'd taken two steps when she turned back to Bernard Flett.

"I am grateful for the friendship you showed my father," Em said.

"He was my great-great-grandfather's shooting buddy," Bernard Flett said. "Passed down through the generations."

Em grinned. She raised a hand to wave "good-bye." He gave her a nod and turned into the house.

"Nice to meet you, Martha."

Bernard's words were immediately followed by the squeak of the closing door. The lock clicked, and Em walked to the car. She got into the driver's seat. She set the manila envelope on the seat behind her.

"What was that?" Mary Ayer asked.

"My father was murdered," Em said.

"Oh, Em, I'm so sorry," Mary Ayer said. "I can't imagine how you feel. You just got him back."

"It's weird," Em said. "I never gave him a thought. He had been a part of my life, my father, some three hundred years ago. Then, *wham!* He's in my life in such a wonderful and miraculous way. And now..."

Em lifted a shoulder in a shrug. Mary Ayer rubbed Em's arm in sympathy. Em looked out across the house and its lands. Glancing at Mary Ayer, she moved to start the car.

"Can we do what we'd intended?" Mary Ayer asked.

"Good question," Em said. "At this moment, I don't think so. I mean, we can try it, but he got in with this key. We don't have the key."

Em made the shape of a small square.

"Brass," Em said.

"Maybe it's in there," Mary Ayer said.

"Maybe," Em said. She grabbed the manila envelope and put it on her lap. "I was going to wait until we were back in our room to open this."

Mary Ayer raised her eyebrows in encouragement. Em nodded. The manila envelope had her name scrawled across the front. She turned it over to see that the flap was taped down. Using the car key, she loosened the tape.

"I don't know what will happen when I lift this," Em said. She glanced at Mary Ayer and back at the envelope. "The last time I spun in a circle for what seemed like forever and went back to 1978."

"I can handle it," Mary Ayer said.

Em flipped up the envelope. Nothing happened. She looked inside the manila envelope. She pulled out a stack of papers.

"His will," Em said. "Wow, you know what that means?"

"Not sure," Mary Ayer said. "What does it mean?"

"He's really dead," Em said.

She passed the pack of papers to Mary Ayer and looked inside the manila envelope. In the dim light of the car, she saw set of keys, a pocket watch, a ring, and a black rawhide necklace. Em made a wish and tugged on the necklace. The square brass medallion popped out of the items below. Em sighed her relief.

"Is that it?" Mary Ayer asked. "The key?"

"This is it," Em said. She peered into the envelope. "The rest of this is going to have to wait."

"We're going tonight?" Mary Ayer asked.

"Gets dark around 3:30 p.m. this time of year," Em said with a smile. "We're in Scotland."

"Lucky we brought our warm clothing," Mary Ayer said with a smile. She clapped her hands together. "I'm excited."

"Me, too," Em said. She backed out from her father's driveway. "Next stop?"

"A nice cup of tea," Mary Ayer said. "Have you noticed how much better tea is here than in the US? I'd completely forgotten."

"I have noticed," Em said. "We have time for a cup of tea before heading back to the hotel. We'll change and be back here at dusk."

"Our adventure begins with a cup of tea." Mary Ayer grinned at Em.

Em glanced at her and smiled before driving to the locals tea shop.

Chapter Twenty-seven

"What did the statue say to you?" Mary Ayer asked Em.

They were walking along a ledge on the cliffs above the elders' cave. Em took a few steps and turned into a shallow alcove in the rock wall. She set down the heavy duffle bag she'd been carrying.

"The statue?" Em asked to stall for time.

She unzipped the duffle bag, and Mary Ayer bent over to start putting on her gear.

"In Laos," Mary Ayer said.

"Well. . ." Em said. Mary Ayer looked up at her. "It was weird."

"'Weird' is a word for it," Mary Ayer said with a grin.

"What did he tell you?" Em asked and dropped to a crouch.

She grabbed a thick sweater and handed it to Mary Ayer.

"You think we'll need this?" Mary Ayer asked.

"It's a cave," Em said. "Cold and wet. I was freezing the entire time I was there last time."

Mary Ayer nodded and began dressing. Her head had just popped through the hole of the pullover sweater when she grunted.

"You're always like this," Mary Ayer said as she threaded her arms through the sleeves of the sweater. "Why can't you tell me first?"

"If I'm always like this, then you should be used to me," Em said.

Mary Ayer laughed.

"I've always been this way, Mary," Em said. "I hold my cards very close to my chest. It used to drive my mother crazy. She could never find the meaning for it."

"Just the way you are," Mary Ayer said with a nod. "Let's see..."

Mary Ayer looked off at the sea.

"First he said — I mean I heard it in my head, of course — that I serve the world best when I am helping other people," Mary Ayer said. "I made the decision right there to make certain you took me with you to Orkney. I thanked him for his wisdom; then, just as I was leaving, he said..."

Mary Ayer turned to look at Em.

"What did he say?" Em asked. She held out a headlamp to Mary Ayer, who scowled at the light. "It's better to be able to see than to have perfect hair. After all, who is going to look at us? Certainly not anyone living."

Nodding, Mary Ayer took the headlamp.

"The statue then said that I must be willing to give up my life for yours," Mary Ayer said. "He said my life was against the order of nature. I said something like, 'You're one to talk.' I heard him chuckle. When I was outside, he said in my head, 'Willingness to let go will be the only thing that will save you in the end.'"

"He said something like that to George and to Alice," Em said as she pulled a balaclava over her head. "Definitely weird."

"Yes, it was, but he said something like it to most of us," Mary Ayer said. She grabbed a thick, handknit hat from the duffle bag and then asked, "Do I need anything else?"

"Knife," Em said. "They're in the side pocket. You sure you don't mind carrying the backpack?"

"Not at all," Mary Ayer said.

"We leave our phones here," Em said. "All electronic gear."

Mary Ayer nodded. She dropped down to the duffle bag. Em gave Mary Ayer her phone. Mary Ayer put her phone in the bag next to Em's.

"I think we're ready," Em said.

"Except you were going to tell me what the statue said," Mary Ayer said.

Em sighed and looked up at the stars.

"What could be so bad?" Mary Ayer asked.

"I'm not sure what it means," Em said.

"Tell me, and maybe I can research it when I'm down there," Mary Ayer said with a nod.

"Fair enough," Em said. "First, he greeted me as if we'd known each other a long time or possibly were the same kin..."

"You think he is?" Mary Ayer asked.

"Possibly," Em said with a shrug. "Then, he said what Argos the Kind said when I was in the cave."

"'You were the destroyer and the savior, the future and the past'?" Mary Ayer asked.

"Great memory," Em said with a smile. "Yes, that's what he said. I don't think I could have come up with the exact words."

"I reviewed all of my notes this morning before we

came," Mary Ayer said. She leaned in. "I seem fierce, but really, I'm terrified."

"I know," Em said.

"I know you know," Mary Ayer said with a smile. "Okay, what else did he say?"

"He said that the coming battle would require all of my resources," Em said.

"He specifically said, 'coming battle'?" Mary Ayer asked.

"Yes," Em said.

"That's not so strange," Mary Ayer said.

"It's what he said next," Em said. Mary Ayer gestured for her to continue speaking. "He said to follow my heart and my intuition. Even if they seem to lead to the ruin of everyone, my heart was pure and my intuition true."

"Wow," Mary Ayer said.

"Then he said, and I quote, 'Do not be swayed by the opinions and words of others. *You* are the only one who *can* see the truth.'"

"I see what you mean," Mary Ayer said. "He said that only you are *capable* of seeing the truth."

"Right," Em said.

"Do you think he meant that you're the only one who *will* see the truth?" Mary Ayer said.

"No," Em said. "I think he meant that I have to see the truth first before anyone else can see it."

"Sure," Mary Ayer said with a nod. "Other people will see the truth after you've seen it."

"I asked him how I could see the truth," Em said. "And he repeated that I should follow my heart and intuition. So it's kind of circular."

Mary Ayer shook her head.

"I asked everyone what he'd said to them," Em said.

"And?" Mary Ayer asked.

"They mostly make sense," Em said.

"Oh, I see what you're saying," Mary Ayer said. "When you add what he said to you to what he said to everyone else, none of it makes sense."

Em nodded.

"What's your intuition say now?" Mary Ayer asked with a grin.

"That we've spent too much time up here," Em said. "We need to get moving."

Mary Ayer looked around to see if anyone was coming. Even in the dark, they could see miles in every direction.

"No one is coming," Mary Ayer said.

"It's not who's coming that's the problem," Em said. "Ready?"

"I . . ." Mary Ayer said.

Em grabbed her friend and willed them into the community cave at the entrance of the interior elders' cave. Like she had with her father, they landed on the thin shelf, covered by the cave roof and open to the sea on one side. Mary Ayer squelched a startled scream, and Em stepped back from her. She walked to the six-foot ocean channel that separated them from the entrance to the cave.

"I tried to use love to get into the community cave," Em said. "This is clearly the entrance."

"Aren't you afraid to awaken the beast?" Mary Ayer asked.

"I have a feeling that I should see it again," Em said.

"Great goodness, why?" Mary Ayer asked in horror.

"I looked up the serpent when I was in the library," Em

said. "My father and Weni told me they'd never seen it before."

"What was it?" Mary Ayer asked.

"I'm not sure," Em said. "There wasn't anything in the library about this creature. Then I saw this old map — Olaus Magnus's Carta Marina of 1572, to be exact. It had a drawing of this serpent off the coast of Norway."

"Very near here," Mary Ayer observed.

"Exactly, and the serpent looked exactly like the creature who attacked us here," Em said. "Down to the very last detail."

"What does that mean?" Mary Ayer asked.

"No idea," Em said. "Since my father and Weni had never seen it, I wondered if I had called it."

"You?" Mary Ayer asked.

"It was my foot that went into the canal," Em said with a nod. "It was about to catch my foot when my father knocked me over."

"But why would you. . . I mean, it. . ."

"I think it wants to talk to me," Em said. She held her arm out.

"Talk to you?" Mary Ayer asked.

"If it doesn't work, just send it on its way," Em said. "My father did it with a 'Be Gone' spell."

Em looked up at Mary Ayer. Her friend looked cold and terrified. Mary Ayer bit her lip and nodded.

"You are a brave woman," Em said. "Now, stand back."

Mary Ayer scooted away from Em.

"Farther," Em said.

"I won't be able to hear," Mary Ayer said.

"Listening spell," Em said with a touch of impatience.

"Oh, good idea," Mary Ayer brightened. She scooted to the edge of the shelf.

"Here goes nothing," Em said.

She stuck her hand into the ocean channel that separated the shelf from the community cave. She barely had time to take a breath before the creature with razor-sharp teeth, a long, serpent-like snout, and an enormous snake-like body flew out of the water. This time, the creature made no effort to take hold of her. He simply looked at her and then gestured to Mary Ayer.

"What is that?" the creature asked.

"She is my friend." Em swallowed back her terror. "My family."

The serpent stretched out over her head toward Mary Ayer. Em watched in horror as he stretched more than nine feet without his tail leaving the water.

"Don't move!" Em yelled.

"I couldn't if I wanted to!" Mary Ayer said.

Mary Ayer screwed closed her eyes and clutched her hands to her chest. Her body shook from head to toe. The serpent's nostrils flared, and a great *"whoosh"* sound echoed off the cave roof. The ocean rose and fell seemingly under the control of the sea snake's breath.

"You are a good person, Mary Ayer Parker," the serpent said in a voice so deep that the very sound of it held the quality of an earthquake. "I will allow you to live."

"What did it say?" Mary Ayer screamed.

The serpent's head turned toward Em. She was standing at the ready.

"It said you were a good person and that it would allow you to live," Em yelled over the ocean waves.

"Good to know," Mary Ayer yelled back. "Thanks, scary monster!"

"Are they all like this one?" the serpent asked.

"They?" Em asked.

"Your abominations," the serpent said with such a boom that the cave shook.

"Yes," Em said. "Kind, loving, generous people who strive to be good."

The serpent seemed to smile. His head seemed to nod in approval.

"Sir," Em said. "Why are you here?"

"You *are* different," the serpent said.

"The last person who said that was a. . ."

"Demon," the serpent said. "Yes, he was."

Em felt an overwhelming sense of futility. She was tired of being afraid, and she'd been terrified for months. While the other witches were enjoying a renewal of their lives, Em had been working to prepare for the coming demon war and all that it would entail.

"Agh!" Em yelled in frustration. "What do you want from me?"

The serpent seemed to laugh. Em snapped her fingers, and she was holding a sword known to have killed many serpents.

"I will chop your head off," Em said with a growl.

"Be calm," the serpent said, seeing the sword. It gave the sword a respectful look and moved back. "There's no need for that."

"I am not Eve," Em said. "I am not a young, naïve girl to be trifled with."

"No, you are a 'gospel woman,'" the serpent said with a

hiss. "'Martha of Truth.'"

"I demand that you tell me the truth, serpent," Em said.

The serpent stared at her for what felt like an eternity. The waves crashed against the small, rocky shelf. Out of the corner of her eye, she saw a wave drench Mary Ayer with bone-chilling sea water.

"Do you know the truth, Martha?" the serpent asked.

"I know it when I hear it," Em said.

"Yes, only you know what is true," the serpent said.

The serpent began to slip back into the water.

"I demand that you tell me the truth!" Em yelled.

The serpent stopped moving. He was so still that Em thought he might have been turned into a statue.

"You cannot go inside," the serpent said finally.

"Why?" Em asked.

"You are blocked from them," the serpent said.

"Why?" Em asked. She brandished the sword, and the serpent moved back. "Tell me why!"

"It's not for me to tell," the serpent said. "You are allowed to speak with. . ."

"My father?" Em's words echoed with more longing and sorrow than she would have liked to give away.

"Your father can be returned to you, Martha of Truth," the serpent said. "But not today. You are allowed only what you can claim."

"'Claim'?" Em asked.

"Call to you," the serpent said. "As with me — you need only to think my name. . ."

"Argos," Em said.

With a nod, the serpent slid back into the water.

"Em!" Mary Ayer screamed. "Watch out!"

A naked, teenaged version of Argos jumped across the channel. He was fit, a little on the muscular side, and light on his feet. His skin was light brown, and his hair was in short, tight braids. He looked as if he hadn't bathed in a long, long time. When he growled and gnashed his teeth at Em, his teeth showed stains and signs of wear. He swung a heavy club in Em's direction. She easily stepped away from his blow.

"Be gone!" this Argos screamed in ancient Hebrew. Em cast a spell so that she could speak and understand his language. He smashed at her with the club again. "Be gone, spirit!"

"I am no spirit," Em said. "I am flesh like you!"

The young man stopped moving. He reached out to touch her face. She let him feel her flesh before stepping back. She sent the sword away with a snap of her fingers. He looked at her with a mixture of fascination and horror. Feeling sorry for the young man, she pulled off her balaclava and then her sweater. His jaw dropped in horror and fascination at her ability to remove these garments.

"Put this on," Em said and held the garments out to him. He looked at them.

"He's no more than a child," Mary Ayer said. She scooted over and took the garments from Em. "He's just like my boys."

Mary Ayer helped the young man put the sweater over his naked flesh. When she'd finished, Em had taken off the shell pants she'd been wearing over her thick fleece pants. Mary helped this young Argos into her shell pants. Em cast a spell so that Mary Ayer could understand and speak with the young man.

"You are very cold," Mary Ayer said. She kissed his cheek. "I had six boys, just like you."

"Like me?" Argos asked.

"Just like you," Mary Ayer said. "I'm Mary. This is Em. She is your kin."

The young man turned and looked at Em. She gave him a soft smile.

"You look like me," Argos said.

"I do," Em said.

"I would have never noticed it," Mary Ayer said. "Let's get somewhere warm."

Argos pointed to the cave, but Em shook her head. She touched his and Mary Ayer's arm. In a breath, they were sitting in their hotel room on Rousay.

"I need a cup of tea," Em said.

"I'll get it," Mary Ayer said and walked toward the little kitchen in their room. Em cast spells so that no one could hear or see them at the hotel.

"But. . ." Argos interrupted her.

"I promise to bring you back when we're done," Em said.

She smiled and finished the spells. Em grabbed a thick wool blanket from the top shelf of the closet and wrapped it around the young man. He sunk into the warmth and stared off at the wall.

"Aren't you freezing?" Mary Ayer asked Em in a low voice.

"I'm okay," Em said. "Strangely warm. Like I was born for this moment."

"I feel the same," Mary Ayer said. "I think that's why I helped him."

Em touched her arm and went back to the young man.

Mary Ayer made a pot of tea. She took a package of digestives from her purse and brought them over. She opened the pack and gave it to Em.

"Please tell me your story," Em said. She took a cookie from the package and made a show of eating it while the young man watched. "We've come a long way to hear about your life."

"I..." Argos looked at her and then at Mary Ayer. "What are you?"

"We are women," Mary Ayer said.

"Have you seen a woman before?" Em asked.

She held out a cookie to the young man. He took it in his fingers. He took a tiny bit of the cookie to test it. His face lit up with delight.

"Have them," Mary Ayer said.

Argos ate cookie after cookie. When the tea was ready, Mary Ayer poured a cup for herself and Em. He shook his head at the liquid.

"Have you seen women before?" Em asked again.

"Mother," Argos said. "Sister."

"You had a mother and a sister?" Em asked.

"A long, long time ago," Argos nodded. "Are you of the serpent?"

"No," Mary Ayer said quickly.

"How would I know?" Argos asked.

"You would feel it here." Em pointed to his heart. The young man nodded. "Listen to your sense of knowing. Ask yourself, 'Who are we?'"

Argos closed his eyes for a moment.

"You are friend," Argo said. "Family."

"Yes, we're your family," Mary Ayer said. She touched

his shoulder before hugging the young man. "Are you warm enough?"

He nodded.

"Can you tell us what happened to you, son?" Mary Ayer asked.

"Happened to me?" Argos asked.

"Tell us about your life," Em said. "Where do you come from?"

She held the tea under her nose for comfort.

"I was born in a beautiful place," Argos said. His face lit up with joy. "Fruit fell off the tree. We hunted and fished with great ease. I spent my days with my father and brothers hunting for food. My mother and sisters prepared everything. We were never hungry. We were never cold."

Argos tucked his nose into the blanket and instinctively shivered.

"I think I have been cold for an age," Argos said. He looked at Em. "At home, the nights were warm and clear. Water was clear and plentiful. We lived in peace and with much joy."

"Were there many of you?" Mary Ayer asked.

"A family tribe," Argos said. "My mother and father, my mother's sisters and their mates, all the children. I knew of other members of our family, but if they existed, I never met them."

Argos nodded.

"It was perfect in every way, except. . ." Argos nodded.

"Except?" Em asked.

"There were two trees," Argo said.

Mary Ayer gasped. She covered her surprise by putting her hand over her mouth.

Em blinked.

"It was forbidden to go to the trees," Argos added.

"Why?" Em asked.

"There was an ancient warning that if you ate from the fruit of either tree, everyone would die," Argos said. "The trees were the altars for all of our ceremonies. Elders buried our dead near one tree, because it was known to create great transitions. Elders left offerings to the other tree, as an offering was known to increase a person's understanding of the world. The trees were so sacred that no child was allowed to even view them."

Argos stared off into space for a moment. Em and Mary Ayer's eyes caught over his head. Em nodded in agreement. He was talking about Eden.

"Everyone knew this to be true," Argos said. "We saw these trees interact with the world. Their roots went deep into the soil, and their braches nearly touched the heavens. They were given to us by the great I am, the creator. To most of us, they *were* the I am."

"Did the trees have names?" Em asked.

"*haChayim*," Argos said with a nod. "And *ha-da'at tov va-ra*."

"The Tree of Life and the Tree of the Knowledge of Good and Evil," Em translated.

Argos nodded in agreement. The young man shook his head and began to cry.

"What is it?" Mary Ayer asked.

"I should have never. . ." the young man said.

He collapsed into his sorrow.

Chapter Twenty-eight

Mary Ayer caught Em's eyes over Argos's head. Em shook her head that she didn't know what to do. Mary Ayer gave an agreeing nod and put a comforting arm around Argos's shoulders. They waited for the young man's sobs to abate.

"What did you do?" Em asked.

Argos looked up at Em. His face was wet with tears and his nose running. As if he were a boy of five or six, Mary Ayer led him to the bathroom, where she helped him blow his nose and wipe his face. Unfailingly kind, Mary Ayer showed him the toilet and stayed to help him urinate. She even endured a few rounds of him flushing the toilet to see how it worked. She then helped the young man take a warm shower. When he returned, he was more centered and smiling.

While they were in the bathroom, Em laid out clothing that would fit him. She had to choose carefully, as these may be the only clothing Argos would have for at least a thousand years or more. Elder Argos had known her when she'd arrived with her father. She was fairly certain that the events that were happening now had happened in his past. Using magic, Em brought a pair of George's favorite fleece-lined jeans and a long sleeved T-shirt from Boston. She decided to give him the wool sweater he'd been wearing.

While he was showering, she infused the sweater with magic so that it would last him a long, long time. Mary Ayer helped him dress.

When he was finally comfortable, Em asked him the question she was fairly certain they had come all this way to ask.

"What happened to you?" Em asked

"I. . ." the young man opened his mouth.

A buzzing sound filled the air. Em saw the young man's mouth move, but she couldn't hear what he'd said. She looked at Mary Ayer, who shook her head. Em reached out to touch Argos.

They were transported from Orkney to a warm, beautiful settlement. Twenty family dwellings sat in a circle around a large fire pit. There was a goat or possibly a sheep on a spit over the coals of a fire. The warm breeze carried the smell of ripe fruit and flowering trees. The sun was just beginning to rise.

Em and Mary Ayer stood next to Argos. Their young friend looked as if he were five or six. His skin had shifted from suntan colored to a rich chocolate brown. His hair remained in tight braids.

"Argos!" A woman's voice called from one of the dwellings. "Argos!"

The boy looked up at Mary Ayer and then at Em. His face broke into a bright grin, showing white teeth. He ran to the hut. They heard a woman chastise the young boy for making her worry. She led the boy out to the fire and began working on his hair.

"They can't see you," a man's voice said.

Em looked to her left and saw the elder Argos standing

between herself and Mary Ayer.

"So we can't change this past," Em said.

"You cannot," Argos said. He turned and reached to hold Mary Ayer's hands. "Your kindness healed a very broken part of me. I carried it with me for a millennium. I believe it's why I became 'Argos the Kind.' I was kind because I learned from you that kindness was powerful. Thank you."

Embarrassed, Mary Ayer could only nod. He kissed Mary Ayer's cheek, and they turned back to watch.

"He is a wicked boy," his mother said to his father. Her voice chided the boy but was kind.

"I am not!" Argos said with a laugh.

"He is a boy," his father said with a chuckle.

"This boy will be the death of me one day," his mother said. "I have too much to care for to deal with his adventurous attitude."

His father laughed.

"Don't give our eldest son so much grief, my love," his father said.

"And why not?" his mother asked.

"He will be a leader someday," his father said. "It's good for him to have a chance to get to know our area."

His mother shot a dark look at Argos's father. His father laughed at her gloom.

"I will take him with me today," his father said.

"Oh no, you don't," his mother said. "The boy will slip away when you are preparing for the hunt."

His father kissed his mother.

"Don't worry," his father said. "He is a boy and will be a great man."

Argos's mother scowled to show her doubt, and Argos screamed a laugh. She gave him a hard kiss on his cheek.

"I love you, my boy," his mother said.

"It's time, my love," Argos's father said. "He needs to take his place among the men. They need to know him so that someday he will be able to lead them."

"Please, Mama!" the child begged.

She relented with a reluctant nod. The worry on his mother's face made his father laugh. She smiled at the sound of his laughter.

Around them, the settlement was beginning to wake to the new day. People joined the small family at the fire pit. While Em, Mary Ayer, and the elder Argos watched, they ate a meal of the cooked meat and what looked like yams. Argos's mother brought her three other children out to the fire. She began breastfeeding her infant son. Argos's father was cleaning his hunting gear and arranging for the hunt. Soon the fire pit was surrounded by young children, mothers with babies at their breasts, and men preparing for the hunt. They seemed incredibly happy.

Although the children called to him to join their play, Argos stayed close to the fire ring. It was clear that he did not wish to miss his father's invitation to go on the hunt. When the time came, his father led the men of the village — including young Argos — from the village. The men carried spears, bows and arrows, and knives. Argos stayed close to his father so as not to miss anything.

Based on seniority and status, the men traveled in a line three across. Argos and his father were at the very front of the line. The men traveled five or six miles until they reached another, less-formal settlement. Like the other boys, Argos brought his father a fizzing, fermented drink and gave him the food Argos had carried from the settlement. The men lit the fires and settled in for the day. A few men practiced their hunting skills, while others told stories and drank the fermented drink. Argos's father was counseling the other men near the fire.

"We aren't going hunting?" Argos asked. His voice rang with disappointment.

"Not today," his father said. "Today we do the important work of building our community."

His father gestured to a line of men waiting to speak with him. Argos scowled.

"What shall I do, father?" Argos asked. He saw his great adventure of going on the hunt disappear before his eyes.

"Practice your hunting skills," his father said with a dismissive wave of his hand.

"But I am an expert archer," Argos said. "I can throw a man's spear with great accuracy. I'm able to wrestle a man twice my size."

"You are my son," Argos's father said with pride. "Now, continued peace in our settlement requires that I help these men resolve their issues. You may stay with me or go practice with the other boys."

"Yes, father," Argos said.

Argos ran to join the other boys, but Argos was not welcomed. He was much younger than the other boys and the leader's son. After a half-hour of trying, the boy left the group of boys. He found a spot in the shade of a tall tree, where he could watch the other boys play. Jealous and lonely, Argos returned to the fire circle, where his father had been holding court, but found no one. Argos discovered his father sound asleep in his midday nap.

Unwilling to disturb his father, Argo decided to go exploring. He bypassed the area where the boys were playing by going in an entirely new direction. He found a clear trail and struck out on his own.

"Uh, oh," Mary Ayer said.

Em, Mary Ayer, and the elder Argos had been silent observers of this day.

"Mischievous hands are the devil's workshop," Em said, putting a spin on the old saying.

"Indeed," Argos said.

They followed young Argos along the path. A happy boy, Argos whistled a nameless tune as he walked. He reached a wide-open area and two enormous trees. The trees seemed to compete with the clouds for space in the sky. The trunks were at least ten feet wide. Both trees were heavy with fruit. Argos stopped to take a drink from the stream that encircled the entire area before entering the space. The young boy touched the memory stones placed for those who had died. He stood on the altar and looked out onto the open space. The bright look on his face reflected his delight.

"I was sure that I'd found an unknown place," the elder Argos said. "I planned to return to my father. You can see..."

The elder Argos pointed to the young boy standing on the altar.

"I was sure my father would be so very proud of me," the elder Argos said. "And that was not an easy feat."

They watched the boy wander to the trees. He looked up into one tree before going to look at the other. He wrapped his arms around the second tree and marveled at its size. He went to check the first tree. Amazed by the wonder of the trees, the young boy watched them dance in the wind.

The wind brought him the scents of the luscious fruit. One tree was growing round, orange fruit while a mixture of fruit grew on the other tree. Some of the fruit was large while some was small. The fruit covered the rainbow in colors. While he watched, the fruit in this second tree shimmered in the wind. Only then did he realize that he was hungry.

As was common for the boys in his settlement, Argos ate fruit for his midday meal. Uncomfortable with the shimmering fruit in the second tree, Argos reached into the first tree and filled his arms with round, orange fruit. He sat down under the shade of the tree. The fruit was sweet and easy to eat. When Argos had finished his pile of fruit, he fell into a deep sleep.

"Did you dream?" Mary Ayer asked.

"If I did, I don't remember now," the elder Argos said.

The sun shifted in the sky at unnatural speed. The day had slipped into afternoon before the young Argos awoke from his nap. Panicked at being late, Argos grabbed the fruit pits left over from his feast and ran toward the men's settlement. As he usually did, Argos threw the pits away at random. He slid into camp just as the men were packing up for the day.

"I had no idea where I'd been or, truly, what I'd done," the elder Argos said. "I felt no guilt. When my father asked me if I'd enjoyed my day, I told him I'd had a wonderful day. We made plans for me to spend the next day with him. I felt proud of myself. I would no longer have to spend my days with the women and children. I had transitioned into manhood early."

"You were no more than a child," Em said.

"I still should have known," the elder Argos said. "Everyone in the settlement knew the story and the dangers of the trees. But I was too busy running around and exploring that I'd had no time for stories told by old men."

"You truly didn't know," Mary Ayer said.

"I had no idea," the elder Argos said. "And I didn't have any idea what had happened until centuries later, when I read the history of Tribe of Israel."

"The bible," Em said, and the elder Argos nodded.

"The five books of Moses, the Torah, which became parts of your bible," the elder Argos said.

As if on fast-forward, the scenes unfolded before them quickly. The young boy greeted his mother with much love. His mother insisted on holding her young son for at least an hour. Because he knew he was returning to the men tomorrow, young Argos allowed his mother to cuddle and baby him. That night, his father announced to the entire group that his young son had transitioned to manhood.

The celebration was large. They were not only celebrating not only a boy's journey into manhood, they were celebrating their next leader. Every household brought out their best food, wine, and beer. They ate, drank, and danced until the moon was high in the sky. Argos's mother carried him to bed. A tear ran down her face as she kissed his cheek.

"I am proud of you, my beautiful son," Argos's mother said.

Argos fell asleep in his bed. Argos's mother went to her own bed, where her infant son lay next to her husband. She picked up her son before realizing that he was dead. Screaming, Argos's mother tried to wake her husband. Unable to wake him, Argos's mother shook Argos's father. He was also dead. Mothers' screams now echoed throughout the settlement. Argos's mother ran to where her other children were sleeping. The two younger children had also died in the night. Argos's mother collapsed at her children's bedside. Able only to crawl, she forced her body to crawl to Argos. She died at his feet.

All the while, the young Argos slept.

The sun was just breaking over the horizon when the child awoke. Getting out of bed, he saw his mother first. A crow was picking at her face, and flies covered her mouth and eyes. Horrified, Argos went from one family member to the next. He ran out into the settlement. House after house, he saw the same sight. Every member of their settlement had died during the night. Scavengers were starting to feast on their bodies. Without an attendant, the fire had gone out. Some large carnivore had carried off the meat prepared the night before.

Argos was completely alone.

The scene began to fade for Em and Mary Ayer. They were suddenly standing in the icy night air on the thin shelf outside of the elders' cave. Em wrapped her arms around herself to keep warm. Mary Ayer moved in close.

"I stayed at the settlement for a couple of hours," the elder Argos said. "Maybe a day. The predators terrified me.

Whether it was a true memory or something created by the tree, I remembered that my father mentioning another settlement of people like us. I left my home to find them."

The elder Argos looked at Em and then at Mary Ayer.

"I got in a low boat and started up the river," the elder Argos said. "In my memory, one minute I was stepping into the small skiff, and the next moment I was in the cave on Rousay. I have no memory of how I got here. My grief and guilt knew no bounds. I may have willed myself to this desolate place. But more likely, the world's currents brought me here."

The elder Argos nodded.

"You ladies are the first people I'd seen since leaving my settlement," the elder Argos said.

"And yet you've aged since then," Em said.

"We do age — you and I," the elder Argos said. "It just takes a very long time to do it."

"What happened?" Mary Ayer asked.

"I would think it would be evident," the elder Argos said.

"I think we want to hear you tell us," Em said.

"I took fruit from the Tree of Life," the elder Argos said. "By taking this fruit, I gave myself immortality and killed everyone I'd ever known. In a breath, they were all dead."

"What about Adam?" Mary Ayer asked. "Eve?"

"Long after my time, I'm afraid," the elder Argos said.

"But. . ." Mary Ayer's mouth fell open with surprise.

Em scowled to cover her own shock.

"You're probably wondering why I shared all of this," the elder Argos said.

Unsure how to respond, the women nodded.

"All of life has a split — light and dark, good and bad, life and death," the elder Argos said. "By eating the fruit from the Tree of Life, I dismissed the death from my life. I stand on the side of life. So do you, Em, and by extension, you, too, Mary Ayer."

Em and Mary Ayer nodded in unison.

"This split tears a hole in life itself," the elder Argos said.

"The demons," Em said.

"The demons are the other side of life," the elder Argos said. "Human beings are children of Adam and Eve. They are both light and dark."

"Demon and us," Em said.

"Exactly," the elder Argos said. "This outcome was not seen by me or anyone else for a long, long time. I lived and loved. Over time, I created others like me. We formed a vibrant community. All the while, I had no idea — truly not even an inkling — that our opposite lingered in oblivion. Slowly, over the millennia, the demons found a way into this world. One at a time, they have killed every single one of our kind."

"We must fight them with everything we have!" Mary Ayer said with intensity.

"Yes," the elder Argos said. "Should you defeat the demons, we shall be restored. Your father. Every single one of our kind will be restored."

"You believe it's possible to defeat the demons?" Em asked.

"Yes," the elder Argos said. "Only you can do this."

"And what happens to my witches if I defeat the demons?" Em asked.

The elder Argos shuffled his feet and looked at the

ground. He took a breath and looked at Em.

"You must do this," the elder Argos said with great intensity. "There is no other recourse."

Mary Ayer gasped.

"I understand," Em said.

"But Em, you can't," Mary Ayer said. "He's saying we will die! We will all die!"

Rather than respond, the elder Argos looked away. Em shifted so that her back was to Mary Ayer.

"Thank you for showing me," Em said. She put her hand on his arm. "Thank you for letting me know what this is all about."

He gave her a slow nod, and she smiled.

"Em, you can't!" Mary Ayer said to Em's back.

Em glanced over her shoulder to Mary Ayer. Reading her look, Mary Ayer crossed her arms and fell silent. Em turned back.

"I wore that sweater for a long, long time," the elder Argos said with a soft smile. "When Levi Strauss wanted to start his business, I gave him the startup capital. I brought sheep to Orkney."

He nodded to Em before shifting to partially face Mary Ayer.

"Thank you for your kindness," the elder Argos said. He reached out and stroked Mary Ayer's cheek. "You saved my life in so many ways."

With that, he looked at Em and nodded his good-byes.

"Good luck," the elder Argos said. "You must vanquish the demons. Until then, you are the only living of our kind. I look forward to embracing you again."

The elder Argos hopped over the six-foot canal and

disappeared into the cave. The ground began to shake.

"Hold on!" Em yelled.

She reached out for Mary Ayer. They held onto each other while the earth shook. Across the channel, the cave roof began to crumble above the community cave.

"Get us out of here!" Mary Ayer yelled as a large boulder obscured the community cave's entrance.

Em took a breath and willed them to their hotel room. They held onto each other for a moment.

"What was that?" Mary Ayer asked.

"The cave is shut to us," Em said.

Mary Ayer pushed away from Em.

"I can't believe it!" Mary Ayer said. "We need that library! We are completely lost without it. How can we find a way to save us all without it?"

Em gave her a grim look.

"What?" Mary Ayer asked. "You can't possibly be thinking of destroying the demons."

Em gave Mary Ayer a long look.

"What is it?" Mary Ayer asked. Her voice edged toward panic. "What are you going to do? What are we going to do? This is horrible, just horrible!"

Mary Ayer grabbed Em's shoulders and gave her a little shake.

"What are we going to do?" Mary Ayer said.

"I promise you this: I will do everything in my power to find a way," Em said with a nod. "No. I *will* find a way to save us all."

Mary Ayer hugged Em tight.

Chapter Twenty-nine

"There you are," Alice Parker said as she came out onto a wide stone balcony off the library in the back of the castle in Scotland.

Em turned in her seat to watch Alice walk toward her. The balcony was so dark that Alice had to make a light in her hand so that she could see.

"I've been looking for you," Alice said. "Are you hiding out here in the cold and dark?"

"I'm sorry," Em said, turning back toward the ocean. "I wasn't trying to hide. I'm just..."

Shrugging, she turned to Alice and smiled.

"Please," Em said. "Why were you looking for me?"

Alice put her hands on her hips and scowled at Em.

"Why, Martha Emogene Panon Rich Corey Peres Burroughs..." Alice said. She smirked at listing out all of Em's names.

"Just 'Em,' please." She waved her hand at all of the names. Alice grinned.

"Well, whoever you are, you're depressed!" Alice said.

"Depressed?" Em asked. She squinted her eyes and thought for a while. "No, pensive — not depressed."

"Pensive?" Alice said with a laugh. She moved between Em and the stone half-wall to sit in the chair on Em's right. "Yes, that's not depressed at all."

Em glanced at Alice and grinned.

"What are you pensive about, my dear?" Alice asked.

"Oh, you know," Em said.

"Having to choose between your beloved hanging buddies and an entire race of people, most of whom you've never met?" Alice asked.

"Something like that," Em said.

"Mary Ayer is confident you'll pick your people," Alice said.

"My people?" Em asked. "Who would that be? The family I've spent the last three hundred years with or a family that I'm related to by genetics?"

"The much superior, almost God-like, and incredibly rare people from Rousay," Alice said.

Em looked at Alice.

"You're not seriously thinking about it," Alice said.

"I'm..." Em stopped talking and looked out over the crashing waves. "Watching the surf."

"But..." Alice said.

"Every time I'm here in Scotland, I wonder how I could have ever forgotten that I love it so much," Em said. "It is my very soul."

"And not Boston?" Alice said with a smirk to indicate that she was willing to play along with Em.

"I love Boston," Em said. "It's my home. But Scotland..."

Em sighed.

"I know what you mean," Alice said. "Were you talking to George?"

"He calls on Sunday nights," Em said.

"How is he?" Alice asked.

"Cold," Em said with a laugh. Alice laughed. "He's going to meet us at home when we get there. I guess there are some big storms coming in."

"A little snow has frightened the good Reverend?" Alice asked.

"I'll let you tell him that," Em said.

Alice laughed. Em smiled. They watched the water for a few minutes before Alice reached across to grab Em's hand.

"What are you stuck on, Em?" Alice asked.

Sighing, Em shook her head.

"Me, Alice — your daughter, best friend, constant project, much loved Alice," Alice said. "You've always been able to talk to me."

"I'm not exactly sure where to start," Em said.

"Start where you are," Alice said. "What's going on with you? I don't believe for one minute that you're going to toss us out because some guy you don't even know — who killed his entire family, no less — told you to do it."

Em raised her eyebrows and nodded.

"Was it the serpent?" Alice asked. "Or the demons?"

Em scowled for a moment. Letting her think, Alice held her tongue.

"It's me, I think," Em said. "Both the serpent and the demon told me that I was 'different.' I don't know what that means. The demon said that he was keeping Weni and my father away from me. Why? And Argos was so disappointing."

"How so?" Alice asked.

"Honestly, I don't think I would have thought about it if

I hadn't met the youngman version of him," Em said. "But he was. . . primitive. He lacked basic reasoning skills."

"Mary Ayer told me he flushed the toilet over and over again," Alice said. "And not because he thought it was cool."

"He couldn't understand the connection of pushing the button and the flush," Em said. "She basically had to take the toilet apart, and, even then, he didn't get it."

"Simple cause and effect," Alice said with a nod. "That's the cornerstone of morality."

"Exactly," Em said. "And he's the one who set up the immortals' society."

Shaking her head, Em shrugged. She turned to look at the waves. She was so lost in thought that she was startled when Alice spoke again.

"You think it's because he never ate from the other tree?" Alice asked.

She put her hand on Em's arm to steady her.

"The Tree of the Knowledge of Good and Evil?" Em winced. After a moment, she nodded her head. "I've wondered."

"But you can think through things," Alice said. "You understand cause and effect. You and George are the smartest people I've ever known."

"That's why it's confusing," Em said.

"What's 'confusing'?" Mary Ayer asked as she came out onto the balcony. "Goodness, Em! It's freezing out here."

Em snapped her fingers, and Mary Ayer was wearing one of Em's knitted sweaters, a hat, and a pair of thick socks. Mary Ayer touched the wool.

"It's so soft and warm," Mary Ayer said.

"Em's knitting is the best," Alice said, touching the sweater she had on.

"I made a bunch of stuff for this trip," Em said. "You're welcome to it."

"It looks nice on you, Mary," Alice said.

"Thanks," Mary Ayer said. "Can I keep the socks, too?"

"Of course," Em said. "And the hat."

Mary Ayer walked to the balcony wall.

"Now what was confusing?" Mary Ayer asked. A short woman, she easily leaned on the half-wall separating the balcony from the surf. "You can't seriously be confused as to whether to save us or all of these people you don't know."

Mary Ayer's voice held her anger and hurt.

"Em's trying to figure out what to do!" Alice said.

"What's the issue?" Mary Ayer said. "Those people went the way of *Homo Erectus* and all the other ancestral humans. We are here and now."

"I know what you're saying, Mary," Em said. "And you're right. When you look at it that way, the answer is obvious. I wouldn't bring back a dinosaur. Why would I bring back this community?"

"Right, why?" Mary Ayer asked.

"To start, my father happens to be one of them," Em said.

"But. . ." Mary Ayer said.

"Em thinks that Argos didn't eat from the Tree of Knowledge," Alice said.

"Like Adam and Eve did?" Mary Ayer asked. "But. . ."

"Listen," Em said with such intensity that Mary Ayer turned to look at her. Alice's hand returned to Em's arm.

"The truth is that I don't know. Anything, really. And there's no one for me to ask. Not a living soul."

"But I don't get what you don't know," Mary Ayer said. "I mean, I'm really good at finding out things. Really good at it. If I know what you're missing, then it's nothing for me to find what you need. So you could just ask me."

"What do you know about the Tree of Knowledge of Good and Evil or the Tree of Life?" Alice asked.

"Other than what's in the original five chapters?" Mary Ayer asked. "I mean, I've read them in the Greek."

"Other than that," Em said.

"Why..." Mary Ayer stammered. "Nothing. I mean, almost every culture has a story about a Tree of Life. It is always described the same way — the branches of the tree reach up past the sky while its roots dive deep into the earth. But that's not really what you mean. Gosh, I don't even know where I'd start to look for information."

"Caves at Mogao?" Alice asked.

"No, I've been there," Mary Ayer said. "I mean, I'm a witch, right? I've been to undiscovered manuscript libraries all over the world, including Egypt and Israel."

"Ethiopia," Em said. "That's where the Garden of Eden is supposed to have been. We could go there and..."

Em shook her head.

"What?" Alice asked.

"Argos said that he didn't understand what had happened until he read the Talmud," Mary Ayer said. She nodded. "I've read that in every ancient language."

She scowled.

"Sorry, I don't know," Mary Ayer said.

Alice gave her a kind smile. Em raised and dropped her

shoulders to indicate that she was in the same place.

"We weren't able to interact with anyone when we went back," Em said.

"Maybe that's something Argos did," Mary Ayer said.

"I don't think so," Em said. "I think that there are some events that simply cannot be changed. Maybe changing them would affect too many things. Maybe they were fated or had to happen. Or maybe. . ."

"They didn't happen at all," Mary Ayer said.

"Maybe what we saw didn't happen in real time but rather was a story created around what actually happened," Em said. "I mean, what do you remember from being five?"

"At this point, very little," Alice said.

"I'd believe that Argos ate the fruit from the Tree of Life. I believe the fruit gave him immortality," Em said with a nod. "I even believe that everyone he knew died. I'm just not confident that he didn't kill them himself. That's certainly what he's asking me to do. And remember what they used to do with non-birth immortals."

"Burn them in the fire," Alice said with a nod.

"Right," Em said. "Argos created the elder community in his own image. That's truth. I'm pretty sure that the story he showed us is *his truth* — but not the literal truth."

"Then we need to find out more about Eden and. . ." Mary Ayer said.

"No," Em said with the power of finality. "This isn't about Argos. It's about us. We don't need to find out more about him."

"We need to find out more about us," Alice said.

"Right," Em said. "I hate to say it, I really do, but I think we need to go back to our own Eden."

"You're not suggesting. . ." Mary Ayer said.

"I am suggesting just that," Em said.

"If we need to go to Salem Village, then we'd better just go," Martha Carrier said from the doorway. "We go together. We leave right now. If we think about it too long, we'll chicken out."

"Get what we need," Mary Ayer said. "And we get the hell out of there."

"No dilly dallying," Em said. She looked at Alice. "No staring at your husband or going home."

"But. . ." Alice said. She licked her lips like a greedy child in a candy shop. "I. . ."

"No," Martha Carrier said. She came out onto the balcony and put her hands on Alice's shoulders. "If we could, I'd say, 'Go for it,' but we can't. Seeing John would change everything. He won't be at home when you come to get him. Em won't have a ride into Boston. You got to spend the *rest of his life* with him and watch your children have grandchildren. Do you wish to risk that?"

"No," Alice said with a firm shake of her head. "No way. No."

"Then we go, figure out what Em wants, and get the hell out of there," Martha Carrier said. "Em, can you make us invisible?"

"I think so," Em said.

"Okay," Alice said. "I understand. But I'm going to need help."

"No, you're not," Em said. "John didn't go to your hanging. Remember? He was trying to get out of town before they came after your kids."

"I told him to do that," Alice said with a nod.

"You begged him to," Em said.

"So we agree?" Martha Carrier asked. "Did that jerk Cotton Mather go to your hanging?"

"He only went to yours," Mary Ayer said.

"Figures," Martha Carrier said. "What are you looking for, Em?"

"I'm not sure," Em said.

"Then how will we know if we've found it?" Alice asked.

"Good point," Em said.

"Tell us what you think you need," Mary Ayer said.

"Well. . ." Em said with a nod. "Because I was arrested in April with Rebecca, I didn't get a chance to see the whole thing unfold."

"I did," Alice said.

"Me, too," Mary Ayer said.

"Okay," Em said. "Then maybe we have that covered. Good. The only other thing was that I had this memory come back, or maybe it was a dream. In it, I saw my demon standing in the crowd at my hanging. Just before I died, he said something like, 'Now it begins.' I want to see if he was really there."

"And if he is?" Martha Carrier asked.

"I want to figure out *why* he was there," Em asked. "Was he involved in the trials? Did he make the entire thing happen?"

"Oh, no, Em," Mary Ayer said. She took a big breath to start lecturing. Seeing everyone's faces, she said instead, "He didn't make it happen."

"Unless Cotton Mather was your demon," Martha Carrier said. "He certainly was mine."

"It's plausible," Em said with a smile.

Martha Carrier nodded.

"Okay," Mary Ayers said. "You need to get a feel for what Salem was like from the perspective of a townsperson, and you want to see if your demon is at your hanging."

Em nodded.

"Anything else?" Mary Ayer asked.

"I think we'll know it when we see it," Em said.

"Is that okay with everyone?" Martha Carrier asked.

"Em's never been wrong," Alice said. "If she says we'll know something, then we'll know it."

Em smiled at Alice's loyalty.

"I agree," Martha Carrier said.

"Me, too," Mary Ayer said.

"Okay," Em said.

As she stood up, their dress transformed into standard Puritan housewife wear.

"In case we're seen," Em said.

Before they could respond, she reached out and touched Mary Ayer and Alice. Martha Carrier was quick enough to grab Em while keeping her hand on Alice. In a flash, they were standing in a muddy puddle on the road to Gallows Hill.

"Did you have to change my shoes?" Martha Carrier asked. She looked down and changed back into her hiking boots.

"Ghastly," Alice said, as she changed hers as well.

"Are we invisible?" Mary Ayer asked.

A mother and father trudged by them with their young children.

"Good Lord, the smell," Martha Carrier said. She went

to the side to throw up. "Rotten flesh, manure, body odor. Did we ever bathe?"

"You can smell the bodies rotting in the crevice," Em said. "Our bodies."

"They could all smell us," Mary Ayer said. "The stench of rotting human flesh hung in pockets around the town. You'd walk down any street, and the scent would assault you. The smell filled your nostrils and mouth. You could taste it in everything you ate. People wore scarves over their mouths so as not to smell it. It was a constant reminder of what had been done."

"And what was to come," Martha Carrier said.

"So many of our friends and family were in prison," Mary Ayer said. "My friend Rebecca... I felt like I could smell the distinct scent of her rotting body — day after day, rotting a little bit more every minute that passed."

Mary Ayer stepped back so another dismal family could walk by.

"I felt so wretched that I hadn't saved her," Mary Ayer said. "But how?"

"Why aren't these people working?" Em asked. She gestured to the many families trudging through the mud and muck toward Gallows Hill. "It's September! Harvest time! Get to work, you hypocrites!"

"Wow," Alice said. "You really don't know."

"Know what?" Em asked.

Alice, Mary Ayer, and Martha Carrier shared a look.

"During the trials, the entire region stopped functioning," Mary Ayer said, finally.

"What do you mean?" Em gave an angry sniff. "When Henry was alive, I was ridiculed for my ungodly laziness.

'Who did I think I was? An aristocrat?' 'God smites those who don't grow their own food.' 'You will rot in hell for not farming, Martha Rich.' Blah, blah."

"That's just it," Alice said. "If you didn't attend the trials, you were suspect. If you didn't give testimony, someone was bound to give it about you. Everyone was terrified for their lives. No one had time to plant that spring or summer. There was nothing to harvest in the fall."

"And if you planted, you were instantly suspect because you weren't attending the trials," Mary Ayer said with a nod toward Alice.

"You were in Boston with Isaac, so you don't know," Martha Carrier said. "Once it was over, there wasn't any food around. Your son, Benoni, had a hard time feeding us that winter."

"Our farm went fallow when John left," Alice said.

"Any food that was available was obscenely expensive," Mary Ayer said. "Benoni was able to afford it only when you and Isaac sent money."

"The food you brought from Boston was often all we had for the month," Martha Carrier said.

"It was a terribly cold winter, too," Mary Ayer said. "Most families spent their money on food. Many couldn't afford to keep warm. Entire families froze to death in their beds."

"All because they were obsessed with the trials," Em said.

"All because they were bullied into participating," Martha Carrier said. "It was a blight on the entire community."

"Oh, come on! Where are the soldiers forcing them to

do anything?" Em gestured to the families moving along the mud road. "They're not forced to do a thing! They're here for the thrill of watching someone else suffer. It's like reality television for the bored Puritans of Salem Village."

"I never went to the trials," Alice said. "I never liked gossip. John didn't, either. And I didn't give two shakes about church politics. It's one of the reasons they picked me up — because we worked our fields instead of attending the trials."

"To set an example of what happens when you don't go along," Mary Ayer said.

"And everyone knew this?" Em asked.

"If you didn't smell it day in and day out, someone was whispering that you were in danger," Mary Ayer said. "The pressure was tremendous. Think of it this way: They arrested you — a wealthy Puritan woman in good standing at the church — and they hanged Rebecca. Everyone was fair game."

"They accused one hundred and eighty-five people, Em," Martha Carrier said. "That doesn't count the people who confessed rather than be charged."

"There weren't that many Europeans living here," Em said under her breath.

"About three thousand in the entire Northeast," Mary Ayer said. "The trials involved almost ten percent of the entire population between Maine and New York. That's everyone."

"The people who were charged were either testifying against their neighbor or being tortured until they confessed," Martha Carrier said.

Em gave Mary Ayer a grim nod. For a moment, they

watched a mother herd her two boys up the muddy hill.

"We should get going," Em said.

They started up the hill. Em and Mary Ayer slipped and almost fell while Alice and Martha Carrier made it up easily. They'd gone only a few feet before Em and Mary Ayer changed their shoes as well. They found a spot on a small rise near the back of the growing crowd.

"They're talking about Giles," Alice said about the family standing next to her. "Everyone is horrified."

"They should be," Em said with a sniff.

"Em," Alice touched her shoulder, "if you want to really see what's going on, you have to open your heart and let go of the chip on your shoulder."

Surprised, Em turned to look at Alice. She gave Em a compassionate nod. Em looked up at the heavens and nodded.

"I'm not back five minutes, and I'm right back to who I was in 1692," Em said.

"We love you." Alice hugged Em.

Martha Carrier put her arm on Em's shoulder. Mary Ayer was busying looking around. She turned to them.

"We're coming," Mary Ayer said.

The crowd shifted as word that the cart carrying the "witches" was almost there. A group of angry young men and women moved to the front of the crowd, while most people shifted back. Women tucked their children into their skirts. They could hear the jeering, abusive men who'd followed the cart from the jail in Boston. The young people on the hill took up the abuse.

The women in the cart, including Em, Mary Ayer, and Alice, were pelted with rotten vegetables and fruit, feces, and horrible words. Em stood at the front of the cart in angry defiance like a wooden figurehead on the front of a galleon. Terrified and hysterical, Alice clung to Em's shoulder. Mary Ayer was near the back. The cart got stuck in the mud and almost capsized. A few strong men helped keep the cart moving.

"That happened to us," Martha Carrier said. "But I don't think we had this much... vitriol. Most of it was focused on George. I hate to say it, but at the time, I thought he deserved it. I didn't even know the man."

The Alice Parker on the cart was hit in the forehead with a clump of human feces. On the cart, Em wiped Alice's face with her sleeve. She said something into Alice's ear.

"What did you say?" Martha Carrier asked.

"She told me not to let them take my last moments from me," Alice said. "'Don't let them steal our last moments on this beautiful earth from us.' She'd been saying that the entire trip to Gallows Hill. And truly, it was a gorgeous day — not too hot, with a lovely breeze. Above the noise and the stench, I could smell the open ocean. Everything was green from the recent rains."

Alice nodded.

"When I hanged, I focused on the glorious oak tree above and ocean wind," Alice said. "The shimmering leaves and warm sunshine. They did not take that from me."

"Me, either," Mary Ayer said. "The water in the creek. The glory of the day, itself. The God that awaited me. That was my hanging."

The look of gratitude on Mary Ayer and Alice's faces

brought tears to Em's eyes.

"What the hell are you doing here?" An angry voice came from Em's left.

Em turned and gasped. Her demon was marching straight toward her.

Chapter Thirty

Em reeled back in horror. Her feet caught on her long dress, and she stumbled.

"And you're pregnant!" her demon said as he continued in her direction. "I told you what would happen if you added to your ranks! Now you're giving birth to another immortal! Do you have any clue of what you've done?"

He was ten times bigger than she remembered and that much more horrifying. Em's hands went to protect the new life growing inside of her. Her mouth fell open to scream, but no sound came out.

"Em?" Alice asked.

"Em!" Mary Ayer said. "What's happening?"

Too terrified to speak, Em raised her hand and pointed. Mary Ayer and Martha Carrier looked at where she was pointing. Alice grabbed Em's shoulders from behind to keep Em from falling down. Mary Ayer and Martha Carrier shook their heads. They caught Alice's eye. She shook her head.

"We can't see it, Em," Alice said in a kind but worried voice. "Is it your demon?"

Em nodded. She swallowed hard and tried to ground herself. She could not fight the demon in this panicked state.

"Mary? Martha?" Alice asked.

The women shook their heads. The demon took a final angry step, and Em stepped back. Alice jumped into the path of the oncoming demon. Martha Carrier stepped right to Alice's side. They linked arms with each other. Mary Ayer linked arms with Martha Carrier, creating a formidable wall of witches.

The demon reared back from them. His cloven feet dug into the muddy ground. He jerked his head back with such force that he tipped backward. He wavered for a moment before the weight of the horn in the center of his forehead was too much. He fell on his rear with such a force that the witches felt the air move and a slight tremor in the earth.

"What was that?" Mary Ayer asked. She looked at Em. "Em!"

Lost in her own world, Em gave Mary Ayer a glazed look. Her eyes were blank with shock.

"He fell," Em said in a toneless voice.

Without warning, Em pushed Martha Carrier forward. The line of witches weaved forward with the force. Martha Carrier took a step forward and then another. The demon scooched back to get out of the way.

"Em?" Martha Carrier asked.

"I'm so sorry," Em said. "I had to see."

"What, Em?" Mary Ayer asked. "What did you have to see?"

"I had to see if he could touch you," Em said in the same dead voice. "He's moving away from you."

"Stupid fucker," Alice said.

She jumped toward the demon. The creature screamed with terror. He ran off into the crowd. Alice chased him for a moment before rushing back to Em's side. She put her arm around Em.

Em grabbed Martha Carrier and Mary Ayer. In a breath, they were all standing on the balcony in Scotland. Em collapsed in a heap.

"What the hell?" Martha Carrier asked. She leaned down to Em. "What just happened?"

Em stared at the stone floor of the porch. Alice crouched down to her side.

"Come on," Alice said. "Let's get her inside. Mary, can you make some tea?"

"First," Mary Ayer said. She clapped her hands, and they were wearing their own clothing again. "Thank God."

Mary Ayer gave a nod and left to make tea. Em grabbed Martha Carrier's ankle. Martha knelt down to her.

"I'm so sorry," Em said. Tears of guilt and sorrow fell from her eyes. "Please, you have to believe that I never, ever would have risked. . ."

"Oh, Em," Martha Carrier stroked Em's cheek. "I know."

Martha pressed her cheek against Em's.

"How did you know?" Martha Carrier asked.

"I realized that, every time I'd fought the demon, you and the other witches were there," Em said. "I saw him alone only in my dreams. Every other time, you or the others were with me. I wondered. . ."

"That's enough," Alice said. "She's pregnant, in shock, and frozen to the core. She needs tea and warmth. Martha, get her other arm."

Between Alice and Martha, they got her inside the castle's library. Mary Ayer had started a fire on her way to the kitchen. Alice fanned the flames, and the fire roared to life. Martha Carrier and Alice situated Em in a cozy armchair next to the fire. Martha Carrier brought a thick wool blanket and draped it around her. They stepped back and looked at her.

Em was completely lost in thought. Her eyes focused on the fire. Her lips rubbed against each other as if they were sanding each other smooth.

"What should we do?" Martha Carrier asked in a low voice.

"Leave her alone for a moment," Alice said in a low tone. In a more directed, louder voice, she said, "When the tea's ready, we'll make her talk to us."

"I heard that," Em said.

"You were supposed to," Alice said.

Martha Carrier smiled at Alice but held her tongue.

"Come on. Em made some of her triple-ginger cookies," Alice said. "We'll have them with our tea."

She hooked arms with Martha Carrier, and they left the room. A few minutes later, Em heard them laugh. She let out a breath. With her breath, her sorrow came flowing out. Her mind flashed through a horrible slideshow of the sights, sounds, and sensations of her hanging day. She wept for herself, before weeping for her community. It had never occurred to her that this thing — this Salem Witch Trial thing — had happened to everyone. She was so lost in her sorrow that she didn't realize that Martha Carrier had returned until she spoke.

"Should I call George?" Martha Carrier asked.

Em shook her head and tried to reel in her sorrow.

"You've never grieved," Martha Carrier said. She knelt

down next to Em's chair. "The year we spent in the barn, you were off in Boston trying to make a life for us. We were a wreck. We didn't have to stay together. We did because we were too grief-stricken to do anything else. You've never had a chance to feel all of it."

Tears still falling from her eyes, Em could only look at Martha Carrier. Em gave a slow nod.

"Have you ever talked to anyone about it?" Martha Carrier asked. "About all of it? Henry and George and Giles, the Indians, and all of the crap that happened after Salem Village? Have you told anyone the whole damned thing?"

"I wouldn't know what to say," Em whispered.

Em shook her head. Martha hugged Em. She sat at Em's feet to give her company in her sorrow. By the time Alice returned, Em was more stable.

"Where did you disappear to, Martha?" Alice asked in a playful voice.

Seeing Em's sorrow and Martha at her feet, Alice gave a slow shake of her head. She set down the tray with a pot of tea and cups she'd been carrying and went to Em. Alice sat on one of the arms of the chair and put her arm around Em.

"What's going on?" Mary Ayer asked as she entered the room.

"Em's sadness caught up to her," Alice said. She mouthed, "Finally."

Mary Ayer nodded. She set down the tray with plates of various cookies on it. She took a seat on the other arm of the chair. For a few moments, they sat in close communion with Em. When Em felt a little clearer, she took a breath.

"How about some tea?" Em asked. She wiped her eyes.

"Of course." Alice kissed Em's cheek and went to pour tea.

Martha Carrier held up a box of Kleenex, and Em blew her nose. They were silent until Alice brought tea. They fell into a companionable silence while they enjoyed their warm tea and bright fire on a cold January night.

"Did you get what you needed, Em?" Mary Ayer said in a soft voice, breaking the silence.

"I believe so," Em said.

"Can I help with anything?" Mary Ayer asked.

"I'm not sure, Mary," Em said. "Probably. I'm not sure what, though. I have to think it through first."

"Can you tell us anything?" Alice asked.

"I don't ever want to go back to Salem Village," Em said.

"The smell alone will keep me away!" Martha Carrier said with a laugh.

"I have to say. . ." Alice started. She sniffed back a tear. "I think of that time as the best days of my life. Everything was exactly how I wanted my life to be. But. . ."

Alice nodded. Her face broke out into a wide smile.

"I loved my John and my babies, but good Lord, just the smell alone was awful," Alice said. "The people were so horrible. . ."

"Small minded," Mary Ayer said with a companionable nod. "I don't think I would have ever thought that until we went back."

"We were all so caught up in our fight with the church," Em said.

"King James and his horrible bible," Martha Carrier said. "We were so sure."

"About everything," Alice said with a nod.

"Exactly," Em said.

"You have to remember, though," Mary Ayer said. "At that time, most real information was managed by the Royal Family. We didn't have the kind of freedom of information that we have now. We didn't know about other places in the world. We only knew about ourselves."

"It was a different time," Em said.

"Did you see Ann Putnam, Junior?" Martha Carrier asked.

"No!" Em said with a startled laugh. "Was she there?"

"With her other horrible accusing compatriots, may they rot in hell forever. Even George Jacob's miserable granddaughter was there," Martha Carrier said. "I wanted to scratch their eyes out."

"Oh, I did that," Mary Ayer said.

"You did not!" Em said in incredulous surprise.

"Oh yes, I did." Mary Ayer nodded. "They clearly didn't need eyes to make their determinations of the world."

"Or to murder twenty people," Martha Carrier sniffed.

"Did you really hurt them?" Alice asked.

"Permanently disfigured one or two of them," Mary Ayer said with an angry sniff.

"Are you ever going to tell us what you did to Ann Putnam Junior's parents?" Alice asked Em.

"Why are you always so sure that *I* was the one who did something to them?" Em tried for an indignant voice, but it came out as a laugh.

"Who else could it have been?" Mary Ayer asked. "We were together in the barn. Alice was on some island off the coast of North Carolina. It had to be you."

Smiling, Em shook her head.

"Oh, forget her," Alice said. "It was probably Isaac, anyway."

Em snorted a surprised laugh.

"Isaac did something to the Putnams?" Mary Ayer asked. "Peaceful, wonderful Isaac?"

Em shook her head. Martha Carrier got up from her spot at Em's feet.

"Is there more tea?" Martha Carrier asked.

"Under the cozy," Mary Ayer said. "I thought we could use at least two pots."

Martha Carrier gave Mary Ayer a soft smile. She touched Em's shoulder before going to the tea tray. Alice picked up the plate of cookies and passed it around. Soon they were eating cookies and drinking tea. They had settled next to the fire when Mary Ayer gave a big sigh. They turned to look at her.

"So what did Isaac do to the Putnams?" Mary Ayer asked.

"I will never tell," Em said. "After all. . ."

"How do you know it was him?" Alice, Martha Carrier, and Mary Ayer said.

They laughed and settled in with their tea and cookies. After a few minutes, they were chatting and laughing about their return to Salem Village. Em looked from face to face and felt overwhelming gratitude for her witches. She smiled and joined their conversation.

. . . . .

"Tell me again," George said.

He pulled the covers back from the bed. Em came out of

their bathroom wearing her bathrobe. She had a towel around her wet hair.

"I will tell you that bathrooms are truly wonderful," Em said. "Showers are the stuff of dreams."

"Five minutes in Salem Village gave you quite the perspective on modern life," George said with a laugh.

He got into bed and pulled the thick comforter up to his chin. Seeing that she wasn't quite ready to join him, he scooted back to sit with his back against the headboard.

"It was. . ." Em turned to face him, ". . . life changing, *and* it was more than five minutes."

"It sounds awful to me," George said. "Why did you go back to that moment?"

"I saw the demon," Em said. "You remember — I had that dream where I saw him. . ."

Em stopped talking and smirked at him.

"You know all of this," Em said.

"I know," George said. "I thought you might need to talk about it some more."

"Why?" Em asked.

She raised her lip to indicate that she wouldn't mind never talking about it again. He smiled at her deception, and she grinned.

"Tell me again," George repeated.

"Tell you what?" Em asked coyly.

George rolled his eyes.

"Tell me about my son, Martha," George said.

"Benoni?" Em said with a grin. "I thought we weren't sure he was your son."

Groaning, George fell face down on the bed. He was there so long, Em wondered if he'd died again.

"George?" Em asked.

She touched his shoulder. He didn't respond. Concerned, she climbed onto the bed.

"George?" Em asked.

She shook his shoulder. He reached up and grabbed her. She squelched a scream. She let him pull her to the bed. He gave her a hard kiss on her lips.

"Did you get one of those picture things?" George asked.

"A son-o-gram?" Em enunciated the syllables.

"Yeah, whatever," George said. "Where is it?"

"You'd have to let go of me," Em said.

"Never," George said. "I will never let you go."

"I'm so glad," Em said.

She kissed him, and he smiled.

"Tell me again," George said for a third time.

"Okay! Okay!" Em said in exaggerated exasperation.

He let her go and rolled onto his back. She didn't say anything. After a few moments, he was groaning again.

"I wanted to see how long you'd wait," Em said. "You know girls who give it up too soon are thought to be hussies."

"Yes, you're right — almost four hundred years is way too early," George said with a laugh.

Em laughed. She reached into her pocket and gave him a copy of the sonogram. He squealed with delight at the sight and then fell silent.

"I have no idea what I'm looking at," George said. "Why was John's so much clearer?"

"Because John had one of his 'people' fix the picture with one of those programs," Em said. She took a few steps on her knees until she was near his head. "Here's his little head. His nose is big like yours."

"How do you know it's a boy?" George asked.

"Ann left that part out," Em said. "No pervy stuff."

George laughed. For a few minutes, he focused only on the image. He kissed the picture and then kissed her belly.

"Why aren't you bigger?" George asked. "Is there something wrong?"

"Nothing's wrong," Em said.

"But Mary Eastey is huge."

"She's pretty tiny," Em said. "She's almost a month ahead of me."

"Why?" George asked.

"I think she got pregnant when I was on Rousay," Em said. "Then you remember how crazy things were when I got back. We weren't terribly active."

"But why aren't you all huge like Mary?" George asked of Mary Eastey.

"I was about like this with the other boys," Em said. "I only got bigger the last month or so. I think it's because I'm fairly tall."

"That counts?" George asked.

"I have no idea," Em said.

"When do you see Ann again?" George asked.

"You mean, she wouldn't answer your questions at dinner?" Em asked.

She couldn't help but smirk at him.

"I know! Can you believe it?" George asked. "After all we've been through, she said she wouldn't break 'doctor-client confidentiality.'"

"I guess you'll just have to trust me," Em said.

"Oh, Em, I do trust you," George said. "I also have a lot

of questions. I mean, when I had children before, it was this big mystery. My wives became pregnant, and they dealt with it. Plus we didn't even know until the baby was almost here. And even then, it didn't have much to do with me. But now, I get to be in the room! I get to watch him grow inside you! I get to be a part of the whole thing!"

George cheered with glee.

"What about your homeless brethren?" Em asked. "Are you saying you're not heading out again?"

"I. . ." George stopped talking. "Shit, I didn't even think about that. Crap."

He looked at the photo again.

"What am I going to do?" he said with great despair in his voice.

Em laughed at him. She unwound the towel on her head and rubbed it against her hair.

"It's not funny," George said. "This time of year, I'm the only thing that stands between them and certain death."

"I know," Em said. "That's why I didn't tell you."

"I've already forgiven you for that," George said.

"Forgiven me. . ." Em chuckled and went back into the bathroom to brush her hair.

"I could be really mad!" George yelled after her.

"You're not," Em yelled.

When she came out, George was lying on his back with his eyes closed. He held the sonogram against his heart. She slipped off her bathrobe and into bed. When he didn't move, she turned off the light. He rolled over and draped his arm around her. She kissed his forehead. Without much thought, she fell into a sound sleep.

She was standing face to face with her demon.

"You think you can hide from me!" the demon yelled in her face. "You think you can add to your ranks and I won't know about it!"

"I... I..." Em swallowed hard. She tried to ground herself to be ready to fight him.

"Three babies!" the demon said. "Three!"

"We were already pregnant when you made your ultimatum!" Em yelled back.

Proud for standing up for herself, she gave him a solid nod. The demon gave a cruel laugh.

"You think that matters?" the demon asked.

"I thought it might," Em said.

"It doesn't," the demon said. "What you add, I will take from you a hundred fold!"

"What does that mean?" Em asked. "Why do you always talk in riddle and then tell me I'm stupid for not understanding? Speak plainly, and then maybe I'll understand you!"

The demon snickered maliciously.

"Juno will rise tonight," the demon said, and disappeared.

Em awoke with a start. She sat up in bed and turned on the light.

"Em?" George asked.

Outside, the wind began to howl. The edge of the coming snowstorm was just hitting Boston. Gusts of wind rattled the windows in her front room. She ran out to see what was happening. Snow was so falling fast that the Common was invisible to her. The wind took up her demon's howl. The snow increased.

"What is it?" George came out of the bedroom. "Lord,

have mercy. This is more than a blizzard."

"He said 'Juno will rise tonight,'" Em said.

"This snowstorm is called 'Juno,'" George said with a nod.

"When did they start naming snowstorms?" Em asked

George shrugged and shook his head. A gigantic snow-shaped demon bashed against the windows. George's hands went to his ears.

"What is that sound?" George asked.

"My demon," Em said.

"Since when did you get a demon?" George asked. "Did you purchase it from the demon store? Call it from hell with a spell? Or..."

"George!" Em said.

"He's some kind of creature tied to you," George said. "You don't know that he's a demon."

"You've seen him!" Em said.

"I have not had that pleasure," George said. "Certainly, if I had, I'd make sure he left you alone. I've been to war plenty of times. There's no enemy that can..."

"Alice saw him!" Em said.

"Alice spends half her time reading your mind!" George yelled back. "She saw him and the other demons through your eyes. So did the other witches. You let them in your mind so they won't force you to talk to them."

"You've never seen him." Em was so surprised that her mouth dropped open. "What about at the meeting?"

"You mean John Parker?" George asked.

"No, the demon," Em said. "What about when we battled him on Gallows Hill?"

"Your demon is John Parker?" George asked.

"No," Em said. "There's a demon that. . ."

"So you've said," George said.

"You saw him step out of John Parker," Em said in an incredulous voice.

"Never had the pleasure." George gave her a murderous look.

The entire building shook with the force of snow and wind. There was a great *"Pop!"* and the power went out.

The storm hit Boston.

Chapter Thirty-one

The snow beat down like an unnatural timpani. The evil in the snow seemed to be fighting to infiltrate the walls. George's cell phone screamed with an emergency weather alert. Em turned on the television, and every channel was broadcasting warnings about the storm. Some of the older weather prognosticators preached calm while their younger brethren screamed and sweated.

The snow continued to fall.

"Em," George's voice was soft. Em's head jerked to look at him. "I have to... I..."

"I know," Em said.

She jumped back, and Sarah Wildes appeared in the place she had been standing.

"I did it!" Sarah Wildes beamed at Em. "I didn't know I could, but..."

She looked up to see that Em and George were gawking at her.

"Em, there's something wrong with this storm," Sarah Wildes said. "Something terribly wrong."

Someone pounded at their front door.

"Em!" Alice's voice came from their door. "It's Alice!"

George went to open the door. There was another *whoosh,* and Mary Ayer Parker showed up in their living room.

"Ha!" Mary Ayer said.

"Well done, Mary!" Sarah Wildes said. She raised her hand. "High five!"

Mary Ayer slapped Sarah Wildes's hand, and they hugged.

"Are you here for. . ." Sarah Wildes said.

"The storm," Mary Ayers said.

Em grabbed Sarah and Mary Ayers and pulled them to her. Martha Carrier materialized.

"Martha! Jump to me!" Em yelled.

Sam Wardwell turned up a moment after Martha Carrier moved.

"What the hell?" Em asked.

"I saw the television," Sarah said. "Were you watching television?"

"Me, too," Sam said. "Em. . ."

"Yes, there's something wrong with the storm," Em said.

"What's with the storm?" Susannah asked as she, Alice, and George came in from the front.

"It's Em's demon," George said.

"Shit," Wilmot said as she ran into Sam.

He grabbed onto her, but they both stumbled out of the way as Elizabeth Howe appeared in the same spot. George's cell phone rang a beat before Em's rang. He answered the phone and went into the bedroom.

"Hello," Em said into the cell phone. "Elizabeth! You have to move!"

Elizabeth jumped out of the way just a moment before Margaret Scott appeared. Elizabeth grabbed Margaret and pulled her out of the way of Ann Pudeator, who arrived in front of the television.

"Martha! What the hell!" Giles' angry voice came from Em's cell phone. "Martha Corey, I demand that you speak to me at once."

"Giles," Em scowled into the phone.

"I can feel your scowl, Martha," Giles said with a laugh in his voice. "Bridget is upset, and frankly, I woke up with terror in my heart for you. Are you in trouble, Martha?"

"It's the storm, Giles," Em said. She looked up to see everyone watching her. She rolled her eyes at the phone.

"Fine," Giles said. Bridget's worried voice came from the background. "Bridget is pregnant, Martha. She cannot come to you."

"Stay there," Em said. "We'll call you as soon as I know something."

"You give me your word," Giles said.

"I give you my word," Em said. "You will be part of the solution."

"Enough said," Giles said and hung up.

She was about to put her phone down when John Willard called. The phone call went about the same way. Mary Eastey was upset and wanted to come. John wouldn't let her come, but he was worried as well. What was wrong? She felt a hand on her shoulder and turned to see Mary Eastey.

"You okay?" Mary Eastey whispered.

Em nodded. Over the phone, she assured John that she would call him when they had a plan. She was hugging Mary Eastey when she hung up the phone with John.

"You should go back," Em said. "He'll freak."

Mary Eastey rolled her eyes and kissed Em's cheek.

"I hate to be on injured reserve for something as dumb as being pregnant," Mary Eastey said.

"You are almost four hundred years old!" Em said.

"You're one to talk!" Mary Eastey said.

"Go," Em commanded.

Mary Eastey laughed and disappeared. When she looked up, most of her witches were standing in the living room. George came out of the bedroom.

"What can we do?" Alice asked.

"I think that's a good question," Em said.

"You don't know?" Susannah asked.

"I have no idea," Em shook her head. "The demon found out that I, Bridget, and Mary Eastey were pregnant."

"Me, too," Elizabeth and Sam said in unison.

"Yay!" Alice hugged Elizabeth and Sam.

"I didn't know that," Em said.

"He seems to know only what you know," Wilmot said. "That's curious."

"He knows what he's doing with this storm," Em said. "Sarah? Susannah? Can you guys put your heads together?"

They both nodded.

"Martha Carrier? Margaret? Can you look at logistics?" Em asked. "The city will be shut down, but we may need to get out of here."

"You bet," Martha Carrier said, and Margaret nodded.

"Sam? Can you check everyone's homes, particularly the old ones?" Em said. He nodded and disappeared.

"Elizabeth? Do you still keep track of our cars?"

"I do," Elizabeth said with a wave of her hand. "I have the spreadsheet on my phone."

"Wilmot? Can you call Sarah Good?" Em asked. "Giles and John both called, but I haven't heard from her. Let's make sure she's not in trouble. Can you go if she needs help?"

"Of course," Wilmot said, with pride in her voice.

"Mary Ayer? George is going to need help," Em said. "You know how he is when he's overwhelmed. Can you. . .?"

"Got it." Mary Ayer nodded and left the room to find George.

"Everyone, please think hard about what we can do to fight this thing," Em said. "Or mitigate the damages. He said he would take a hundred fold what we were creating. We cannot lose four hundred humans. Don't forget Giles and Bridget. They are at Bridget's mansion across the Common. John and Mary Eastey will help, too. John's just worried about Mary. They will do whatever we ask. I'm sure there's a bunch of things I haven't thought of. Just. . ."

Everyone nodded. The witches began talking amongst themselves. George came in from the kitchen.

"Can you find out about the storm?" George asked. Em gave him a hard look. He smiled, and said, "Yes, I know it's precognition. You're better than anyone else, even though you refuse to do it."

Shaking her head, she sighed.

"It makes me sick," Em said. "Every time. My father said it's common for our family. I won't be of any use to you later."

"The others can fill in until you've recovered," George said.

"I don't know," Em said.

"Do it!" George commanded.

"George, really..." Mary Ayer put her hand on his arm. He looked at her and shook his head.

"Lives are at stake because you're fighting with this creature," George said.

Em sighed. Even though he was acting crazy, he was right. She'd brought this curse to her beloved Boston. She should do everything in her power to make this right. Closing her eyes for a moment, she gathered her strength. She took a deep breath and let go of the present in a long sigh. She took another breath and paused for almost a full minute.

"If we fight him, the snowstorm will last for three days, but he will return. The snow will return," Em said in a flat, deep voice. "If we do not fight, he will take the entire city back to the beginning, back to 1692. The land will fall into the sea. Thousands will die. All services will be lost. That's what he wants. He wants to take us back to the beginning."

Em blinked. She took a breath, and then another. She blinked. Her eyes looked up at George for a moment before everything went dark. She felt herself crashing toward the ground.

"Fuck," George grabbed at Em.

"THIS WILL BE THE FINAL BATTLE OF THE SALEM WITCHES," Em's flat, deeper voice boomed.

As if she were suddenly coated in butter, Em slipped from George's hands. Her body hit the floor.

Em groaned and rolled onto her back. She felt

movement, but it was too dark to see who was there. She felt George grab her hand.

"Em," George said.

She moaned in response.

"I'm so sorry," George said. "I forgot about the baby, and. . ."

Em rolled toward his voice. He was kneeling next to the bed.

"Ann's been here with her crazy machine," George said. "Our son seems to be all right, but Ann's angry with me for pushing you. You're just always so tough, so strong. It never occurred to me that you'd get so sick and. . ."

When Em squinted, George stopped talking.

"Say something," George said.

"Hi," Em grunted.

George clutched Em. She felt moisture on his cheek. She sputtered and pushed at him.

"Need some. . ." Em started to say before she threw up.

George laughed and held her tighter.

"Get off me, you crazy man," Em said with a laugh.

Laughing, he helped her up. George held her on her feet as the wind battered the building. He followed her into the bathroom.

"Go," Em said.

"You know I can't leave you," George said.

"Go!"

"You might be sick again!" George said.

She lit an electric spark, which chased him out of the bathroom. The door slammed with a satisfying *wham!* Laughing, he leaned against the door. She lingered in the bathroom to spite him. When she came out, Ann

Pudeator was waiting for her.

Ann checked her heart and listened to the baby. She ran Em through a variety of tests to make sure she was all right. Em tried to be patient, but the steady tap of snow against the windows reminded Em of the demon's promise.

"You've been out for a day," Ann said. "Promise me that you'll rest."

"Scout's honor," Em said.

Ann raised her eyebrows and laughed at Em.

"Try to keep your great ideas to yourself," Ann said to George.

Ann pointed a finger to George. He raised his hands as if she were holding a weapon. Shaking her head at him, Ann left the room. Em looked at George. He'd changed his shirt and washed the vomit off his neck.

"Is everyone still here?" Em asked.

"Most," George said. "A group of them went to Bridget's. They're opening her house for people who don't have electricity or power. Neighbors are dropping blankets and food there. It should be a wild community event. Your Isaac has rallied his flock, as well."

"It sounds really fabulous," Em said.

"Sarah sent an email out from the shop," George said. "Less than an hour later, we had twenty slow cookers full of soup or stew. She's organized a knitting brigade. Sam has sorted out snow clearing by neighborhood. Ann's working to support emergency services. And the rest... well, they're generally awesome."

George gave her a proud smile.

"We have the nicest friends," George said. "Everyone has chipped in."

"And Sarah Good?" Em asked. "She wasn't here and hadn't called when I passed out."

"She's stuck in Washington," George said. "She's fundraising among her rich friends. They are trading convention visits to get the hotels to donate rooms for those who are out of doors. She also has raised enough money to buy rooms. They've found enough rooms for most of my people."

"We can put money into that." Em smiled.

"We're feeding everyone," George said. "The elderly... the vulnerable... Susannah's filling the 'in need' list. Ann's already delivered two babies in the middle of the store."

"Nice of us," Em said.

"Of course," George said. "When you're up and around, I'm heading out to get my folks indoors."

Despite her sinking heart, Em gave him an encouraging smile.

"You said that we needed to fight the demons," George said. "Do you remember?"

"I think so," Em said in a vague voice.

"We aren't sure how to do that," George said. "Mary Ayer and Wilmot have been around the world looking for information about how to fight demons. They should be back any minute."

Em shrugged.

"You just have to remember that they want to help," George said.

"They're being annoying?" Em asked.

"Pull-your-hair-out annoying," George said.

"Good to know," Em said.

"Listen," George said. He sat down next to her on the

bed. "I wanted to talk to you about something."

"Susannah or Ann?" Em asked.

George flushed bright red. Shaking his head, he looked away.

"I need to tell you something," Em said.

George's eyes flicked to her.

"Do you know why they arrested me?" Em asked. "In Salem Farms, I mean."

"To break people's resistance to the trials?" George asked.

"You really don't know," Em said.

"Because Giles was a demented old fool when he first talked to them?" George asked.

Em shook her head.

"What are you saying, Martha?" George asked. "And why are you saying this now?"

"I have this feeling that the next weeks will change everything," Em said. "I don't want all of this life and living to end without you knowing the truth."

"What 'truth,' Martha?" George asked. "Which 'truth'? That I loved you completely and was stupid enough not to make you leave Henry? Not to marry you right then and there? That I was too bullheaded to let you pay my debts, or that I was so certain they would pay me for my services or at least match the debt with what they owed me? Is it 'truth' that I was too vainglorious to see that nothing I could say would change their minds? That the entire escapade had nothing to do with witchcraft or godliness but rather. . .?"

Em put her hand over his, and he stopped talking.

"The only 'truth' that I have found is my love for you,"

George said with a shrug.

"They wanted to know where you were," Em said. She was so ashamed that she couldn't look at him. "They tortured me for a month until they started on Thomas and Benoni. I finally... I finally..."

A tear ran down her face.

"Of course, you did," George said.

"They dragged you from your dinner," Em whispered.

"I knew they were coming," George said. "Like the fool I am, I assumed that they would be reasonable. I wanted one last meal with my child and wife."

"You knew they were coming?" Em asked.

"I knew the moment they arrested you," George said. "But yes, I was warned as soon as they entered the county."

"You knew they arrested me to find you?" Em asked.

"Of course," George said. "I wanted to turn myself in so that you wouldn't suffer, but..."

He scowled at her.

"What?" Em asked.

"I don't know 'what,' Martha," George said. "I didn't. I knew that you were the only person who knew where I was. I knew that you were suffering terribly. I..."

George sighed and shook his head.

"I'd sent you away," Em said.

"You told me to leave and never come back," George said. "If I had known about Benoni or that the trials were coming or that living with you, day in and day out, would make me the better man I longed to be..."

George gave her a sad shrug.

"I'm so sorry," she said.

"You have nothing to be sorry for," George said. "You

were tortured for weeks. They came after your children. Everyone breaks down at some point, Martha. Everyone. They were willing to find everyone's breaking point. Good Lord, they pressed Giles to death!"

She held her arms out, and they hugged.

"I will tell you, my love," George said. "I never will forget how I felt the moment I entered that filthy jail and found you there. I knew there was a God in Heaven because I got to spend my last days by your side."

"And if it all ended tomorrow?" Em asked.

"I will thank the Lord for giving me so many perfect days and years," George said.

He kissed her.

"I'll talk to Susannah and Ann," Em said.

"You're sure?" George asked.

"They want a baby," Em said. "Sam is already helping Elizabeth and a few of the others. John won't. Giles wants to wait until Bridget has their child. It makes sense that you could help out."

"You'll let me know?" George asked.

Em gave him a quick nod. He kissed her.

"I love your generous soul," he whispered.

There was a tap on their door.

"That's Mary Ayer," Em said. "I need to get up. Will you help me?"

George gave her a soft smile. Even though pregnancy hadn't made her large, she'd grown out of most of her clothing. She had to guide George to clothing that she could still fit into. He helped her out of bed. The moment her feet hit the floor, a blast of wind shook the building to its foundation. Em bounced back onto the bed.

"What was that?" George asked.

"It's the demon," Em said. "You might not be able to see him, but you can feel his wrath."

George glared out the window.

"At least you know I'm not making this up," Em said.

"Oh, Em, I never thought you were making this up," George said. "You're too. . ."

"Boring?"

"Honest," George said with a smile. "Real, grounded, present. . . beautiful."

Em touched the side of his face. For a moment, their eyes caught, and their deep love for each other passed through their eyes.

"Throw me my clothing," Em said.

He tossed her a pair of his jeans, an undershirt, and one of his thick flannel shirts. He helped her get dressed while she lay on the bed. He grabbed her snow boots from the closet and set them next to the bed.

"It's worth a try," he said and gave her a soft smile.

She sat up and slipped one foot into a boot. When nothing happened, she slipped the other foot into the second. She smiled and stood. The wind and snow pummeled the building. George moved to help her sit down again.

"No," Em shook her head. "This is my fight. I need to get to it."

"It's our fight." George pulled her to him. "I'm sorry I put that burden on you. I was ridiculous. If some creature has a fight with you, he has a fight with me. Doesn't matter if it's Cotton Mather or a demon from hell. Your battles are mine to fight."

"Ours, too," Mary Ayer said.

Em looked up to see Mary Ayer standing in front of Susannah, Ann, Alice, and Wilmot. Alice came forward to hug Em. Soon Em was surrounded by her witches. The wind picked up, and the snow drove against the building, but they stood within the strength of their love for each other.

"George! George! George!" said a deep male voice, breaking their silence. The spirit of Martha materialized in Em's bedroom dressed as Michael. She was wearing his US Army fatigues. For all of her feminine ways, this aspect of Martha's spirit was all male.

George looked up from his position in the middle of the witches.

"Stop fucking around, Captain!" Michael said. His voice was so deep that it seemed to shake the air around them.

When George turned to look at the spirit, the witches shifted away from each other.

"You remember Martha?" George asked. "This is her more masculine side, Michael."

"Shut the fuck up," Michael said. "And listen."

"I'm all ears," George said.

The witches turned toward the spirit.

"Those demons have taken the little red-haired Irish girl," Michael said. "The one who lives across the way."

"The key stealer?" George asked.

"One and the same," Michael said. "They are torturing her poor, wretched soul. She's only a child."

"Why would they do that?" Martha Carrier asked.

"They got your friend Buford," Michael said. "That's how they got the girl. You know how protective he is of her. Like she was his child."

"The red coat?" Em asked.

Michael nodded.

"You don't want to know what they're doing to him," Michael said. "They tried to get Martha, but I intervened. They can't get me here — inside this building. I got inside only because I'd held Em's purse. Out there, I'm..."

Michael's hands went to cover his ears.

"I can hear her scream," Michael whispered.

"As owner of this building," Em said. She stepped forward to put her hands on Michael's shoulders. "You are welcome here, Martha and Michael."

"How will I be able to help?" Michael asked.

"You are anchored here, now," Em said. "You will return here no matter where you go. The witches are the same. They will not be able to get you now. When you're ready, we'll help you move on."

"Save the child," Michael said. "We must save the child and Buford."

"How do we do that?" George asked.

"We'll figure it out," Em said. She turned to the witches. "I cannot ask you to come. It's likely that this is our last battle. I would rather that you stayed here, stayed safe."

"Shut up, Martha," Martha Carrier said. "To the Common!"

With that, the witches disappeared. Overwhelmed, Em took a breath.

"Shall we stand together against our doom?" George asked.

"Nothing would make me happier," Em said.

He took her hand, and they left for the Common.

Chapter Thirty-two

Em landed next to Susannah. Alice, Ann, and Wilmot were standing in the Central Burial Ground.

"They're gone!" Susannah yelled over the wind.

George walked to the marker and called Buford's name. He added enough magic so that his call could be heard in every dimension. The sound echoed around them. A huge gust of wind and snow knocked George off his feet.

"We need to get to an open area — the Common!" Em yelled. Like a movie-screen witch, she began to fly a few feet off the ground. "Follow me!"

As if they were leaves on the wind, the witches flew a few feet off the ground toward the Boston Common Baseball Field.

"Stay on the field!" Em yelled. "Don't cross the path. The parking garage is underneath there. We won't be able to defend it."

The witches landed in the center of the baseball fields. Martha Carrier appeared.

"I stopped at Bridget's to see if I could grab Sarah Wildes or Margaret," Martha Carrier yelled over the snow. "Ann, there's a woman in labor at Bridget's home."

"I will not leave, Em," Ann yelled back.

"Go," Em yelled. She had to lean forward to make her

voice heard. "We are nothing if we are not in service to human beings."

Overwhelmed by the thought of leaving Em, Ann touched her heart with her hands.

"Go," Em yelled. She held out her arms and hugged Ann. "Listen to the wind. Our struggle will be there. If you're free, come to join us."

Ann blew Em a kiss and disappeared.

"What's the plan?" Martha Carrier yelled.

"Are Sarah Wildes and Margaret coming?" Alice yelled to Martha Carrier.

Martha Carrier shook her head.

"It's crazy at Bridget's," Martha Carrier said. "She could use our help."

"After we kick some demon ass," Alice yelled. She let out a whoop like a high school cheerleader.

"Form a circle around Em," George commanded. He pointed to the ghost Michael. "The energy inside the circle is too much for you. You cannot join us, Michael."

"Roger that," Michael nodded.

The witches linked elbows in a tight circle around Em.

"Stay by me, Michael," George commanded. "I'll keep an eye on you."

"Why, George," Michael said in Martha's voice, "you do love me!"

Still dressed in US military fatigues, Michael suggestively leaned on one hip. George smiled, and the witches chuckled.

"If you're in danger, head to the Mystic Divine!" Em yelled. "You'll be safe there. You, too, Martha!"

There was an enormous *"Boom!"* and the witches gave a

startled scream.

"They're coming!" Em said.

The wind began to swirl around the witches. Another boom came from somewhere near the Boston Common Gazebo. The air around the witches tightened.

"Hold on," Em yelled over the wind. "They are only trying to frighten us!"

The demons flew with ease through the snow.

"I see them," George yelled.

"I do, too," Wilmot yelled.

The demons began to circle above the witches. They screeched and howled, but the witches didn't move. The snow pounded down upon the witches. Em was losing sight of Martha Carrier, who was standing in front of her.

"There's one that looks like Argos!" Mary Ayer yelled.

"There's Bill Panon," Michael pointed to one of the demons above.

"Where?" Em asked.

She followed Michael's finger into the air. The snow battered her face. She squinted against the cold. A dark blur flew overhead. She followed the blur as it flew in the circle above her. When it reached the opposite side of the circle, she recognized the man who had killed her in the Jamaica Plains apartment building. Seeing her face, the man dove down to her and bellowed out a cry.

"Does he look like your father?" George yelled.

"A version of him," Em said. "It's like he's darker or... something."

"Smeared," Martha Carrier yelled. "It's like someone took a painting and ran their hand across it."

"Like they're underwater," George yelled.

"Or we see them through a coat of oil," Wilmot screeched over the noise. "They have no clear edges. They are diffuse and yet still tangible."

"Is it your father?" Mary Ayers yelled to Em.

"No," Em said. "I can't say why, but it's not him."

"They've taken these forms to fool us!" Susannah shouted.

"Resist the demon!" George yelled.

"And he shall flee from you," the witches quoted James 4:7 in unison.

Em struggled to get a good look at the creatures flying above. She thought she saw a blur that looked like Ellen the Watcher. Another demon that looked a smudged version of Miriam of Geography shot by. The next one looked like a shadowy Benjamin the Warrior. The demons swooped down upon them and screeched away into the clouds.

"I recognize some of them," Em yelled.

"Have you seen the red-haired girl?" George yelled.

"No," Em said. "I don't see my demon, either."

With her words, everything became very still. The wind dropped. The only sound was the crisp patter of falling snow. The temperature dropped. The demons had disappeared.

"What was that?" Alice whispered.

No one dared respond. Em began a spell. Her lips moved, but no sound came from her mouth.

"Damn these theatrics," George said. "Show yourself!"

"I'm freezing," Susannah said.

The snow continued to fall, and Em continued her spell. Despite the cold, the field was peaceful. George began leading the witches in his favorite prayer — Robert Louis Stevenson's "For Success" from his *Prayers from Vailma*.

"Lord, behold our family here assembled," George said in a soft voice.

"We thank Thee for this place in which we dwell; for the love that unites us." The witches joined in with the prayer. "For the peace accorded us this day; for the hope with which we expect the morrow."

There was a loud *whooshing* sound that riveted their eyes to the heavens. Em's demon floated down to them. His naked, charcoal-grey rhinoceros skin glistened in the rain. The curly, dark hair of his legs was wet. His cloven hooves seemed sharper than they were before. The jutting horn in the middle of his pronounced brow ridge seemed exceptionally sharp. He stood out like a dark menace among the sea of white snow around them. His claws held the red-haired girl in a tight grip. The child ghost was weeping. A high-pitched squeal grew as the demon flew closer.

"You know the spell to close your ears," Em said. "Use it now!"

The witches yelled out the spell. The demon smiled at Em. He hovered in the falling snow above her.

"They can't hear us now," the demon said with a grin.

"I can't hear him!" George yelled. "Demon — be gone!"

"I can't hear anything!" Wilmot yelled.

"What do you want?" Em asked. As if she were going to punch him, she balled up her fist.

He stroked the curly hair of the little girl, and the girl began to sob.

"*Cabhrú liom.*" The child begged Em to help her in Irish

Gaelic.

"Let her go!" Em demanded.

"The child has no name," the demon laughed. "She belongs to whomever owns her."

"Let her go!" Em demanded.

"No," the demon said with a laugh.

"What do you want from me?" Em asked. She raised her fists to the sky. "Tell me *now*!"

Em's final word held all of the power of her people and history. The demon laughed at her show of strength.

"You do not command me!" the demon said. He raised his hand to point at her. "In fact. . ."

Em opened her hands. The demon gasped as the full blast of a travel spell hit him in the chest. Em grabbed the ghost of the red-haired girl a fraction of a second before the demon soared backward through the air. The demon stretched out his hands to grab the child, but Em held her spirit tight to her chest.

"To the Mystic Divine!" Em yelled.

Em transported the girl back to the Mystic Divine. The store was dark and still. They landed at the same time as George. The child threw herself into George's arms. As the other witches arrived, George and the child spoke back and forth in Irish Gaelic.

"Can you do that thing?" George asked. "Can you root her here?"

"The demon is right," Em said. "Without a name, she's fair game to any strong force that blows by."

"I name you Aileen," George said in Irish Gaelic. "*Aileen álainn.*"

The red-haired girl grinned at being called "beautiful

Aileen."

"What is your name?" Alice demanded of the girl. George translated.

"Aileen," the girl said with a giggle.

Em placed her hands on the child's shoulders and rooted her to the building. George repeated her words in Irish Gaelic.

"What about Buford?" Martha, recently Michael, asked.

Now that the battle was over, Michael had returned to his Martha form.

"If I know Buford, he'll. . ." George started.

The ghost of the British soldier flew through the front window. He checked to make sure nothing was following him before looking around. George went to welcome his friend. Em welcomed him and helped tie him to the building so he would remain safe.

"Should we expect the demons?" George asked.

"No," Em said. "I sent them far from us. Pluto, I think, but I was aiming for the Kuiper belt."

"The what?" Susannah asked.

"It's a belt of small debris left over from the creation of the universe," Wilmot said. Everyone looked at her with surprise. "What? I watched *Cosmos* with Em."

"Our Lord has created a truly wonder-filled universe," Em said.

"When do we expect that they will return?" George asked.

"February at the earliest," Em said.

"Just in time for the Super Bowl," George muttered.

"It's not held here, is it?" Em asked.

George shook his head.

"Then God's team, the New England Patriots, should be just fine," Em said. Under her breath, she said, "Provided they didn't cheat."

"Cheat?" George asked. His face darkened, and he raised a finger to point at her. "Watch what you're saying, woman. Those are fighting words!"

The witches gasped, and Em grinned. George scowled.

"There's that whole ball-inflation thing," Em said.

"The Pats would never cheat," George said with a sniff.

Em laughed out loud, breaking the tension. The other witches laughed. Finally, George grinned.

"What do we do now?" Alice said to change the topic.

"Let's open the store to anyone who needs it," Em said. "If these spirits feel the uncertainty, certainly our community feels it as well."

"Did we keep any of the food that was donated?" George asked.

"We have about half," Susannah said.

"We have plenty of food upstairs," Em said. "I baked a bunch of food so George could take it out with him. The freezer downstairs is full."

"We can barbeque," George said.

"Good idea," Em said."

"Hey, Em." Sam jogged down the stairs toward her. His cell phone was clamped between his shoulder and his ear. "There's so much snow that the city wants to move the snow onto five snow farms."

"What's a snow farm?" Em asked.

"It's a place to store all the extra snow," Sam said. "Most of the sites are parks — Franklin Park Zoo and the golf course there; some place in Hyde Park. They're looking for one in Dorchester. They think they found one in Hyde Park. They're wondering if they can use the lot on Tide Street in South Boston."

"Can you think of any reason we wouldn't?" Em asked with a shrug.

"It will have snow and debris through June?" Sam asked. "We'll lose the parking income."

"We can afford it," Em shrugged.

"I'll tell them to go ahead," Sam said.

Em nodded. Noticing it was still dark in the store, Em waved her hand, and the lights came on. From where they stood, they could see that three young women were standing outside the door. George ran to open the doors.

"Oh, Sam?" Em turned to see if she'd caught him.

He turned at the top of the flight of stairs. He looked at her, but his attention was clearly on the phone. She waited.

"Didn't we help the Port Authority buy those snow-melting tanks?" Em asked.

Sam pointed to her and nodded. He turned and went up the stairs to the apartments.

"What was that?" Alice asked.

"Trying to be a good Boston neighbor," Em said with a smile. "Why don't we crank up the heat, pass out food, and..."

"Give free readings?" Martha Carrier asked. "It's been an age since I played with the tarot. I'd be happy to do readings."

"Great idea!" Em said. "We'll make a festival out of it."

"Oh, good, you're open," Shonelle said from the door.

"What are you doing out in the storm?" Em asked.

Em jogged down to the door. She hugged the girl close.

Shonelle shook in Em's arms.

"I didn't know what else to do," Shonelle said, sniffing back her tears. "There's something just *wrong* with this storm. I was scared, and I thought maybe I could come here, and you'd. . ."

Em kissed her cheek.

"It's always so safe here at the Mystic Divine," Shonelle said.

"I'm glad you've come," Em said. She hugged the girl again for good measure.

"Em?" Wilmot touched Em's arm.

"I need to. . ." Em gestured to Wilmot. Shonelle nodded. George scooped her up in a tight hug.

"They're asking for a prayer session," Wilmot said.

"We can have George do one," Em said.

"They're asking for Elizabeth or Sarah Wildes," Wilmot said. "They lead those big groups. I think most of these people are their flock."

"Let's ask Alice or Susannah to get Sarah Wildes," Em said. "Sam and Elizabeth are working to shore up the houses and clear the snow. I'm sure Elizabeth will come down if we ask."

Wilmot nodded.

"How many years did you do fortunes?" Em asked in a low tone.

"More than a hundred," Wilmot said with a nod. "Not quite two."

"Martha Carrier's setting up tables to give out free readings," Em said. "Why don't you join her?"

"That sounds fun," Wilmot brightened.

Em patted her back, and Wilmot left to find Martha

Carrier. She felt a hand on her back and turned to see Alice.

"Susannah went to Bridget's to get Sarah Wildes," Alice said. "I just couldn't leave you."

Alice hugged Em.

"Are you all right?" Alice asked in Em's ear.

Over Alice's shoulder, she watched Sarah Wildes trot down the steps at the back of the store. She rushed to greet a group of "her" women. Alice leaned back from Em.

"Em?" Alice asked. Her face was a mask of concern.

"I'm okay," Em said. "I. . . wish I knew more."

"What do we need to do now?" Alice asked. She leaned toward Em as a man walked past them. "About the demon, I mean."

"Nothing," Em said. "We have to wait out the storm."

"You're sure?" Alice asked.

"I don't want to go into full-scale battle with these. . . things. . . until I know more of what I'm dealing with," Em said.

"How do we find out?" Alice asked.

"Em?" Mary Ayer asked. "Do you have a minute?"

Em raised an eyebrow and nodded to Alice.

"Can I come?" Alice asked. She blushed and took Em's arm. "I just want to be with you."

"Of course," Em said. "Let's go upstairs."

"There's a bunch of people in your apartment getting food and stuff." Mary Ayer shook her head. "Sam's working on the snow thing."

Em winced at the idea of all of those people in her home.

"Can we go to your office?" Mary Ayer asked.

"Sure," Em said.

They started toward Em's office when George called for Em. She turned to look across the store. Detective Shane Donnell was standing at the entrance. Em stared at him for a moment before waving him back.

"But, Em. . ." Mary Ayer said in a low voice.

"I looked him up after he was here," Em said in a low voice. "He's supposed to have one of the best investigative minds in the country."

"John Willard said he teaches classes at the FBI," Alice said in a low voice.

"I need someone to help me think through all of this," Em said. She looked up and smiled at the Detective. "We were just about to talk about everything that's going on. Would you care to join us?"

"Is the city in danger?" the Detective asked. "We've been getting a lot of calls."

"We took care of the immediate threat," Em said. "It's going to snow for a while, but the evil has been dealt with — for now."

"For now," Detective Donnell said.

"I'm hoping to get a better idea of what will be effective with these creatures," Em said. "Mary here has been researching the situation. Alice brings a wonderful perspective. If you are willing, I'd love to have you assist me in thinking through this."

"Sure," Detective Donnell said. "I got to call my station."

"Fair enough," Em said. "Since there are so many of us, let's go into one of the small classrooms upstairs."

The Detective nodded and took out his cell phone. Em, Mary Ayer, and Alice headed up the stairs.

"I hope you know what you're doing," Mary Ayer said as

she sat down.

"You know that I don't," Em said with a grin.

"We'll do our best," Alice said. "If we can't figure this out, no one can."

Em raised her eyebrows in a nod. The Detective came through the door and shut it behind him.

"Tell me what you know," Detective Donnell said. "Hold nothing back."

Chapter Thirty-three

Mary Ayer had been talking for almost an hour. She stopped talking only when the detective asked a question. Em's mind went numb around the same time she lost feeling in her rear. Alice had checked out a long time ago. Though her eyes were open, Em could have sworn that Alice was sound asleep. Em made a mental note to ask if Alice had used a spell.

Em glanced at Mary Ayer. Em had the distinct feeling that Mary Ayer was falling for Detective Donnell. While he was harder to read, Em thought he was dazzled by Mary Ayer. Em watched the volley of early love unfold. Detective Donnell asked a thoughtful question. Mary Ayer would pause and lay out three or four answers. If Em didn't feel so desperate, she would have been charmed by the entire interchange.

One thing was definitely true – Mary Ayer Parker had worked her rear off to find all of this information in such a short time.

The other thing that was true was that none of the information applied to their situation with Em's demon.

Em patiently listened out of the hope that Mary Ayer had found something, anything that applied. So far, Em had been disappointed. There were demons here and there.

"Here a demon, there a demon, everywhere a demon," Em's mind chanted as she listened to Mary Ayer.

With her foot, Em nudged Alice's chair. Em cleared her throat, and Mary Ayer stopped talking. Mary Ayer looked at Em and blushed. Em smiled at Mary. Alice stretched in her chair.

"Warm in here," Alice said.

Em, Mary Ayer, and Detective Donnell laughed. Alice grinned.

"I'm sorry, Em," Mary Ayer said. "All of this... it's not very helpful, is it?"

Not sure what to say, Em smiled at Mary Ayer. She glanced at Detective Donnell. He was scowling at something on his notepad.

"Detective?" Em asked.

"I wouldn't say it wasn't helpful," the detective shook his head. "No. This was... intriguing."

"How so?" Em asked. "Please, sir, we're interested in anything you have to share."

"Well, after listening to Mary." The detective nodded to Mary Ayer. "May I call you Mary, ma'am?"

"Please do," Mary Ayer said with a smile.

"Ma'am," Detective Donnell cleared his throat, "there's a lot of quality research and valuable information here. You've clearly worked very hard."

"Wilmot helped," said Mary Ayer while flushing with his praise.

"Our Mary is the best," Alice said.

Hearing Alice's voice, Mary Ayer looked at Alice. She took in Alice's encouraging smile and grinned.

"We love her dearly," Em said.

Hearing the subtle threat in Em's voice, the detective's head jerked up to look at Em. She grinned, and Detective Donnell nodded that he'd received her message. He glanced at Mary Ayer, who was smiling at him.

"What can you tell us, detective?" Em asked.

"Well..." The word came as a kind of out breath. Detective Donnell flipped through a few of the pages in his notebook. "Well... it occurs to me that '...light,' '...dark,' these are judgements."

The women fell silent and still. Detective Donnell began to sweat under the intensity of their gaze.

"I mean, to us here in Boston, we think murder is bad or dark, right?" Detective Donnell asked. "But if someone invaded our fair city, we'd murder every last one of them without hesitation and call it justice."

He looked from Mary Ayer to Em, and then at Alice.

"'Light,' 'dark,'" Detective Donnell said. "Mary, here, gave us a lot of information about demons. It seems like humans have always had angels and demons."

"For all of recorded history," Mary Ayer said. "Yes."

"We can agree that we like angels." The detective looked from person to person. "We agree we don't like demons."

"Sure," Em said.

"Since 'light' and 'dark' are what we deem them to be, it makes sense that demons and angels are what we make them," Detective Donnell said. "They are created out of our own hopes, fears, and judgements."

"Collectively," Mary Ayer said. "Some angels, such as the Archangels, come up in stories throughout history."

"Yet you can say that the God Shiva is very similar to the

Archangel Gabriel," Detective Donnell said. "And the Archangel Gabriel is not dissimilar to Perses, the Titan of destruction."

Mary Ayer thought for a moment before nodding.

"There are certain types..." Detective Donnell said.

"Archetypes," Mary Ayer said.

"Right, archetypes," the detective grinned at Mary Ayer. "We need to conceive of these situations as a God or an Angel. *We* have a need to explain our world, and we use these... beings, for lack of a better word, to explain the world around us."

"And our role in it," Alice said.

The detective looked at Alice for a moment.

"You're brighter than you look," Detective Donnell said.

"Is that a compliment?" Alice asked with a laugh.

"From me?" the detective grinned. "Yes. That is definitely a compliment."

"We're more than three hundred years old, sir," Mary Ayer said. "We don't show the wear, but we've lived through a lot."

"Well, that's a question, isn't it?" Detective Donnell asked. "Do you emotionally and mentally evolve?"

"I think so," Mary Ayer said.

"I have," Alice said. "I was so... young, naïve, when everything happened. I... I'm not so young now."

Em raised her eyebrows while she thought for a moment. She nodded.

"Why do you ask?" Em asked.

The detective nodded to acknowledge Em's question. He looked through his notebook for a moment.

"To me," Detective Donnell said as he raised his

eyebrows. He looked at Mary Ayer, Em, and then Alice. "To me, there are two questions."

The detective started flipping through his notebook again. He seemed to settle on two pages that he flipped back and forth.

"And what are those?" Em asked.

"Oh," Detective Donnell said. "Right — you don't know what they are."

"I might," Em said. "What I know is that I don't know what are your questions."

"Ah," Detective Donnell said. He gave a full-bellied laugh. When he stopped laughing, he looked at them again. "You are truly not what I expected you to be."

"That sounds like a good thing," Mary Ayer said.

Detective Donnell blushed and rustled through his book nervously.

"Detective!" Em said. "What are your questions?"

Surprised, he jerked to look at her. Feeling her frustration, his face drained of color. He swallowed hard.

"Don't worry about, Em," Mary Ayer said. "She just likes to know what's going on."

The detective looked at Mary Ayer and then at Em.

"I'm not going to turn you into a frog," Em said with a smile. "I'm upset and impatient with how little I know and how much less I understand. I feel responsible for the people of this city that will have to endure all of this... weather... because of me and my issues. The lives of sixteen of the dearest people I've ever known, not to mention their infants, are in danger. I must resolve this. The sooner, the better, I'd say."

"Yes, ma'am," Detective Donnell said.

"Your questions?" Em asked.

"The first question is one you've probably thought of — why is this happening now?" Detective Donnell asked. "That's kind of obvious, but we don't really know why this demon decided to come after you now."

Em opened her mouth to respond, but the detective held up his index finger.

"Mary, here, said that this Argos told you that the demons didn't come after him right away," Detective Donnell said.

"His demon," Em said. "There seems to be one for every person like me."

Detective Donnell looked at her for a moment before making a note. He looked up.

"Can you tell me again how they got to him?" Detective Donnell asked.

"He said they 'got through,'" Em said.

"'Found a way into this world,'" Mary Ayer said with a nod.

"That's probably right," Em said.

"But you think he's kind of an idiot, right?" Detective Donnell asked.

"Well. . ." Em started at the same time Mary Ayer said, "Yes."

Detective Donnell raised and dropped his eyebrows in a kind of "That's what I thought" gesture. He looked at his notebook for a moment before scowling.

"What if these 'demons' take time to develop?" the detective asked. "Think of a child. Even the most hardened criminal starts out as a happy baby. It takes time for malevolence to develop."

"And then, over time, it fades away," Em said with a nod.

Mary Ayer and Alice looked at Em with raised eyebrows. Only the detective's shuffling of pages could be heard.

"Giles," Em said. Mary Ayer and Alice chuckled. "He's much nicer now than he was just a hundred years ago."

"So let's say this thing came after you," Detective Donnell said. "The next question is. . ."

Detective Donnell looked at Em and then cleared his throat. She raised her eyebrows.

"Why is this thing frightening?" the detective asked. "I mean, what if this thing isn't such a bad thing?"

"You mean like the Goddess of War seems like an amazing, strong woman unless you're at war?" Em asked.

"Athena, yes," Detective Donnell said. "Enyo is thought to also be a Goddess of War."

"Or wife of the God Ares, God of War," Alice said. "Thus Goddess of War in name only. Or possibly his sister with her twin sister as the Goddess of War."

"Exactly," Detective Donnell said.

"The demon did take over the body of a young man," Em said.

"And what?" the detective asked. "According to you, the young man was taken out of his time four hundred years ago only to be dumped into this one. That's enough to make anyone batty."

"You're asking — what if I've got this all wrong?" Em asked. She thought for a moment. "How would I know?"

"No idea," Detective Donnell said. "You just asked me to listen, take in the situation, and present the problem. To me, the problem is that you know a lot about all kinds of demons but don't know anything about *these* 'demons.'

And, the reason you don't know anything about them is that you refuse to interact with them."

Stunned by his words, Em could only stare at him.

"But, he's a demon!" Alice said.

Detective Donnell shrugged.

"The demon that looks like her father shot her," Mary Ayer said.

"Did it kill her?" the detective asked.

"No, but. . ." Mary Ayer said.

"Would he know that it wouldn't kill her?" the detective asked.

"He killed Martha," Em said.

"Now that's a crime," Detective Donnell said. "And we've arrested Bill Panon for it."

"You did?" Em asked.

"He's sitting in our jail awaiting trial right now," Detective Donnell said. His face brightened in a kind of laugh. "You want to talk to him?"

"Maybe when the storm ends," Em said.

"Fair enough," Detective Donnell said. He stood up from his chair. "I should get going."

"Thank you so much for your time, detective," Em said. "I am grateful, again, for your support."

"Of course," Detective Donnell said. "If you need something, just call me."

"If you need help over the next couple of days. . .," Em said.

"I'll call you," Detective Donnell said. "George said he'd head out with me."

Em nodded. Mary Ayer stared at the detective. Alice nudged her chair with her foot. Mary Ayer looked up.

Alice gestured for Mary Ayer to go with the detective.

"I'll show you out," Mary Ayer said.

Mary Ayer got up and followed the detective. At the door, she turned to Em and Alice. She wrinkled her nose in a "Should I?"

"Go for it," Em said in a low voice.

Alice grinned. Mary Ayer beamed at them and went to follow Detective Donnell.

"Ugh!" Alice fell back against her chair. "I'm exhausted!"

"Yeah," Em said. "We need to go out and help."

"In a minute," Alice said. "You must be super frustrated."

"Poor Mary," Em said. "She's busted her ass, and we have bupkis."

Em shrugged.

"A couple of questions," Alice said. "What are you going to do?"

"Try to find the answers to the detective's questions," Em said.

"Let me know if I can help," Alice said.

Em nodded. They heard footsteps in the hallway and looked up at the door. Mary Ayer came in with a big grin on her face.

"He asked me to dinner," Mary Ayer said. "I told him that we were probably eating here. So he's coming tonight!"

Em smiled.

"Nice job!" Alice said. She got up to hug Mary Ayer. "He seems really great."

"George wants to see you, Em," Mary Ayer said. "He's heading out into the storm."

Em got up from her seat. The women walked together toward the store.

"You are making something yummy tonight, aren't you?" Mary Ayer asked.

"I hadn't thought of it," Em said.

"Think of it," Mary Ayer said, with great intensity, which caused Alice to laugh.

"I'm happy for you, Mary," Em said. She leaned in to give Mary Ayer a hug. "Thank you for all you've done. You're a real life saver."

"If I can help — really, anything — I'm there," Mary Ayer said.

Em smiled. She walked ahead to find George. She walked past the area where Martha Carrier and Wilmot were doing tarot readings. The energy in the store was warm and happy. Em grinned. If she'd ever had time to dream what she'd wanted to create, this would most certainly be it.

"Em!" Wilmot said.

Em stopped walking and waited for Wilmot to catch up with her.

"How are the readings going?" Em asked.

"Fun. Really fun." Wilmot leaned close to Em. "I haven't read in this time. The people — they are almost as open as in the '20s."

Em grinned. In the 1920s, Wilmot was a famous mystic who dressed in tight-waisted floor-length, red-velvet dresses which pushed her breasts almost to her chin. She fleeced the wealthy while giving nearly every penny to the desperate poor. Em's eyes flicked to Wilmot's chest, and Wilmot laughed.

"Did you talk to Mary?" Wilmot asked.

Em gave a quick nod.

"We really tried, Em," Wilmot said with a sigh.

"I know," Em said. "It's not your fault. Certainly, you both worked your butts off."

"We want to help." Wilmot's voice held an edge of desperation. "You think that detective is okay?"

"He's a descendant of Lydia's," Em said with a shrug. "He's smart, disorganized, goofy..."

"Sounds perfect for Mary Ayer," Wilmot said. "Are you going to find me a lover, too?"

"Would you like one?" Em asked.

Wilmot lifted a shoulder in a casual shrug. Laughing, Em continued toward George.

"Oh, Em?" Wilmot asked.

She grabbed Em's arm, and Em stopped moving. Em turned to look at her.

"I just..." Wilmot said. "Um..."

Em tipped her head to the side.

"Uh..." Wilmot said.

Wilmot looked like she wanted to melt into the carpet. Em hugged her tight.

"Mammy," Em whispered Wilmot's nickname in Salem Village. "Thank you for caring."

She kissed Wilmot's cheek and started off again. Wilmot trotted to catch up with her. Em stopped walking.

"If you know something — or even think you do — I would love to hear it," Em said.

"I just... well," Wilmot winced and looked up at Em. "Have you ever wondered why he, the demon, I mean, looks like the one we feared? I mean, Alice described the demon you saw upstairs in the classroom. He is the spitting image of the devil we Puritans feared. Maybe it was different in Salem Farms than in Marblehead, where me and my Samuel lived, but. . ."

"What?" Em asked.

"I mean, we believed the devil was real, flesh and blood, cloven feet, furry legs, charcoal skin. . ." Wilmot said with a nod. "I was sure that creature lurked in every shadow. He was the terror of my childhood. What do they call it now?"

"Boogeyman," Em said idly.

"Boogeyman," Wilmot said. "That's right."

"Exactly this one?" Em asked.

Wilmot nodded. Em looked down for a moment to think.

"And. . ." Wilmot said. "The others, the ones we saw on the Common this morning?"

Em nodded.

"You could see people," Wilmot said.

"The elders I'd met," Em said with a nod. "I figured they came because I knew them."

"I didn't see them," Wilmot said.

"But you said. . ."

"I saw demons," Wilmot said. "Shadows, almost smoke, against the pure white of the falling snow. I felt a chill over my very soul. I was frightened, but my eyes could not discern what they were."

"And the one who held the child?" Em asked.

"Wisp of a shadow, more indistinct than the ghost that he was holding captive," Wilmot said.

"Really?" Em asked.

Wilmot nodded.

"You must ask the child," Wilmot said. "George saw what I saw, but Alice, she saw what you saw — that horrible creature holding the ghost. So did Mary Ayer and the girls who went back with you to Gallows Hill. I talked to them when we were setting up, before you talked to Detective Donnell."

Em bit her lip. She was sure that Wilmot was saying something important. She just wasn't confident she understood it yet. She wasn't even sure what question to ask.

"Alice had seen him through your mind before," Wilmot added.

Em's eyes flicked to her face.

"And Mary Ayer had met Argos," Wilmot said. Her head bobbed up and down in a nod.

"Are you saying that they were there for me, only?" Em asked. "That's why I'm the only one who could see them?"

"I don't know," Wilmot said. "Honestly, I don't."

"But?" Em asked.

"I. . . What's clear to me is that these creatures are real," Wilmot said. "If we were of this generation, we might think they were aliens or something like Bigfoot. But we're Puritans, so we see them as demons."

"But they are real?" Em asked. "I'm not imagining them?"

"Oh, no, you're not imagining them," Wilmot said. "They are very real. Malevolent, as well. They're natural, holistic. That's all."

"Like yin and yang," Em said. "I've thought of that."

Wilmot nodded and looked at Em expectantly. Em shrugged her shoulders and raised her eyebrows.

"Oh," Wilmot said. She winced. "I don't mean anything by this. I really don't. I just. . ."

Wilmot swallowed hard.

"Yes?" Em asked.

"I wondered if you see what you want or, maybe, need to, see," Wilmot said. When Em didn't say anything, Wilmot pressed on. "That means that you're a part of this."

"A part of what?" Em asked.

"You are connected to these creatures," Wilmot said. She looked up and sighed with frustration. "I'm not saying it right. . ."

"Thank you for all your help," Em said. She gave Wilmot's forearm a warm squeeze. "I'm grateful."

"Don't you see?" Wilmot said. "If you're part of it, then you know what to do."

Em's mind flashed to the memory of the day they found John Proctor's remains. The transvestite Martha told Em that only she knew the truth. She swallowed hard and squinted at Wilmot. Wilmot nodded and then shrugged.

"That's the best I can say it," Wilmot said.

"Em!" George said as he walked toward them. "There you are!"

Em gave Wilmot a nodding kind of bow before turning to him.

"I need to head out. . ." George said. He looked at Em and then Wilmot. "I'm sorry. Am I interrupting something?"

"We're done," Wilmot said. She grinned at him. "I love giving these fortunes. So fun."

"I know," George said. "People today are so spiritually

open and receptive."

Wilmot gave him a little wave and walked back to where she and Martha Carrier were giving readings. George gave Em a probing look.

"Are you all right?" George asked.

"Good," Em said. She gave him a bright smile. "I'm kind of sad that you're leaving."

"It tears me in half to leave you both," George said. He put his hands over the bump in her belly. "Detective Donnell said they're having the damnedest time getting the homeless inside. They asked for my help."

"Go," Em said. "We'll be here."

"I heard we're hosting a big community dinner," George said. He grinned at her. "You are very kind to do things you don't know anything about."

"Such is the suffering of this witch," Em said.

He grabbed her with such intensity that she gasped with surprise. He held her close.

"I never thought I could love you more," George whispered with great intensity. "But I only love you more and more as time continues."

He let her go. Without saying another word, he turned and walked away from her. For a moment, she could only watch him go.

"Em?" Shonelle asked from behind her. "The register's out of paper, and I can't find any more."

Em watched George for another moment before turning toward Shonelle.

"We'd better go find it," Em said.

She put her arm around Shonelle, and they walked toward the storeroom.

Chapter Thirty-four

Em sat watching the white snow from a window seat in Bridget's Beacon Hill mansion. The sun was finally peeking out from behind the clouds. From where she sat, she watched the sparkling sea of white snow covering the Common and the bright blue sky. She could almost see the very spot where she'd sent the demon to the outer reaches of the universe.

The snow had lasted almost three full days and dropped a record-setting 24.6 inches of snow on Boston. The weather speculators called Juno, the snowstorm, a "freak storm" which was unlikely to happen again. It was the sixth-largest snow in the history of Boston. After all, there hadn't been a snow like this in more than ten years!

Em knew in her heart that her beloved Boston would endure more storms before the battle with her demon was resolved. She only hoped the battle with the demon would not kill them all. She sighed.

"Here it is," Bridget said as she came into the room. "Sorry — everything is a mess since the storm. My staff has their hands full cleaning up. I had to make this myself. I hope it's okay."

"I'm sure it's perfect," Em said while taking the tray from Bridget. "You were very kind to take in everyone."

"It was fun," Bridget said. "Please sit down. When I came in, you looked so..."

"Pensive?" Em asked with a smile.

"Sad," Bridget said. "Resigned."

"I wanted a chance to talk to you and Giles before everyone came over," Em said.

"John and Mary are downstairs with Giles," Bridget said. "Should I get them?"

"Let's have our tea," Em said. "You know John can never resist a hot cup of..."

"Is there tea?" John said from the doorway of the sitting room.

He winked at Em and took the tea tray from her. He took a whiff of the tea and scowled. He set it down on a nearby table. Mary Eastey waddled into the room. She and Bridget exchanged a strained hug over their enormous bellies.

"Did you make this?" Mary Eastey whispered to Bridget. When Bridget nodded, she added, "Why don't I make a refresher? Can you show me where to...?"

Bridget grinned at Em. Mary Eastey picked up the tray and left with Bridget. John gave Em a hug.

"How are you?" John asked. He looked into her face. "How's the baby?"

"Good," Em said. "I'm good. The baby's good."

To convince him, Em nodded her head up and down with some vigor. John shook his head. They knew each other too well for her to fool him. He hugged her again.

"Before the others come," John said in a low tone. "I want to... well..."

Em gestured for him to join her on the window seat. He

took a long look at the view before sitting down next to her.

"We have only a minute," John said. He looked at the door to the room. Em nodded. "I know why you're pulling everyone together."

"You do?" Em asked.

John nodded.

"There's no way for me to publicly support your proposal," John said. "I'll be the usual ass that everyone expects."

Laughing, Em knocked into him with her shoulder.

"Privately," John said. "Between you and me, I've got your back. I just want to. . ."

They heard Mary Eastey and Bridget laughing in the hallway.

"Remember the hand," John said.

"What?" Em asked.

"That's what the statue in Laos said to say to you at this very moment," John said. "After he reminded me that I owe you. . ."

Bridget and Mary Eastey came into the room carrying two trays of with pots of tea on them. Mary Eastey also brought some of her caramel-chip cookies.

"Everything," John said in a low voice. "You have my life."

"And your hand?" Em asked in the same voice.

He nodded.

"Now, what are you two plotting?" Mary Eastey asked. "You're not trying to convince John to be a pirate again, are you, Em?"

"I thought he already was," Giles said as he entered the

room.

Confused by Giles's attempt to make a joke, they turned to look at him. When he laughed, they laughed as well.

"You know me too well, Giles," John said with a grin.

John got up to greet Giles. The men fell into an easy conversation about the upcoming Super Bowl. Bridget passed out hand-painted china teacups while Mary Eastey shared the cookies. Knowing there was a purpose to their visit, they settled into chairs grouped around the window seat. A few minutes later, George jogged into the room. He waved to John and Giles and kissed Em on the cheek before sitting down at the window seat.

"Reverend," Mary Eastey said as she poured him a cup of tea.

She gave him the cup and then passed him the cream. Em stifled a chuckle when he had to bite his tongue rather than complain about adding cream *after* his tea was poured. When he looked up, Mary Eastey held out the plate of cookies.

"Oh, my favorite," George said. "Bless you, Mary."

Mary Eastey flushed and smiled at George.

"Why are we here, Martha?" Giles asked. As he usually did with Em, he gave her an order. "Tell us straight. Don't leave anything out."

As usual for Em, she raised her eyebrows at his order. He winked at her, and she grinned.

"Honestly, there isn't much to tell," Em said. "You know about the demon. You know that Adam and Eve ate from the Tree of the Knowledge of Good and Evil. You are their descendants."

Em looked at each of them as they nodded in agreement.

"My ancestor ate from the Tree of Life," Em said. "This gave me, and, in turn, you, an extended life."

Em looked down at her clasped hands. She sighed and nodded.

"I have learned that when Eve, and then Adam, ate from the Tree of the Knowledge of Good and Evil, they internalized the darker side of themselves. They became both good and bad, yin and yang, opposites but whole." Em refused to look at any of them. George pried her hand away from its mate. He held her hand between his hands. "I have only the one side. Call it good or evil — my ancestors are all one sided. My father was the same way. My mother was a descendant of Argos, the one who actually ate from the Tree of Life. She passed this, for lack of a better word, 'recessive trait,' to me."

"Like blue eyes, Em?" John asked. When Em nodded, he explained to the others: "You know how two dark-haired people can have a blue-eyed person or vice versa? Because blue eyes are a recessive gene."

Mary Eastey looked at Bridget. They both looked at John and nodded. Giles gave an easy nod. John looked confused at Giles's easy understanding.

"I breed world-class racing horses, John," Giles said with a grin.

"Oh, right," John said.

"Please continue, Martha," Giles said.

Em looked up at Giles. Their eyes held for a moment before she looked at each of her witches in turn. She gave a quick smile to George.

"What I'm about to tell you is really more of a best guess than fact," Em said.

She waited for them to interrupt, but they were simply waiting to hear what she had to say.

"I need to combine with the demon," Em said.

"No!" Bridget exclaimed at the same time Mary Eastey said, "Goodness, Martha! That's insane!"

George squeezed her hand tighter, while John and Giles just looked at her. When everyone settled down, George tugged on Em's hand.

"Why?" George asked.

"I can see no other way," Em said. "It's combine with the demon or die. Someone or something has killed every single person of my kind."

"Except the statue in Laos," John said.

"Get to the bottom line, Martha," Giles said.

"You live as a kind of extension of me," Em said. "For example, you were capable of getting pregnant because I was on Rousay."

"We live because you gave us the choice," George said with a nod.

"You are bound to me," Em said. "It's clear to me that if I don't combine with the demons, I will be killed, and you will die."

"But Em, that's crazy!" Bridget said.

"The demons were fighting my father when they killed a quarter of the population in London during the Great Plague of 1665 and at least as many in the Great Fire of 1666," Em said. "I have no question that they will take out the entire city of Boston and, possibly, the entire US. They will exact their revenge on all of Adam and Eve's descendants."

The witches were so still that Em looked up to see if they

were still paying attention. Their attention was riveted to her.

"Are you sure, Em?" George asked.

"As sure as I can be," Em said. "The only way to avoid killing every human on the planet is to combine with the demon who says I belong to him. But. . ."

"What will happen to us?" Bridget asked.

"Exactly," Em said. "If I don't do this thing, you might die. If I do this thing. . ."

Em shrugged.

"You have no idea, do you?" Giles asked. He gave a slow shake of his head.

Em shook her head.

"We could all die," Em said. "We could lose our immortality and stay in this time. We could lose our ability to perform magic. It's possible that we'll be returned to the spot we were when I. . ."

Em's quick breath in shared the quality of a sob.

"Because the demon is repelled by the dark that lives inside you, I feel safe to say that this is likely to kill you," Em said. She put her hand on her stomach. "And I don't know what will happen to our children."

Mary Eastey gasped.

"I won't do anything until we have a chance to talk it through," Em said. "I wanted to talk to you alone because of our children."

"Then we wait until the children are born," Giles said. "It's only a few months now."

"If we can," Em said. "That's my hope. But. . ."

"The demon told you that they would not allow you to increase in numbers," George said in an even voice. He looked up at Giles. "They're not going to allow us to have these babies."

"Please give it some real thought," Em said. "Unless something forces my hand, I will not act until I hear from everyone."

She gave them a sad smile.

"We have an added burden," Em said.

"What about Elizabeth?" Mary Eastey asked. "Sam? Why aren't they here?"

"She lost her baby," Em said. "She was out in the snow when she and Sam checked our houses. That was before I sent the demon away. She miscarried a few hours later."

"From the snow?" Bridget asked.

"It seems like it," Em said.

The witches looked horrified.

"She had seven children in Salem," Mary Eastey said softly.

"And no miscarriages," George said. "That's why Sam believes the snow caused her miscarriage."

"The others will be here any minute," Em said. "George has agreed to tell them what's going on. I've been up since the snow started. I am exhausted. I'm going home to rest. That gives you a chance to talk among yourselves without fear of hurting my feelings."

Looking into each of their faces, Em willed them to know her love for them. When no one spoke, she left the room. They began arguing the moment she stepped out of the room. Their voices chased her from the house. She walked across the Common to the Mystic Divine. Gratefully, the store was quiet. Upstairs, she took off her shoes and climbed into bed. Wide awake and fully dressed, she pulled the heavy comforter over her head. Tucking herself into a fetal position, she began to pray.

Hours later, George came into the bedroom. He stood at the door for a few minutes before going to the bed. He flipped down the covers. She was still hugging her knees, wide awake, and praying. She didn't move.

"What did they say?" she asked.

"As you predicted," George said.

"They won't go through with it and don't want me to," Em said.

"They don't see the necessity," George said. "After all..."

"It's been more than three hundred years," Em said. "Why would we have to deal with this now? When things are going so well?"

"Exactly," George said.

"Thanks for trying," Em said.

She reached for the covers and pulled them over her head. Sometime later, he joined her in bed. Long after he was asleep, she lay in a fetal position, praying.

When the New England Patriots won the Super Bowl, everyone told Em that it was a sign. The demons were vanquished. There was no need to change anything. They joined their human friends and neighbors to celebrate their team's triumphant win.

But the whispers remained. The NFL was looking into something that had happened in January. There was evidence of wrong-doing. Sanctions were likely. Em watched as the best weapons in the demon's arsenal — suspicion and doubt — fluttered after the New England Patriots like confetti in the welcome-home parade.

She knew the very moment her demon and his kind returned to Boston. She saw him everywhere. He whispered in her ear.

"I will kill them all," he said.

At night, her dream life was populated with bleeding, suffering humans. In the light of day, it seemed like the world was either in flames or stuck in limbo. Hatred and death continued in terrorist acts in familiar places such as Yemen, while peaceful communities such as Sydney, Australia, were shattered by death and horror near their homes. All the while, justice for the victims in cases, such as the trial for the Boston Bombing, seemed hopelessly locked in limbo. Everywhere Em turned, she saw the demons venting their rage upon the world.

The death and destruction danced across Em's eyelids every night. Her mind replayed the horror of the London plague or the Spanish Flu. Some nights, she was fleeing the Great Fire and its 1700°C flames. Night after night, she watched helplessly while everyone died around her. She woke exhausted and anxious.

George returned to his service of the poor and desperate. As usual for this time of year, the Mystic Divine was quiet. They kept only a skeleton staff in the store. They used the rest of their employees to help plan events for the next year or work on counting inventory. With Elizabeth back in front of her class, Sarah Wildes ran the planning sessions. Wilmot took care of the inventory. The store was a quiet hum of activity, none of which involved Em.

Em usually spent this week going to plays and eating amazing food with Sarah Good in New York City. This year, she couldn't bring herself to leave her beautiful

Boston. Instead, she used the time she had to clean out her life. Her friends clucked their tongues and told each other she was "nesting." But Em's reasoning was a little different. She didn't want to leave a mess when the demons took her. Because George couldn't care less about possessions, she made quick work of her office and his.

She was now spending her days going through the basement storage room. Sam Wardwell came by once a day to haul her junk to the dump. Alice ran lively eBay auctions of some of the treasures Em had uncovered. Margaret Scott helped Em to anonymously donate items of historic significance to Harvard or the University of Virginia. In the evenings, Em went from house to house, dropping off things she'd kept for each of the witches.

In her own way, Em was saying good-bye.

The end was coming. She could feel it in her bones. She wanted to make sure that these precious people knew that she loved them. They humored her and chalked her sentimentality up to the upcoming birth of her yet-unnamed son.

Denial is a wonderful thing.

The rumors of another snowstorm started midweek. It was winter in Boston. Of course, there was bound to be more snow. As the fear and threat grew in Em's mind, she forced herself to focus on the task at hand.

A day or so later, the weather speculators began to suggest that the oncoming storm would be as big as the one in January. No one listened. After all, there hadn't been a storm like the one in January in more than ten years. How could there possibly be another so soon? Em kept cleaning and organizing the storage room.

The snow began to fall on Saturday, and Em held her breath. She prayed that this storm wouldn't be a replay of the last one. But there was no denying the malevolence of the building storm. The snow picked up speed and strength on Sunday.

Disheartened, Em kept to her apartment. When the electricity went out, she lit candles and hid. Near midnight, she took a long, hot shower. Shivering from the cold, she wrapped herself in a thick towel and grabbed her bathrobe. She made a turban around her wet hair and trotted out into her bedroom. She was almost to the bed when the bedroom door opened.

Giles walked into her bedroom.

"Giles!" Em said. "I just got out of the shower!"

"You're very beautiful," Giles said with a smile.

"What?"

"You always were my favorite wife," Giles said.

"I heard that!" Bridget's laughing voice came from her living room.

Giles turned toward the living room and then back to Em.

"Are you all right?" Em asked. She walked to him and looked in his eyes. "Have you been drinking? Are you feeling... confused again?"

Giles tipped his head back and laughed. Em stepped back from him.

"No, I'm not confused," Giles said. "But I know why you're asking."

Em sat down on the bed.

"What's going on?" Em asked.

"We're all here," Giles said. "It was Sarah, really. Sarah

Good? She has friends at the National Weather Service. It seems like this is some kind of... snow hurricane. I don't know. You'll have to ask her. She told me, but..."

Giles shrugged.

"This thing — the snow hurricane — it's very rare," Giles said. "Very dangerous. It's the kind of storm we sometimes see in the summer. A hurricane, you know."

"But this is snow," Em said.

Giles nodded.

"Sarah tried to get you, but she couldn't find you," Giles said. "She came to our house. Between the three of us, we compelled the others to come over."

"George, too?" Em said.

"Good Lord, Em," Giles said with a grin. "No one can compel that man to do anything."

Nodding, Em laughed.

"I don't know how you put up with him," Giles said. "You should have stayed with me."

"Don't make me go in there!" Bridget yelled from the living room.

When Em laughed, Giles did too. He fell to his knees. Em jumped off the bed and went to him.

"I begged you once to help me," Giles said as he looked up at her. "To be my wife, to care for me. I know the sacrifices you made for me, the sacrifices you've made for me all of these years."

Tears fell down Giles Corey's face.

"Will you forgive us for being stupid and selfish?" Giles asked. Em hesitated. "I'd like to say it was a spell, but it was mostly selfishness. We've fallen complacent in these easy and prosperous times."

Em winced and closed her eyes. She crossed her arms over her heart.

"Will you save the world?" Giles asked.

"I don't know if I can," Em said with a shake of her head. "My father was unable to save his beloved London from plague and fire. I don't know if I can save Boston."

"Will you try?" Giles asked. Em opened her eyes. His face begged her.

"I might kill us all," Em said.

"Then, let's get on with it," Martha Carrier said from the doorway.

Em looked up to see all of her witches, except George, standing in her living room.

"We'd rather die than see Boston destroyed," Sarah Good said. "And I believe you. If Boston goes, the rest of the world will not be far behind."

"But each of you just told me that. . ." Em said.

"We were wrong, Em," Alice said. "Can you forgive us?"

Em looked from face to face before giving a slight nod.

"Can I get dressed first?" Em asked.

They laughed.

"Get out of my bedroom," Em said to Giles.

"We can't find George," Giles said.

"George," Em said and clapped her hands.

"Yes?" George appeared next to their bed. He scowled at Giles. "Giles?"

He glanced at Em before realizing the other witches were standing in their apartment.

"Wha. . .?" George asked. He looked back at Em.

"They want to save the world," Em said.

He nodded. Alice went to hug him. She put her arms

around his neck and then screamed.

"My God, you stink," Alice said.

"If I'm going to die tonight, I may as well die in my native state," George said.

Everyone laughed. Em snapped her fingers, and she was dressed in her warmest clothing.

"Baseball field?" Giles asked. "On the Common?"

"I'll meet you there," Em said. "I need to set out a note for Shonelle. You know, in case we don't get back."

One at a time, the crowd began to thin. George and Bridget helped Giles get off his knees. Bridget kissed Em's cheek before she and Giles disappeared.

"Go," Em said to George. "The snow is dark and horrible. They will need your light."

With a nod, George disappeared. Em retrieved the note she'd written for Shonelle. She set it on her kitchen counter. She grabbed her heaviest jacket and wrapped a scarf around her neck. With one last look at her home, she started out the door. She stopped short. Jogging back to the kitchen, she took a large plastic-lock bag out of the freezer. She tucked it into her heavy jacket and stepped across the threshold of the apartment. On the landing, she wished herself to the baseball field on the Boston Common.

The witches had formed a large circle. Their heads were bowed as they recited the Lord's Prayer. Em went to George. She held him tight. In a story, George would have told her how much he loved her, and she would have given a long expository on how much he meant to her. They would clutch each other and curse their fate.

This was not a story.

She kissed his cheek and walked to the center of the circle.

"I will have you know that you are the very finest people I have ever known in my entire life," Em said in a voice so that the witches could hear her. Margaret and Mary Eastey began to cry.

"Em!" Alice screamed and pointed up.

Looking up, Em watched as the dark swirl of clouds overhead transformed into the serpent she'd met on Rousay. The serpent moved in a slow circle until its head caught up with its tail.

Pop!

There was a loud snap when the serpent caught his tail. The witches gave startled screams. The store let loose. Snow fell with an increasing pitch. The wind whipped at them.

"Stay calm!" George yelled over the wind. "They're trying to frighten us!"

The witches steadied themselves. The demons were now flying in a spiral formation, with the serpent as their boundary. They whipped the heavy snow clouds into a frenzy of snow and ice. Em could no longer see her beloved witches.

"Go on, Martha," Giles yelled over the snow.

"We're still here, Em," George said. "We believe in you!"

"We love you, Em," Alice said.

Em took a deep breath to gather her strength. She took another breath.

"I command my opposite to join me," Em said. "Come with me, now, and we shall be as one."

The air filled with the horrible pitch of the screaming,

raging demon. Like a dark missile, the demon shot out of the sky. He dove into Em at the chest, streaking out of the sky as it streamed into her. Her body screamed with pain. Every cell in her body shrieked. When she was sure she could tolerate no more, the demon continued to pour into her heart, mind, and body, until, finally, there was nothing left of him.

There was a loud *Snap!* when the demon's entirety had entered her body. Her body shuddered. Em looked up to see that the serpent had let go of his tail. She weaved and fell to her knees in the snow.

Thunk!

A loud sound echoed through the Common.

Woozy, Em threw up. Above her, the serpent let loose of his tail. The spiral of wind and snow slowed to a natural pitch. Em fell to her knees and threw up again.

"George! Alice!" She was unable to see them through the snow. "Giles! Anyone?"

Jumping to her feet, she ran to where they had been. She stopped short. The Salem Witches lay, as if dead, in the snow. She was nearest to Martha Carrier. She ripped off her glove and bent to her.

No pulse. Martha Carrier's heart was not beating.

Jumping to her feet, she felt a wave of vertigo that knocked her back to her knees. She crawled to George. Her icy hand felt at his neck.

No pulse.

Em roared at the heavens. Her consciousness slipped. Forcing herself to focus, Em pulled out the plastic bag she'd retrieved from the freezer. Holding it before her eyes, she looked at the two shriveled, dried human hands in the bag.

She reached in and took one out.

"Ablaze!" Em whispered.

With what felt like her last bit of energy, she tossed it to the center of the circle. She repeated the process with the second hand. By some miracle, the second hand landed on top of the first. A bright flame grew out of the shriveled hands.

"Restore to life," Em whispered.

She passed out.

Epilogue

Em drew the sea mist into her lungs. Scotland was always good for her soul. She looked down at the five-month-old baby asleep in the baby sling tied tight against her chest. Grinning, she picked up her bag and took a step off the Orkney Ferry and onto Rousay. She moved aside to avoid getting run over by the flow of people. She scanned the crowd waiting for the Ferry passengers. Her father waved from near the back. He jogged to her. When he hugged her, the baby awoke. Her son opened his dark eyes and looked up at Em. She smiled at him.

"When do the others arrive?" William asked.

"In an hour or so," Em said looking at the North Sea. "We had to charter a car ferry. They only run in the summer."

"They brought their vehicles?" William asked with a grin.

"We have infants and pregnant women and such," Em said. "Renting cars was easier than lugging everything."

"Of course," William said. "And this George? Where might he be? Not still afraid of Scotland, is he?"

Em grinned at the menace in her father's voice.

"He stayed to help the others," Em said. "He wanted to give us some time."

Em laughed at her father's grunt of disapproval.

"I wanted a chance to speak to you before everyone arrived and the celebration began," Em said.

Her father scanned her face and gave her a bright smile. He took her bag and nodded toward the car park.

"I have many. . . questions," William said.

"Really?" Em asked. "I wrote everything down!"

"Yes, well. . ." William blushed.

"You didn't read it," Em said.

"I did read it," William said. "Many times. I still have questions."

"Like what?" Em asked in a frustrated voice.

He nodded to a Range Rover, and she followed him. He opened her door and helped her inside. He took the baby and settled him into a brand-new car seat hooked into the back seat of the vehicle. The boy looked at his grandfather and then fell asleep again.

"Is that a spell?" William asked.

"Because he's sleeping?" Em asked. William nodded. "No, he's a very calm baby. Nothing really fazes him. He likes to sleep this time of day. He'll wake soon enough."

"He's very beautiful," William said.

"He looks like George," Em said.

"I was going to say that he looks like your mother," William said with a grin.

Em smiled at him. She settled into her seat. She held her tongue, so that he could ask his questions in his own time. She watched the open fields set against the sparkling North Sea pass by her window. Her father pulled into the driveway of his cottage.

"Bernard Flett?" Em asked.

"He died right after your visit," William said.

"Demons?" Em asked.

"Probably," William said. "Would have been damned uncomfortable to move back in with him here. 'I saw yer heed, sir.' 'It was an art installation, Mr. Flett.' 'Can't fool an old aboriginal, William. You magicked it.' I couldn't really tell him that my daughter had integrated a demon and caused the return of all of our kind."

"It's a lot to take in," Em said with a grin.

"It's good to see you, Martha," William said.

His eyes welled with tears. Rather than express what he was feeling, he jumped out of the truck. He'd retrieved her child from the car seat before she'd managed to unhook her safety belt. He nodded to her and marched into the cabin. She grabbed her bag and followed him. He settled the child into a brand-new bassinette and gestured for Em to have a seat near the fire. She watched the fire and waited while he puttered in the kitchen. He returned with two mugs of tea. She smiled her thanks and took a cup from him. He set his cup down and went to pick up the child.

"Do you mind?" William asked.

"Not at all," Em said.

"I never thought. . ." William said. "He's. . .."

"Yes," Em said.

"Did you ever talk to my opposite?" William asked to change the subject. "The one who shot you. This Bill Panon?"

"I couldn't," Em said. "He hung himself in his cell the very day I was supposed to speak with him."

"You think the demons did that, too?" William asked.

Em nodded and drank her tea. He squinted and then

looked away. He leaned forward to look at the child. Em smiled. Like everyone who'd met the child, her father was clearly in love with her son. It was wonderful to see. After a few moments, he looked up at her.

"Why did you have dried human hands in your freezer?" William asked.

Em grinned. She took another sip of her tea and set it down.

"They were Hands of Glory," Em said. "The most powerful magical object in the world if taken from a hanging convict, particularly one convicted of witchcraft. I found them when I was cleaning out our basement. I stuck them in the freezer so I'd know where they were if I needed them."

"It's very... revolting. Primitive," William sneered. "Whose hands did you have in the freezer? Yours?"

"No," Em said. "One was George's. It was taken in Salem, as payment of his debt, while he hanged."

"And you got it..."

"Tortured the executioner to find out where it was," Em said. "My husband Isaac killed the couple who had demanded George's hand as payment on the imaginary debt. Isacc loaded them into a wagon to make it look like an unfortunate wagon accident. While he was busy, I spent some time with their daughter."

"Ann Putnam, Junior?" William asked. "The one who testified against you? Started the whole thing in Salem?"

"She saw her way to tell me where George's hand was kept," Em said.

"I bet she did!" William said with a laugh. "What did you do?"

Em grinned but said nothing. William laughed.

"And the other one?" William asked.

"East India Trading Company hanged John Willard as a pirate," Em said.

"Close your ears, son," William whispered to the baby. He kissed the baby's cheek. "Why would they do that?"

"Because John *was* a pirate," Em said with a grin. "They liked to hang pirates and leave them to rot on the rope. They felt it deterred people from being pirates. You can imagine what happened with John."

"He'd have awoken and died over and over again," William said.

"They took his hand," Em said, "and left him to hang. I knew of it immediately, but it took me months to get there. By the time I arrived, he'd been hanging for almost six months."

"God, how awful," William said. His hand instinctively went to his throat. "What did you do?"

"I got him down," Em said. "He found his hand. We may or may not have burned the entire island to the ground. I won't burden you with that story."

"You sound quite a bit like a pirate yourself!" William said.

Em grinned. Realizing she was out of tea, she went to the kitchen to make a pot. Still carrying the baby, her father followed her into the kitchen.

"Your wife?" Em asked. "Justine?"

"She's passed," William said. "Turns out she had a slow-growing tumor. That's why she was blind. My efforts to heal her caused the tumor to grow. They couldn't operate, so we lived out our days here. She's buried in the back."

"Near mother?" Em asked.

"Oh, no," William said. "I didn't want your mother to know I married again. She could tolerate other women but not another marriage."

Em chuckled in agreement.

"Do you have other questions?" Em asked.

William nodded. Em poured the hot water into a pot. He gave her the child so that he could carry the tea to the couch near the fire. Em checked her child before sitting down near the fire. William took the baby from her.

"Does my grandson have a name?" William asked.

"I was waiting for you to ask," Em said with a grin.

"You are your mother's daughter," William said with a laugh. "Please introduce us, Em."

"Nathaniel William Burroughs, meet William Panon," Em said. "He's named after George's father and you, of course. We call him Nate."

"They've landed." William looked in the direction of the ferry landing.

Em nodded. She could feel that her witches had landed on Rousay.

"I have questions, but I'm not even sure how to form the questions," William said.

"Just take a stab at it," Em said.

"Why did you listen to the serpent?" William asked.

"Paul tells the Colossians that 'all things were created by him.' God, of course." Em gave a nod.

"And that means?" William asked. Em grinned.

"If God is in everything, than the serpent is of God," Em said. "That simple thought is what changed my mind about everything."

"How so?" William asked.

"If the serpent is of God, then God was in the act of convincing Eve to eat the fruit from the Tree of the Knowledge of Good and Evil," Em said. "That meant that God wanted humans to be both light and dark."

"And to have knowledge of Good and Evil," William said.

"To be capable of choosing for themselves," Em said.

Em nodded. She poured tea into the mugs. They were silent as they prepared their individual mugs.

"I didn't see it for a long time," Em said.

Her father looked up at her intense interest.

"The bible says, 'Thou shall not suffer a witch to live,'" Em said. "Of course, I'd heard the phrase all of my life. I'd always believed the passage was a mistranslation. It wasn't actually 'witch' but 'poisoner' — someone dangerous to the tribes of Israel."

"The passage was used as the reason to destroy the earth based religions during the Inquisitions," William said. "Our kind lost a lot of people to that very phrase."

"Certainly, the very next passage says you should kill anyone making a sacrifice to other Gods," Em said. "So there's plenty of reason to believe that the passage was mistranslated."

"What do you believe now?" William asked.

"I believe the passage is a pointer straight to us," Em said. "We are not descendants of Adam and Eve."

"We should not live," William said.

Em nodded.

"Argos got it wrong," William said.

"He was five when he ate fruit from the Tree of Life,"

Em said. "He lived a long time, but his mind remained very primitive. He was afraid of the demons, so he assumed they were chasing him to do him harm."

"He knew abominations were dangerous," William said.

"Because they were both light and dark," Em said. "Descendants of Adam and Eve. *We* were the true abominations because we were only one side — light or dark — depending on how you think of it. I will tell you that the demon, or dark side, of me was terrified of the witches."

William nodded.

"How did you survive?" William asked.

"The fire," Em said. "I set the hands ablaze. I'm told that the fire burned like a pyre. Someone saw it and called Emergency Response. We were taken to the hospital. We stayed about a week. They kept me, Bridget, and Mary Eastey a little longer because we were pregnant."

"Your dying wish to restore your witches turned the hands into a pyre?" William asked.

Em nodded.

"So you're still a witch," William said.

"Aren't you?" Em asked.

"No," William said. "I have some senses — intuition — but our family has always been strong in that. You probably would have lost your skill if you hadn't had the hands."

"Huh," Em said. "Maybe. The others still have their powers, too."

William nodded.

"It's always possible that yours will come back," Em said.

"The technology available now is like having magical

powers," William said with a shrug. "I haven't missed it much."

Em watched his face. When he looked up at her, they laughed.

"Sure," Em said, and he smiled. "Maybe it will return."

"Maybe," William said. "Do you think the hands did it?"

"Brought us back to life?" Em asked. "I have no idea. Maybe. We were revived at the hospital after they slowly warmed us up. We were frozen."

She shrugged, and he nodded that there was no way to know.

"How were you restored?" Em asked.

"I'm not sure," William said. "I found myself wandering the fields of Rousay. Naked, of course. And it was February, no less."

He grinned, and she smiled.

"I was alone for only a few moments before I came upon the others," William said. "They were confused and frightened, but. . ."

He gave her a look filled with love.

"Every one of us was restored," William said. "My parents. Argos. Weni. As always, there were some who preferred to return to their rest, which was taken care of. There are about a hundred of us left. Everyone else. . . Well, we invited you and your witches to Rousay for a celebration of our rebirth."

"We can all be in the same space and time?" Em asked.

"Amazing," he said with a nod.

Em smiled.

"You did really well, Martha," William said. "How do you feel?"

"Good, different," Em said. "How do you feel now that you've combined with your other half?"

"Strong," William said with a nod. "Different, yes. Whole."

"Whole," Em said with a nod.

"And your witches?" William asked. "How are they?"

"They are happy," Em said. "They've been released from the curse of being barren. A few women are pregnant, which makes them very happy. The others are exploring modern birth control. I assume that's true in the elder group as well."

William gave a curt nod.

"We don't know if we're still immortal," Em said. "No one's wanted to risk it."

"We are," William said. "At least you and I are."

"Then they would be, too," Em said.

"Possibly," William said.

"How would you know?" Em asked

"We had the usual trouble putting to sleep those who wanted to rest," William said with a grin. "We aren't as fragile as humans."

"Ah," Em said. "The Tree of Life flows through our veins. Good to know."

They fell silent as they finished their tea. Outside, they heard the sound of a few SUVs coming toward the house.

"We don't know how long it will last," Em said.

"Why not forever?" William asked.

"I just don't know," Em said.

"Time will tell," William said.

He stood from his chair. Em followed him to the door of the cottage. In the distance, she saw a row of five Land

Cruisers coming toward them.

"One more thing," William asked.

"Yes?" Em asked.

"Why were you convinced that the demons would kill all the humans?" William asked.

"Your demon killed hundreds of thousands of humans in the Great Plague and the Great Fire," Em said.

"Yes, but it wasn't *all* of them," William said.

"It's something I felt from my other half," Em said. "As you've said, our family is strong in intuition. And I felt that he felt cheated that he hadn't had a chance to live on this wonderful planet — to eat, love, and procreate. He and his tribe were willing to give me a chance because I was 'different.' If I failed, they were going to return the world to primitive living and take over."

"Why did they give you this chance?" William asked.

"I don't think we'll ever know," Em said. "George believes that they, like us, know God — uh, the Creator. They knew the Creator wanted us to be whole and not to live as separate halves. In all likelihood, they knew that, eventually, we would return and that they would have to deal with us. It's even likely that this cycle has happened many times before."

"You think that they've reset time and taken over only to be deposed by us?" William asked.

"It's possible," Em said. "How many children ate from the Tree of Life before the serpent convinced Eve to eat the apple?"

"The serpent? You mean 'God'?" William asked.

"Maybe, maybe not," Em said. "It's a mystery, even to us witches."

William looked off into the distance.

"Do you believe they were acting on our Creator's wishes?" William said.

"Godly demons," Em said.

William shivered.

"What?" Em asked.

"Don't mention that to the others," William said.

"Why?" Em asked.

"Just don't," William said.

"I must ask. . ." Em turned to her father. "Are you going to burn my friends and family alive?"

"No," William said with a laugh. "We're celebrating our return to life. We chose September 22, because it's the day you were hanged. The day you were reborn. The day your witches were created. It is now our most sacred day."

Em blushed and looked away.

"Plus, that was Argos's thing," William said. "You'll be happy to know that he's retired as the head of our people."

"Who's in charge now?" Em asked.

"They're hoping you will take over," William said.

"No," Em said. "I have enough trouble keeping my witches on track."

"I told them you'd say that," William said.

The SUVs pulled up near the house. William started forward to greet the witches. He got only a few feet before the baby awoke. He scowled at William and squawked. William turned to look at Em.

"He doesn't like to be away from me," Em said.

Her father jogged back to return the child. Em slipped him into the baby sling, and Nate fell back to sleep. Em stayed where she was to watch her friends' arrival. As

always, Martha Carrier was out of the vehicle first. She was
on her own after breaking up with Bruce, the coworker.
Ann Pudeator slipped out of the vehicle behind Martha
Carrier. Clearly pregnant, she waited a moment for her
husband. A surgeon, Ann's human husband had
something to say to John Willard about his driving. John
was laughing when he stepped out from the driver's seat.
He caught Em's eye and nodded toward Ann's husband.
She smiled, and John went around the front of the car to
get his son from his car seat in back. Mary Eastey took the
child from John, and they started toward the house.

A very pregnant Susannah got out of the front seat of
the vehicle that George had been driving. She waved to Em
while clearly singing. Sarah Wildes' voice carried when she
got out of the SUV. They were singing the Psalms. Em
smiled. Alice's client-turned-boyfriend got out of the SUV.
When turned to help Alice out of the back, Em scowled.
Em had never heard Alice mention the boyfriend's name.
Before she could ask, Mary Ayer and her boyfriend,
Detective Shane Donnell, got out of the SUV. George's
deep singing voice was heard until her father reached him.
The women continued their song without him. Wilmot
climbed out of the back of the SUV. She called to Em and
waved.

Em scowled. No one had gotten out of the SUV that
Giles had been driving. She was about to make her way
there when George jogged to the car. Sam Wardwell got
out of the back.

"We were locked in," Sam yelled to Em with an
exaggerated roll of his eyes. Em laughed.

Sam's husband got out behind him. Both men helped a

clearly pregnant Elizabeth from the back. Margaret Scott got out after Elizabeth. She waved at Em and went to the back for suitcases. Giles got out from behind the driver's seat. He went around the front of the vehicle to help Bridget out. They embraced and went back around the SUV to retrieve their infant daughter. Sarah Good was talking on her phone as she got out of the SUV. She waved to Em before turning away from the house to finish her phone call.

There they were. The sixteen people who'd been hanged with Em in the Salem Witch Trials. As of today, they'd lived through the ups and downs of the last three hundred and twenty-three years. They were the finest people Em had ever known. They were her family. They were her friends. Em beamed with love for each of them.

George ran across the field to her. He twirled her around and kissed her hard. He slipped Nate from the sling. He kissed the baby's cheeks before setting him back in the sling.

"Your father — he's. . ." George started.

"Yeah," Em said.

George laughed.

"Come on," George said. "Show me around. I'm not sure why, but I've never been to Scotland."

"It is a mystery," Em said with a laugh.

"I want to see everything," Giles said.

"As you wish," Em said.

Suffer a Witch is written by Claudia Hall Christian. While subscribers of Suffer a Witch serial have already asked for another book, there is nothing in the works so far.

Claudia is the author of the Alex the Fey Thrillers, the Seth and Ava Mysteries, and Jornada del Muerto. She also writes traditional serial fiction including the long running Denver Cereal, the Queen of Cool, set in Fort Worth, Texas, and Suffer a Witch. Claudia keeps bees, dogs, and a husband in Denver, Colorado

To find out more, go to ClaudiaHallChristian.com.

You can find her on Twitter and Facebook.
She's a middle child and would love to say "Hello".

Thank you for reading.

Made in the USA
San Bernardino, CA
12 October 2018